Time with Mr. Silver

Elle Nicoll

Rose Hope Publishing Ltd.

Contents

For everyone who likes their heroes pierced and possessive
x

(Please turn back to copyright page for Content Warnings)

Chapter 1

Dax

Three years earlier

"Mr. Dax Anthony Silver, on the count of grievous bodily harm with intent, how do you plead?"

"Not guilty, Your Honor," I grind out. A stabbing pain shoots up my jaw as I clench my teeth.

I drag in a deep breath as the *victim* scoffs from his position across the courtroom. I meet his eyes with a glare that could penetrate bulletproof glass.

I should have killed him. Finished the job when I had my hands around his throat.

The corners of my lips twitch as I recall the softness of his skin beneath my fists that night. The sound his ribs made when they cracked. Like snapping the wishbone after a roast chicken supper that Mom would cook.

Shame, those wishes never came true.

I fight the urge to adjust my collar in the stifling heat of the courtroom. Her Majesty's finest building for justice and they couldn't even fix the damn air conditioning.

A bead of sweat rolls down the back of my neck, but I ignore it. Any movement, any show of weakness, and *he* will think it's guilt over what happened between him and I.

Guilt or fear.

And I feel neither.

I don't feel guilt. The bastard deserved it, and a whole lot more.

And fear? I tear my gaze away from the man in the suit staring at me like something he stepped in, then look over at my sister, Jasmin, and give her a small nod as she stares back at me with wide eyes.

No, not fear... but regret maybe.

Regret, in case this sadistic fucker gets his way and sends me down for something he had coming, she will be alone. Something I promised her she would never be.

My friend, Logan, reaches for her and takes her hand, squeezing it, but her eyes never leave mine as she draws in a breath that makes her shoulders shake.

Not guilty, Your Honor. Not fucking guilty.

"Members of the jury, have you reached your verdict?" the female judge asks. And despite the courtroom being quiet before, a new level of silence descends as the entire room seems to hold its breath. Only the ticking of the clock on the wall can be heard. Each strike sounds like a missile counting down to my fate.

"We have, Your Honor," the appointed speaker of the jury answers—an oily-looking businessman with more money than style. Jury picking by the prosecution, is an obvious tactic. Choose people of the same age, sex, and race as the person I'm accused of harming. And similar social standing in the community, judging from the speaker's smug self-important expression plastered over his face as he flashes me a look of disdain.

Get more sympathy from jury members. Let them re-late to the victim.

I wonder if this jerk has a tidy little side business supplying coke to minors. Oh, and sending fucking dick pics to my sister.

I turn my attention back to the reason we are all here today—Julian Young, owner of Mason's, the UK's biggest overseas spirits import company. Business rival, drug dealer, and all-round asshole.

He purses his lips as he stares at me, his hair slicked back, graying at the sides and around his collar.

I never liked him, even before he put his disgusting, filthy, leery eyes on my sister, and then violated her privacy by sending her those messages. He isn't worthy of breathing the same air as her.

I remember the way his hand landed too low on her back the night of that business dinner as he whispered something in her ear. It made contempt slither over my skin like a swarm of starved locusts. Maybe I should have ignored the comment he made about her, about how it was a shame she was my sister as he bet I would love to fuck an *ass like that*. Maybe I shouldn't have gone postal on him. After all, it resulted in me being restrained by five security guards in front of half of Southeast England's most influential businesspeople.

Or *maybe* I should have broken the other two ribs that escaped my wrath. And smashed his nose to the backside of his head instead of fracturing it. Maybe I should have done that.

The clock continues to tick. He leans in his chair and whispers something to his lawyer as he holds my eyes.

Sly bastard. He's wanted me out of the way since our company outperformed his at last year's industry awards. Slippery fucker tried to get me done for attempted murder, until the charge was reduced to a lesser one.

But I doubt I'm the only one who wouldn't cry at his obituary if someone did the world a favor. The less creeps like him in the world, the better.

"Very well. And do you find the defendant guilty or not guilty?" the judge asks.

Julian straightens. I stare into his eyes.

"Guilty, Your Honor."

His eyes gleam, and he bares his yellowing teeth before his mouth curls into a sneer, and he finally breaks my gaze.

I exhale and draw in a deep lungful of air.

I was holding my breath that entire time without realizing.

"No! Dax!" Jasmin sobs from the seating area.

Eyes whip to her, including Julian Young's son, who is sitting on the opposite side of the central aisle.

Is he proud of his father? Or a fellow criminal—like father, like son?

Although, in the eyes of the law, I'm the only criminal here today.

I can't leave my seat. I can only look on as Logan wraps an arm around Jasmin's shoulders, and she blinks at me, wiping the tears from her cheeks with the heel of her hands and pushing her long, dark hair away from her face.

I love you, I mouth as her face crumples again and her entire body shakes with her sobs.

She drops her face into her hands as Logan holds her tight. He tips his chin at me in a silent confirmation.

He'll look out for her.

We've known Logan since school. His family runs a luxury engineering and design company that his father is readying him to take over. But his father was adamant he worked for other companies first to make sure it's what he wants. So, Logan has been working for me at the distillery Jasmin and I inherited from our grandparents. Our parents were killed in a car accident years ago. And that meant a multimillion-pound company was handed to us when I was twenty-one and Jasmin was fifteen. It's been years of hard work, college night classes, and more business meetings than I can remember, but we've done it. We kept the business afloat, despite not having a clue what we were doing. Jasmin helped out around school hours, but I tried to keep her out of it, wanting her to choose her own future. Not be thrust into one chosen for her.

I wanted her to have freedom. To never lose the beautiful, strong-willed, dreamer of a little sister I had known. For the most part, it worked. We grieved our parents together. Held each other up when the other could have so easily crumbled into ash. We got through it. Day by day. And she still kept her smile that could light up the darkest corners of the earth.

But that smile is a ghost now as the judge reads out my sentencing.

The air leaves my lungs in one harsh burst and tension ripples through my shoulders for the first time since being arrested.

Three years.

Three years of my life I won't be with her, when I promised her I'd never leave. She may be a grown woman now, but all I see is the twelve-year-old girl who was told Mommy and Daddy were never coming home again.

She looked to me then, her big brother, barely eighteen, with fear in her eyes. And it was simple. I had to protect her at all costs. We had to stay together.

And now I've failed her.

I clench my jaw again, unable to take my eyes from her crumpled frame as the officers come to lead me away.

Julian Young will fucking pay for this.

Chapter 2

Rose

Present day

"YOUR HOUSE OR MINE, Babe?"

Stale beer fumes fill my nostrils as I stare up into the glassy eyes next to me. The weight of his arm around my shoulders is like a noose, making my chest tight and my breathing labored.

"All right there, Romeo. Mind if I steal my girl back?"

My best friend, Casey, sidles up to us and expertly maneuvers me out of his grasp. My drunken partner of choice for the evening mutters his disappointment.

"Thanks, Case." I incline my head and rest it on top of hers; an easy feat, considering I'm five inches taller even without heels.

"Please... as if he stood a chance, anyway. You always go for the weird ones, Ro..." She trails off.

Ever since Gareth.

That's what she's thinking. I know it. Ever since Gareth, my childhood sweetheart, spectacularly dumped me days after I gave him my V-card, and my life turned to shit. I wanted to wait until we were married. Call me naïve or old-fashioned or whatever. But the old me used to believe in true love and soulmates.

The old me.

I snort and lose my balance, wobbling as the night's cocktails swirl around in my stomach and cause my head to spin like I'm on a ride at Staten Island Fair.

Casey tightens her grip on my waist as we exit the club, and the night air of New York hits me like a slap in the face, making my stomach roll again.

A girl stands shivering, arguing with the bouncer about going back inside to find her purse to get a cab home. I don't wait to hear his excuse about why she can't go back in. I pull a twenty from my purse and press it into her hands.

"Always get home safe. That's what my dad used to say," I slur.

"Thanks." She smiles as I bat her words away with a swipe of a drunken flailing hand.

"It's nothing."

I lean into Casey's side as she pulls me away further down the sidewalk.

"You're too nice, Ro." She sighs as she scans the street.

"You and I both know that's not true." I clasp a hand over my mouth as I belch, and my neck burns.

Casey blows out a breath, probably too tired to argue with me. We've had this conversation before.

Many times.

"Looks like our ride home just found us."

I follow her gaze to the blue sedan pulled up by the curb. Brett glares at me from the driver's side. I lift one hand and wiggle my fingers in a wave, attempting to curl my lips into a semblance of a smile, instead of the grimace that has settled there.

"He shouldn't be here," I mutter.

He winds down the window and calls to us. Casey answers for me as a fresh wave hits me, forcing me to bend over at the waist and hurl the night's liquid courage all over the sidewalk. She rubs my back with one hand, gathering back my hair with the other.

I groan and straighten up, wiping the back of my hand across my lips, and look over at Brett through bleary eyes.

"Hey, big brother." I grimace.

He looks at Casey, then back at me, his mouth flattened into a grim line.

"Get her in the car, Case. It's time Rose went home."

I roll my eyes, which makes my head pound.

"Come on, Case," I whisper. "Time I went back to serve my sentence."

After dropping Casey off, and me drunkenly whispering—which was more like slurred shouting—about how I didn't want her to leave me, and then trying to cling on to her as she exited the car, Brett drives me the rest of the way home in silence.

Stone-cold silence.

I glance at him twice, at his stupidly handsome face, all mad and unsmiling. And at his giant biceps as he steers the wheel and uses the wheel-mounted hand controls to accelerate and brake. Either he ignores me on purpose, or he's too busy concentrating to notice me watching him.

I rest my face against the cool glass instead, staring out the window.

Please, God, if you're listening... let tonight be the night aliens abduct me and take me far, far away, where I'm not the family fuck up anymore.

"Stay there." Brett side-eyes me as he parks on the driveway and kills the engine.

"I can help," I slur, grabbing the door handle clumsily on my second attempt and launching the door open, almost falling out onto the ground.

"Rose, I said wait," Brett snaps as I open the back door and grab his folded-up wheelchair.

It gets wedged between the seats, and I yank at it, cursing under my breath.

I hate this thing. I hate it with a passion. But what I hate the most is that I'm the reason Brett needs it.

I pull hard, and he hisses as it comes free and flies out, knocking me on my ass and landing on top of me, cracking me on the cheekbone.

"The fuck, Sis!" he growls as tears sting my eyes and my cheek throbs. "I told you to wait. You okay?"

I lift my head and meet his heated gaze. His eyes soften as he looks at me spread out on my back. I push the chair off me and stand, straightening up as I swallow the lump in my throat.

I can't bear to look into his eyes when I know what is there...

Pity.

Pity for the sad and pathetic mess his younger sister has become.

"What's going on?" Mom says as she hurries from the front door and over to us in her slippers.

"I was—"

"She drank too much again." Brett reaches for the wheelchair, grabbing it from where it's landed by the driver's door, and opens it up with one hand before sliding himself effortlessly into it using his strong arms.

Mom looks at me, her eyes glistening with unshed tears. "Rose... Why are you doing this to yourself?"

"I'm not doing anything, Mom." I sway as I walk ahead of her and Brett and into the house. Only a single lamp is on in the hallway, and I stumble as I step through the door, momentarily losing my bearings in the dim light.

I grab on to the hall table, but misjudge the distance, and send a frame skittering onto the floor. The glass smashes into a thousand tiny, splintered pieces.

"Oh!" Mom sobs as she appears behind me and scoops the frame up.

She turns it, and nausea washes over me, taking with it the blood from my face as I stare at the photograph of the five of us.

Smiling.

Back when we all had something to smile about.

"I'm sorry, Mom," I whisper, swallowing the dry lump in my throat.

She pats at her eyes, the earlier unshed tears losing the battle and dropping down her cheeks in silence.

"Go to bed, Rose. It's late."

She traces her finger over the photograph, lingering on Dad's face, then turns and walks to the kitchen.

"Let me clean it up, let me..."

"Leave it." Brett sighs behind me.

I say nothing, just nod.

Then I climb the stairs slowly, using the wall for support and go straight to my room, lying on the bed while the room spins around me.

"It's got to be worth a try though, right?"

I stall, my hand hovering over the door handle as my older sister's voice flows out from inside the kitchen.

"We have to do something, Mom." *Brett.*

"I don't know. It's so far away."

I squeeze my eyes shut as my mouth goes dry at the anguish in Mom's voice.

"What do you think, Reed?"

I lean closer to the closed door. My soon-to-be brother-in-law is here as well. Which is only to be expected. Him and my older sister, Harley, have been joined at the hip ever since they started dating when he was running in the election for mayor of New York last year. A position he won with a record share of the votes.

I really am the only fuck up in the family.

"I think it could be good for her," he says.

I roll my eyes. Always diplomatic. Maybe that is what years in politics does for you.

I take a deep breath and open the door. Four pairs of eyes fly to me.

"Busy discussing what a trainwreck I am?" I walk over to the refrigerator and grab a carton of orange juice. Fetching a glass from the cabinet, I pour it in and take a sip, sighing in relief as its cool sweetness eases the rough hoarseness that a night of too many cocktails has had on my voice.

"Don't talk about yourself like that, Rose," my sister says from her seat at the kitchen table. Her fiancé, Reed, lays a hand on her shoulder and squeezes. "We were just discussing how to help you."

I snort as I drain the rest of my juice.

"Drowned me at birth?" I mutter.

Mom's eyes plead with mine as I look into them.

"I'm sorry," I breathe, my shoulders dropping. "I'm fine, honestly. I just had one too many last night, that's all."

"It's every weekend." Brett looks at me from under his brow from where he's sitting between Mom and Harley.

"Not every—"

"And some nights in the week," he finishes, pushing his head into his hands and running his fingers back through his hair. "We love you, Sis. We want you to stop blaming yourself."

My throat burns again.

"How can I do that? When we all know it's my fault we are even having this conversation." I walk to the dishwasher and put the glass inside.

"There's a new job that Harley's friend has told her about," Mom says suddenly.

I freeze with my back to them, my spine stiffening.

"We think it would be good for you," she adds.

"I have a job."

"You *had* a job," Brett says.

I turn, crossing my arms over my chest.

He's right. The accounting firm I work for made cutbacks recently. Of course I was the one who didn't make it. Friday was my last day.

Damn. Why didn't I lead with that? Say that last night was just me letting my hair down after losing my job? I could have explained the cocktails away easily. They'd have bought it.

I look back at their stony faces.

Or maybe not.

"Fine. Give me the details and I'll look into it." I turn my back on them all, unable to take any more of their grim, pitying looks.

I fetch out a knife, plate, some bread, and the peanut butter to make a sandwich. I unscrew the lid of the peanut butter and spread it over the bread.

"It's in England," Mom says.

The knife falls from my hand, clanging loudly against the plate.

"As in New England?" I turn to her.

"As in, the UK," Brett says, staring at me as Mom watches me closely.

I look between the two and then to Harley, and finally Reed.

"You want me to go to England?" The room falls silent, the uncomfortableness thick and stifling as it weaves itself through the air.

"We think it will help you. A new place, fresh scenery, a break from here," Mom suggests.

She doesn't sound convinced herself, so why the hell should I be?

"You've already set this all up?" My mouth drops open as one guilty look between my sister and brother confirms it. "Fuck."

"Rose!" Mom chides.

"You're sending me away?" It makes perfect sense, though. I wouldn't want me here either, after everything I've done.

"Of course not. We just want what's best for you. We love you." Mom's voice reverts to its usual octave of helplessness tinged with heartbreak.

Maybe I should curse again. I would rather her be angry at me than feel her sadness radiating from her like a beacon in every word and look she gives me.

"You just need time, Rose. Time to find yourself again... to *forgive* yourself," she whispers with sadness in her eyes.

Time... if it were that simple.

Brett remains silent.

Reed is standing behind Harley. He loves her more than anything. It's in his eyes, and my heart squeezes that she has found that with someone. It reminds me of the way Dad used to look at Mom. And how she looked at him.

I take in the two empty chairs at the kitchen table. One is mine. The other...

The Jacobs family.

One short.

I would do anything to fill that seat again. But that's impossible.

I would also do anything to see Mom smile again.

One question leaves my lips, "When do I leave?"

"I'm going to miss you so much." Casey swipes at her eyes again as she pulls back from our hug.

"I'm going to miss you too. But it won't be forever. Just until I find myself, or forgive myself, or whatever shit I'm supposed to be doing over there."

When I get upset I get this burning, aching lump in my throat like a damn marble made of acid. But no tears. Never tears. I haven't been able to cry since Brett got knocked down by a speeding driver. Not even when Dad—

"Well, do it fast." Casey sniffs. "I need you here, Ro. It's been you and me since we were five. From sandbox to casket, remember?"

A lopsided grin stretches across my lips as I pull her in for another hug.

"Yeah, I know. No one else has been there for me like you. You're the bestest friend a girl could ask for."

She clutches me tighter. "No, Ro. That's you. You're the bestest friend. I'm going to call and text you every day."

"Okay." The burning lump prevents me from saying much else.

I pull away and lift the carefully wrapped package from the top of my drawers, setting it down on my pillow and smoothing over the cloud paper with one hand. Then I rest the note atop.

I love how happy he was the day we took this. I'm sorry about the frame. I love you. —Rose.

"She'll appreciate it," Casey says, her eyes resting on the wrapped-up replacement frame. She went shopping with me this week to find one the right size for the one I broke.

If only everything that needs fixing could be done with a trip to the store.

She reaches over and grabs my hand. I squeeze my eyes shut until Mom calls up the stairs.

Time to go and find myself.

Whatever the fuck that means.

Chapter 3

Rose

I SCAN THE DEPRESSING, gray parking lot.

One Atlantic Airways flight, two trains, and more hours than I care to think about, spent squeezing my five-foot ten frame into seats, with legroom designed for some miniature being—definitely not an actual human—and I am aching. And cranky.

The sky chooses this moment to welcome me on my first visit to England in style—with a downpour of freezing rain. Cursing, I pull my suitcase along the front of the countryside train station. There isn't even a dry, indoor seating area. I have officially fallen off the grid in the middle of nowhere.

Leaning against the wall, I wrap my arms around myself. I'm in the right place. I just have to wait.

Ten minutes pass, and as the rain stops, a sleek, silver Range Rover pulls into the small parking lot and slows to a stop alongside me. The electric window rolls down, and a guy leans over from the driver's side.

"Rose?"

I peer into the car and inhale the leather interior.

"Dax Silver?"

His green eyes sparkle in amusement.

"Not even close."

He jumps out the car and heads around the hood, giving me time to assess him. He must be in his thirties. Wavy brown hair, a broad frame indicating he works out, and he smells incredible.

He holds out a hand to take my bag, and I instinctively pull it toward me. The man I've come to work for is called Dax Silver. This guy may be handsome, but he isn't who I was expecting. And serial killers can be good-looking, too.

He bites his lip, then tilts his hand in greeting.

"Logan. I work with Dax."

He drops his hand and reaches into his pocket, pulling out a pink card.

"Here."

It's a British driving license with the name Logan Rich on it and a picture of him looking a little younger.

"And if you're thinking of any rich jokes, I'll be impressed if you have one I haven't heard before."

I raise my brows at him.

A smile stretches his lips as he puts the license back in his wallet.

"I'm from the Silver Estate, I promise." He steps to the side and tips his head toward the lettering on the side of the car. *Silver Estate Distillery* is emblazoned on the side in fancy, metallic lettering.

I didn't notice it before, too busy freezing my tits off and wondering why the hell I agreed to come here.

For Mom, Brett, and Harley, a small voice says in my head. *For your family.*

"Okay." I allow him to take my bag.

He grins and then opens the passenger door for me. "Ladies first."

My eyes never leave him as he places my bag in the trunk then rounds the car and gets into the driver's side.

"Bit of advice now that you're in England"—he glances at me before driving off—"get a brolly."

"A what?"

"An umbrella. You're soaking."

My clothes are sticking cold and soggy, like mud on a shovel. Of course I need a *brolly*.

"Thanks for the tip. So, what do you do?"

"Apart from abducting lone females from country train stations?" He smirks at the hint of a smile forming on my lips. "I run the estate's communications team. Manage the PR side of things, the open tours, events held on site, that kind of thing. And you're here to fill the new accounting role," he states.

"I am."

He reminds me of my brother, Brett, able to strike up a conversation with anyone, always upbeat, no matter what shit's been dealt his way.

"Great. We need all the help we can get. Dax has been back at the helm for over six months now, but we're still building things back up, you know? Me and Jasmin, we kept things going, but it wasn't the same without him."

"Why? Where's he been?"

"You don't know?"

"Should I?"

He shrugs his shoulders.

"I guess not. Not if you're not from around here. Thought you would have googled your new company before coming, though."

That would have been the logical thing to do. But I was too busy alternating between being mad at my family for sending me away to wondering how much I'll miss them when I've never traveled outside of the States before.

"It wasn't exactly my choice to come," I jibe. Way to win points with one of my new superiors, but I don't care. I didn't pick this job or this place. And judging by how at ease Logan seems and the way he's chuckling at my response, he doesn't care about my lack of business etiquette either.

"Dax implied as much."

"He did?" I figured my new boss must know something about my situation if this job is a favor to Harley's friend. With any luck, he will be okay to work for, and I can get out of here and back home as soon as possible. Mom might be happier then, knowing I've had time away like she wanted.

"You just need time to find yourself, Rose. Forgive yourself."

Some people don't deserve forgiveness. Not when their crime is unforgivable.

"He sure did," Logan says, turning down a small country road.

"So where was he, then?" I ask.

"Oh, Dax? In prison," he says as casually as if he's discussing directions.

"Jail?" I deadpan as I study his face. No suppressed laugh, no glittering eyes. Nothing to suggest he's joking.

"Yeah," he says. "For grievous bodily harm. It was attempted murder at one point, but that got thrown out. The whole case should have, frankly. He's innocent."

"Right."

I've seen enough of people's ugly sides, my own included, to know that there is usually no such thing as 'innocent.' We are all guilty of something.

Logan sighs. "The Silver Estate is... you'll see. I think you're going to like it here."

"Mmm."

He glances at me, then smiles.

Outside, blurs of green hedges pass us until we pull up to the junction of a main road, and Logan signals left, taking us a short distance before pulling up in front of a giant silver metal gate with the estate's logo displayed across it.

"I'll be the judge of that," I say, staring up at the imposing gate.

"I'm sure you will." He smirks, pressing a remote control.

Then he drives through, submerging me deeper into my *temporary* home.

My first night is... quiet. That's the best word to describe it. It was already getting late when Logan dropped me off last night. As part of the job, I've been given a small cottage in the estate's grounds to live in while I'm here. It's cute. Quaint. The floors slope on the upstairs landing.

Resembles walking on a rocking ship when I go to the bedroom. The kitchen looks like it was hand carved, and the only thing visible from the windows is green. Grass. Trees. More grass.

Maybe that's why they sent me here so that I can't go anywhere or do anything. I know Mom and Brett were getting sick of me going out so much and seeing me stumble home. Harley, too, although she doesn't live with Mom, so she's usually the one who nags me the least.

I pull on my over-the-knee boots. I'm wearing them with a smart, skater-style dress that flows out from my waist, so it's an appropriate attire. I wore it at my old job, but judging by the gray mist that had settled over the grass outside this morning, I'm questioning whether rubber boots might be a better option.

There was a note left by Jasmin—one half of the Silver siblings—that said she would collect me in the morning and give me my induction. And a delicious-looking pie in the refrigerator, which I devoured half of before crashing out last night.

I'm stuffing my perfume into my purse when there's a knock at the door.

"Rose?"

It's hard not to smile at the dark-haired beauty standing at my threshold. She's grinning at me like we are already BFFs. First, Logan. Now, her. People are cheery around here. Maybe it's a British thing. Or maybe they're drinking the product on the sly all day long.

I sniff subtly. No, no alcohol. Definitely a British thing.

"I'm Jasmin Silver." She holds out a hand, and as I extend mine, she pulls me into a quick hug. "It's so nice to meet you. Ooh, nice boots."

"Thanks." My smile widens.

"Are you ready for your induction and to meet the team?"

"Yes, umm, that sounds great." It sounds less like a lie than I thought it would. I'm here now. After a good night's sleep being stuck here doesn't seem quite as depressing. If everyone is as nice as Logan and Jasmin, then my stay might even be bearable.

"It won't take that long to whizz around the estate," Jasmin says over her shoulder as she walks down the path, and I follow behind. She's wearing Louboutin stilettos, their red soles flashing with each step she takes.

Okay, this is a good sign. I won't have to trek across half of the muddy English countryside while working here if she wears shoes like that to work.

"It's a hundred acres. Most of it is forest and fields. The main distillery and offices are all close together, though, so you'll spend most of your time there. Of course, if you fancied some time away for yourself, then feel free to take one of the fleet cars."

"Oh, okay, thanks," I say as we approach another gleaming silver Range Rover with the estate's logo on. It unlocks without Jasmin pressing the remote. They must keep Range Rover in business.

"Don't mention it. It's fine," Jasmin says as we climb in and she starts the engine. "Although stay on the estate if you don't have a license. We don't need the police visiting." The smile drops from her face momentarily.

"I can use my US license for a year as a visitor."

"Oh, great." She lights up again. "Well, in that case, please make yourself at home. Use whatever you want, go wherever you want. I can take you into town on the weekend if you like. Show you around the area?"

"That sounds great, thanks."

She breathes out in a rush, her words spilling out. "Honestly, it's the least we can do. I was so happy to hear you were coming to help us get on top of the accounting. We've gotten behind with my brother..." She chews on her bottom lip. "There's a lot of catching up to do. And you come highly recommended."

"I—Thank you."

I take my work seriously, but I'm hardly at a level that warrants Jasmin's enthusiasm. Harley really must have pulled in the big favors to get me this job.

Either that or my family wanted to get rid of me. I don't blame them.

Jasmin floors the accelerator. We pass a group of trees and turn onto the estate's main driveway. At least, that must be what it is, because up ahead is the largest, regal-looking country house I have ever seen, complete with circular driveway and a central fountain shooting water up into the sky like a bouquet of crystal droplets.

"I'll take you to the distillery and warehouses." She points to another set of buildings off to the side. It's obvious they aren't original, like the main house. But they've been constructed in such a way they look like it, with matching sandstone bricks and large white sash windows. "Then we can head into the offices, and you can meet the rest of the team and Dax."

The next hour I am rendered speechless as I take in the Silver Estate in all its glory. I've never been inside an actual distillery before, and the building housing the giant stills was just incredible. Jasmin told me they produce over thirty gins here. But their largest contract is for one called Aunt Iris's Blend, which originates from California. One I've drunk myself on many occasions.

The mention of it makes my stomach clench with a pang of sadness. *What are Brett and Mom doing right now?* New York is five hours behind us, so they must be sleeping. At least, Mom will be. Brett must be working out. He has a physical therapist who he sees daily, but he still insists on extra workouts by himself to build his strength up since the accident.

I follow Jasmin up the sweeping staircase in the main house where the offices are. We've greeted the rest of the team, including Logan, who came with us when Jasmin showed me the orangery—a room with all glass walls and a glass ceiling where they host tasting events. The house is beautiful. It's kept its internal features like the oak staircase and molding around the ceilings. But the office rooms are modern and bright. Welcoming.

We head up to the second floor where Jasmin shows me my office setup. It's full of boxes of old paperwork that needs sorting out. A small accounts team does payroll and invoicing downstairs, but she said they need me to go over all the books for the last three years and make sure everything looks okay before I move on to the daily stuff. I have no idea what state things will be in. It could take me weeks. And some things might be a little different with the UK tax and laws, so I need to get my head around that.

The more Jasmin tells me about the role, the more I want to ask what the hell I am doing here. I know it was some favor to Harley through her friend, Maria. But I've no doubt there are people better suited.

"Oh, damn, he's not here," she says as we walk into another large office space, one with views from the window over the sweeping driveway and fountain. "His car is outside..." She pauses, her brow wrinkling before she spins and heads toward the door. "Relax, Rose, grab a drink." She points to a sideboard set up with a fancy coffee maker. "I'll go find Dax and then you'll have met everybody."

She's gone before I can protest. It doesn't feel right making myself at home in my new boss's office and using his coffee machine. What if he's one of those uptight stuffy suits that doesn't like his things touched?

Every piece of furniture is positioned with precision. There's even a giant tropical fish tank with sparkling glass sides.

Yep, definitely a stuffy businessman.

I walk over to a high-backed chair set facing the window. Everything else in the room is set up for business. Cold and detached. But this chair feels different. For a start, it's alone. No matching partner. It's angled perfectly to see all the way out of the window and across the grounds. The old leather seat is worn and depressed in the center as if it's spent many hours being a comfortable haven for someone.

Even though it feels like I'm invading Mr. Silver's privacy, I sink into the chair, letting out a deep sigh as it welcomes me like an old friend.

I rest my head against the high back and cross my legs as I gaze out the window.

The view is incredible. The cottage I'm staying in is even visible, peeking out from behind the trees.

Approaching footsteps outside have me ready to spring to my feet. But something in the deep growl that's with them has my ass gluing itself firmly in place.

"You just need to be there.... It's guys we've used before."

The owner of the growl lets out a frustrated sigh, and I picture him sitting in this chair. It's the perfect place to sit and calm the anger so heavily seeped into his voice.

This is awkward. The chair shields me from his view, but I should get up. It's got to be Mr. Silver. And he's about to find me hiding in his office, eavesdropping on a private conversation.

I uncross my legs and prepare to stand.

"No. They may as well be chasing their own fucking tails. Useless pigs," he hisses.

Abort.

Maybe if I stay seated, he'll leave and never know I was here.

Chapter 4

Dax

I END THE CALL and toss the phone on my desk.

Fucking Marcus. He has one simple job. Make sure the crates get picked up. It's all been arranged. All he has to do is help load them onto the truck and then fuck off home. He reckons he saw a cop car near his house earlier and now he's pissing himself. Stupid fucker. He needs to grow balls. Happy enough to spend his cut, flashing it around like a complete dickhead. But one little squad car passing and he's ready to run home for Mommy. And he wonders why he's given all the shit jobs. Something I've learned about this world over the past few years—you've got to earn respect. And with that comes trust. Fortunately for me, I've got both.

I flick through some papers on my desk without taking a seat. My spine straightens as a scent catches my attention. *Sweet and feminine.* It's suspended in the air like an image on a Polaroid before it has time to develop.

Whoever she is, she was here recently.

"There you are." Jasmin waltzes in and stalls, flicking her eyes around as if she's looking for something before she walks over to me. I wrap an arm around her and kiss her on the cheek; the phone call and Marcus's incompetence forgotten.

I inhale before she pulls away. Jasmin's wearing her usual scent today—*Tom Ford*. It's not the one I smelled a moment ago. That alluring scent has drifted away with the displacement of the air. *Shame.*

Two and a half years in a men's only jail and you get good at recognizing when something smells like a vanilla fucking cookie wrapped in petals is nearby.

"She was here. I left her here." She looks around again. "Rose?"

I lean back against my desk, wrapping my palms around the wooden edge.

Rose Jacobs. Logan said he had dropped her off last night. The latest addition to the Silver Estate's staff. A more unusual hiring, but I was asked to repay a favor I owed, and I'm a man of my word.

I look around my office, my eyes landing on the chair by the window.

"New girl!" I snap, my sudden outburst echoing off the walls and making Jasmin jump. She turns to scowl at me, and I curl my lips into a smile. She may be twenty-five now, but I still love to mess with her sometimes.

Be nice, she mouths, as movement in my peripheral draws my attention back to the chair and the tall blonde emerging from behind it.

"Dax. This is Rose."

I stare at the woman in front of me. Her long hair falls in waves over her shoulders, framing a face that has an elegant beauty to it, a slightly upturned nose, soft-looking lips, and large blue eyes.

"Nice to meet you," she says as she reaches me. I inhale sharply, my grip on the desk tightening. *Vanilla and petals...*

Frowning, I take in her outfit. A dress that probably should be longer, but due to her height, falls mid-thigh, showing a hint of smooth, tanned skin, before meeting a pair of black over-the-knee boots.

Jasmin coughs and I snap my eyes back up, reaching my hand out.

"Dax Silver."

As our skin connects, a spark of static electricity jolts us.

"Rose Jacobs," she replies with a furrowed brow.

"You know how to balance books?" I ask, gripping her hand in mine. Jasmin sighs. She hates me cutting to the chase with business. She's much more of a relationship builder with our staff. She wants to make them feel at home, ensure they're happy here. I think it stems from her being left so many times over her life. She hates it when people leave. This is her way of trying to make sure they never want to.

But this is business. Most people only want you to believe they're your friend. They only care about themselves and their own agenda.

"Yes." She holds my gaze, tightening her grip on my hand. "You have no worries there."

"I just need to worry about you hiding and listening into private phone calls, then?"

Her lips flatten into a line, and she pulls her hand away. "I wasn't hiding."

"But you *were* listening?" I narrow my eyes as her lips part, and she stares at me.

"Right, that's introductions done." Jasmin breaks the growing tension in the air, and I turn my back on Rose, picking up the folder on my desk.

"Nice to meet you, Miss Jacobs. I'm sure Jasmin can help you settle in," I say, effectively dismissing her.

The two leave as Jasmin whispers something about me not being that bad once you get to know me.

But she's forgetting this is a favor.

I have no intention of getting to know Rose Jacobs.

None at all.

Over the following days, I only catch glimpses of Rose a few times. Meetings take me away from the estate, and it's approaching her finishing time as I walk into the office on Friday afternoon. Jasmin has insisted on giving me regular updates though, saying Rose is settling in fine and getting on well with the rest of the staff.

I've already discarded my jacket and tie and rolled the sleeves of my black shirt up as I stride down to Rose's office. Her computer is still powered up, but she's not at her desk. I walk into my office. I always leave it open. Jasmin and Logan come in and out and sometimes work in here, despite having their own adequate offices. They say mine has the best view.

"No hiding in the chair this time, then?" I say as my gaze lands on Rose, bent at the waist, admiring the fish in the tank.

She straightens, her eyes dropping to my forearms and the full inked sleeves that cover the skin there.

"I wasn't hiding."

"So you said." I drop the folder I'm carrying onto my desk next to some accounting reports.

"It's not a full analysis, by any means. But I thought you might appreciate an update on what I have done my first week."

"Okay."

"So, what was it?" She juts her chin and folds her arms across her chest.

"What was what?"

"The reason you agreed to take me on. You must have one. I know my sister's friend pulled a favor."

Her blonde hair's swept forward over one shoulder. Defiance lights up her blue eyes. But for all the forced strength she's exhibiting, there is an undercurrent of pain screaming out underneath. She might be able to fool other people. But I've always been good at reading others. And I recognize a person who has something weighing heavily on their soul when I see one... A kindred spirit, I suppose.

I lean against the desk, crossing my legs at the ankle as I hold her gaze.

"It was Daisy Anderson. She's the owner of Aunt Iris's recipe."

"Your bestseller?"

"A global bestseller," I correct her. "It's served in the best hotels and bars around the world."

"I've had it before. It's nice."

"Just nice? It's triple distilled." I snort, earning a glare from her.

"You didn't answer my question. Why did I get this job?"

I rub my hand around my jaw. She's persistent. She will keep at me until I give her something.

"After I was sentenced, our contacts cut ties with us. The business would have gone under and left us with nothing. Aunt Iris's Blend is the reason we survived."

She doesn't react. Someone must have told her. It's hardly a closely guarded secret. The trial headlined the local papers for weeks.

I don't tell her that Daisy, the owner of the original recipe, had her own reasons for believing I should never have gone to jail. She told me she knows what evil looks like, and it isn't me. Her story is a wild one. But it isn't mine to tell.

"I will always be indebted to the Anderson family for choosing to place their faith and trust in me. So when Daisy said Maria reached out to her because she knew someone who needed some fresh scenery and had an eye for figures, I agreed to take you on."

Her shoulders soften, and her arms drop. "Maria is my sister's best friend. She used to work with someone called Daisy in California. That makes sense now. I guess I should be thanking you for taking me on as your charity case."

I cross the distance to her, and slam to a halt before inhaling.

Vanilla and petals.

"Listen. You aren't a fucking charity case. I'm not here to save you. Only you can do that," I hiss, failing to disguise the anger in my voice.

She stiffens again, lifting her eyes to mine, ever so defiant. She pulls her shoulders back and takes a deep breath.

"Good. Because I don't need saving. And certainly not by you," she declares.

The overwhelming urge to kiss her smart mouth strikes me like a hot poker to the heart, and I retreat quickly, dropping my hands to my hips.

"The workday ended ten minutes ago."

"So it did."

The light in my office dims as gloominess takes over the sky, and rain pours down. Rose glances at the window, then leaves.

She walks from the cottage every day. The thin blouse and short swishy skirt she's wearing won't last two seconds in the rain before she's soaked through and freezing.

I curse myself as I walk to the closet in my office. She's someone's sister, and the idea of Jasmin getting a chill or...

I grab the umbrella and march to Rose's office where she's turning off her computer.

"Here." I drop it on the desk. My lips twist at her soft expression.

Don't look at me like that, baby. I'm no fucking white knight.

"The idea of you getting wet is..." My eyes have a mind of their own and wander to her sheer blouse and the outline of lace beneath.

Fuck. Her wet... her long legs—Shut the fuck up, Dax.

"Thank you. I'll bring it back to you tomorrow."

"Tomorrow's Saturday."

"Monday, then."

I clear my throat and glance at her once more before I leave. "Have a nice weekend."

"You too, Dax," she calls behind me.

Her saying my name invokes a million images in my head that have no place there. Not now. Not ever.

Fuck doing favors for other people.

Chapter 5

Rose

I DROP THE GIANT knocker, letting it bang loudly against the thick, painted wood and step back, craning my neck to look at the house. Jasmin said Dax has converted the top floor to an apartment. Apparently, he never likes to be too far from work in case there's a problem. Guilt for being away for two and a half years—Jasmin's words.

I bang the knocker again before cursing myself inwardly as I spot a keypad. It's been cleverly concealed away from the main door, hidden behind one of the giant stone pillars. Still, it's a stupid place to put it. Difficult to spot unless you already know it's there. Maybe that's his reasoning. Judging by Dax's lack of friendly enthusiasm, I don't expect he likes to encourage visitors.

I press the buzzer. This is a stupid idea. He said to return his umbrella on Monday. But after going out with Jasmin last night to some local bars where she told me how incredible Dax's apartment is and how the view is even better up there, my curiosity was piqued. I've always loved being up high. Dad would take me, Brett, and Harley on walks to the highest point in our town and point out our school and all the places we visited down below.

Somehow being up high and looking down makes your troubles seem smaller.

I turn away seconds before the front door opens.

"Leaving already?"

I spin back around. Dax leans against the doorframe, arms crossed.

"Um..."

I let my eyes rake over his fitted black jeans and bare feet, before moving up to his black t-shirt. The sleeves are shorter than when he rolls his shirt up at work, and more of the full tattoo sleeves on each of his arms are visible. An intoxicating array of images stretch over his corded muscles before disappearing beneath the fabric. But his neck grabs my interest the most. There were hints of ink there beneath his work jackets, but it always felt too rude to stare. Now I can't stop myself. He has the most beautiful, intricate design of entwined leaves and flowers covering his skin. And there's even a bird. There's more to discover the longer I stare.

"Let me guess. You have virgin skin?"

I drag my eyes back to his.

"What did you call me?"

He chuckles. And it's deep and gravelly... and sexy as sin. My lower stomach clenches involuntarily as a flutter runs through it. He's staring at me intently and all of him is... it's... *He looks like sex.*

"I said I bet you have virgin skin. I wasn't asking if you've never fucked before."

My head jerks back. This is my boss. A man who's barely spoken since I started working here a week ago, except to grunt in response to the accounting updates I have given him. And now he's standing here, looking like a rock god, and using the word 'fucked' like it's a normal thing to discuss with someone you hardly know.

I let my eyes wander over his tattoos again. He couldn't be more different from my ex, Gareth, if he tried. Gareth was the typical clean-cut, fresh-faced boy next door. Someone safe and dependable. Only he wasn't. Not in the end.

I shake my head. Why am I even thinking of him now? We could never go back to where we were, not that I'd want to.

"Good. Because that's obviously none of your goddamn business," I fire back.

He rests his arm up against the doorframe, and his eyes twinkle as he smirks against his fist, rubbing his thumb over his lips. He hasn't shaved today. The extra scruff suits him. All the business shirts and jackets... he wears them well. But here like this, something tells me this is the real Dax standing in front of me right now. It's like he's shed some of his usual harshness when he's stripped of his suit.

But either way, I'm not about to stand and discuss my sex life with him and give him something to laugh about.

"Here." I thrust the umbrella into his hand and turn to leave.

"Hey." He grabs ahold of my wrist, gently curling his large hand around it to prevent me from leaving. The same static electricity that passed between us the first time we met crackles again, sending energy buzzing up my arm.

I turn back and frown at him.

"I'm sorry. I just like seeing that spark fire up I was told you have."

My skin bristles. My family must have told him more about me than I realized. It's something Harley has been the most vocal about. How she misses my feistiness. She said it's been absent so much since Brett's accident and since Dad passed. She said she always loved how despite being the youngest, I was the one most likely to get into a scrap, standing up for her or Brett.

I haven't felt much like fighting for anything in a long time.

"You've spoken with my family."

"Not much." His eyes hold mine. "But I wanted to know who I was trusting into my business, even if you being here is a favor."

I wince at his harsh reminder. I am here as a favor. Because I've let my family down. Because Mom lies awake every night, worrying about me and all the late nights and partying. All the toxic behavior that living with crippling guilt brings.

I've let so many people down.

"Breathe," Dax says softly.

I stare into his eyes, my wrist still held in his warm grasp. His deep brown irises are a stark contrast to his blond waves. I've never met anyone with such naturally dark eyes and light hair before.

"I can feel your pulse racing." He strokes his thumb over the inside of my wrist, pressing lightly against the pulsing vein there. The gesture is calming. He holds my gaze until I have to look away so I can do as he says—*breathe.*

I shouldn't have come. This is weird.

"See you on Monday." I pull my hand away.

He grabs it again, tugging me toward him. Heat radiates from his body as I stand before him, my chest inches from his.

His voice drops, softening like velvet, as he looks at me. Not many men look down at me with me being so tall, and This feeling... it's... nice. It's nice to feel like the one who could be wrapped up in strong arms and treasured.

"Come and have a tour. I know Jasmin told you I have an even better view from my apartment than from the chair in my office." He smirks again, and the corners of my mouth lift in response to the glint in his eyes. I'm beginning to see what Jasmin keeps telling me. Away from work, there's a man with a sense of humor, and maybe even a heart beneath all that ink and those incredible eyes.

"She only told me that last night when we went out for drinks."

"Yeah, I know." He looks at me in puzzlement. "I spoke to her this morning. We went for a run together. We talk every day."

The smile slides from my face.

"I used to run with my brother before he was knocked down by a speeding driver. He uses a wheelchair now," I confess in a trembling voice that sounds nothing like mine.

Dax rolls his lips, his eyes dusting over my face with a hint of something that better not be tenderness. I don't deserve it. He wouldn't feel sympathy for me if he knew it was my fault.

I take my hand back from him again, skating my fingertips over my wrist where he held it.

"Come on. I'm not getting any younger here, Rose." He smiles softly and tips his head to the open doorway. I walk ahead of him, grateful he doesn't ask me more about Brett.

Dax's apartment is amazing. It's neutral and calming, decorated in mostly white with lots of cushions scattered on the sofa, and modern art on the walls. Maybe Jasmin decorated it for him, because it's a stark contrast to the 'bad-boy' image he portrays, dressed in black with tattoos covering the majority of his body—the parts I have seen, that is.

He's kept all the original features, like the ornate ceiling roses and the cornicing around the top of the walls. And his bathroom has the most amazing claw-footed free-standing tub positioned in front of one of the giant windows. I bet he spends hours lying in it, staring out over the fields. I know I would.

But the roof terrace blows me away. Chest-height stone pillars join together, surrounding the edges of the space, making it feel like being encased on top of a castle. The floor is decked, and planters fill the space with greenery.

"You can see the cottage from up here." I rest my hands on top of the stone and look over at where I'm staying.

"Feel free to come up here should my office chair no longer suffice for your viewing and listening pleasure."

I side-eye Dax. I refuse to give him the pleasure of a reaction. He's trying to fire me up again. He admitted as much on the doorstep before I came inside.

"Why do you have fish in your office? You don't strike me as a Nemo fan."

He turns to me, his brows raised, and I bite back my smile. He was expecting me to counter his comment with my own, but instead, I've turned the conversation firmly back onto him.

He places both hands on the stone guard rail and looks out across the driveway toward the estate's main gate.

"I find them calming. My anger took me away from Jasmin, and I promised her I would find ways to control it so it wouldn't hurt us again."

"Took you away?"

He glances at me with a stormy gaze before he looks away again.

"Yeah. Being locked up has drawbacks." His lips twist into a grimace.

"Oh." I have no right to ask Dax personal questions. And now I've ruined what was turning into a nice afternoon in his company. It's the most time we've spent together since I've arrived.

I follow his line of sight over to the main gate where one of the Range Rovers is coming through.

"It's Logan. We have some work things to go over."

I chew on my lip. Everything about this afternoon has suddenly turned heavy and stifled. And I hate it.

"I'm sorry, I—"

"Don't worry about it." Dax sighs, then pushes off from the guard rail and turns toward the roof stairs. I follow him down through his apartment to the front door to meet Logan.

"I've got my own key for the main door, you dick," Logan says as Dax opens it wide. "Oh." Logan's gaze lands on me, and a grin spreads across his face as he looks from Dax to me and back again.

"Hi Rose."

"Hi, Logan."

"We've got work to do," Dax snaps, frowning at Logan and then darting his eyes to me briefly. "You okay getting back?"

"I'm only…" I motion toward the trees that sit in front of the cottage.

He looks at the sky. "It'll be getting dark soon. I'll watch from upstairs until you get inside."

"Why would you do that?" The words tumble from my mouth, earning a dark glare from Dax.

He cocks a brow as he continues to stare at me, repeating, "I will watch."

The intensity in his eyes makes heat fire in my cheeks.

I walk out the door and turn back to face him. "Um, okay."

I stand stunned as he tips his chin and then closes the door. How can he go from friendly host, to deep in thought and moody, to weirdly over-protective, all in the space of ten minutes?

I walk back to the cottage quickly as dusk settles. The entire way, the hairs on the back of my neck are standing to attention, uncomfortably aware that he is watching my every move.

I get to the front door and pause. Should I wave? Show him I'm here? No, that's stupid. He knows I am. He's watching.

I take my keys from my bag and fumble with them, dropping them to the floor. *Stupid.* I bend to retrieve them quickly, not paying attention to how I do it. *Shit.* I stand and smooth my dress down. It's fine. He's too far away. No way did Dax Silver see my ass in the lace thong beneath my dress. Not unless he has a telescope hidden up there in his comfy-ass apartment.

I take a deep breath, opening the door with steadier hands.

No, definitely no telescope that I saw.

I walk inside and flick the sitting room lamp on, looking out the front window and up to the main house where the lights are on in half of the upstairs windows. The one on the far left is his bedroom. I only saw it quickly on the tour. It felt odd spending too much time in there. The only thing I remember is he has a four-poster bed. A modern one with voile drapes around it.

The light in it flicks off. *Is that where he stood to watch me?* The idea of Dax Silver standing in the window of his mansion, dressed in black, his biceps tensing beneath his tattoos while he watches me, sends a shiver up my spine.

Only, with the way he blows hot and cold, I'm not sure whether that's a welcome shiver or not.

Only time will tell.

Chapter 6

Dax

"Let me see the message again."

Rose's face lights up as Logan passes her his phone. She and Jasmin bend their heads over the screen.

"She's definitely flirting."

"Absolutely. You should flirt back," Jasmin agrees, and the two of them break into giggles.

I lean back in my chair, a smile playing on my lips as they chat and laugh at things. It's so good to see Jasmin happy again. Seeing her here like this with Rose, it makes my chest swell with pride and relief that she can still smile the way I always remembered. I haven't seen it in a while. Maybe Rose's arrival is what's brought it on.

"You can't put that!" Rose gasps as Jasmin types something into Logan's phone.

He grabs it, and his brows shoot up his forehead. The girls shriek with laughter at his reaction.

"You"—he points his phone at them both—"are both filthy."

"Me? It was all her." Rose's cheeks flush.

"How much did you put on the bar tab?" Logan says with a smirk, leaning across the table.

My shoulders vibrate as I laugh softly. It's the first work night out I've taken the entire team on since I got out over six months ago. It's long overdue, and judging by the merry faces filling the restaurant and bar we've overtaken in town; it's appreciated.

Logan winces as one of the warehouse guys down the other end of our table sings loudly.

"I used to like this song. Now my ears will bleed whenever I hear it."

I chuckle, rubbing my thumb over my lips as Jasmin and Rose head over to the small dance floor by the back of the large space.

"She's got some moves." Logan watches Rose as she circles her hips in time to the music while wearing another short dress that shows off her long legs.

He turns when I don't respond.

"Don't," I grunt before he opens his mouth.

He holds his hands up. "I said nothing."

"You didn't have to."

"Only... When was the last time you went on a date or—"

"Fuck off."

He smirks into his drink as he drains his glass. "I'm just saying."

I swirl the deep amber liquid around in my glass. It's top shelf brandy. It's hitting the spot for now. But when you run your own distillery, you get kind of picky. At least, that's what I'm putting the creeping sourness over my tongue down to.

"Yeah? Well, don't." I *would* tell him he knows why I cannot get involved with Rose—or anyone even if I wanted to. But I can't say that. Because he doesn't know why. No one does. And that's the way it's got to be. This job is too dangerous already. I can't get caught and lose my life. I already lost some of it three years ago.

"Who were the girls texting on your phone? The same woman you told me about? From the dating app?" I ask, steering the conversation away from my dick and onto Logan's instead.

"Yeah. Cherry 69."

I snort as I drain the rest of my glass, grateful for the distraction. Logan has been using this dating app for months now, thinking he has exhausted Surrey's pick of eligible women to date. And now he's casting the net wider. The bastard gets loads of matches, too. He's a good-looking fucker with a certain charm about him, I guess. And he knows it. He's never had problems picking up women the entire time I've known him.

"She's probably some hairy biker from Glasgow."

He screws his face up before pointing at me. "No. She's a nimble twenty-one-year-old yoga instructor from London. Look."

He thrusts his phone into my face, and a new picture of the woman he's shown me before fills the screen.

"No way is she a yoga instructor with tits like that."

I chuckle as Logan turns the screen back around, hearts practically appearing in his eyes. He's a tits man, no doubt about it. You could stick a nipple on anything, and he'd be circling it, panting and whining like a puppy.

"Isn't that discriminatory to yoga instructors?"

"Logan, those tits are photoshopped. I'm telling you. If they were real, they'd be declared a country and would need their own border control. No way can she walk, let alone do a downward dog."

He frowns at the image, tilting the screen. "Fuck. You're right." He throws the phone down on the table and stretches his hands behind his head. "Back to square one."

"I think you need another drink." I laugh as I stand, following Logan's gaze to the dance floor. Jasmin and Rose are holding hands, dancing, heads thrown back, singing with their eyes closed.

I head over to the bar and order two more brandies, keeping my gaze firmly locked on the girls. The song ends and moves into another one I know Jasmin hates. She waves a dismissive hand in the air and then pulls Rose over to the bar, slamming into it on unsteady feet next to me.

"Hey, brother." She giggles and then orders two waters, fanning herself with one hand.

"All right, sis? Just water now, yeah?"

She rolls her eyes, turning to whisper to Rose, although she's tipsy and her whispering voice is even louder than her regular one. "Are all brothers such party-poopers?"

My eyes meet Rose's. She expertly hides most of her flinch at the mention of brothers. But not all of it. For a brief second, something flashes in her eyes. Something so raw my gut twists in response. It's gone almost as soon as it appears.

"Ugh. Really?" Jasmin sighs as the DJ plays another song by the same artist. "That's it. I'm not dancing to this all night." She knocks back her water and slams it back down onto the bar. "I'll be back." She strides off toward the DJ booth.

Rose whips her head around after her, losing her balance and swaying into me.

"Sorry."

I clasp her upper arms, steadying her.

"You okay?"

"Yeah. Sorry," she breathes, looking up at me.

Her pupils are dilated from the alcohol and her cheeks are flushed a warm pink. Her usually wavy blonde hair is straight tonight, reaching almost as far as her tiny waist. I gaze at her pouty pink lips and brush some loose strands of hair away from her eyes. She's like a doll. A delicate, porcelain doll. One I could break far too easily.

"Only water for you now, too."

Her brow wrinkles, and she opens her mouth—

My phone rings in my pocket, cutting off whatever it is she's about to say.

I pull it out. *Marcus.* Fuck's sake, what's wrong now? This is an easy job—shifting some product to the next county. Wait until we get onto the big stuff, like the international shipments. He needs to get his big boy pants on if he thinks this is the life for him.

"I've got to take this," I say.

She nods at me, turning back to her water, and I head outside.

"What is it?" I snap.

"I... um..." Marcus sniffs.

I clench my teeth.

"Spit it the fuck out," I hiss.

"Some guys came by. Two of them. Big ugly fuckers. They knew Mr. Young."

Mr. Young.

Fuck. Him sending someone to sniff around a small job like this is not a good sign.

"I'll be right there."

Chapter 7

Rose

I WRAP MY ARMS around myself, curling my torso in, trying to heat up. I don't know how I lost everyone. One minute we were all leaving the club we ended up in together, the next I was in the taxi line minus anyone I recognized. I've been into town on nights out with Jasmin before, but I've never seen the taxi line that busy. People were stealing cabs off each other left, right, and center. It's a miracle I even got one.

I stare up at the Silver Estate gate. They look even more imposing at night, lit up with the additional bathe of moonlight. I pull my phone out again.

Come on, Jasmin.

She texted me when I was in the cab, worrying over where I was and I told her I was safe, so she said she was making her way home, sharing a cab with Logan. They both live near the estate, so they should be home now too.

I check the time—three in the morning. I texted her over ten minutes ago now asking what the security code is for the gate. I've only ever come through it in a vehicle that's got an automatic sensor in, so the keypad on the stone wall to my right is as good as useless.

I shiver. I can't stay here all night. *Maybe I can—?* The top of the black metal gate is spiked. No. I don't like the idea of being impaled, even if I could climb that high.

I shuffle over to the keypad. *Damn you, Jasmin. Now I'll have to wake up that confusing brother of yours.*

My finger hovers over the call buzzer.

Dax disappeared tonight. Took that phone call and then stormed off. I saw him through the bar window, face like thunder, dark eyes almost black as he growled something into the phone. I wouldn't want to trade places with whoever was on the other end of the line.

Jasmin said he had probably used it as a ruse to leave early. Apparently, he isn't a big socializer anymore. She didn't say it in so many words, but she said enough for me to know that if Dax made one wrong move—being drunk and disorderly, get into a heated argument, or a scuffle, the way I've seen so many people do on nights out after a few drinks—then he could be straight back in jail.

I guess they are less lenient if you are caught offending a second time. However, I don't agree with her it was a ruse. I saw his face when he was on that call. He looked ready to murder someone.

"Damn it," I mutter, jabbing the button and squeezing my eyes shut.

Ten seconds pass.

Maybe he's not home yet.

"Rose?" His voice slices through the night air from the intercom. "What the hell are you doing out there?"

I pop my eyes open and look up. There's a security camera trained right on me.

"The taxi dropped me off and left. And I don't know the passcode. Can you please buzz me in?"

"Wait there," he snaps.

Like I'll go anywhere else.

I look over my shoulder to the dark, deserted country lane behind me. Ordinarily, I would love this if it were on screen in a movie. The moment before the stupid girl gets caught by the psychopath. But that's from my sofa in my pajamas. Standing here now while strange English animals snuffle and squawk, hidden from sight, is not doing it for me.

I shuffle closer to the gate.

How long does it take to press a button?

I turn back to the gate and squint as headlights approach, casting me under a spotlight, as they stop inches from the other side of the gate.

It slowly slides to one side as the front door of the Range Rover flies open and Dax jumps out. He marches over, leaving the door wide open behind him. He's wearing black sweatpants and a half zipped up hoodie.

He slams to a halt in front of me, his eyes scanning over me ruthlessly.

"What the hell, Rose? You're fucking shaking." He unzips his hoodie and peels it off, leaving his chest bare as he curses under his breath.

He loops his arms over my head and throws it around my shoulders, pulling the edges together over my breasts. His eyes simmer with anger as they meet mine. But I recognize something else there too. *Concern.*

I've spent years having my family and other people around me back home look at me with concern in their eyes. But not like this. Theirs was always tinged with sadness and hopelessness at how much they think I have changed since Brett's accident and losing Dad. I always felt some eyes—of the interfering neighbors—held blame in them, too. Much like mine when I look into a mirror.

But Dax? The concern in his eyes burning right through me right now isn't because he's remembering who I was once. He's thinking about who I am now. Standing here in this moment. Not the me I was before Brett was knocked down and hurt while out looking for me. Not the me I was before the stress of it all brought on my Dad's heart attack that killed him.

Just me. Here. Now. Alone and cold.

And it makes something inside me unfurl like a forgotten leaf, so far into spring that the other trees are all in full bloom and hope had all but gone.

I glance at his naked chest, covered in tattoos. They glow in the headlights like magical inscriptions carved into honeyed marble.

"It's nothing. I just got a little cold," I say to his pecs.

"What am I going to fucking do with you?" he growls, his voice softening.

I look up into his eyes and he is staring at me. The light catches his hair, highlighting the golden strands that are all mussed up and falling forward.

"You shouldn't be out alone at night. It's not safe." His eyes roam over my face and then body like he's checking I'm okay.

"Did I wake you? Were you in bed?"

He looks at my mouth and then back to my eyes and licks his lips. "Yeah."

"Alone?" I blurt, frowning the second it leaves my lips.

A grimace takes over his lips.

"You could have buzzed me in. You didn't have to get out of bed."

And leave whoever was there with you.

The idea that I interrupted Dax's night has my stomach churning with humiliation. Is she watching us on the camera now? Will he go back and tell her what the stupid new girl did? Will they laugh about me being so stupid and getting locked out?

He moves to the passenger door and opens it. "Get in the car. I'll drop you back."

"You don't need to do that, I can walk."

He sucks in a breath. "Rose..."

"It's only over there." I point to the tree line, all draped in pitch black.

"Get in the fucking car!"

My skin prickles as I walk to the open door. I dip past his naked chest and slide into the seat as he drags in a heavy breath.

He slams the door behind me and stalks around the hood, all the muscles in his upper body moving in perfect harmony with one another.

He throws himself into the driver's seat, his presence taking over the car.

Tension seeps into every space as he sits.

Just sits.

He doesn't drive away. He wraps his hands around the steering wheel, taking deep breaths, his eyes focused on the gate outside the windshield.

After an eternity, he finally speaks, his voice a rough whisper.

"I've seen what men are capable of, Rose. I've heard them talk." His eyes squeeze into slits as he keeps facing straight ahead. "Promise me you won't be out alone at night again?"

My heart beats steady and strong, centering me as I stare at him.

"Promise. Me. Please."

His voice loses all power as he looks at me. Waiting.

And for the first time, there is a vulnerability in Dax Silver that I've never noticed before.

And for all its raw beauty, it's fascinating.

Beside me is a man with hidden depths so dark I can never hope to understand them. Every curve of ink on his skin tells a story. A story about a man who loves his sister fiercely. A workaholic who has fought to keep a business afloat when people turned their backs on him. A man who has spent time away... locked behind bars... *caged.*

Who are you really, Dax Silver?

"Okay." I whisper. "I promise you."

"I think you'll love it. I've heard it's not gruesome, but it's jumpy. You'll totally shit your pants." Casey laughs as I prop my phone up on the sofa and grab the remote.

Her green face fills the screen. It's face mask and movie night. Something we used to always do when I was at home. Although, it's face mask and movie *afternoon* for her with the time difference.

I grab my bowl of popcorn and pull my legs up underneath me as I get cozy. The estate cottage has a comfy sofa. It's a corner one covered in cushions and a big old fleecy throw blanket. Jasmin said they usually rent the cottage out for short-term holiday rentals, but when Dax gave me the temporary job, he said I should use it. Maybe he thought I would feel like a fish out of water being so far away from home by myself. Whatever his reasons, I'm glad. I'm getting used to the weird nighttime noises and having my own space. I mean, I love Mom, but how many twenty-five-year-olds still live at home? After Brett's accident, I wanted to be there with him. Before I realized, it had become too hard to leave. Even though now I'm thinking leaving was the best thing I did. For me. For everyone.

I flick the TV on.

"I've missed this." I smile at Casey's face on the screen.

She wraps her own blanket tighter around herself. "Me too."

This is good. It's not the same as her being here, but it's still so good to see her face and hear her voice. She's been filling me in on the new guy she's started dating. She's been single for years. Up until now, she's been adamant she doesn't want to be in a relationship, being on the verge of tears if anyone ever pushed the subject. She never explained why, besides saying who needs a man when you have friends. And I didn't push it any further because it made her so upset. Maybe me moving away has given her the time to finally date—we were almost inseparable. Whatever the reason is, I'm happy for her.

"Oh, what?" I groan as the TV screen freezes and then goes blank. I flick it back on again and the same thing happens, leaving me staring at a black screen. "Hold on," I say to Casey, getting up and checking the plugs. I switch them off, then on again, but the stupid thing does the same again.

"You aren't on some middle-of-nowhere meter there, are you? One you have to put coins in or crank up?" Casey laughs.

"No." I sigh, flopping down onto the sofa.

"Can Jasmin help? Maybe it's happened before."

I grab my phone. "I'll text her and ask."

Me: Hey. The TV in the cottage keeps shutting off. Do you know if it's done it before?

Jasmin: Strange... it's usually fine. Don't worry, I'll sort it.

Me: Don't come all this way for that. It doesn't matter.

There's a delay before her reply comes in.

Jasmin: Not me, I'm at the hairdresser's. And I've already messaged him. He's on his way.

Me: Logan?

Jasmin: Dax.

Shit.

"Case? I'm going to have to go." I jump up off the sofa and take the stairs two at a time up to the bathroom. "I'll call you back if it's working again soon, okay?"

"Sure."

"I'm sorry."

"It's fine." She smiles. "I just miss you, that's all. Speak to you later."

"Yeah, later." I smile back. "Case?"

"Yeah?"

"Sandbox to casket."

She grins. "Sandbox to casket. Love you."

I end the call and bend over the sink, scrubbing off the bright green clay mask. Thank God I'm in loungewear and not my actual pajamas. Harley has a thing for ugly pajamas she thinks are cute and bought me a short set with cartoon singing waffles all over them to bring with me. I've never been so grateful for a cropped hoodie and leggings before. Not that I'm bothered what Dax thinks. But he is my boss, and well... singing waffles.

There's a knock at the door. I grab a towel and scrub my face dry, tossing it onto the side of the sink so I can go answer it.

How does he get everywhere so fast?

I open the door, and there he is. Black shirt open at the neck, blond waves pushed back off his face, and deep brown eyes that connect with mine instantly.

He fills the doorway, the scent of his aftershave floating into the cottage and making me inhale a little slower. A little deeper.

He smells heady, and dark, and... expensive. The way he smells at work. It's different to how he smelled last night when he dropped me back in the dark. Last night, he smelled warm. Of warm skin that had gotten out of bed. It was his smell. His own scent.

"You going to let me come inside?"

"It's not a problem. I don't want to interrupt whatever it is you're doing." I look at his suit again and the way the black open collar makes his neck tattoo look even more incredible. The leaves, the bird's feathered wings. So intricate. *So beautiful.*

"What I'm doing right now is waiting for you to invite me in, Rose." His eyes stay fixed on mine. "Do you want my help or not?"

So we're back to moody, sarcastic Dax again? I would love to throw a comeback at him. But I want his help. I need to call Casey back and laugh as we scare ourselves stupid watching a horror movie together. I want to not think about anything else for a blissful ninety-five minutes.

I open the door wider, and he raises a brow at me.

"Yes." I hold his gaze. "I want it."

Chapter 8

Dax

ROSE STANDS NEXT TO me, so close I can smell her. *Vanilla and fucking petals.* Why couldn't Daisy have asked me to give a guy a job for a while? Not a tall, blonde with shapely legs I can finally see all the way to the top of in the pair of skintight leggings and short hoodie she's wearing. A blonde with a smart mouth and a smart mind.

Her hair is piled on top of her head today with strands falling around her face. And she's not wearing any make-up. The urge to wrap her up and protect her hits me like a sledgehammer. She shouldn't be here. She doesn't belong anywhere near the shadows I exist alongside. The world I inhabit would be like black tar on white silk for her. Sticky, insipid, ruining the hint of purity and innocence her eyes still hold. Even though she tries to hide it, I see it. Rose Jacobs has a pure heart with pure intentions. Something that doesn't mix with my world.

She's chewing on her bottom lip, humming gently as she watches me flick through the TV settings with the remote. I tense my jaw to stop myself from telling her to stop.

To stop fucking torturing me.

I alter the TV's automatic shutoff timer back to 'off,' so it won't keep turning off, and then scroll through to the movies.

"What were you trying to put on?"

"Oh." Her brows shoot up. "That one."

She points to a horror movie I've seen. One where a woman is made to watch as each of her friends are ended in front of her, and then told to run as the killer counts down, giving her a brief head start in the deserted snowy town they're in.

"Really? Not a rom-com girl, then?"

"Did I ever give that impression?" She huffs, crossing her arms and making her hoodie ride up, exposing a flash of smooth stomach.

"With that smart mouth? No." I avert my gaze and set the movie up so all she needs to do is click play.

"What? Horror movies are more realistic."

"You think you're more likely to be chopped up by a psycho with an axe than fall in love?"

She turns to face me head-on; her arms still firmly crossed over her chest like a shield.

"Movie love doesn't exist. Fairytales don't exist. But murderers and psychos are real," she says, as though that explains everything.

"I guess hanging around deserted country lanes at night alone increase your chances of meeting one," I mutter, placing the remote on the sofa.

She ignores my dig about last night. I still can't believe she would be so careless with her own safety. If anything had happened to her...

"Attraction is just dopamine." She sniffs, tightening her arms around herself. "Cause and effect, nothing more. A perceived high in our body from a chemical change. That's what love is. Just a chemical."

"Chemical, sure." I allow myself the brief indulgence of staring into her light blue eyes. "Whatever you say."

She follows behind me as I walk to the door.

"You don't agree?"

I turn, leaning back on the closed door, crossing my arms over my chest, mirroring her pose as I sigh. Like usual, she isn't going to leave this.

"Look, it's not for me to tell you what love is. That's for you to decide. You want to not believe in it? Fine. You want to think it's a load of shit? Fine. You want to marry the first guy who tells you he loves you? Fine. You want to live alone with a load of cats and have a house that reeks of piss? Fine. It's your life, Rose."

Anything is fine with me.

I'm lying out of my ass. The idea of her having anything less than what she deserves and what will make her happy is like a gut-punch.

She's better than all of it.

Her mouth drops open, her forehead wrinkling before she snaps it shut and glares at me.

"I like cats."

"Okay," I say slowly. Not the reaction I was expecting.

"And I would have married him if he'd asked."

Hang on, what?

"Who?" I grit, hating the fucker already. If there's a guy who Rose could have seen herself marrying, then why is she here arguing with me on the other side of the Atlantic? Why did she need time away? Daisy never mentioned an ex. Just family issues since losing her dad.

"It doesn't matter." Her shoulders drop as she looks away. "He wasn't who I thought he was after everything."

I maintain my position, leaning back against her door with my arms crossed, studying her. From the outside, I probably look calm. But inside, I'm burning up with rage from the way her body and voice have crumpled. I hate to see women upset. Maybe it's the big brother in me.

"And who was that?" I ask, not sure I want to know the answer.

Rose brings her shining eyes back to mine and shrugs her shoulders. She's trying to play it down. Whatever happened with this guy obviously hurt her. This is the most rattled I've seen her.

"My ex, Gareth. We were together since I was eighteen. I thought we were going to have it all together, you know? Marriage, kids, house in the suburbs." She looks at the floor, pushing at a piece of fluff on the carpet with her toe. "Then one day, he said he was taking a promotion in Washington. Alone." Her brows quirk as she continues fussing with the carpet. "We'd only moved in together the month before, and we had... we'd..." She sighs with a humorless laugh. "Never mind. That's too much info. Let's just say he knew... He knew a while before he told me. And he let me believe differently. I made choices based on what I thought we had. When it was all a lie... I was stupid."

"No, you weren't. He was a prick."

Her eyes widen as they pop up to meet mine.

"He was," I state again, because she needs to hear it. What kind of guy takes a new job and moves states without talking to his long-term girlfriend first?

A prick, like I said.

"I..." She studies me, uncrossing her arms. "Maybe he was. But I still made mistakes I can't take back now."

"So move forward. You can't change the past, but you can carve your future."

She stares at me again like I'm talking another language she doesn't understand.

"You have no idea about the mistakes I've made, Dax. And I don't just mean letting Gareth..." She screws her face up, squeezing her eyes shut as her voice cracks. "Letting him trick me like that. I've made a lot. I've fucked up and hurt people. Sometimes I think I don't deserve to—"

The waver in her voice as she pauses before those next words has me closing the gap between us in one lightning step. And I grasp the back of her neck with one hand, pressing my lips to her forehead with the other.

"Don't finish that sentence. Don't you fucking dare."

She freezes in my grasp.

"Breathe," I whisper against her skin, my lips still against her forehead.

She relaxes enough for her body to sink a little closer to mine.

I keep my hand on the back of her neck, my thumb curled round to monitor her pulse.

It's racing.

"Breathe," I repeat.

I hold her as she uncurls her arms between us and rests her hands on my chest. She takes in shaky breaths as I slide my other hand around her waist and flatten my palm against her lower back.

And I hold her like that, in the silence of the cottage, the two of us, both broken in our own ways, until her heart rate slows and her breathing calms.

I let my eyes fall closed as I drink in her scent. Commit it to memory for later. For when I'm alone and can let my imagination run wild.

"You are so much more than that. You're not the mistakes you've made. You're not responsible for the mistakes he made, either. Don't let anyone ever tell you otherwise."

I press a kiss to her forehead. It's a habit. I've always done it to Jasmin if she's ever upset.

Only, this is Rose.

"They don't," she says, her voice faint. "They don't. It's *me* who tells me. It's why my family wanted me to come here. They say it's all me. That I need to forgive myself." Her voice drops again, and if I weren't so close with my body pressed to hers, then I would miss the words. "Some days I can't even look at myself in the mirror. I just see the cause of so much pain."

I slide my lips from her skin, dipping my head so our foreheads almost touch.

"Look at me."

She presses her lips together, keeping her eyes down.

"Look at me," I urge softly.

Slowly she lifts her gaze to mine, looking up at me through dark lashes. Her eyes are dry, but they're glassy, and fuck if my heart doesn't die right here. The heart I wonder if I have. Only, I must. Because the pain in my chest at the hopelessness in her eyes is like a dagger slicing through it.

"You are beautiful. Exactly as you are. We all make mistakes. I've made a fuck ton."

She gives me a small smile, and I shake my head gently.

"But they're gone. They're done. Don't waste breath trying to change something you can't. Use it to do things differently from now on."

I return her small smile as she sniffs and nods at me. "Yeah. I guess."

"I want you to look in the mirror and see what your family see. What I see."

"What's that?" Her breath mixes with mine as our lips hover inches apart.

"Someone worth saving."

I squeeze the back of her neck gently and kiss her forehead again before letting her go and turning to open the door before I do something else. Something my body is screaming for, but my mind is holding me back from.

She isn't mine to touch. She isn't mine to kiss. She isn't mine to taint and ruin with my life and all its ugliness.

And it needs to stay that way.

I turn my back on her and stride through the door.

Rose Jacobs doesn't belong near me with her virgin skin any more than I belong near her with my stained hands. Those two worlds don't mix. They couldn't be farther apart if they tried. Like truth and lies. Justice and Revenge. Love and hate. *Hard, cold, silver, and soft, sweet, flowers.*

Nothing about us belongs near the other.

"Call Jasmin if you need anything again, okay?" I say over my shoulder.

"Dax?"

I turn and look straight into her clear blue eyes.

Fuck, why have I no willpower? I should be in the car driving away.

Her brow furrows as she stares at me. Seconds ago, she was in my arms. She feels the turn in atmosphere—the sudden change in me as my head takes over, *damage limitation*—that much is clear by the way her mouth is parted in a perfect O.

I'm sorry, Sunbeam. Don't look at me like that.

I give her a tight smile, then climb into the Range Rover and drive away.

Chapter 9

Rose

IF THE WRITERS OF the dictionary need a new adjective for confusing, then they could put Dax Silver's picture there. After the weird, but strangely comforting moment we shared at the cottage yesterday, he's been avoiding me. Although, I can't prove it. He could have been out for meetings all day, but it feels like he's distancing himself from me on purpose.

I take a sip of my white wine and tune back into the conversation Jasmin and Logan are having. We've come out after work to have dinner. I couldn't be more grateful that everyone else on the estate is lovely. And these two... I will miss them so much when I return to New York, because they have been my rocks since I arrived.

"You cannot be serious?" Jasmin grabs Logan's phone from him, swiping through it.

"What?" I ask, wanting the distraction. Now it's not just home and my own guilt taking over my head, but thoughts of Dax hot-and-cold Silver, too.

Jasmin rolls her eyes. "Logan thinks this is a good chat-up line." She tilts the phone screen so I can read the messages between him and *MissFoxyFarnham.*

"Still using this dating app, then?" I lean forward, reading the exchange.

LoadedLogan31: When can I take you out?

MissFoxyFarnham: I'm seeing someone new. I'm about to delete this app.

LoadedLogan31: Don't let a boyfriend ruin your chance of meeting your future husband.

"First of all, that name." Jasmin throws her head back and laughs, her long dark waves falling down her back. "Loaded Logan?"

"What?" Logan stares at us both. "My name's Logan Rich. So... rich... loaded, and also..." He arches one brow. "Loaded. You know what I mean?"

"Eww." Jasmin straightens in her seat, her lip curling in distaste before holding a hand up. "No is all I am going to say about that. But secondly, Logan, that's such a douchebag thing to say."

"I thought it was quite witty," he mumbles into his glass.

Jasmin rests her forearms on the table and leans toward him. "You're telling me that if this girl says yes that you'd actually want to take her on a date? If she's happy to cheat on her boyfriend, then she would do the same to you, you idiot."

Logan frowns into his glass before placing it on the table and opening his mouth to speak.

"And don't"—Jasmin holds up one finger—"say some shit about how she would be so satisfied by you she wouldn't need to look elsewhere. Because I'm telling you, if a person cheats so easily with no regard to anyone else's feelings, then they will always cheat. Won't they, Rose?"

She turns to me, inclining her head to Logan.

"Yes," I agree. "Absolutely. Cheating ruins everything. It's vile and it's selfish, and it wrecks lives."

Jasmin raises her brows, maybe not expecting me to be so passionate on the subject. But pleased nonetheless as she tips her head back at Logan in a told-you-so manner.

"Where's your brother when I need him?" Logan pipes up with a chuckle. "I'm outnumbered two to one here."

"I don't know. Taking care of some things he said he had to do. Besides, don't think for one second he would support this little dick-led notion of yours." Jasmin looks at Logan pointedly. "He knows better than that."

"He's scared of you, you mean?" Logan laughs, earning himself a slap around the bicep from her.

"Shut up, idiot." She smirks. "Thankfully, my brother is more mature than this one, despite them being the same age," she says. "Dax has always been in control, but since he got out, he's been even more serious. I wish he would loosen up a little. He works too hard."

"He's just worried about the business, with him being away from it for so long." Logan turns serious.

"I know. But we managed, didn't we? Besides, I'm not convinced that's all it is. I'm amazed he came for the staff night out the other week. He never comes out with us anymore."

Jasmin's right. I've already been out with her and Logan multiple times for drinks and to a club since I arrived. And the staff party is the only night Dax came, even though I'm sure Jasmin invites him every single time.

"He's thirty-one years old, and he's a hermit. He's either at work or out at meetings. Being in jail changed him. He's obsessed with the idea that one wrong move and he could be back there. So he never goes anywhere. Or does anything." Jasmin drops her chin into her hands on the tabletop, her shoulders sagging. "It worries me. He should be doing the things he missed out on. He's always had to be the grown up. Thinking he had to look after me. He never got to be stupid and make mistakes like most teenagers. The first one he made landed him in jail."

"What happened? Sorry... I mean, it's none of my business," I say with an apologetic smile.

I don't want to admit that I know he was sentenced to three years for grievous bodily harm with intent, thanks to Google. But the news articles didn't tell the story behind his motive. Only that he had laid into a guy at some big business dinner event. Why would he do that unless he was provoked somehow?

"Don't worry, it's not a secret. But it is a complicated story." Jasmin sighs, pressing the heels of her hands into her eyes. "It was my fault."

"It wasn't. The guy deserved it." Logan turns from Jasmin and fixes his gaze on me. "There's a guy, Julian Young. He runs one of the country's main import and export companies for wine and liquor. The Silver Estate didn't bother him until Dax and Jasmin took over."

"But since our grandparents passed and we inherited the business, things got... messy," Jasmin adds. "He was jealous that Dax secured the sole production rights for Aunt Iris's Blend. It was a huge contract. Julian wanted to win it and then outsource production to overseas to keep costs low."

"Rake in the cash," Logan snorts.

"He was always making digs at Dax whenever he saw him at business events. But Dax ignored him. Until Julian got drunk one night at an event and got a little handsy with me, then sent me a delightful selection of dick pics from the men's restroom."

"Gross." I recoil.

"So gross," Jasmin agrees. "Dax saw my phone. I was standing with him and had no idea what I'd been sent. He marched right over to Julian in front of everyone in the room and I saw Julian say something quietly to him, then the next second, all hell broke loose."

"It was impressive." Logan smirks.

"It was awful." Jasmin scowls. "Dax was like a man possessed. I've never seen him so mad. He just kept hitting Julian over and over. Julian smashed a glass and went for Dax, and then Dax broke a chair over him."

"Dax was awesome. The cock deserved it."

Jasmin flashes Logan a stern look that shuts him up. "He might have deserved it. But the law doesn't see it like that. Dax threw the first punch. He approached Julian. And Julian was the one who needed surgery for internal bleeding. Dax barely had a scratch on him."

"Yeah, and Julian was unconscious," Logan says.

"He tried to get Dax charged with attempted murder. He would have been gone for years." Jasmin's lower lids pool with water. "I'm sorry." She sniffs, wiping them away. "I hate thinking about it. Two and a half years felt like a lifetime. The idea that… I just can't bear to think about it."

"I'm sorry I asked." I wrap my arm around her, and she squeezes my hand.

"Don't be. You work with us. You're our friend. You should know what happened."

"Dax served two and a half years of a three-year sentence. They let him out early for good behavior," Logan says.

"He *is* good." Jasmin wipes her eyes again with one hand, still holding mine with the other. "He's amazing. Honestly, Rose. Don't let this change the way you see him. I know he looks like this bad guy with all his tatts and moodiness. But he's got the biggest heart. He'd just turned eighteen when we lost our parents. He had to look after me. He had to grow up fast. His whole life has been about doing the right thing and thinking of others before himself. I just wish he'd realize that he needs to put himself first now. I want him to be happy."

"He's lucky to have you." I rest my head on top of Jasmin's head, and she sighs.

"*I'm* lucky. I don't deserve him." She sniffs and wipes her eyes again with a laugh. "This sure got heavy."

"I'm so sorry I asked." Guilt pulls at my chest.

"Stop. I won't hear it. I'm fine. Everything's fine. Brothers, eh?" She laughs again, and I smile because I know what she means. I love my brother, Brett, more than anything. He's always put me first, too. He was out looking for me that day Gareth dumped me. He shouldn't have even been walking on that road. I'm the reason he was.

My smile slips. *I'm the reason.*

"I hate to break up all the fun," Logan says. "But *Miss-FoxyFarnham* just messaged me back."

"What did she say?" Jasmin straightens, her voice suddenly filling with energy.

I straighten up too, grateful for the change to a lighter topic.

Logan's eyes light up and his brows shoot up his forehead as he reads the message. "She said, I have a girlfriend, not a boyfriend." He grins as his fingers fly over the screen typing out a reply.

"Please tell me American men aren't such dicks?" Jasmin says loud enough for Logan to hear, but he's far too busy studying his phone, his cheeks glowing.

I bite my lip, pushing Gareth firmly to the back of my mind.

"I wish I could."

Jasmin and Logan drop me off at the main estate gate, after buzzing it open for me, and I walk up the main drive toward the turn off for the cottage. It's still light. After Dax's warning the other night, had it been dark, then I would have asked them to drop me at the front door. But I like the walk. It's not far. And the estate is beautiful. The main drive is lined with these weird-looking trees called monkey puzzles. They have long textured branches that hang down like monkey tails. I guess that's where they get the name.

I step back so I can stare at one of the trees.

That's when the main gate whirrs and a silver Range Rover without the estate logo on the side glides through. It drives right up to me, only slowing to a stop because I'm standing in the road. If I wasn't, then I get the distinct impression it was about to drive past me.

I look through the windshield and lock eyes with dark brown. Dax stares back, his eyes holding mine as he swipes his thumb across his lips and licks the corner of them.

I walk over to the driver's side window and wait as it slides down just enough that the top half of his face is visible through the tinted glass.

"What happened to your face?" I stare at the beginnings of a bruise shading the contours of Dax's cheekbone and unease gnaws low in my stomach. Something isn't right. "Roll the window down. Now."

His eyes flash with something before he presses the button, and the glass slides all the way down.

"Dax?" I gasp as I take in his face. His cheekbone is bruised and his lip split, blood staining the crease at the corner of his mouth.

"It's nothing." He looks through the windshield, his hands flexing on the wheel. His knuckles are grazed, his right ones swollen.

"Where have you been?"

He shakes his head with an empty chuckle. "This isn't your fight."

"What's that supposed to mean?"

He snaps his eyes to mine and they're dark and glistening. "It means go home."

"No!" I'm fed up with him ordering me around, thinking he knows best. My family sent me here, thinking they know what is best for me. Other people are always telling me what to do.

Be kind to yourself, Rose. You need time, Rose. It wasn't your fault, Rose.

I march around the hood of the Range Rover and yank the passenger door open.

"What are you doing?" Dax grits, his jaw tensing as I climb into the passenger seat and slam the door shut.

"Hanging out with a jerk, it would seem," I mutter as he glares at me.

"A jerk?" he growls.

"Yeah." I look at the fresh blood running from his lip again. "One with a face that's too pretty to be banged up like that. Now drive, please." I fold my arms and face straight ahead, waiting for him to argue, to contradict me. To make me get out of the car and leave me here as he kicks up gravel and dust in my face.

"What am I going to fucking do with you?" he mutters.

It's the second time he's asked himself that.

I get under his skin. I must by the way he reacts to me sometimes. But I bet it's not half as much as he gets under mine.

Dax hot-and-cold Silver.

He shoves the car into drive without saying another word.

Chapter 10

Dax

"So, ARE YOU STILL not going to tell me how this happened?" Rose asks as she presses an ice pack wrapped in a washcloth to my cheek.

My eyes pinch at the corners, and I ignore the sting in my skin.

"Fine." She huffs. "Suit yourself. Hold this." She places my hand over the ice pack so she can press another washcloth to my split lip.

"You've done this before?" I ask, watching the way her blue eyes narrow as she concentrates.

I'm sitting on the sofa in my living room, and she is on her knees between my legs, smelling and looking like too many thoughts I cannot entertain. She's wearing a white t-shirt and another of her short, loose skirts. They flow around the tops of her thighs, swishing as she walks. Not that I watch. At least, not all the time.

"My brother, Brett, would get into the occasional fight when we were younger," she says, dabbing at the corner of my mouth to loosen the dried blood. She frowns as her eyes wander over my face again, her dark lashes fluttering over her cheeks each time she blinks.

She's so beautiful. Pure and fucking beautiful. I can't tell her I had to put a guy in his place earlier today who thought it was okay to steal the product for his own use. She'd run out of here faster than he was snorting it up his nose when I caught him.

I look down and flex my fingers. Rose follows my gaze, her frown only deepening at the sight of my red knuckles. It's a good thing she can't see the other guy. This is nothing.

"I bet he was keeping the boys away from you and your sister. That's what brothers do."

"Did you do that for Jasmin? Scare them all away?" Her lips curl into a smile.

"Of course I fucking did."

She laughs softly.

Beautiful and pure.

Not for you, Dax.

"Brett did do that for me and Harley," she says, turning her attention back to my lips. I should do this myself. But her doing it, taking care of me... it's... nice. "He was always looking out for us both. And us for him, too. We were all really close once."

"Once?"

Any remnants of her laugh dies in the air as her face closes off.

"Yeah. Things change. But I guess you know this already. You agreed to give me the job. You must have heard from my family why they thought I needed time away?"

She pauses, her hand hovering over my skin as she hesitates.

"Perhaps. But I haven't heard it from you."

She inhales slowly, and her long blonde hair catches the light, framing her face as she lifts her eyes. They're clear and bright and make something lodge in my chest that shouldn't be there. I can't look away. I shouldn't be asking her these things, encouraging her to open up to me. To bare herself. It's not fair. Because I can never do the same. I can't tell her who I really am.

I can't tell anyone.

"I..." She shakes her head and looks down at the cloth in her hand. "Brett was run down by a driver in broad daylight, over three years ago. The guy never stopped to check if he was even alive. Just left him at the side of the road like he was nothing. He was too busy racing home to his wife to stop his mistress from telling his wife about their affair. And after, the stress of it all brought on Dad's heart attack that killed him. The doctors never said that was the cause. But we all knew."

I listen as she continues to blot my lip, her eyes now focused on her task again.

"I'm sorry."

Her lips twist into a tight line and she exhales through her nose.

"It's my fault. Brett was out looking for me that day. Me and Gareth had a fight and I stormed off. I just went for a walk, and I called Brett in a mess telling him how stupid I felt. He came out to look for me. That's why he was there. That's why he got hit."

"That wasn't—"

"My fault?" She shakes her head, keeping her eyes down. "That's what everyone keeps telling me. But I...

and the thing with Gareth... I just felt so deceived. So... *so stupid.* Gareth told me he was offered this new job in Washington. It was really good for him. More money, more responsibility. He wanted to take it. I was so happy. I thought he meant both of us. I thought he wanted me to go with him. I even thought he was about to propose, you know? Make it a totally new chapter for us. But he didn't. Instead, he told me he was going alone."

"He was a selfish prick, Rose," I say with conviction because it's the truth. And also, he was a fucking fool. I mean, look at her. Listen to her. It doesn't take a genius to see how wonderful Rose Jacobs is. She's smart, witty, gentle, and beautiful. Far too good for a prick named Gareth.

"You already told me that. And I agree." She smiles and bites her bottom lip.

"I can tell you a third time if it keeps you smiling."

She freezes and looks me in the eyes as something passes between us. Something unspoken, but significant. Something I should not be encouraging. And something I definitely shouldn't be so fucking happy about. There's even a warmth spreading in my chest.

She tucks her hair behind one ear and continues cleaning me up, her eyes darting to mine and away again.

"Do you think I'm uptight?" she whispers.

I pull my brows together, ignoring the tenderness in my cheek as I frown.

"Why are you asking me that?"

"It's something Gareth said."

I grit my teeth. *Fucking Gareth.* The bastard deserves to have his ass handed to him.

"What did he say?" I growl, not even trying to hide my murderous tone.

"He..." Rose averts her eyes from my face again. "You have blood on your shirt." She points to the dried red spots on the front of it. I know it isn't mine. Typical that I wore a white shirt today. If Marcus kept his asshole friends in line, then I wouldn't have needed to ruin it.

I rip it open and pull my arms out, tossing it aside onto the floor.

"What did he say?" I ask again, but Rose isn't listening. Her lips have parted as she studies my skin, sweeping her eyes over it, taking her time as she gazes at my tattoos. I have a lot. It's kind of an obsession. My entire chest, back, arms and neck are covered. And I have them running around one thigh as well. Most people think they're too much.

"They're stunning." Rose gazes at the compass on my chest, set to west for the sunset. She drops the cloth onto the sofa and looks at me.

I nod, answering the silent question in her eyes.

She reaches out, and with a featherlight touch, traces her fingertips around the circumference of the compass, before following a twisting branch from it, covered in leaves that snake down my side. My muscles tense and spark with heat and energy from her touch. But she's too lost in her own world as she explores me to notice.

I suck in a breath and take the ice pack away from my cheek, dropping it onto the cushion next to me. I place both hands on Rose's rib cage and wrap them around her gently, sliding down her body until my thumbs rest over her hip bones. They look so wrong there, inflamed, bloodied knuckles against the pure white cotton of her t-shirt. And I'm kidding myself if I think I should allow myself to indulge even for a second, in the complete, intoxicating rush that having my hands on her gives me. I held her in the cottage. But that was different. She was upset. It was instinct.

This time, it's pure selfish indulgence.

I should move them. I should.

I curl my hands and squeeze, holding her tighter.

She continues stroking my skin, small murmurs of awe and delight escaping her lips as she discovers something else.

"Do you have them on your back as well?"

"I do." I clear my throat, unable to take my eyes from hers. I make no attempt to move forward for her to see, but she's content to continue her exploration of my front, her comfortableness growing as she adds her other hand and allows both to roam all over my bare skin.

Her eyes dart side to side, a small smile playing on her lips as she notices something new. I flex my fingers on her hips and it takes all my willpower not to tear her t-shirt off and start my own exploration of her.

"There are so many," she says. But where I am used to that being said with an edge of surprise and distaste, Rose's voice is only warm with sincerity. "Which was your first?"

I twist my arm so she can see the eagle on my left shoulder. She immediately places her fingers to it and smiles as she strokes its wings as though the feathers there are real and soft to the touch.

"It started on my eighteenth birthday. Mom took me. It's not that she wanted me to have one, exactly. But she always supported me and Jasmin in whatever we wanted to do. She probably thought I would regret it and never have any more." I smile. She always encouraged me and Jasmin to make our own decisions. I had no idea we would lose her soon after that day.

"After her and Dad died, I got the compass. And then it just kept going. I like that they're permanent. Memories can fade. But these never do."

"I think I understand that." Rose smiles softly as she glances at my face before looking back at my chest. "I can't decide which I like best. I think maybe..." She runs her hands up over my collarbones and to my neck and the small bird hiding amongst the flowers and leaves there. "I think maybe this one. I like the way the rest are covered by your suit at work, but this little man wants to be seen." She strokes the small hummingbird and the muscle in my jaw works on overtime beneath her soft touch. "Maybe I should give him a name."

"Like what?" I stare, transfixed at the delight swimming in her eyes.

"I don't know. Chirpy?" She giggles, then bites her lip, looking back over my chest again. "I love how free you are, Dax. How you've chosen all of these for you."

My heart stalls. *Free? She thinks I'm free?*

"I'm not that strong. I listen to other people too much." Her voice falters.

"You mean, Gareth?" I hiss, hating that I'm saying his name again. Hating that he's inside her head. That he's the cause of her entire posture changing as the delight in her eyes dims until it's extinguished.

"I thought we were the real thing. I thought it was forever. The old Rose believed in love. The old Rose wanted to wait until she was married." She scoffs. "How ridiculous is that?"

My hands burn against her hips as what she's saying sinks in. Yet, I still can't bring myself to move them.

She keeps stroking my skin, as though the distraction makes it easier for her to talk.

"Gareth said of course we were headed that way and it shouldn't matter. We had just moved in together and he said that was worth celebrating. And I agreed. I'm weak, Dax. I'm stupid and I'm weak. He knew when we did it that he was going to leave. Maybe he didn't know what date the new job would start. But he must have known it was a possibility that he would get it. I think he always knew that he wanted to go alone. He just wanted to see what he was leaving behind," she murmurs. "Maybe if I had been better, he would have asked me to go with him, who knows."

If she had been better? Jesus Christ.

I fight down the rage simmering inside me, threatening to erupt. I fight it down with everything I have.

I inhale slowly.

What can I smell? Vanilla. Petals.

What can I see? Long, dark lashes, clear blue eyes.

What can I hear? Her breathing, soft and gentle. My pulse hammering in my ears.

Breathe. Breathe.

"You're saying you've only ever been with him?" I ask softly, aware that if I give even my voice one ounce of the fire licking at me, it could be game over. I'm holding on by a thread.

She nods, her pupils dilating as she looks at me. "Just the one time."

Jesus fucking Christ.

"He said he didn't really understand why I was so uptight about it. That it wasn't a big deal. I wasn't *his* first. I started to wonder if there was something wrong with me. If I wasn't passionate because I wasn't battling with myself daily to resist. But... I... I just wanted to wait. Mom and Dad did. She told me once. And I guess I looked at how in love they were, and I romanticized it. I made it bigger than it needed to be in my head."

"You are passionate." I grasp her hips tighter, leaning closer to her as I will my heart to stop racing. "There is nothing about you that doesn't evoke the word passion when I look at you. Fuck. Passion and you are the same in my mind." I drag in a breath, our faces inches apart.

Her eyes pop wide with surprise, but I continue, gripping her beneath my fingers, splaying them out where they wrap around her body.

"Any man would be lucky to call you his, Rose. And none would be worthy." I dip my forehead toward hers. "None," I whisper.

She stares at me for a few precious, silent seconds, her lashes dipping slowly as she looks at my lips and subconsciously licks her own with a gentle swipe of her tongue. Then she frowns, her eyes still on my mouth.

"I went out a lot... back at home, I mean." She chews on her lip. "I would flirt with guys. I don't know why I did it. Just to prove to myself I could, I guess. To prove they wanted me, even if Gareth didn't anymore. I never went home with any of them. I just... I wanted to feel something."

Tightness threatens to take over my chest again and I take in a slow, deep breath.

"He was a prick, Rose. A boy who didn't know anything other than his own selfish fucking ego. You deserve a man who understands the most valuable thing isn't what you do to please him. It's how *he* makes you feel."

"That's the most romantic thing I think I've ever heard anyone say. Who are you, Dax Silver?" She smiles, but it doesn't mask the hurt that's in her eyes. Nothing can hide that.

"It's better you don't know." I ease back from her, so our faces are no longer almost touching and drop my hands from her hips and onto my thighs instead.

She laughs softly. She thinks I'm joking. But I'm not. I knew it before, and after what she's told me, it's even more glaringly obvious. I should not be anywhere near her.

"How do you feel?" She strokes my neck, leaning close again, closing the space I created between us. "You say it's all about how you make someone else feel. How do I make *you* feel?"

She looks at me with honest, innocent eyes, searching mine for something I can't give her.

"You..." I look at her lips. "You make me..." Then lower, to her breasts, her hardened nipples visible through the thin fabric. *Fuck.* She's so close to my cock, which is hard as steel between my legs. A couple of inches closer and her lower stomach will be pressed right up to it. I clench my hands into fists against my legs. "You..."

Her eyelids grow heavy, and she's expecting me to kiss her. I know it.

But I can't.

I fucking can't.

I have no goddamn right to bring her into my shitstorm of a life.

"If I tell you that, then I'll have to put you on the first plane back to New York," I grit, sounding harsher than I intend to.

Her eyes pop wide. "But—"

"Thanks for cleaning me up. I appreciate it." I grab my hoodie from the back of the sofa. I pull it on and zip it up.

She jerks back onto her heels, which allows me enough space to step up from the sofa and hold out a hand to help her up.

She shoves it aside and is on her feet in a split second. "See you at work, then," she snaps.

The pinch at the corners of her eyes has me stepping into her space again until our chests graze one another's. I keep my eyes on hers as I take her chin between my finger and thumb.

"You make me feel, *Sunbeam*. That's all you need to know."

"Sunbeam?" She stares at me, her eyes alight with energy.

I open my mouth, then close it again as I swipe my thumb over her bottom lip, following its path as my chest squeezes.

"Dax?"

I keep my lips sealed together, and when I say nothing, she shakes free of my grasp and stalks toward the door. I don't try to stop her or call after her as she slips through it.

And then she's gone.

And even though it's for the best, it still stings like a bitch.

I spend the rest of the evening pacing up and down in front of my bedroom window, staring over at the cottage and the light in the front room. I pace until the light turns off and the one in the upstairs bedroom goes on. *Her bedroom. What's she doing in there? What's she thinking? Maybe she's packing? Maybe she's going to leave.* She should. It would make things simpler.

Bile rises in my throat, then retreats as the light goes out. She's not going anywhere. At least, not tonight.

And yet I still pace for another two hours, my eyes trained on the front door of the cottage.

Just in case.

Chapter 11

Rose

"Are you sure he said it was for me?"

"It's what he said," Larry, one of the estate's groundskeepers, replies, as he props the giant bubble-wrapped package up against my bedroom wall.

Why would he send me a gift? Why would he send me anything? After yesterday, Dax's feelings couldn't be clearer. *"I'll have to put you on the first plane back to New York."* It doesn't matter what else he said. I'm fed up with riddles. He thinks about me going back to New York. He doesn't see me staying here long term. Not that I was ever meant to. A fact I'm sure he's ecstatic about.

"You want me to unwrap it?" Larry asks.

I smile at his kind, older face. He reminds me of Dad, a little. The way his eyes twinkle as he smiles.

"No, thanks, Larry. I've got it."

I see him out and then go to my bedroom and stare at the giant object.

I fetch scissors and cut through the layers of protective plastic, tearing them away and discarding them on the floor. It's therapeutic in a weird way. Like shedding dead skin to reveal the new, smooth, fresh one below. One that hasn't been scarred with mistakes.

I sit back on my heels as I peel the final layer back.

Blonde hair and blue eyes that almost look too big for the face they're a part of stare back.

Me.

He's sent me a mirror.

A giant, gilt-framed mirror that must be hundreds of years old. It's probably one of the original ones from the main house.

I run my hands around the intricate carvings of the frame, a mix of leaves and flowers. And at the top center—a bird. *Like Dax's neck tattoo.*

Taped to the top right corner of the frame is a handwritten note.

Look in it and see what I see. What the world sees.

I stare at my reflection. What is that supposed to mean? What he sees? What the world sees? Dax Silver is the most confusing man, no, most confusing *person* I have ever met. Why would he send me this? He's so moody and intense. But then I know he can be tender too. He calms me in a way no one else can. When he holds me and tells me to breathe in his deep voice, it's like a wave of warmth flows over me, easing all the tension away. It's like he gets me somehow. Like he gets what it's like to feel at war with yourself inside your own mind. But then he says and does things that contradict it again and throw me through a loop.

I stand, straightening my white flowy dress. I've teamed it with heeled sandals today and have my hair up in a high ponytail with a thin white ribbon tied in a bow. I bought the dress when I went shopping with Jasmin. She said it was too cute not to get, and I agree. I didn't even realize most of my wardrobe had turned dark in color since losing Dad. Not until I unpacked my suitcase here and my wardrobe looked like it belonged to a grieving widow from centuries ago.

I purse my lips, looking in the mirror one final time as I grab my purse.

Right now, there is only one thing I am sure of.

And that is, the more time I spend with Dax Silver, the less I understand him.

"Did Larry bring the mirror to you?"

"Mmm-hmm."

I purposefully don't look up at the open doorway of my office.

"I see," he murmurs.

I carry on typing the figures into the report I'm working on, but he stays standing in the doorway, so I glance up for a split second, then away again. He's wearing a suit, his bird tattoo on full show where the neck of his new white shirt is unbuttoned.

He ripped the last one off, remember?

I press my thighs together and bite the inside of my cheek, continuing to ignore him. That was hot. I know he didn't intend for it to be an act of seduction—he couldn't get me out of there fast enough afterward. However, a man that looks like Dax Silver *ripping* his shirt off... I doubt anyone is immune to that. And his tattoos... I've never seen anything more beautiful. I could have stared at him all night and traced the curves of ink over his skin with my fingertips had he let me. I found them mesmerizing. So detailed. Each having a story behind it. Marking a moment of how he felt, how he thought at that point in his life. Like a diary portrayed in images instead of words.

"Don't you like having it in the cottage?" he asks, his deep voice floating over from the doorway and causing me to mistakenly glance up and locking eyes with him.

Light blue meets deep, deep brown.

"It's a beautiful mirror." I look back at the computer screen.

"That's not what I asked."

I groan internally as he walks into my office, around my desk to where I'm sitting, and leans back against it, crossing his legs at the ankle.

"It looks more like it belongs here. In the main house," I explain.

"It did. It's from my mother's childhood bedroom."

I stop typing and turn in my chair, giving him my full attention. His lip looks better today, but the bruising across his cheekbone is coming out more, and it's bizarre, but it works for him. He has a classically handsome face—sharp, strong jawline, high cheekbones, straight nose. Eyes that look equally stunning when they're either amused or stormy. And those blond strands that he pushes back from his face, but inevitably fall forward a few times a day and dust his forehead.

The bruise only makes him look sexier. Edgy. Protective.

He's what Casey would call a 'hot as fuck, pretty, bad boy'.

"Your mother's room?"

Dax never takes his eyes off me as he speaks. "What used to be. The entire house has changed as the business has grown. But the mirror was still here. She always said it was the one thing she missed."

"Not your grandparents, then?" I laugh, stopping abruptly as a shadow passes over Dax's features, his brows dropping low over his eyes.

"No, they fell out before I was born. Mom hadn't spoken to them in years. Jasmin and I met them for the first time after they found out Mom had passed away."

"Really?"

"Really." He shrugs, crossing his arms over his chest as he continues to pin me with his gaze. "But that's not a story for now. I want to know why you don't like the mirror."

"I never said I don't like it." I shuffle in my seat. He's so close. His aftershave is calling for me to take a large inhale. He always smells so good. But the scent underneath is making my stomach flutter. It's clean and fresh, and something else. Maybe it's just him. He smelled like this yesterday when I was close to him. A scent that makes me think of lying together in clean sheets with bare skin when the sun is shining outside. Warm and masculine, and... *sexy*.

"I sent it to you because the cottage doesn't have a big one. Jasmin likes a full length one when she's getting dressed. I thought you might too." His eyes drop over my white dress and to my bare legs.

I fight to keep my unwelcome shiver at his appraisal small and unnoticeable.

"And the note?"

He lifts his eyes from my legs. "You need to stop looking at yourself through these warped lenses you have in place. Your ex was an undeserving prick. Your brother's accident wasn't your fault. And neither was your dad dying," he says without a shred of empathy in his tone.

Wow.

"I'm not trying to be an asshole, Rose."

"Aren't you?"

He doesn't flinch. Instead, he looks directly at me like he can see things no one else can. Like he can read the hidden parts of me as if they are printed on my skin. *Like tattoos.*

"I understand what blame can do to you. I left Jasmin. It's always been the two of us. Then I went and lost my head and got locked up. Away from her."

I look into his eyes and the hint of vulnerability is there again, like the night he let me in the gates and told me I shouldn't be alone in the dark. That he knows what men talk about. *What they talk about in jail? What they did to be there in the first place?*

"What was it like there?"

"In jail?"

I nod.

"I hope you never find out." He looks at me as I wait for more, then exhales slowly, his shoulders dropping. "It was... long. It felt long. And with all those men? Some days, it... fucking stank." He cocks a brow and smirks.

I press my hand to my lips to hold in my giggle, and he uncrosses his arms and pulls my hand away.

"You have a beautiful smile. Don't hide it."

I freeze, staring at him as he holds my hand, lowering it to the desk inside his. His eyes don't meet mine, they're on my hand in his. Fair skin held by bruised and scratched knuckles. He still hasn't explained what happened to him yesterday. And the more I consider how it is he got hurt, the more my mind has been running away with me. Jasmin said he's good, that he was protecting her that night he assaulted that guy. Was he protecting someone again last night? Or protecting himself?

My first day here I overheard him on the phone. He was angry and said something about pigs. *Cops.* But it could be nothing. I mean, why *would* he like the cops? They locked him up when he was looking out for his sister. And the more time I spend with him, the more I see what Jasmin says and am inclined to believe her when she says he has the biggest heart.

You have a beautiful smile. Don't hide it. A shiver runs through me.

Dax clears his throat. "I never meant to upset you yesterday. But we work together. And I'm not a man you should want to know any more about than the basics required to do your job. It's better this way. Believe me."

What if I'm wrong and he's right? What if there is a darker side to him I'm better off not knowing?

But despite the conviction in his voice, his eyes tell a different story. Their deep brown shines with genuine remorse as he looks at me. And my gut tells me he's wrong.

He might think he's bad, or think he needs to tell me he is. But he did one thing to protect someone he loves. Other people may judge him for it. But I'm finding it hard to let him paint that picture of himself no matter how much he thinks he needs to.

I lift my chin. "I don't believe you. I'm sorry, but I don't. You don't see what I see in you, either."

His gaze remains on our hands as he traces circles over my wrist with the pad of his thumb.

"You don't know me. Not really."

"I know you're a man who protects his family. Who would do anything for them. That you run an incredible, successful business, which you've already doubled the profits of since you came back to work. I know that your staff trust and respect you."

I wait for him to say something.

His eyes dart up to mine before he looks away, a crease furrowing deep into his brow as he presses his lips together, deep in thought.

He lets go of my hand and places it onto the desk.

"Keep the mirror, Rose."

He pushes off from the desk and strides out of my office.

"I can't believe you told him you've only had sex once. And it was with Gareth."

"I know. I feel so stupid."

"Oh, Ro." Casey shakes her head at me as we have our daily catch-up video call.

I don't know what got into me the other night. I think it was seeing Dax hurt, and then seeing all his tattoos. It felt... intimate, I guess. I'm not usually one to overshare, but with Dax, it pours out. Maybe it's because he listens. He stops talking and he *listens.* I don't recall Gareth ever listening like that. But then, we were younger, and it was before Brett's accident and before Dad died that we were together. Maybe I had less that I needed listening to back then.

And I cannot believe I leaned so close to him, thinking he might kiss me. *Hoping* he might. I'm not even sure how I feel about him. I have no idea what's going on in his head. He blows so hot and cold. Yet, in that moment, all I wanted was to see how it would feel to have more than just his hands on me.

I shuffle in my seat. The way his fingers flexed against my hip bones while I cleaned him up, wrapping around me and holding me like I was precious. Like I wasn't a total screw up. *I wanted to keep feeling like that. And more.*

"I know that face, Ro. Are you still wondering if he's in some sort of trouble?" Casey asks.

"No... Yes," I say with a sigh.

I told Casey about the blood. She thinks Dax must have gotten into a fight. And it makes sense. Someone hit him, judging by his cheekbone. But Jasmin said he barely goes out to bars anymore. And he hadn't even had one drink as far as I could tell. Which means it wasn't a stupid drunken fight. But something else.

"Maybe it's an underground fight club," Casey suggests.

I adjust the phone on the car's dashboard so I can see her better.

"What? No." *But... it would explain the bruised knuckles.* "I don't know what happened. And it's none of my business what he gets up to after work."

"Yet here you are."

"It was your idea." I scowl.

She laughs. "Relax. I'm kidding. You're not doing anything wrong. If he sees you, just say you were taking a drive to look at the countryside."

I look out of the Range Rover's windshield. Jasmin said I could borrow one whenever I wanted, but I checked anyway, and she said it was fine. She's off on some massage course or something that she wanted to do tonight. And Logan is on another date. So I don't need to worry about either of them seeing me parked up behind the trees at the turn off for the cottage staking out the main house like a crazed stalker.

"You can just see where he goes and then go home. You want to know he's safe, don't you?"

I suck my bottom lip into my mouth and chew on it. She's right. I want to know he's safe. Yesterday could have been much worse. If he is going to some fight club to let his anger out, then it could all get ugly. He said the night he beat that guy up who tried it on with Jasmin he lost his head. What if someone else loses their head and takes it out on Dax? I'm sure he can hold his own. I felt just how thick and solid his biceps were yesterday when

I was admiring his tattoos. But still. What if some of these guys he might be meeting are actual psychopaths?

"You don't think he really could be mixed up in something?" My stomach churns. "You know? Like something illegal?" But even as I say the words, I can't bring myself to believe them.

"Why would you say that? Because he's been in jail?"

"No... I..." I stare at the estate's main gate. "When I spoke to Jasmin earlier, she said Dax told her he'd done it at the gym, going too hard on the punch bag. He said it swung back at him."

"I mean, it could be true," Casey says.

I shake my head, looking at the phone screen. "It's not. He would have come home in his gym gear. He was in his suit."

"He might have showered at the gym."

"He had blood splatters on his shirt."

Casey's brows shoot up. "Check you out, Detective. I'm impressed."

I give her a small smile.

"Whatever it is, Ro, even if he lied to his sister, it doesn't mean anything. People have secrets. Some have really bad ones. But it doesn't make them bad people for lying to those they love. They just don't want to hurt them."

I wrinkle up my nose as she watches me.

"I don't know. A lie is still a lie. Why not be honest? Deal with it together?"

Casey rolls her lips and blinks a few times. "I guess. I mean—"

"He's coming," I gasp, immediately lowering my voice as his Range Rover glides gracefully down the driveway and toward the main gate.

"Go," Casey urges. "Go put your mind at ease. And then call me as soon as you get back."

I nod, my gaze darting back to the Range Rover as it goes through the now open gate.

"I will. Love you."

"Love you too."

I hit end call and wait until the Range Rover turns right onto the road.

Then I follow it.

The road ahead is empty as I exit the estate and turn right. I drive to the first bend, taking it slowly. I'm not used to the roads here in England. They're all so narrow and bendy. And the grass banks either side of the road are higher than the Range Rover's roof.

I hit the brakes as I round the corner.

A few meters ahead, there's a small passing place where the road widens. And in it, Dax's Range Rover.

He leans back against it, legs out in front of him, crossed at the ankle, arms folded over his broad chest. His head is turned in my direction.

Waiting for me.

I roll the car forward until I am level with him, and then lower the front passenger window.

"Hi. Nice evening for a drive." I laugh nervously.

His eyes glitter and he arches a dark brow. "Isn't it? And it looks like we are driving in the same direction as well. Even though town and practically everything you would drive to is that way." He tips his chin in the direction we've come from.

"I wanted to look at the view." I stare at him, blinking as I fight the urge to look away. It will only make me look guiltier. *Do not blush. Give nothing away.*

"You're a shit liar, Sunbeam." He exhales, tipping his chin up and looking at the sky.

I tighten my hands on the steering wheel as I stare at him. He's in all-black tonight. Black sweatpants, black t-shirt, black hoodie.

Because he's going somewhere dark? Like an underground fight club?

I inhale slowly. I'm being ridiculous.

"Back up."

"Sorry?" I look at him in confusion.

He brings his eyes back from the sky and onto mine, and my breath hitches as they make contact, a trace of amusement making fine lines appear at their corners.

"Back it up. And park it behind mine."

"The car?" I glance over my shoulder out of the back window at the widened area of road.

"You want to know where I'm going, right?" He unfolds his arms and straightens up from his car.

"I... that's not what—"

"Park it. Unless you want me to climb in there with you and sit you on my lap so I can show you how to make it fit."

"I can do it," I snap back. *How dare he insinuate I can't park. Make it fit... Sit me on his...*

My cheeks are hot as I swing the Range Rover back into the space and slide out, walking over to him. I glance at his face as he holds the passenger door open for me, but it's set. No hint of anything that might give me a clue over how pissed he is that I followed him.

I should have stayed further behind. He wouldn't have seen me.

He climbs into the driver's side. "I knew you were there before I left the house. If you wanted to know where I was going tonight, you should have just asked me."

He puts the car in drive, and we continue down the road.

"Would you have told me the truth?" I look over at him as he drives.

His brow creases. "Of course I would."

"And what about where you were last night? Before you came home with blood on your shirt?"

A muscle in his cheek twitches.

"Yeah. Thought so." I sigh and look out of the side window.

"It's better you don't know where I was, Rose."

"Better for who?" I huff.

God, he's infuriating. I hate being told what is good for me. Everyone around me thinks they know what I need. The only reason I am even here, in England, with him, is because my family thinks they know what is best for me. They're all trying to fix me. Because I am a problem. I'm THE problem. The root cause of all the family shit.

"You're overthinking it." Dax glances at my face as he drives. "I just go to some places that are not the kind of places you should be."

"And what sort of places are those?" I snort.

He flicks his gaze over me. "The kinds of places where the men there won't be content with only looking at those incredible legs of yours."

I look at my over-the-knee boots. I'm wearing them with an oversized sweatshirt dress. It almost meets the top of them when I'm standing. I only have skin on show right now because I'm sitting.

"The way *you* like to look at them, you mean?"

My stomach flips. *I did not just say that out loud.*

I'm bluffing. I've seen Dax glance at my legs before. But I assumed it was my outfit choice. Not my legs.

Those incredible legs. Why would he say that?

His chest rumbles with a deep laugh and I turn to him in surprise. His brilliant white teeth are visible as his lips part. I've never seen them like this before. They look even whiter against his dark clothes and inked skin.

They're perfect... like the rest of him.

"What's so funny?" I blurt.

"You."

"Me? What's funny about me?"

He looks straight ahead. "You're right. I have looked at them. I'm not going to lie and say I haven't. I've looked at them and thought a whole host of things I shouldn't be thinking. All of which include them being wrapped around me." He shakes his head, his laugh gone. "But that's never going to happen."

My core flutters, then promptly crashes and burns. Was that an admission of being attracted to me? Or just another of his riddles?

"Why?" I push.

He shakes his head. "Because I will never allow it. That's why," he hisses, back to moody Dax again.

Oh.

Then he turns up the radio, drowning out the confused whirl of my own voice in my head.

Dax hot-and-cold Silver. Telling me things that evoke entire butterfly armies to leap into life in my stomach in one breath, and then blasting them all with toxic bug poison the next.

He's right. We *should* never happen. He's far too complicated. And I came here because my life is already complicated enough. I don't need to add to it.

I stare out of my window, and we drive the rest of the way in silence.

Chapter 12

Dax

Rose wrinkles up her nose as I open the car door for her, and she looks over at the giant woodland cabin.

"You'll see."

I take her hand in mine and lead her over to the open doorway.

"What is this place?" Rose looks at the neat line of shoes on the wooden deck that wraps around the cabin.

I pull her up the steps and drop to one knee on the deck in front of her, running a hand up her inner thigh, my fingers dusting the smooth, exposed skin.

"Dax, what are you—?"

I hold her gaze as I take the zip of her boot between my fingers and slide it slowly all the way to her ankle.

"No shoes inside."

She glances to the door of the cabin again, then back to me, lifting her foot from her boot and placing it down, then shifting her weight as I remove the other one for her.

"Oh... right."

I stand and yank my sneakers and socks off, placing them down next to hers.

"Come on."

I walk us inside, and Emma, the class instructor, waves a hand in greeting, walking over to us.

"Hello, Dax."

I smile at her. "Emma, this is Rose. Rose, Emma."

"Hi." Rose smiles at Emma shyly, her eyes darting around the room at the mats laid out on the floor.

"Is this your first sound bath?"

"Um..." Rose looks at me, then her eyes land on the large circular gong and various sized singing bowls set up at the front of the room. "Oh, yes. I've heard of them, but I've never been to one."

"Well, Dax is a regular. I'm sure he can help you get set up?"

I nod.

"It's an hour-long meditation," she says to Rose. "I will use the gong and bowls to create sound frequencies that help to rebalance your inner vibration. Think of your inner self as having a frequency. When your vibration is running to optimum, the signal is clear. But many things in our daily lives can imbalance us—whether it be something emotional we are holding on to, or something physical. I would ask that once you're settled, you set yourself an intention for today. Think about what you need help with. What seems out of balance. The more specific you can be, the more you will take away with you tonight. Some people find it quite an emotional experience, so I have tissues at the front should you need them." Emma squeezes Rose on the forearm and then moves past us to speak with another participant.

"I won't need tissues. I never cry," Rose murmurs as she continues to gaze around the room. "Do you come here a lot?"

I take us over to two side-by-side matts with rolled up duvets and pillows next to them.

"Once or twice a month."

She sits down on one of the matts, looking around the room at the twelve other spaces that are already filled.

"And what intention do you set? Sorry." She brings her clear eyes back to mine. "I shouldn't ask that."

"It's fine." I lay her pillow out and unroll her duvet. "I use it as a method to control my anger."

"You have a lot of that?"

I encourage her to lie back onto the pillow and pull the duvet up over her.

"Sometimes." I give her a small smile. "But mostly, it's to keep Jasmin off my back. She doesn't want me to almost kill someone and get locked up again."

"Oh." Rose gazes up at me, and I brush a strand of hair from her eyes.

"Turns out, I enjoy them. But don't tell her that." I smirk as I take my position and Emma starts the class.

For the next hour, I bathe in vibration and sounds that pull me from my body and let me relax. To clear my mind of work. Of Julian Young. Of revenge. Of all things underhand and impure and ugly and dirty that I am involved in. They all drift away until I am left with the incredible inner calm I feel when I am here. Only this time, it's infused with the scent of vanilla and petals. And it calls to me like nothing ever has before.

"How did you find it?" I ask Rose as the class ends and everyone else leaves.

She's lying on her back, her eyes open with her lids hooded. She looks serene, the usual tightness around her eyes gone.

"I felt it through the floor."

"The vibrations?"

"Yeah. And I... you'll think I'm weird."

"Try me."

"I just... I kept seeing clouds. Kind of like I was dreaming. But I wasn't asleep."

"That's not weird. You were in a meditative state."

She inhales, then lets it out slowly. "Dad used to look at the clouds with me when I was a kid. We would watch for shapes. The weirder, the better." She smiles. "If I ever worried about anything, he would tell me to look for the silver lining. He said there always was one. We always planned to go up in a hot air balloon together, because I said I wanted to look and find it."

Rose's eyes dart to Emma at the front of the room as she stacks up the singing bowls.

"It's fine. Take your time," I whisper.

The rest of the class have left already. We are the only two here, along with Emma, who knows when it's someone's first time, they might need that little extra time to come back from wherever they went. She continues packing up quietly. But Rose is already on her knees rolling her duvet up.

"Thank you so much," she calls to Emma as she stands.

Emma smiles and walks over.

"How did you find your first time?"

"It was incredible," Rose breathes with complete sincerity. "The vibrations through the floor were odd at first, but then I kind of got lost in the sound, like it was only me here and no one else. I saw memories like a movie playing in my head. Ones I haven't thought about in a while."

"That's great. It's a very powerful thing. The more you do it, the more you'll be able to bring those feelings of peace and calm with you into each day. And call on them when you need them. It was lovely to meet you, I hope to see you again. Bye, Dax."

We head outside and retrieve our shoes. Rose has a faraway look on her face as she stares off through the woods. It's getting dark.

"Do you want to try something else I sometimes do after a class?"

She smiles. "Sure."

"I just write it?"

"Yeah."

"Whatever I want?"

"Whatever you want."

She chews on her bottom lip, her bare legs spread out over the grass lawn behind the main house. "So I could wish for a new life?"

I frown as I hand her the small notepad and pen.

"If you had a new life, then you wouldn't be you anymore."

"You say it like it's a bad thing." Her hand catches mine as she takes the pad, and a fission of electricity darts up my arm.

"It would be for me."

Her lips part and she rounds her big blue eyes on me.

"Write it down, Sunbeam," I say, turning away. "It's time to let that shit go."

She scribbles something down on the pad, tears the paper off, and hands me the pad and pen. "If I'm doing this, then so are you."

"I know." I write on the pad, ripping it off and folding it up.

"So now we burn them?" She looks at the small campfire I've set going.

"You can say something if you like."

"Will you go first?" Her voice drops and she looks at me, hunching her shoulders in toward her chest.

I unzip my black hoodie and place it around her. The day was warm, but as the sun is now low in the sky, the temperature has dropped.

I hold her gaze, then turn to the fire, letting its glowing flames dance in my eyes as I picture the face of the man I hate. The man who took me away from my life for two and a half years.

"To putting things right," I say as I flick my paper into the flames. It catches right away, curling up and shriveling into black ash.

Rose watches me and then takes a deep breath.

"To forgiveness." She tosses her paper into the fire and her choice of words slashes me like claws across the heart.

Forgiveness.

Here she is, so beautiful and so fucking pure in her spirit that she's wishing and hoping for forgiveness.

While all I am wishing for is a slow and cruel revenge as I see the look in the man's eyes who I hate as I destroy everything that matters to him.

Another perfect example of why I am no good for her and the sooner she goes back to New York, the better.

"I know you are fulfilling a favor by giving me the job here. But I still don't know what miracle my family thinks is going to happen by me coming here." She picks at the grass. "It's not like me being here will bring my dad back or make Brett's injuries disappear."

"I don't think they are trying to change the past. No one can do that."

"Well then, what do they expect?" Her voice pitches as she looks at me and then lets out a deep sigh. "What do they expect me to *do?*"

I wish I could clear away the haze that's in her eyes, falling like a cloak over her, weighing her down.

Guilt.

I recognize it. I understand it.

"They want you to live your life. Not to blame yourself. It's self-destructive, Rose. It serves you no purpose at all."

"But it is *my* fault."

My chest clenches, a burn running through it, so hot that I may as well have embers from the fire smeared across my skin. *She truly believes it.*

"Has your mom told you it's your fault? Or your brother, Brett? Your sister?"

"Of course not. They aren't monsters."

"That's just you then?"

She looks at me in confusion.

"You're your own monster. Placing this fear inside yourself. What's so wrong with living your life? Why are you afraid to move on?"

"I..." She opens her mouth, shaking her head as she blinks rapidly. "I..." She narrows her eyes as she looks back at the fire. "Why should I be allowed to? Dad doesn't get to live his life anymore. Brett doesn't get to live his like he used to. All because of me."

"Stop. Just stop." I scrub a hand down my face and lean my elbows on my knees where I am sitting. "I've seen people's darkness. I've watched people who like to hurt others, and the way they take pleasure in it. That's not you. None of it was your fault. But you're too scared to admit it."

"I'm not scared." Her eyes widen. "It *is* my fault." She jabs a finger against her chest. "Mine. No one else's. Brett was out looking for me. He was run over because of me. Dad had a heart attack because it all got too much."

"No."

"Yes!"

"Brett was looking for you because Gareth was a shit to you. He got hit because some driver was speeding and not paying attention, too wrapped up in his own life to care about anyone else. Your dad had a heart attack because life is just fucking unfair. Not because of you!" I drop my head into both hands and pull at my hair, relishing the sting as I pull the roots. If only I could tear the idea out of her head that she is to blame. Tear it out as easily as I could the roots from my head if I only pulled hard enough.

"No," she whispers.

"Yes." I drop my hands and spin my head in a rush, pinning her with a wild gaze. "Yes," I say again, my voice forceful and loud. "You watch horror movies because it's easier to see it. To detach yourself from it, instead of having to look at yourself. Use the fucking mirror I sent you, Rose." I suck in an angry breath, my chest shaking with the effort to rein in my anger.

But it's not anger aimed at her. It's anger aimed at everything. The way she blames herself. The tightening in my chest that renders me almost breathless when there's hurt in her eyes... in her voice. The way I left Jasmin alone for two and a half years. The way I'm supposed to be a free man, yet my life feels less like my own than when I was locked up. The way I can't touch her. Not in the way I want to. Because she doesn't deserve to be dragged into my shit. And it's anger for the way her eyes linger on me sometimes. It's anger for the way my heart somersaults when they do. The way it screams out for me to touch her. To see just what those lingering looks mean. See just how far she would let me take it.

But I can't give her what she deserves.

I shouldn't be losing myself like this. I should be talking to her. Trying to stay calm. But I know her well enough now to know that will never work. She will never listen. Not until she's ready. If I want her to move on, then I must give her time.

"What good is looking in a mirror going to do me?" Rose moves forward so she is kneeling next to me, staring at me, searching my face for answers. She's so close. Close enough that my eyes shutter closed as I inhale her scent with one deep breath, clenching and unclenching my hands where they rest on my legs.

"You need to see what everyone else sees. You have to see it and believe it."

"And what is that?" she cries. "Because all I see is a mess. Someone who ruined so much." Her voice breaks, and she screws her eyes shut, but no tears come.

That familiar tightening wraps around my chest like a vise, and I reach forward and grab her, pulling her into my arms until we fall back onto the soft grass together, me on my back, her against my chest.

"Don't." Her voice is muffled as I hold her into my side. "I don't deserve your sympathy. I don't want it."

The tightening is joined by a burn as she melts into me like she was always supposed to fit there.

"You think this is for you?" I press my lips to her forehead. "This is for me, Sunbeam."

"Shut up."

"It's true." I sink a hand into her hair and dip my nose into it, inhaling slowly. "It's all for me. You think you're fucked up? You're the perfect person for me to hold, because you won't see just how fucked up my life is."

"It's not." Her voice softens and she wraps an arm around my waist.

"You have no idea. You have no fucking idea."

"So tell me," she breathes. "Tell me about you, Dax. I want to know everything."

No, you don't, Sunbeam. Not everything. Trust me.

My arms stiffen around her, and she looks up at me, her eyes dry and red. If laying a little of my shit out for her to see distracts her for a while, then it'll be worth it. Anything would be worth it to not have this unbearable burning in my chest when she looks at me like this.

"Jasmin told you Mom and Dad died," I state, because she knows this already. "After they died, our grandparents got in touch. They must have found out about us somehow. We'd never met them before. Mom told me they were dead to her."

"Why?"

I relax a little as Rose's face softens and she watches me, waiting for my next confession.

"Mom said they were controlling. Overbearing. Nothing she did was good enough. No one was good enough. She told me when I was older that Dad wasn't my biological dad, only Jasmin's. But it didn't matter to me. He's the only dad I needed. He was there since I was a baby. But Mom told me she had another boyfriend once. And she knew my grandparents would never approve. His family had no money. My grandparents ran the distillery. It was hugely successful. They moved in different circles. They were snobs. So Mom lied about her surname so he wouldn't know who her parents were, and she was planning to run away with him."

"That must have been so hard for her. To make that decision."

I blow out a disgusted breath. "Not as hard as when he fucked off and left her pregnant and alone. Left her with a baby and no relationship with her parents. No support. No family. Nothing. She moved away, like they had planned to do together. She did it all alone. A single mom. She needed that freedom from her parents. She was stubborn. It's where Jasmin gets it from."

"She didn't go back home?" Rose looks up at me, her eyes already having lost their earlier redness.

I shake my head, dusting my lips over her forehead, breathing in vanilla and petals which helps more tension to leave my shoulders.

"No. She thought they would blame her for getting pregnant and being a single mom. It wouldn't have been acceptable to them. She never even told them I existed. That bastard broke her. Left her with nothing," I spit. "Moved back and married some other woman. They had a baby within a year. If Mom ever considered coming back for a moment, she told me the thought of seeing him again was enough to keep her away. She couldn't face the thought of being rejected by both him and possibly her parents if she were to come home."

"I'm so sorry, Dax. That sounds so awful for her. For you."

"Don't be. She met Dad, and they had Jasmin. We were a regular family. A happy one... Until they both passed away. Our grandparents heard what had happened and found me and Jasmin. We began building a relationship with them. Then they died as well, and it was the two of us again, only we inherited the estate to run."

Rose tightens her arm around me. "That's one hell of a story. You've both done so well. The business is thriving. And I should know. I've seen the books." She gives me a small smile.

"Maybe. But then I fucked it up by smashing in a guy's face. I let Jasmin down. She lost everyone. And then she lost me too." I clench my teeth and drag a breath in through my nose.

"I don't think she sees it like that. It wasn't your fault."

I snort. "That's my line. If it's not my fault, then whose is it?"

"The guy who made those comments. The one who sent Jasmin the photos," Rose says immediately. "You know I'm right."

I sink my nose into her hair. "Just like I was right when I said it was Gareth's fault, or the driver's fault."

She falls silent in the crook of my arm and lays her head back down on my chest. The weight of it there brings a new calmness, and I allow my eyes to close as we lie together for a while until Rose speaks.

"After Brett's accident, I started having this recurring dream. I would be running away from something I couldn't see. Then I'd get inside the front door, but no matter how many times I turned the key, it would never lock. Whatever it was would reach the other side, and I would wake up as I watched the handle press down, knowing they were coming for me."

I open my eyes and look down at her, but she's gazing at the fire which has almost burned out.

"Do you still have it?"

"Sometimes. But do you know what was scarier for me?"

"Tell me."

She twists her head to look into my eyes. "Seeing you covered in blood the other day. I sat with Brett for weeks in the hospital afterward. Seeing people hurt... I just... I don't want to be cleaning up your blood again, okay?"

If only I could promise her. But I can't. What I do is dangerous. And there's every chance there will be blood. Hopefully, not mine next time.

"Okay, Dax?" she repeats when I don't respond. She pushes up to a sitting position and stares at me, and more than anything, I yearn to pull her back down into my arms again. Instead, I sit up and slip a hand around the back of her neck, pressing my lips to her forehead again as I exhale.

"Dax? Promise me," she whispers, gripping the front of my t-shirt in both hands.

"I don't make promises I can't keep. I wish things were different. *You* make me wish they were."

"What's that supposed to mean?" She pulls away from me.

I stare at her lips, then back up to her eyes.

I can't go there with her.

"Nothing. It means nothing."

Chapter 13

Rose

I SLAM THE FRONT door of the cottage, my fingers tingling with rage. I want to hit something.

Him.

I want to hit Dax square in the jaw. Hit the bastard for being so fucking infuriating and complicated.

"I wish things were different. You make me wish they were."

What does that even mean? Does he think I'm too innocent for him because I've only had sex once with Gareth? When Dax has probably had sex with loads of women in his life. Especially since coming out of jail. He's probably been making up for lost time. But Jasmin said he hardly goes out to bars. Where would he meet anyone? Maybe he has a little black book of hook-ups he calls.

Like I care!

I stomp upstairs to my bedroom, dragging my boots off my feet and ripping his hoodie off, throwing it over the mirror so it hangs, obscuring my reflection. The last thing I want to do is look at myself in it. Not when that's what he wants me to do.

I pull off my dress and get into my pajamas and go to the bathroom to scrub my face and brush my teeth. Every movement is jerky and exaggerated by how wound up I am. He wouldn't even let me storm off in a sulk earlier. All I wanted was to walk back alone under the night sky and clear my head. But he wouldn't hear of it because it was dark. The bastard followed two steps behind me the entire way despite me trying to speed up and lose him. He stopped at the bottom of the path to the cottage.

I peek out between the drapes before I throw myself onto the bed.

Gone. He's gone.

Idiot. Stupid, complicated, confusing... caring... attentive... sexy idiot.

I grab my cell phone from the bottom of the bed where I threw it and unlock it to call Casey. But my willpower loses out, and I bring up Google instead, and search for *Dax Silver, Silver Estates.* The first few entries are about the court case and him getting released. But further down there is a magazine article written about the estate and the gin tours it hosts. They've put a picture of Dax and Jasmin in. They're at some posh function from the looks of Jasmin's evening dress and Dax's tuxedo.

I zoom in on him. His eyes are dark, and his blond hair is styled neatly back from his eyes. But his tattoo is still visible. A hint of dark, delicate leaves winding their way around his neck. The feathers of a tiny bird.

Damn you, Dax Silver. Damn you for being so beautiful and difficult all at once.

I run my hand down my body, stroking circles over one nipple as I travel south, burying it inside my panties where my hot skin is slick with arousal. I slide a finger inside myself, biting my bottom lip as I stare into Dax's dark eyes. Never have I met someone who makes me want to scream with both frustration and pleasure simultaneously.

I pull my finger out and spread my wetness around my clit, stroking it in quick circles with the pads of my fingers. I'm too worked up to take my time. And thanks to a fear of the luggage scanner at the airport, I didn't pack my vibrator. I've heard stories of them going off in cases and security officers unpacking them.

"Mmm," I moan as a rush of moisture runs out of me and my nipples tighten. "You're a bastard," I hiss at Dax's picture. "A moody bastard who blows hot and cold. I bet you think I'm too boring for you..." I slip two fingers inside myself and use the back of my thumb to rub my clit as I finger-fuck myself. "But I can still make myself come. I'm not as helpless as you seem to think I am."

I speed up, my back arching off the bed as I hold my phone above me and stare at his picture like he is over me, pushing inside my body, every muscle rippling beneath his tattoos as he pounds into me with none of the restraint he shows every time I see him.

"Just like that," I murmur, my lids heavy as I stare into his eyes.

I suck in a breath as every muscle draws in, tightening into a ball in my core. Then I explode, coming in a rush that makes me cry out his name as my body spasms

around my fingers, sucking them in, desperately squeezing in the hope they will turn into his.

I drop my mouth wide and pant as I hold his eyes and
a second orgasm hits me, making sweat bead on the skin
between my breasts. I keep coming in waves around my
fingers, staring into deep brown, looking at beautiful art
upon skin, until my body wilts into the mattress with a
final shudder.

I toss my phone to the side and squeeze my eyes shut.
Fuck you, Dax Silver.

"Jasmin, I need you to go to Brighton with me this afternoon to sign some papers at the lawyers.'" Dax's deep
voice booms from the hallway.

He strides into his office in a black suit and black shirt,
his step faltering as he sees me standing to one side. I
came in to chat to Jasmin. Now I wish I hadn't.

"I can't. I have the hairdresser's," Jasmin replies.

I frown. I'm sure she went last week. And the week
before.

Dax's eyes drop over my outfit. I have a fitted black
pencil skirt on today and white silk blouse. The skirt
goes down past my knees.

He frowns before turning to Jasmin.

"They need a signature from me and one other senior
employee."

"Take Logan."

"He has a date later," Dax grits.

"So, take Rose." Jasmin shrugs. "She's senior in accounts."

My spine straightens, and I pull my shoulders back as I stare at her. *Look at me, Jasmin. Look at me so I can signal that is a terrible idea.*

"Rose is busy."

"I'm busy."

We both blurt at the same time.

I glare at Dax, and he looks back at me, a muscle in his jaw tensing.

"So now you can be busy together." Jasmin kisses Dax on the cheek and then smiles at me. "See you later, Rose." She walks out of the office leaving the two of us staring at each other.

He clears his throat, his Adam's apple moving in his neck, making the edge of the bird's wing appear like it's fluttering.

"I need to get these papers done today. Can you come?"

"I thought you said I was busy." I arch a brow.

It's easier being pissed at him. When I'm pissed, I don't have to think about how tender he was when I was cleaning him up, resting his hands on my hips and looking at me like I was the most precious thing he had ever touched. I don't have to think about how when he says "*breathe*" and tells me he can feel my pulse in my wrist, it calms me like nothing else. I don't have to think about him kissing my forehead, and how his skin touching mine sets a burst of energy off inside my core, like a bunch of fireworks.

And I don't have to think about how I came twice last night while holding his picture above me and imagining he was fucking me so deep I would feel deliciously bruised today.

"Are you?" His deep brown eyes penetrate me.

"I suppose I can make time if you want me to come."

"I do," he replies without missing a beat. "But I won't force you. I want you to feel comfortable, Rose. But there's no one else I would rather be with. Believe me."

I search his eyes, narrowing my own. I can't work him out. *No one else he'd rather be with?* Yet, he can easily hold me on the grass last night with his lips pressed into my hair, saying I need to live my life, with conviction in his voice, and open up to me about his family's history, and then tell me he can't promise me a thing, all in the same breath.

"I never know what to believe with you, Dax. You're a puzzle with no solution."

His gaze darkens and he stalks over to me.

"Don't," he hisses.

"Don't what?"

He looks into my eyes, his mouth set in a grim line.

"Don't make out I've lied to you. I've never lied to you, Rose."

"You just talk in riddles." I snort.

He clasps my chin in a flash, leaning so close his breath warms my lips, and they part of their own accord. *Traitors.*

"I told you. My life. It's fucked up," he rasps.

"So is mine. That's just an excuse. Just admit it. You don't like me," I say, stopping myself before I wince at how pathetic I sound.

His brows shoot up his forehead, and he falters, his head jerking backward.

"That's what you think?"

"It's what you tell me every time you go all weird and cryptic. Just forget it." I try to twist out of his grasp, but his hand tightens on my chin, holding me in place.

"You came here to make your life better. Not to complicate it. What kind of person would I be to steal that chance from you?" He screws his face up, his eyes roaming all over me before coming back to hold mine. "I *can't* touch you, Rose." His chest heaves against mine as he hisses, lowering his lips so they brush against mine. "I can't touch you. Even though all I want to do is *fucking* touch you. It's all I think about night and day. It consumes me, Sunbeam. It fucking *owns* every moment."

He breathes against my lips, so light, my brain barely registers it, before it's gone. He steps back and shakes his head, looking at me in regret.

"Be ready to leave in half an hour."

I've always wondered what the beach would look like in England. Whether it would be pebble or sand. This one is sand. A long, golden stretch of it along the coastline, with a giant pier housing a fairground reaching out into the rough sea.

I've been to the local town plenty of times now. But the lawyer Dax needed to see was here, further away. He drove us down as I stared out of the window, and he stayed silent. It wasn't much better at the lawyer's, with him only speaking about work things and the paperwork we had to sign. It was all a rush because there was an accident and we got stuck in traffic. They stayed open for us, but it's already late, so we will probably be heading back soon.

I look along the sidewalk to where Dax is on the phone, his brow furrowed as he shakes his head, his body language tense as he stares at the ground and paces up and down. He looks up and locks eyes with me for a split second, then barks something into the phone and ends the call.

"The road is still gridlocked." He walks to where I am sitting on a bench and turns, hands on his hips to look out at the sea. White crests swirl and crash against the base of the pier as the wind picks up more.

"A slow drive back, then?"

"We could get some dinner. It might give it time to clear."

I look up at him. His hair matches the sand, golden and warm. But everything else is dark. His black suit, his black shirt, the closed expression on his face.

My stomach growls as if on cue and one side of Dax's lips twitch.

"Dinner it is, then," he says.

"Fine," I mutter as I stand, smoothing my pencil skirt down over my hips.

We find a restaurant and eat together. I make small talk about work, which Dax engages with. But it's stifling, sitting at a table with him, surrounded by couples and people on dates while we are sat like two total strangers, each not wanting to say what they are thinking to the other.

I walk out onto the sidewalk, sucking in the evening air in relief as Dax pays and we leave.

"You ready to go back?"

"Sure," I reply, looking off up the street so I don't have to meet his eyes.

"Rose."

"What?" I snap, turning to face him.

He shakes his head, his eyes dropping to my lips.

"Don't."

"Don't what? I'm not doing anything."

"Why are you acting like you can't stand to be around me? Ever since last night..." He lowers his voice and steps closer as a couple pass us. "You've been acting pissed at me."

"Because I am pissed at you."

"What did I do?" His eyes darken.

"You..." I search for the right words. *You confuse me? You infuriate me? You turn me on like no one ever has before and it annoys me?*

"Come here." He grabs my wrist and pulls me down a small alleyway.

"What? Ow, Dax, that hurts."

"Shh." He presses his fingers to my mouth, and I stare at him as he pushes me against the wall, shielding my body with his as he cranes his neck, looking around the corner of the wall to the main street.

"Yes... yes. I know how to do it. I have Mr. Young's file here."

The voice grows closer.

I pull Dax's hand away from my face. "Why are we—?"

"Be quiet," he hisses, his eyes widening as the voice continues to increase in volume as whoever the guy talking on the phone is, gets closer.

"Shit," Dax mutters underneath his breath.

"He was my mate. Not anymore. The fucker deserved it. Could have lost me my job... Yeah, well, he'll heal. Number one rule, don't steal the product."

The man must be seconds away from passing the top of the alleyway where we are standing.

"Dax?" I whisper as he pulls his head back from the corner, his jaw tight as he presses his lips together and sucks in a sharp breath. "Do you know him—?"

Movement at the top of the alley catches my eye, and in a flash, Dax twists his body, turning his back to the man. Then he grabs my face in his hands and crashes his lips onto mine, pulling me into him.

I freeze as his warm lips connect with mine. But then my body takes over, and I part my lips, groaning into his mouth as I welcome his tongue to mine and sink my hands into his hair.

He kisses me with all the passion and dominance I expected a man like him to kiss with. His lips, his tongue, his breath, all mixed with mine in the perfect pressure that has heat pooling low down in my core and making my thighs clench together.

I whimper against his lips as he nips mine between his teeth, sucking in a breath and then kissing me hungrily again, his hand gripping my face and tilting it up toward him, so he has me exactly where he wants me. I press my breasts against his chest, my nipples tightening into painful peaks, aching for his attention.

"Dax..." I tug on his hair, pulling him closer.

And then suddenly I'm cold.

I slump back against the hard stone wall, panting, as he steps away from me and looks out of the alleyway again.

"He's gone. That was close. Fuck," Dax hisses, his attention gone from me as I grip onto the wall for support.

"Did you... did you kiss me because you didn't want him to see you?" I pant, my heart hammering as he finally drags his eyes away from the street and back to mine. "Did you?" I snap.

"You don't understand. That guy... if he'd seen you—"

"I don't give a fuck!" I cry, shoving him in the chest as humiliation crashes over me like a wave, making my head spin. Here I am kissing him with everything I have and feeling things, feeling... And to him, it's *nothing*. A tool to prevent him having to talk to someone he wants to avoid.

I shoulder-pass him out onto the street.

"Rose." He grabs my arm, yanking me back against the wall and cages me between his arms.

"Let me go." I shove at his chest again, but he doesn't move.

"I can't tell you why. But believe me when I say, if that guy saw you with me tonight, it could cause a whole fuck-ton of trouble that we don't need."

I search his face for clues as I lower my voice. "Who is he? Tell me."

Dax holds my eyes, and for a moment, my heart lifts. He's going to be honest with me. He's going to say something that makes sense for once. He's going to—

"He's no one you should think about again, Rose."

My stomach sinks and I shake my head in disgust. "Take me back. I want to go back to the cottage."

Dax looks at me, his brow furrowed as he studies my face. But I can't look him in the eye. I don't want to. Not when all he's going to do is hide the truth from me.

"If that's what you want," he says.

"What I want is for you to stop treating me like I'm helpless. You think I'm this broken girl who can't do anything for herself. Who can't cope with the truth."

"I don't," Dax grits. "Believe me, I know how capable you are. I just don't want you caught up in my shit." He screws his face up and curses.

The back of my neck grows hot, and I take in a breath as my heart races with how close we are. I can't believe my body is still reacting to him like this. Like it would swoon at his feet if he were to kiss me again.

Pathetic.

"You know what? That's fine. Because I don't care about it. I don't care what shit you're into. I am done trying to figure you out." I duck under his arm and stride off up the street.

"Rose?" He falls into step beside me. "Rose. Please."

"Please what?" I keep walking.

"Don't be like this. I just want to keep you safe."

Heat lances through my veins. He wants to keep me safe. It's all about him. What Dax wants. What Dax says.

"You think I'm some hopeless loser," I hiss. "You think I can't handle anything. You'd wrap me in fucking cotton wool given the chance."

"That's not true... Rose." His tone has taken on a darker edge, dripping in warning.

"No!" I grind to a halt and spin to face him. "I am sick of everyone else making decisions for me. Telling me what I need. What I should do. Treating me like I am damaged. I thought you were different."

"I never told you I was." He leans closer to me, his eyes falling to my lips and up again. And I hate the way my treacherous body still tingles under his gaze.

"Then I guess that makes me a fool." I sneer.

He tips his head back to the sky with a curse. "You know I don't mean it like that. I just... You have to trust me when I tell you that I will do nothing but complicate your life."

"Trust you?" I snort, anger bubbling in my gut. "Just like that? When you are literally telling me nothing that makes sense."

I spin and stalk off up the street again. A neon light up ahead calls to me.

I need a drink. A strong one.

I walk straight past the doorman as he holds the door open for me, as Dax storms in behind me. I glance back in time to see him take some money out of his wallet and hand it to the woman at the reception desk we pass.

I thought this was a bar, but it must be a club if Dax has had to buy our entry.

I follow the sound of music to a set of double doors, a huge security guy on one side dressed all in black with a face like stone. I snort internally. Dax fits right in.

"Rose?" Dax snaps, trying to get me to stop.

I walk up to the doors and smile sweetly as the security guy holds them open and tells me to enjoy myself.

"I want to get a drink, Dax. Then you can drive us back and fuck off and do whatever it is you want to."

I walk into the club and look around.

The lighting is low and sexy and has a red tinge to it. A long bar is to one side of the room, and various small booths and intimate cocktail tables with plush velvet chairs are spaced around.

In the center of the room is a stage. With a pole on it.

I dart my eyes around the tables and booths again. Women in small ribbons of material—silky, sequined, lacy—are walking around, stopping to talk to customers. Bending at the waist and exposing tight, toned legs as they whisper in the ears of those seated.

I stall, my legs freezing in place.

"You wanted a drink, Sunbeam," Dax growls in my ear as he comes up behind me, so close that his breath fanning over my neck sends a shiver up my spine. "So let's get one."

I glance around, trying not to be obvious that I am staring at all the beautiful dancers with exposed flesh as Dax places his hand on my lower back and steers me toward a small booth.

I slide into the seat, and he sits opposite me, his expression dark as he leans back, watching me take in our surroundings.

"First time in a strip club?" He quirks a brow, a sinful smirk on his face.

He's changed from moments ago. Because now he has the control. And the bastard knows it.

"No." I scowl, even though it couldn't be more obvious. I'm fed up with him thinking I am this helpless girl he must protect. A girl who can't look after herself.

"Okay." He nods at a waitress as she approaches, and she leans down so he can whisper in her ear.

Fire pricks at my veins as she giggles and places her hand on his chest before walking off.

I glare at him through slitted eyes as she returns and places two clear drinks down in front of us. Dax thanks her, but his eyes stay trained on mine.

"So. Not your first time then?" His eyes glitter as he stares at me.

He's enjoying this. *Jerk.*

"Nu-uh." I pick up my glass and down half of it, hiding the smile on my face as Aunt Iris's blend hits my tongue, the lemon and tonic in the glass complimenting it perfectly. The last thing I want is for him to think I approve of him choosing my drinks for me, even if he does pick well.

Dax swirls the gin in his glass before taking a sip, his eyes on my face the entire time.

"You won't mind if I buy a dance, then?"

"Be my guest," I snort, sitting back and folding my arms over my chest.

"Good." He smiles.

Images of me getting on my feet and slapping it off his face fill my head, and I smile back.

"Good," I echo.

Stupid jerk. If he thinks I'm going to sit here and be bothered by one of these women grinding on him, he's got another thing coming.

I do not care.

"Which one?" He tilts his chin, turning to look around the room.

I tear my eyes away from his neck tattoo and follow his gaze.

"How about her? The blonde with the big tits? I like blondes."

I screw my nose up and shake my head as he smirks at me.

"Or what about her? The redhead in the leather dress? I bet she's got some dirty moves."

He sniggers as I scowl.

"You pick, Sunbeam. Tell me who you would choose."

My body tenses at the challenge held in his darkened gaze.

"Fine," I snap.

I look around the room. All the women here are beautiful. There are a mix of figures. Some curvier than others, some with huge breasts spilling from tiny skin-tight dresses. Others with smaller chests, and incredible toned abs on display in cutaway lace outfits.

"Her."

I look over at the beautiful girl with porcelain skin and long, dark hair. It's poker straight and shines like glass. She's wearing less makeup than most of the other girls. She doesn't need it. She has a natural beauty that makes her look better with less. And I like her outfit. It's a pink silk fitted dress with a thigh high split and matching scarf. But the material is covered in black flowers and birds.

Similar to something else I'm drawn to, despite wanting to fight it more than ever tonight.

I look back at Dax as he purses his lips and sweeps his gaze over her appreciatively. Something acidic simmers low in my gut.

"Good choice, Sunbeam. She's stunning."

His words hit me like a whip.

Not sexy. Or hot. *Stunning.* He's really going to enjoy this.

"Don't close your eyes. Watching is the best part." Dax smirks at me again and raises a finger, beckoning the girl over.

She slinks over. It's the best way to describe the sensual rock of her hips with each step she takes as she comes to our booth and over to Dax. She leans down until her lips are practically touching his, and then she turns her head, and her lips brush his ear as she whispers something.

He turns and smiles at her, all perfect white teeth, his eyes holding hers, then he tips his chin, inviting her to lean closer so he can whisper something in her ear.

She smiles and nods as I sit glued to my seat on the other side of the booth. I'm going to have to sit and watch Dax have a lap dance from this gorgeous woman, no doubt getting a raging hard-on as she climbs all over him. He's going to let her get closer to him than he ever lets me.

Sourness creeps over my tongue, so I pick up my glass and drain the rest of my drink.

The dancer turns away from Dax and walks over to me. I stare at her as she drops to her knees in front of me.

"Hi," she breathes.

"Hi," I reply.

"He said he wants me to dance for you. Is that okay?"

I look over her shoulder. Dax's eyes pinch at the corners, and he spreads both arms across the back of the booth seat as he places me under an intense gaze. A muscle tenses in his jaw and he inhales slowly through his nose. Waiting.

Does he think I'll say no? Stay safely trapped in my helpless bubble where I don't do anything.

I look back into her eyes. They're a beautiful rich green.

"Yes. It's okay. If it's okay with you, I mean."

She giggles and places her hands on my thighs. "It's okay with me. I'm Midnight."

"I'm Rose."

She smiles at me. "That's a pretty name. Do you mind if I lift your skirt a little? It helps me to dance if I can widen your legs."

"Oh. Sure." I look down at my tight pencil skirt. Of all the days I choose not to wear one of my short, flippy skirts, it would be today.

Midnight slowly slides both hands up from my ankles, stroking my skin. As she reaches the hem of my skirt, she pushes it up over my thighs.

"Lift," she purrs. And I obey, rising from the seat a little so she can slide it right to the top of my thighs. "You have amazing legs," she says as she slowly unwraps the silk scarf from around her neck and places it between my legs where my skirt has been pushed right up. "No one can see. But just in case." She winks.

"Thank you," I whisper, unable to take my eyes from her as she rises to her feet between my legs and slowly begins to rotate her hips to the music.

She dances as though her beautiful, elegant limbs are connected to the music. Turning and swaying, her hair swishing and dusting a heady, floral perfume around us as she moves. I can totally get why people pay to watch now. She's hypnotic, and that's not even taking in the fact that she's going to take her clothes off any moment. It's the way she's moving just for me, her eyes holding mine whenever she's facing me. Like this moment is all for me. She is focused on me and my pleasure.

She smiles and then turns her back to me, reaching up with pink glossy nails, and slowly easing the zipper on her dress down until the top of a thin lace thong is visible. Then she spins to face me again and lets her dress drop to the floor, stepping out of it.

My lips part as I stare at her.

Dax is right. She is stunning. Her breasts are round and perfect with pale pink nipples, and her hips curve out, the pink lace of her thong worn high on them, accentuating her waist.

"Have you ever had a dance from a girl before?" Midnight asks as she twirls slowly in front of me and then leans close, rolling her body down over mine.

I follow her every move with my eyes, loving the way she moves so freely, so seductively, so confidently.

"No," I whisper as she rolls against me again, bringing her breasts level with my face.

"Well, thank you for letting me be your first." She smiles as her hair falls onto my blouse, some of it touching the bare skin where my top buttons are unfastened. It caresses my skin in one fluid move as she rolls up again and then slowly places one leg, then the other, either side of me on the seat so she is straddling me.

I keep my hands down, my palms flat against the sides of my thighs as my breathing quickens.

"Don't worry. It's okay if you touch me by accident. It's just not allowed as a general rule."

"Oh, okay." I nod, relaxing a little as she hovers in my lap, rolling her hips slowly and exploring her body with her hands, roaming from her hips up to her breasts and squeezing them, then sliding them back down again and dipping them inside her panties.

She moans softly and then takes her hand out and slides off my lap, standing up between my spread thighs and spinning around.

She hooks her thumbs under each side of her lace thong and bends in half, sliding it off and giving me a full face-height view of her perfectly smooth pink pussy. Then she straightens up and lowers herself back onto my lap, facing away from me, where she continues to roll her body as she rests her back against my chest.

"Do you and your boyfriend come to clubs a lot together?"

She runs her hands up and strokes both breasts, arching her back away from me, before dropping it back down and writhing on me gently. Her skin is soft and smells of the same heady floral perfume.

"He's not my boyfriend. He's my boss," I say as she hooks one leg over my thigh and spreads hers, placing her hand between them and stroking herself.

"That's why he hasn't taken his eyes off you this entire time, then. Because he wants you but can't have you." Midnight giggles softly and I glance up.

Dax is watching me, his eyes burning with a deeper intensity even for him. Midnight is spread open, naked, and touching herself on my lap. But Dax's eyes are dark and fixed on mine as if she isn't even here. His tongue slowly darts out, licking along his lower lip, so subtle it could be easily missed. Heat spreads in my cheeks as he watches me. I take a deep breath, becoming aware of Midnight as she moves away from me and retrieves her dress, slipping it back on.

I break Dax's gaze and look up at her, handing her the scarf and gently pulling my skirt back down.

"You're a beautiful dancer."

She bends down and dusts my cheek with a soft kiss.

"And you were a pleasure to dance for." She glances to Dax and back. "Enjoy the rest of the night with your boss." She smiles and then walks past Dax. He holds up some folded notes in one hand and Midnight plucks them from his fingers as she leaves.

I stare after her, energy dancing in my stomach.

"You looked like you enjoyed that."

"I did. She's beautiful," I confess as I bring my eyes back to meet his.

He stands and holds his hand out to me. I hesitate before taking it and let him pull me to my feet.

"Did *you* like watching her?" I breathe as I stand and come face-to-face with him.

His voice lowers. "You know the answer to that."

"She was naked." I bite my bottom lip, narrowing my eyes at him. "*So* naked."

"And she may as well have been a fucking trucker called Keith for all I care," he growls.

I tilt my head and study him. "Why did you pay her to dance for me, then? If you weren't interested in watching her."

"Because, Sunbeam," he murmurs, low and gravelly in my face, "I wanted to see what you look like when you're turned on. I wanted to see if your cheeks would flush like they are now. I wanted to see if your lips would part and go a deeper shade of pink like they are now. I wanted to watch you and imagine if your cunt was dripping and if you could feel your pulse beating in it." His chest rises and falls with labored breaths. "I wanted to see it so I can imagine it when I'm in bed tonight."

I gasp quietly, and he turns his face away from me with a soulless chuckle. When he looks back, he pins me in place with glittering eyes.

"Is that what you want to hear? That I want you so fucking much when I look at you? But know I can't ever have you? Is it?" He leans into me, pressing his lips to my ear, sounding out each word slowly. "I'm more trapped than when I was in fucking jail."

"Dax?" The air leaves my lungs as he pulls back, and I catch a hint of the haunted look on his face before he masks it with a scowl. "Dax? This is... I don't understand. Please. Talk to me." I search his eyes, but he just glances at me and then tightens his grip on my hand. "Where are we going?"

"You wanted to go back," he grunts. "So I'm taking you back."

We walk back to the car in silence and Dax drives us back with the radio playing. The entire time, my head spins so hard that I'm dizzy and confused by the time he drops me back at the cottage. I climb out into the night air and walk to the front door. He won't leave until he sees that I'm safely inside.

I pause as I unlock it. Maybe this was his plan all along. Distract me with a lap dance so I didn't ask any more questions about the man we saw, and why he pulled me into the alley to avoid him. *Why he kissed me.*

But it backfired on him because I pushed him. I always push him. I feed off getting a reaction from him. Because it's the only way I know he feels something. He can't deny me that. He may be hiding things from me. But when I push him, he can't hide the way his body reacts to mine. The same way mine does to his.

And now I know Dax feels it as much as I do, I intend to push him more. I'm fed up being treated like I'm fragile. Having everyone else tell me what I need. I want to scream. I am so sick of it.

Fighting with him makes me feel something other than guilt for a change. I thought him being tender, and all the intimate moments we've shared meant something. But now I'm questioning whether I imagined them. Whether it was all an illusion.

But I do know this. Fighting with Dax stops me from feeling like a failure. The one who screwed everything up.

If that's all he will give me, then I'm taking it.

Fighting with him is all I have right now.

I step through the front door and resist the urge to look back at him before I close it.

Chapter 14

Rose

"HOW WAS THE VISIT to the lawyer?" Jasmin asks, placing a steaming mug of coffee down on my desk.

"It was fine. We got the papers signed." I click out of the report I'm working on and pick up the mug, inhaling the steam. "Thank you."

"So my brother didn't seem weird?"

"What do you mean?"

"I met him for a run this morning and he was the grumpiest asshole. Which only usually happens when he's worried about something. The last time he was this bad was before... before the trial began." Jasmin sighs, perching on the edge of my desk.

"I..." I frown into my mug as I take a sip. "He did start acting weird. There was a guy coming toward us on the phone, and he pulled me down an alley to avoid him."

And kissed me. Fake kissed me.

"What did he look like?"

"I didn't see him. He sounded... I don't know. He was talking about product and stealing it. And he mentioned a Mr. Young."

Jasmin pales, her eyes widening. "Julian Young?"

"I don't know." My stomach twists into a knot as the name registers. "Is he the guy who—?"

"The guy who got Dax sent to jail? Yeah." Jasmin closes her eyes, running her fingertips over her forehead. "Yeah, he is."

"Maybe this guy was someone Dax recognized from the trial, and he didn't want to see him. It would make sense."

"The only thing that makes sense is that if Julian Young's name is ever mentioned, then there's trouble," Jasmin says.

"Have you ever seen him? Since Dax got out? Has *he* seen him?" The idea has goosebumps prickling up my spine. What would that be like for Dax? Seeing the man who began the chain of events that led to him losing two and a half years of his life?

"Dax hasn't seen him." Jasmin drops her head back and blows out a breath toward the ceiling. "And hopefully, it'll stay that way. Although he isn't far away. His business is in the next county."

"What does he do?"

"He runs an import and export company. Mostly overseas liquor. Rum, brandy. Wine."

"Not gin?"

Jasmin scoffs. "No. Not gin. A fact he's never let go. He was so pissed when Dax won that contract with Daisy Anderson to produce it here. Julian wanted to outsource it overseas where labor would be cheaper, and then transport it globally using his company."

"But Daisy chose you and Dax, not him."

"She chose Dax." Jasmin shakes her head with the beginnings of a proud smile "He and her husband, Blake, hit it off and she liked something about Dax. She said she had learned to be a good judge of character. And Dax passed whatever personal test she had set. Either that, or she felt sorry for us. Two orphans being thrown into a business we had no idea how to run. Dax was only twenty-one, and I was fifteen when our grandparents died and we inherited the estate. He did it all himself. We got by fine. But it was years later when we won that contract things really improved, and the business started thriving. Dax barely had time to enjoy it before he got convicted."

"You guys are incredible." I reach over and squeeze her hand. "You've done an amazing job. And you've made more profit than predicted. Dax told me that you both want to give the staff a bonus."

"Yeah. They've been great. The ones who've stuck with us."

"Well, looking at your figures, you can easily do it. You could even give them more if you wanted to."

She smiles at me and squeezes my hand back, taking in a deep breath. "Thank you, Rose. You coming here has been great for all of us."

"How'd you figure that?"

She laughs.

"Well, apart from being a lady-boss at your job, you've done something to Dax. He may be moody still, but... I don't know. He's here. He's present. I used to look at him when he first came out and wonder if part of him was left behind. Still locked in that cell. But recently he's been...

Dax again. Mostly the grumpy version. But I see the way he looks at you. He likes you being here. You don't treat him like a criminal. You don't judge him. And you also don't take his shit."

"I have a brother who likes to mess with me. Believe me, I know how to not take shit. He sat on the TV remote for three hours once so me and Casey couldn't put a movie on when he wanted to watch a soccer match. He let us turn the house upside down looking for it, and it was under his ass in his wheelchair the entire time."

"He sounds like a typical brother." Jasmin laughs.

"Yeah. I guess he is." I blink back the sudden stinging in my eyes.

What if I haven't been fair to Brett? Here I am complaining that my family tell me what to do, and all think they know what I need, what's best for me, treating me differently since Brett was hurt. What if I've been like that to him? We've still had our normal moments living together, getting on each other's nerves. But they've been far fewer. I've shut him out. I've blamed myself for what he's been through. When maybe I should have been speaking to him instead. Have I made him feel like a victim? By always seeing his injuries and blaming myself for them?

Have I hurt him even more?

Jasmin's phone rings, and her face illuminates as she looks at the screen.

"I need to take this. I'll catch you later?"

"Sure." I smile weakly as she leaves, then pick up my phone and dial Mom's number.

I just want to hear their voices.

Brett answers on the third ring.

"Hey, Sis. Harls? Rose is on the phone. Hang on, I'm going to put you on speaker."

"Okay."

"Hi," Harley pants. "Sorry, I just ran in from the back-yard."

"She and Reed were out there making a porno on Mom's sun lounger.

"We were not," she gasps.

"Could have fooled me. Your lips are permanently attached to him."

"Ignore Brett." Harley giggles. "He's just jealous be-cause he has this new physical therapist he has the hots for, and she's not interested."

"It's not that," Brett grumbles. "She says she can't date me because of some stupid patient and therapist rule."

"Really?" I snort, smiling at their squabbling. This was always the three of us before. Winding each other up. Dad had to play peacemaker so many times.

"I've got it all worked out," Brett announces. "I'm going to ace the program she's got me on, and then when I smash it and she isn't my therapist anymore, I'm going to ask her out."

"Uh-huh," Harley quips.

"I am. She knows it. I've told her."

"What's this girl's name?" I ask.

"Lena," Brett replies.

"I'll keep Lena in my prayers tonight for having to put up with you." I laugh.

There's a pause before Harley and Brett break into surprised laughter. They aren't used to me joining in with them now. I can't remember the last time I cracked a joke.

"How are you doing, Rose?" Harley's voice softens. "Are you... are you happy there? We miss you."

"I'm..."

I glance up at my office doorway as something dark catches my eye. Dax walks past with Logan, on the way to his office. He looks straight at me as he passes, his eyes burning into mine. I can't bring myself to smile or nod or acknowledge him in any way. I just stare back until they pass.

"The people are nice. Especially Jasmin. You guys would love her. Casey would too."

"Have you spoken to Casey in the last couple of days?" Harley's voice is quiet, and I strain to hear her.

"Not since the day before yesterday. Why?"

"Oh... well, it's..." Harley fumbles.

My skin prickles. Casey and I talk every day. But when I tried to call her after getting in last night, her phone went to voicemail. And she hasn't texted me back today.

"Has something happened?" Coldness creeps over me, turning my stomach. The same way it did when the cops turned up on our doorstep that day and asked if we were Brett Jacobs' family.

"She's fine, she's fine," Harley says. "It's just... we found out something. She said she would tell you herself. She swore she would."

"What?" The coldness drops another degree until pain joins it, twisting my stomach inside out.

"She was..." Harley starts and then stops.

"She was the other woman," Brett says matter-of-factly.

"What are you talking about?" I sit forward on the edge of my seat.

"The guy who knocked down Brett, the one who was speeding home to his wife," Harley whispers. "Casey was the one who—"

No.

"No!"

"I'm so sorry, Rose."

"You're wrong."

"We're not." Brett sighs. "We're not, Sis. We wouldn't tell you unless we knew for certain."

"She is my best friend," I hiss. "Why are you lying?"

"We're not. I wish we were," Harley says, her voice wobbling.

"What even...?" I screw my face up, my hand flying to my mouth.

"She said it was over before that day, before she even knew what he had done," Brett says.

I shake my head, my ears ringing as I rip my hand away and gulp in air, my chest tight.

No.

"She would have told me. It's been years."

"We're so sorry, Rose," Harley whispers.

"Whoever told you, they're lying."

She wouldn't do this. Sandbox to casket.

"A couple of friends heard the guy's wife saying things after a few drinks. She didn't know who it was, but the stuff they overheard... they said it had to be Casey," Brett says.

"She admitted it all when we saw her yesterday. She even seemed..." Harley sighs. "I don't know... like it was a relief to finally come clean."

"I haven't spoken to her... I ..." My vision blurs, my heart racing.

She didn't. She couldn't have.

"She would have told me!" I cry. "She's my best friend. She would have told me."

There's no way she could have been seeing someone, especially a married man, and be keeping it a secret from me. We tell each other everything. And I would have noticed, I mean...

But Gareth and I were going through that rough period. It lasted months. Moving in together, and the... the sex... I thought at the time it would all help. That we just needed to show each other how committed we were. That it was a dip that would pass.

I was distracted. I didn't see Casey as much... but I was still there. She couldn't have hidden this from me. She wouldn't.

"You're liars!" I shout down the phone. "You're talking about Casey like she would do that to me. She wouldn't. She's been there for me forever, every time I've needed her."

"Exactly," Harley says gently. "Exactly, Rose. How could she have told you after she knew what he did? What he did to Brett? To our family? To you?"

"She wouldn't do it."

I hold my free hand out in front of me. It's shaking. I suck in a breath through my nose and hold it still. But it trembles again in a split second, then turns into a full shake once more.

"Sorry, Sis. We didn't want to be the ones to tell you. She said she was going to," Brett says.

"But we could tell by the way you sounded when you called that she hadn't." Harley's voice is full of concern, and I can just picture her looking over at Brett with wide, worried eyes. The two of them feeling sorry for me again. Poor fucked up little sister. Never being able to move past that day that cost us all so much.

The day that was my fault... only... was it?

If Casey was ... No! She couldn't be. But if she was? Then...

I have to know.

"I've got to go." I hang up before Harley and Brett can say anything else, and immediately dial Casey's number.

It doesn't even complete a full ring before she answers.

"Rose, I was about to call you, I was—"

"Is it true?" I scream, my voice breaking.

"I—"

"Don't lie to me. Don't lie to me again!" I screw my eyes up so hard they sting as colored spots pulsate behind my eyelids.

"I was going to tell you. I just didn't know how. I'm so sorry." Casey breaks down sobbing.

I fold forward over the desk as the air leaves my lungs in one sudden whoosh, like I've been punched in the gut.

Casey continues sobbing. "I'm sorry, Ro. Please... I'm so sorry..."

I stagger to my feet and grab my purse.

I end the call, cutting off her frantic cries as I swipe a set of car keys up from the desk and race out of the office.

Chapter 15

Dax

"YOU GOOD WITH ALL this?" Logan asks as I flip through his proposal for some additions to the next estate open day he's running.

"Yeah. You and Jasmin have both run more of these days than me, I know you've got it covered."

Logan tips his head to the side with a grin. "We couldn't just sit on our asses while you were away in Her Majesty's finest five-star luxury now, could we?"

I smirk. "Bastard."

Logan and Jasmin are the only ones who can make jokes about me getting sent down. It's a dark humor we all share sometimes. We started doing it because the alternative of getting all depressed and shit when we talk about it isn't top of anyone's wish list.

Especially mine. Two and a half fucking years of my life… gone.

They both stuck by me through everything, keeping the business afloat. I owe everything to them. And I intend to pay them back. I know Jasmin wouldn't be okay with my methods if she knew just how I intend to do it. But she will understand when it's done. And so will

Logan. But right now, it's better for everyone the less they know.

Especially Rose.

Rose.

I grit my teeth as I hand the proposal back to Logan. Rose has no idea what she's getting into by pushing to get to know me. She wouldn't want to know me if I told her what I do. Maybe I should tell her. At least that way, she might leave. Go back to New York where she's safe from it all. Safe from me. But I can't... I'm a selfish bastard. Because as much as I am no good for her, I can't let her go, either.

I want her. I want her so much it fucking hurts to breathe when I see her.

Especially when she looks at me with that fire in her eyes. I knew she had it. It's coming back, brighter every day. And I'm a moth to the fucking flame.

My phone starts ringing.

"Great. I'm going to find Jasmin to go over some things. Catch you later."

"Yep." I nod at Logan as he leaves and pull my phone from my suit pants, checking the caller ID.

What the fuck now?

"What?" I bark.

"You're ready, right? You're coming down now?"

My jaw ticks. Fucking Marcus. He couldn't organize his way out of a wet paper bag.

"You can handle this. It'll be good practice for the big shipment."

"I know, it's just... with Mr. Young—"

"Forget about him," I snarl. "Or are you pissing yourself just hearing his name?"

"Fuck off—"

"Listen to me." I drop my voice. "Don't worry about him. Just do your damn job."

Marcus sniffs down the line. "You coming to gimme a hand or what?"

Jesus. How this guy hasn't been killed already, I have no idea. It's a miracle he makes it out of bed, let alone survives with the company we keep.

"I can be there in—"

"You're liars!" Rose's voice cuts through the air like a knife, forcing all the hairs on the back of my neck to stand to attention. "Is it true?"

The pain in her voice as she screams and bangs about in her office down the hallway makes my stomach roll.

"Marcus. You'll have to wait. Something's come up."

"What? Come on—"

"I said, you'll have to fucking wait." I throw my phone down on the desk and fly out of the room, my jacket flapping behind me as I run to Rose's office.

Empty.

Something's happened. She shouldn't sound like that. Her voice...

Where is she?

"Rose?" I yell, racing down the stairs to the ground floor. Someone points to the front door.

I tear through it.

Gravel and dust kick up into a giant cloud, engulfing the air in front of the main house as one of the estate's Range Rovers speeds off down the driveway.

Rose? What the fuck happened?

Her blonde hair cascades down her back where she's sitting slumped over her drink at the bar. If I didn't sense the hurt radiating from her in waves, pulling me to her, then I could stay here and watch her. Stay here all fucking night. Admire the way her hair shines, the platinum highlights in it glistening. Watch the way her lips part as she takes a sip of the clear liquid in the glass she's gripping so hard, her knuckles are turning white.

No matter what she does, Rose Jacobs is fucking beautiful.

And I would cut out anyone's tongue who dared say otherwise.

"Aunt Iris on the rocks." I nod at the bartender as I slide onto the bar stool next to her.

"How did you know I was here?" She sniffs, keeping her eyes on her glass as she turns it side to side in her hand, watching the light catch on the rim.

"The car has a tracker."

She turns to me, her eyes dull, and it's like someone just ripped open my chest with their bare hands and poured salt inside.

"Oh." Her mouth flattens into a grim line as she turns back to her drink, sighing heavily. "You know how you said that your life was fucked up?"

"Yeah?"

She tips the glass again and then downs the remainder of it. The bartender places my drink down, and I signal to him to get another for Rose.

"Mine definitely out-fucks yours as of today."

"What's happened?" I lean closer to her, my body turned to her, tuned in to her every movement. To the pinch in the fine lines by her eyes as she screws them up and drags in an uneven breath. To the small shake in her fingers as she wraps them around the fresh glass that is placed down. To the forced swallow before she speaks.

"She's been lying to me for years. She's the only person I trusted."

"Who has? Rose?"

She turns to me. "Casey. It was her all along. She knows what that man did to our family. She's the reason he was speeding down that road. He was having an affair with her."

"Brett's accident?"

"She's my *best friend*, Dax. How could she do that? How can you lie to someone every single day? Look them in the eye and know you played a part in them losing everything?"

"How did you—?"

"She admitted it. Said she's sorry. She hasn't stopped texting me." Rose reaches to her phone on the bar and hands it to me. "I've switched it off. Don't let me have it back yet. I'm afraid of what I might do if I turn it on and see her name again."

I slide it into my jacket pocket, then take her hand in mine.

"What do you need?" I place my thumb over her wrist and stroke her vein as it pulses against my skin.

She looks up at me and her eyes pinch at the corners, and tension lines form a V between her brows. "I need to get wasted."

I frown and shake my head, rubbing my thumb back and forth over her pulse as it beats faster. "That's not going to help. Trust me."

She rips her hand from mine, her eyes flashing.

"Trust you?" She leans forward until we are almost nose to nose. "I'm done with trusting anyone," she spits. "Look where it's gotten me."

She leaps up from her stool in a flash and begins fighting her way through the bar toward the exit. It's late afternoon, but the space is packed with people who've left work early for the weekend. Many are standing and watching a giant screen with a wrestling match on.

"Rose!" I chase after her, shouldering past a throng of bodies and getting dirty looks as I force my way through.

"Watch it, mate."

"You fucking watch it," I hiss, glaring at a guy in a wrinkled suit and a pint in his hand. He scowls and steps back near his mates.

Yeah, thought so, fucker.

That's one thing jail taught me. How to give someone a look that means they won't want to mess with you. Not unless they're a crazy fucker with a death wish.

"Rose!"

She squeezes in front of a group of men and their eyes follow her. One reaches out and curls his fat fingers around her forearm.

"What's the rush, love? Stay and have a drink with us."

His eyes drop over her body, stopping on her legs in her short skirt and heels as he licks his lips.

"You want to lose your fucking fingers?" I hiss in his ear as I come up behind him and grab the back of his neck with one hand.

He stiffens but can't turn his head as I have him in a vise-like grip. I squeeze harder.

"I said, do you want to lose those filthy fucking fingers?"

"What the hell?" he gasps as his mates just stare at the both of us. *Pussies.*

"If you don't want me to rip them the fuck off"—*squeeze*—"then I suggest you take them off *my* girl. Right. Now." *Squeeze.*

He drops Rose's arm like it's a grenade.

"Now, apologize," I snarl.

"Sorry. No harm meant," he chokes out as I give him one final squeeze and then throw him away from me and into his mates who are staring with their mouths open like fucking idiots.

"Let's go, Rose." I grab her hand and pull her outside.

"What was that?" She turns to me, eyes wild the moment we step through the door, yanking her hand from mine.

"He's lucky he still has his hand. He was touching you without your permission." I inhale slowly to ease the wild thumping in my chest.

Her mouth drops open and her eyes go round. "I mean the 'my girl' crap? I'm not your girl."

"You sure as fuck aren't anyone else's." I step forward into her space until our chests almost touch. She glares up at me but doesn't move away.

"Throw that in my face as well while you're at it, huh? Poor pathetic Rose who's only ever gotten laid once in her life."

"Don't." I shake my head, my eyes holding hers as I suck air in through my nose. Forget trying to ease the thumping in my chest. There's a full-on herd of wild buffalo in there now, stampeding against my ribs.

"Don't what?" She screws her face up, jabbing a finger into my chest. "Did I say something you don't like, *Boss*?"

I grab her hand in mine and pull her hard against me.

"Don't talk about yourself like that. Why are you even thinking about him?"

She snorts, her eyes glittering. "Gareth. Casey. They're both liars. And what does that make me? The stupid idiot that listened to them."

"You're not," I whisper, lifting my other hand and snaking it around the back of her neck, pressing my thumb over the hammering pulse beating next to her windpipe.

She leans closer until her lips are almost touching mine, and I breathe in vanilla and petals. One more inch and I will be kissing her. Feeling her soft lips against mine again, just like in the alleyway. Blood races to my dick as her eyelids fall closed.

My beautiful Sunbeam.

I apply pressure to the back of her neck to bring her to me. She's so close that our lips dust together.

"Don't worry," she breathes as I part mine, ready to close the final miniscule space keeping us apart. "You don't have to fake-kiss me tonight."

Then she shoves hard against my chest and spins out from my grasp, storming off up the street.

"Rose!"

"Leave me alone, Dax," she cries over her shoulder as I catch up with her.

"Will you stop, please? You're upset. I'm not leaving you here by yourself."

"Like you care!"

"Of course I fucking care! The town is full of pricks like that guy back there who wouldn't think twice about putting his hands all over you."

"So what?" She wraps her arms around herself as she rushes down the street with me by her side. "Maybe that's exactly what I need tonight. A distraction with a man like that. In fact"—she turns suddenly and marches back in the direction we came from—"I'm going to go back there now and talk to him."

"The fuck you are." I grab her arm and pull her to me. Her eyes are shining with undisguised pain, thinly masked by two drinks and a whole lot of anger.

She fists my shirt as she glares at me, then narrows her eyes with a grimace. "I think he's *exactly* what I need tonight, Dax. He can help me erase the memories. Replace Gareth's fingerprints as the last ones on my skin." Her eyes drop to my mouth as I grind my teeth so fucking hard my brain throbs in my skull.

"That's what you want? To hide away with someone like that?" I spit. "Separate your body from your soul and be a hole to fuck? Get on your knees and suck that prick's tiny cock?"

She gasps quietly as I hold her close and bring my lips to her ear to whisper.

"We both know you won't, Sunbeam. Because as much as you lie to yourself about dopamine and love being just a chemical, you still want it all. There's a tiny part of Rose Jacobs that still believes."

"Stop." She pushes against me, but I don't let go.

"You know how I know?" I dust my lips down the silky skin of her neck to her collarbone and back up, fighting to stay in control as she shivers from my touch. "Because all those men you told me about, that you'd flirt with when you went out. You never went home with any. Not a single one. And I'm not about to let you start tonight."

"What are you going to do, Dax? Break every man's hand in town tonight that I speak to? Go back to jail?" Her words are sharp and jagged, aimed to hurt me. But I would rather she fight with me than do anything else with another man.

"No. I'm going to do this."

I bend at the knee and hoist her over my shoulder, wrapping an arm around her legs to secure her in place.

She bangs her fists against my back. "Put me down. Dax! Put me down."

"I'll put you down when we get to my car," I growl.

"You're a bastard! The worst boss ever!" she screams, drawing attention from some guys that have spilled out from one of the bars on the opposite side of the street.

"What's going on?" one yells.

Rose's attack on my back ceases.

"You want them to call the cops and send me back to jail. Now's your chance. Tell them I'm taking you against your will." I slow my pace as we draw level with the group of men, and she lifts her upper body away from my back.

"Nothing. Mind our own business," she shouts at them, flopping herself back down again with a cross between a frustrated scream and a sigh.

I stroke her thighs with one hand. "Thought not. Now let's get you home."

Chapter 16

Rose

THE RANGE ROVER HASN'T even come to a complete stop before I throw open the door and jump out, leaving it wide open behind me.

"Rose!" Dax flies out of the vehicle and is behind me in a flash.

"I'm back now. So you can fuck off!"

I slide my key into the cottage's lock and turn it. Dax stands behind me and wraps his hand over mine.

"You know why I had to bring you home." His breath fans over my neck, and my nipples harden despite wanting to hate him right now.

"This isn't my home."

I turn to face him. His dark eyes are there, waiting to capture mine and make it impossible to look away as they reach right down deep inside me and make me feel both exhilaration and a strange calmness all at once.

"You brought me back because you think you have some claim over me. Some right to say what I do. When you don't. You have no right to anything. So go on," I say, trying to sound braver than the churning that's happening inside my stomach at the thought of being alone once he leaves. "You can go now."

I turn back to the door, opening it.

"I can just go back out if I feel like it, anyway. This time without being spied on by your fancy car trackers."

"You wouldn't," he grits, and his eyes are dark and stormy as I turn and glance at him.

"I might."

Then I slam the door in his face before he can move and collapse back against it, my chest heaving.

Who the hell does he think he is? He storms into the bar, does his whole listening and caring act that he's so good at, and then acts like a prize jerk and orders me to come back. No, make that, swings me over his shoulder and physically carries me back. Asshole.

I *should* go back out tonight. It's still early. I can call a taxi. What's the alternative? Stay in and drink alone? And it would serve Dax right for thinking he can boss me around. We aren't at work now.

I head upstairs and pull my work blouse and skirt off, throwing them into the laundry hamper, then get a short black dress out with a skirt that swishes when I dance. I can call Jasmin. She might be up for hitting a club. Somewhere with strong drinks and music loud enough that I can't hear my own thoughts. It's *exactly* what I need. Dax knows nothing. The complicated bastard.

I take my time fixing my hair and touching up my makeup.

Damn it. He still has my phone. I gave it to him in the bar. *Shit. Think. Think.*

I can call on the cottage's landline. I must have something with Jasmin's number on somewhere. Some estate paperwork or something.

A loud, incessant banging comes from downstairs.

"Rose? Open the door."

My skin prickles with irritation. "Go away!"

I've been inside awhile. *Why hasn't he left yet?*

"Open the door before I break it down!"

I stomp downstairs to the door and rip it open so hard it's a miracle it stays on its hinges.

"What?" I spit.

His eyes drop over my outfit and darken. "You're serious? You're actually going back out?"

"What if I am? It has nothing to do with you." I'm trembling with anger, my fingertips pulsing by my sides.

"Don't go." Dax's voice drops to a deep rumble, and the shine in his eyes makes my chest tighten. "Don't go back out tonight. Don't let another man touch you. Not tonight. Not ever. The thought is driving me fucking *wild*. Please..."

He sucks in a breath, looking to the sky with rapid blinks.

"I'm going to lose my fucking mind here, Rose." He brings his eyes back to mine, and my breath stalls as he looks so deeply into mine it makes my head spin.

"Why are you doing this?" I grasp the door frame for support, my stomach clenching. "One minute your life is too fucked up. The next you're fake-kissing me and buying me lap dances and telling me you think about me when you're in bed at night. What do you *want* from me?"

"It wasn't fake... The kiss. Nothing with you has ever been fake." He screws his face up, pressing a thumb and finger into his eyes. "But I'm involved in some serious stuff. Stuff that you shouldn't be anywhere near. You're too good for any of it."

Here we go again. I roll my eyes and step back inside, grabbing hold of the door. "Goodnight, Dax."

"Wait." He puts his foot inside the frame and pushes it back open. "Wait."

The two of us stand, breathing hard, staring at each other.

Light blue meets deep brown once again.

Then his gaze drops to my mouth.

"Come here," he growls.

He closes the distance in one stride, grabbing my face in his hands and backing me up against the wall before crashing his lips onto mine.

I'm pinned in place by his hard body, heat radiating from it as he angles my face and kisses me with a force that makes my knees buckle. If it weren't for being pressed so tightly against him, I would be a puddle on the floor.

He groans from deep in his chest as he coaxes my lips apart. He slides his tongue inside my mouth, licking, sucking, and stroking me into oblivion. I should push him away. Tell him that I'm not letting him mess with my head anymore.

But I can't.

Every nerve ending in my body is alive for the first time in my life, energy racing through my bloodstream as he groans into my mouth and nips at my lips with his teeth before sinking into the kiss again.

He slides his hands back from my cheeks and threads his fingers into my hair, his voice sliding over me. "Touch me, Rose. I need to feel your hands on me. Show me I'm not the only one in this."

He opens his eyes and the hint of vulnerability he hides so well is there. It breaks any lingering resolve I'm gripping on to. With him, it's lost. I have a pull to him that I can't explain. It's not logical. But it's all-consuming, and despite the hot and cold signals he gives me, I can't fight it any longer.

"You're not..." I pant, our lips grazing each other's. "You're not alone. I'm right here with you."

Then I slide my hands up over his chest, wrapping them around the back of his neck and pull him to me.

I kiss him back with everything, pouring out all my frustrations, all my energy I've spent fighting with him. I kiss him until I'm moaning into his mouth and arching away from the wall to get closer to him.

And he matches me, stroke for stroke, moan for moan, breath for breath, until I swear a part of each of us will always be fused with the other.

If a kiss ever had the power to end the world. Then this is it right here.

"Jesus Christ, I've wanted to kiss you properly for so long." Dax tugs my hair, tilting my head back so he can pepper kisses along my jaw and to the sensitive skin beneath my ear. "It's felt like fucking eternity, Rose," he whispers in my ear, sending heat tingling through my core and making my already soaked panties wetter.

"Is that all you want? To kiss me?" I slip my hands down to rest against his shirt as he groans and kisses and sucks my neck.

"You've no fucking idea." His lips against my skin send a vibration all the way to my toes until I'm balling the fabric of his shirt up in my fists and trying not to explode with pleasure as he continues kissing and sucking and groaning into my neck.

I push away the briefest flash of nerves. They don't belong here.

Him. Here. Now. This is exactly where I am supposed to be. I know it.

"Upstairs," I breathe as his lips return to mine and he kisses me again. He pulls back just enough to focus on my eyes with a questioning look. "I want you to take me upstairs, Dax. I want you to show me what you've thought about doing to me."

His brows pull in for a second and then relax again as he searches my eyes.

His are exquisite. Not just deep brown, but a warm, rich golden-hued chestnut brown that somehow lightens and darkens, altering depending what mood he's in.

I gaze back as he strokes my cheeks with his thumbs. Our frantic draw to one another pauses momentarily as he holds me in his arms, making way for something deeper, something we will never come back from. *Something I want to run straight into.*

"Are you sure?" His brow creases again as his whisper caresses my skin with the tenderness of someone I know I can give this to.

Gareth may have been my first. But that was just biology. A physical act. He never looked at me like Dax does. Like I'm the most precious thing he's ever seen. He never held me like he can't believe I am really in his arms. And his skin touching mine never made me feel like I would die if I were told I would never feel it again.

Not like Dax.

"You won't break me," I whisper, blinking up at him.

He searches my eyes one more time, and then he lifts me, holding me underneath the butt so I have to wrap my legs around his waist.

I don't know how he makes it up the stairs so gracefully while kissing me as if he needs me to breathe. But he does. He carries me to my bedroom with his lips moving from mine to my neck, my collarbones, my jaw, my cheeks, and back again. Everywhere he can possibly reach in this position.

We get to my room, and he pauses, burying his nose into the hair behind my ear and inhaling.

"I've loved your scent since that first day I met you in my office." He inhales slowly again. "Vanilla and petals. I've wanted it all over me. On my hands, my lips..." He kisses my neck. "My cock."

I shudder as he lowers my feet to the floor and slides his hands up my legs, dusting the inside of my thighs and cursing as his thumb drags over the soaking lace of my panties. He takes his hand away and pulls his jacket off and discards it. Then he rolls his shirt sleeves up.

"I've wanted it fucking everywhere," he groans, bringing his hand back to my thighs underneath my dress and slipping his thumb inside the edge of the lace, swiping it through my swollen skin. "Jesus, Rose. You're so wet."

I gasp as he places one hand against my lower back, steadying me as he continues his slow exploration inside my panties. His lips stay on my neck, kissing and mur-

muring about how hot and wet I am, and it's all I can do to stay upright and not buckle at the intense throbbing that's overtaken my pussy.

"Is this okay?" Dax asks with a low voice as he stretches the lace away from my skin and circles his thumb over my entrance.

I grab onto the front of his shirt for extra support. "Uh-huh."

"I need to hear you say it."

"Yes," I gasp as he circles again and my thighs tremble.

"Good girl," he breathes.

Then he pushes his thumb inside me, sucking in a sharp breath as I cry out and my body releases a new burst of wetness, coating it and running out onto his palm.

"Shit, that's so fucking hot. You're dripping all over me."

"I know." I tighten my grip on his shirt and moan as he circles his thumb inside me again, the sound of my arousal thick in the air.

He abandons my neck and moves to face me, looking at me with lust-filled eyes. Then he glances at something to the side and takes his hand back from inside my panties.

"Turn around."

He holds my hips and spins me slowly, pressing my back into his chest as he moves us to face the giant mirror propped against the wall.

"I sent you this because I wanted you to look at yourself and see what I see... just how *fucking beautiful* you are." He sweeps my hair back over one shoulder so he can kiss my neck, his eyes holding mine in the reflection. Then he uses both hands to slide my dress up until the black lace of my panties shows. "Look, Rose. See what I see when I look at you."

My eyes lock with his as he slides his hand down inside the front of the lace and pushes one long finger straight inside me. I gasp and fall forward, but he catches me gently with one arm and curls his hand up around my throat, holding me in place as he watches me in the reflection.

I stare back as he kisses my neck. His shirt sleeves are rolled up, the thick veins in his inked forearms bulging as he finger-fucks me with delicious long, slow strokes which make my inner thighs tremble, and my legs grow weak.

"Look at yourself. Look at the way your cheeks flush when you feel pleasure. Look at the way the blood makes your lips darker as they part... as you moan. You're the most beautiful woman I've ever seen, Rose."

I swallow, my neck contracting against Dax's hand, and he strokes his thumb over my racing pulse.

"I..." I gasp as he adds another finger and uses his thumb to rub circles over my clit at the same time as he quickens his pace and fingers me harder.

"You want me to make you come, Sunbeam?" He sucks on my neck, his eyes blazing into mine.

"Yes."

I suck in a breath as he groans against my skin, holding me tighter to his chest, as he pushes his fingers deeper inside me, curling them until they connect with my G-spot and I cry out.

"Look at yourself. Look how fucking breathtaking you are."

I drag my eyes from his and refocus on my face. I am flushed, like he said, my lips darkened and parted as I draw in a breath and hold it. My hair is cascading down one shoulder, and the skin of my bare arms and legs is pale and smooth.

And *virgin*.

My skin appears stark in contrast to Dax's. Inch after inch of untouched, unmarked skin, wrapped inside two strong, muscular arms covered in dark ink, flexing as they work me. Controlling every sensation in my body. All at their mercy. His hand around my throat even has flowers and vines on it, and then there's his neck, my favorite of them all... barely visible from his position behind me, except the tip of one feathered wing running up toward his ear.

He presses his lips against my ear. "Come on my fingers."

I let go of the breath I'm holding in a rush and immediately suck in another as my body tightens, pressure pulling my core tight. I move my gaze back to his eyes as I shake and shudder.

"Soak my hand, Rose. Let me feel just how wet this perfect pussy gets when you let go."

I moan, my eyes glued to his, and then I release, exploding around his fingers in a crashing wave as we stand in front of the mirror. Two people locked in a moment.

Moisture pricks at the corner of my eyes, and I blink it away as he continues fucking me with his fingers, drawing out every last drop of my orgasm as I ripple and pulse around him, my body sucking on him greedily, my wetness spreading onto my inner thighs.

Dax kisses my neck. "Incredible. You're incredible."

I whimper as the waves finally begin to subside. My body sinks back against his chest, tension leaving every muscle and euphoric bliss washing over me.

"Oh my God." I take a slow, deep breath. "That was—"

"Good after so long?" His eyes close as he smiles and presses his nose into my hair. Then he inhales.

"No," I murmur. "I mean... no one's ever... I have... plenty of times, but just me... alone, I mean."

Dax's eyes pop open and pin onto mine in the reflection, his upper body tensing.

"Are you saying...?"

I bite my bottom lip. I said too much. I shouldn't be mentioning my sexual past—or lack of it—when we are here like this. Together.

"Rose?"

"I just mean I've only ever orgasmed alone before." My cheeks burn, and I attempt to turn my head, but Dax keeps it fixed in place with his hand still around my neck.

"No one's ever given you an orgasm before?" His eyes are the most intense I've ever seen them.

I shake my head as much as his grip on me allows. "No."

His brows shoot up. Then they pull low, making his eyes appear even darker.

"Dax? What are you think—?"

"I didn't know," he whispers. He slides his fingers from me and clutches my hip bone, turning me in his arms so that I'm facing him. Then he holds my chin with his other hand. "But now that I do..." He brushes some loose strands away from my face. "I'm going to make every single first one count."

I frown as he kisses me on the lips.

"There's only one first, Dax. And it's already yours."

He kisses my neck, at the same time as sliding his hand underneath my dress and cupping my soaked skin in his palm. I moan loudly, unable to hold back.

His voice rumbles against my neck as he slides his hand around to cup my ass.

"That was the first for my fingers. The next one's for my tongue."

Chapter 17

Dax

"The next one's for my tongue."

Rose looks at me with wide eyes. She's so fucking beautiful, it makes my chest hurt.

And so fucking sexy, it's got my cock throbbing painfully.

She's letting me touch her. Letting me be the first person to give her body true pleasure.

Gareth was a fucking idiot to lose her.

"What about you?" Rose murmurs as I kiss her neck again, relishing the way my lips slide over her skin like it's silk. And her scent? Fuck, it's amazing. I can taste it on her skin. *Drink it the fuck up.*

"Don't worry about me. This is for my pleasure."

I walk her backward to the bed, stopping as the white sheets graze the back of her legs.

"Arms."

She lifts her arms above her head without hesitation, allowing me to pull her dress up over her head until she's just in her black lace bra and panties. Her nipples harden inside the fabric, calling to me.

"This is *definitely* for my pleasure," I groan as I unhook her bra and pull it off, freeing her breasts into my waiting hands. Her eyes drop to where I'm rubbing my thumbs back and forth over her pink puckered skin.

I squeeze her nipples gently, and she gasps as her upper body trembles.

Sensitive nipples? Fuck...

I push her down so she's perching on the edge of the bed, then drop to my knees on the floor in front of her and let my eyes roam hungrily over every curve of her.

"Panties off, too." I reach forward and she lifts up from the sheets enough for me to slide them all the way down her long legs.

I press them into her hand.

"Feel how wet you made them."

She gazes at me, closing her fingers around the fabric.

"Don't you mean, how wet *you* made them?"

I growl as I pull her knees apart and dive onto her, kissing her smart mouth, and sinking one hand into her hair.

"I don't know where to fucking start." I pull back. "Maybe here?" I place both hands on the bed, caging her in and lick over her collarbone, moving down until I'm sucking one of her tight, perfect nipples into my mouth. I groan as I roll my tongue over it. "Or here?" I switch sides, and she moans, arching up into my mouth.

"There," she breathes as I swirl my tongue faster and suck harder.

"Or maybe here?" I drag my lips down the soft skin of her stomach and straight between her legs, making her jump. Then I lick down her slit with one long swipe of my tongue, until I reach her asshole, and she tenses, closing her legs around my head.

"Fuck," I groan, placing my hands on her thighs and holding her wide open as I lick forward, grazing her entrance with the tip of my tongue.

She sucks in a breath as I groan again. She tastes as good as she smells. Like fucking nectar on my tongue. A heady combination that will render me addicted to her.

I couldn't give her up even if my life depended on it.

A fact that is stabbing me in the heart right now.

I'm too selfish to have kept away.

And I sure as fuck am too selfish to let her go now.

I suck up a rush of her wetness and drink it down with a deep growl of appreciation. Then I settle my lips around her clit and suck gently.

"Dax." Her breathy moan speaks directly to my cock, and it weeps in my boxers.

"You ready to come on my face, Sunbeam?" I flutter the tip of my tongue against her clit and slide a finger inside her.

She shudders, holding herself up on one arm as her other hand drops to my hair and she curls her fingers through it.

"Mmm."

"Tell me," I whisper around her clit as I suck it again.

"Yes."

"And you're going to watch, aren't you?" I look up, my lips never leaving her as I swipe my tongue over her again.

Her lashes flutter, and she bites her bottom lip. "Yes."

"Good girl." I smile against her and suck again, my cock leaking even more as her eyes widen and her mouth drops open. "I want you to watch yourself in the mirror.

Watch how beautiful you are when you're being given pleasure. Watch how much you deserve to be worshiped like this. With me on my knees at your feet." I add another finger and stretch her open gently. "Watch how desired you are and what you fucking do to me."

"Okay," she breathes, her cheeks flushed. Then she lifts her gaze from mine and looks over my head at her reflection.

I close my eyes and dive into her, kissing, sucking, fingering, groaning, drinking, worshiping. Every damn thing I can do to her as she quivers and swells against my mouth, her wetness running down my chin.

I pull my fingers out, suck them clean and replace them with my tongue, fucking her with it as her hand twists in my hair and her ass lifts off the bed. I push her back down and pull my tongue back, moving back to lick circles over her clit as I sink my fingers back inside her again and suck in a sharp breath as her hot, tight, walls ripple around them and pull them in further.

"Dax," she moans. My cock throbs harder at the pleasure dripping from her voice.

I increase my pace in response.

She sucks in a breath, tugging my hair at the root as she pants.

"Dax."

"Do it." I bury my face in her and press my tongue harder against her clit.

She whimpers, "Fuck."

Then she comes.

She comes all over me, covering my lips and face in her orgasm. She clenches and releases around my fingers and shudders against my tongue. She grips my hair so hard my scalp burns, and she pulls me closer and grinds onto me.

She lets go completely.

"Fuck!" she cries.

I open my eyes and look up. She's watching herself in the mirror, just like I instructed her to. Her mouth is open, and her eyes are glittering as her chest rises and falls with fast breaths.

I suck on her clit, and she drops her head back and looks at the ceiling as she shudders again.

I continue sucking and kissing her gently until her breathing slows, and she sighs quietly. I can't take my eyes off her for a second. The release from her calms the raging storm that's often inside my head. Just watching her like this makes everything still somehow. Nothing else matters. Nothing except her and the flush in her cheeks and the light in her eyes as she finally brings them back to meet mine.

She watches as I press gentle kisses to her skin and take my fingers from her body. Then she smiles and sighs happily, and fuck if my soul doesn't pledge its eternal promise to worship her.

For now. For tomorrow. For all time.

I am totally fucked for this girl.

"Kiss me, Dax."

I press my mouth to her swollen flesh one final time, then rise to my knees, wrapping my arms around her waist and pulling her to me. She places her legs around me and crosses her ankles behind me, holding me close as she snakes her hands up around my neck, parting her lips as I lean forward to kiss her.

"I can taste myself," she murmurs as I swipe my tongue through her lips to meet hers.

"You taste incredible."

She kisses me again with her arms wrapped around my neck, and it's like a fucking deep bass has started playing in my chest.

She's holding me like she never wants me to leave.

"Are we going to have sex now?" she whispers against my lips.

I moan at the innocence in her tone as she sucks on my bottom lip with a soft sigh.

"We don't have to do anything you're not ready for. We can take our time. I'm patient." I stroke her hair away from her face, cupping her cheeks.

She searches my eyes and clear blue shines back at me. "I guess you learned to be patient. Being where you've been. Until you came home, I mean. Then I guess it was different." Her forehead wrinkles as she looks at my lips.

"It's not been different, Rose. Not until now."

She lifts her eyes to meet mine. "What do you—?"

"There's been no one. Not since before I got locked up."

Her eyes widen and then narrow almost immediately.

"I'm telling you the truth." I rub my thumb back and forth over her lower lip. "There's been no one in over three years."

"The same as me," she whispers.

I rest my forehead against hers. "The same as you."

She takes a second to process my confession, and then she's all over me, her lips crashing onto mine, her hands grabbing at my shirt as she fights to take it off. I pull it from my suit pants and rip it off over my head before swooping back onto her lips again.

"You're sure?" I groan between kisses, grabbing handfuls of long blonde hair as I devour her mouth.

She grabs for my belt, moaning loudly as I kiss along her jaw and suck on her neck.

She undoes my pants and forces them and my boxers down over my thighs, wrapping her hand around the base of my aching cock and moaning my name.

She's sure.

She slides her hand up to my tip, then stops. "What's that?" She leans back and looks down at my cock. The head of it is covered in pre-cum, which makes the silver bar that runs down through my urethra and out below the rim on the underside of my head shine.

"A piercing."

She looks up at me, her eyes wide. Then she stares back at it again.

"Does it hurt? I mean... what does it... how does it feel?"

She rubs the tips of two fingers over the top end of it, rotating the bar, and I curse with a deep growl as it sends a vibration buzzing through the head of my cock.

"It feels fucking amazing. Especially when you do that."

I look at her delicate hand stroking it, spreading wetness over one end of it, and then dipping below to rub wetness on the other end as well.

"I like it." Rose bites her bottom lip and gives me a shy smile. "I like that it feels good for you if I touch it."

"It'll feel good for you too." I take her chin between my thumb and forefinger and dust her lips with a kiss. "I promise you, Sunbeam. It'll feel good inside you."

"Okay." She bites her bottom lip, her eyes bright. "I believe you."

Her words stab at my heart.

Not many people have chosen to believe me in recent years. Not many at all.

But she is willing to give her trust to me so easily.

All I have to do is give her my word. And it's enough.

"Lie back."

I move us up the bed and lower Rose onto her back. She pulls me over her immediately wrapping her arms around me, kissing me, and pushing her breasts against my chest.

"I want to feel it." She spreads her legs around my hips and lifts them until my cock nudges at her entrance.

"Have you got condoms?" I don't have any in my wallet. *Stupid.*

She stops kissing me. "Can you wear them with a piercing?"

"Of course. I always have."

"I..." She looks between my eyes. "No."

"It's all right." I move back a little. "We can wait."

"No." She pulls me back to her. "I... Please, Dax." She looks at me with pleading eyes. "I don't want to stop. If you're—"

"Clean?" I finish for her, and she nods.

"And so am I... then?"

"I am. I had tests before I went away." I stare at her, trying to get a read on what she's thinking.

"I have the injection, so I'm not going to..." She inhales and glances at my cock, and the fucker laps up her attention like a puppy and wags at her, smearing pre-cum over her inner thigh. "I want to feel it with nothing between us. I want to feel *you*, Dax."

Her pupils dilate as she breathes my name, and I press forward with a low moan, catching her lips in another heated kiss.

She's obliterated any last shred of willpower I might have had.

"Hold on to me," I say against her mouth as I kiss her again.

She wraps her arms around my neck as I lift one of her thighs and press just the tip of myself into her tight, wet heat.

I hiss at the contact as her body grips on to me greedily, holding me tight, in warm, wet ecstasy.

"I can feel it." She smiles as I circle the head of my cock inside her so the hard metal strokes her walls. "More," she whispers.

I push forward, giving her another two inches, and she moans as I circle again, stroking her inside, getting her ready to take all of me.

"You okay?"

She bites her lip and nods as I push another couple of inches inside her with a deep groan.

Fuck, she feels incredible stretching around me. So wet. So hot. So *tight*.

"Dax."

I stop pushing immediately. "I'm almost halfway."

I dip my head and kiss her, holding still inside her so she can get used to me. She parts her lips with a whimper, letting my tongue slide inside her mouth. I kiss her, my cock held snugly inside her as she melts into me, relaxing more the longer we kiss. Then she lifts her hips toward me, inviting me to push another couple of inches inside her.

"That's it, Sunbeam. You're taking it so well," I hum against her lips as I keep kissing her. My cock throbs where it's seated, partway inside her tight body.

"There's still more?" she pants as I slowly circle again, kissing her neck behind her ear as my arms shake with the force of holding back.

"Quite a bit more," I admit as the head of my cock throbs with the need to move inside her.

She threads both hands into my hair and moans as I suck the point on her neck where her pulse is beating rapidly. "Okay. I'm ready."

"You sure?"

"Yes." Her voice is breathy with an edge of excitement. "Don't stop until you're all the way inside me."

I catch her lips in mine again, and my balls tighten, pulling up to my body as I push forward, stretching her around me. I push deeper as she writhes beneath me, pulling at my hair, a gasp falling from her lips. I push and keep pushing, until finally I am all the way inside her, being gripped tightly.

"Fuck, you feel incredible." I drag in a shaky breath as my balls tingle.

Rose wriggles beneath me, clenching her sweet cunt around me.

"Don't."

"What's wrong?"

I bury my face into her neck. "Just give me a second."

Fuck, I'm going to lose it any moment. Lose it and spill inside her. Fill her up until it's pouring out of her.

I breathe deeply. What can I hear? What can I smell? What can I taste? Breathe. Breathe.

"Okay." I bring my face back to hers and kiss her. "Okay."

Then I begin to move, slowly at first, afraid I will hurt her. She's so tight, it may as well be her first time. I could hurt her if I get carried away.

The last thing I want to do is hurt her.

She moans and wriggles beneath me, widening her legs and lifting her hips to meet each gentle thrust I make into her. She's so wet that it makes it easier.

So fucking wet.

"More, Dax. Please."

I look into her eyes, bright and trusting, and then I take both of her hands in mine, threading my fingers with hers and pressing them against the sheets above her head as I drive into her with more speed.

"How's that feel?"

"Amazing." She tips her head back as my cock is coated in a fresh wave of arousal from her. "It feels amazing."

I clench my teeth as I alter the angle so the top of my piercing will rub against her G-spot.

"Dax." Rose gasps, lifting her head from the mattress as I pull back and thrust in again, hitting the new spot. "Dax... that's..."

She drops her head back to the bed, moans overtaking her parted pink lips as I fuck her in delicious long, deep, rhythmic strokes, relishing the way her body welcomes my aching cock with such enthusiasm, squeezing it on every intake.

"I want you to watch me this time." I thrust into her, and her pupils dilate. "I want you to keep your eyes on mine as you come on my cock."

"I don't know if I can like this," she pants. "It feels..."

I thrust a little harder until my balls kiss her skin.

"It feels so... so good, but I haven't ever..."

"I'll take care of you."

I let go of her hands and rest on one forearm, sucking my thumb, before sliding it between our bodies and circling it over her clit.

I continue to thrust into her, letting her stretch around my cock as I stroke her swollen clit until she's panting and grabbing at my shoulders, her nails digging into my skin.

"You ready to come for me now?"

"Yes." She nods furiously as I increase my pace, my balls slapping against her body. Each connection threatens to make me blow. I've never been so fucking turned on in my life.

"Good girl."

She sucks in another breath and then her chest starts to tremble.

"Eyes, Rose," I urge gently.

She brings her gaze back to mine as the first contraction hits the tip of my cock making my balls twitch. I dip my chin, watching as she loses all sense of reality until all she can do is gaze at me, cry my name, and come hard on my cock, soaking it.

"You're so fucking beautiful." I keep stroking her clit as she comes around me.

The head of my cock burns with need inside her as my piercing rubs against her hot flesh.

I groan like a wild animal as the last wave of her orgasm passes and mine begins. I release forcefully, filling her with streams of hot cum that race from my balls and up my cock with the power of a tsunami.

It may have been three years, but I remember sex. And it has *never* been like this before. It's not the fact that it's my first time without a condom, and that I'm filling her with me.

It's not even the fact she's so ridiculously tight and wet at the same time.

Her body might be the stuff of wet dreams.

But it's more than that.

It's her.

Her spirit. Her feistiness. But equally, her tenderness, too. That inner beauty that makes her glow brighter than the fucking sun.

It's all her.

Rose watches me with vibrant blue eyes, her cheeks flushed from her own release as I spill inside her, losing any sense of control. I grab her face and crash my lips to her, sucking in giant breaths.

"Fuck…" I growl into her mouth. "Fuck, Rose…" *Thrust. Thrust.*

"Dax," she murmurs, kissing my lips as I struggle to breathe.

My balls throb as they pump out the last of the most powerful orgasm of their existence and I groan as my cock pulses one final time and then releases its hold over me.

"Rose." I gulp in air and then return her kiss. "Fuck." I exhale slowly and then sink my face into the crook of her neck. "You're everything. You're fucking everything."

Chapter 18

Rose

I LIE COCOONED IN Dax's warmth as his body covers me.

His heart is hammering in his chest against mine. And we lie with him still deep inside me until both of us have come down enough to talk without the need to draw in extra air.

"Fuck," he sighs gently, moving his arms to hold my face between his hands.

He rests his forehead against mine and breathes in slowly before kissing me tenderly on the lips.

"Are you okay? I didn't hurt you, did I?"

I smile and move a strand of blond hair from his forehead.

"No. You didn't hurt me."

Relief washes over his face as he kisses me again. Then he stops and rises onto his forearms to pull out of me.

I don't hide my wince fast enough and Dax is on me in a shot, cupping my face again.

"Rose?" His brows knit.

"I'm fine."

He looks between my legs. "Shit. You're not."

He jumps up from the bed and rushes to the bathroom, then comes back moments later with a warm washcloth. He kneels between my legs and presses it to me gently, a frown marring his handsome face.

"You're bleeding. Not much but... Jesus." He scrunches his face up and wipes me with the cloth again.

"Show me."

I prop myself up on my arms and Dax holds the cloth up. The tiniest smudge of pink is on it. It's barely noticeable.

"I told you I'm fine." I smile, but he frowns and looks between my legs again.

"I would never forgive myself if you got hurt because of me." He blinks and keeps his eyes focused between my legs, where a delicious ache is setting in.

His eyes pinch as he cleans me up carefully. He says I am the beautiful one. But it's him. He's taking care of me like I'm hurt when I'm really not. But he's not going to listen, so instead I lie back and enjoy the attention he's giving me.

He's completely focused on me. Before, his eyes were burning with desire for me. And now, they're full of adoration and concern.

How can I be a fuck up if someone can look at me in this way? How can I be the failure I've cast myself as these past few years if I was those things? Then no one would want me, surely? No one would desire me.

My breath catches as Dax looks up and locks eyes with me.

If everything that has happened to my family was my fault, then no one would be able to look at me the way he is right now, like he sees my soul and thinks it's perfect.

Like he wouldn't change anything about me. Not a single thing.

Blood rushes in my ears and my chest flutters as his lips move.

"What?"

"I asked you what you were thinking about? You look so serious." His lips flatten. "It *does* hurt, doesn't it?"

"No." I sit up, warmth spreading in my chest as I reach out and stroke down the side of his face and along his strong jaw. "For the first time in three years, it doesn't hurt quite so much."

Then I smile.

His face softens until he's smiling back. Then he wraps me in his arms and kisses me.

"Let's take a shower."

He pulls me up from the bed, walking backward with my hands in his, all the way into the bathroom. We get to the shower, and he lets go of one hand long enough to turn the water on, and then he takes hold of it again, pulling me in under the hot spray with him.

"You going to let me wash you?"

I bite my lip and stand on my toes, kissing him as the water runs down over our mouths. "Only if you let me wash you. I haven't seen the tattoos on your back yet."

Dax stiffens, the muscles in his broad shoulders tightening. "Okay. But I'm going first."

I stand happily, my arms draped over his shoulders as he takes my shower gel and lathers it up between his hands before running them all over my body. He groans as my nipples harden when he washes my breasts, and his cock stiffens against my ass as I look at him over my shoulder while he washes my back. But despite the intensity his eyes have taken on, and the deep groans coming from his chest, he is the perfect gentleman, washing me gently with large, warm hands.

"Now you."

I take the bottle from him and squirt some into my hands. I'm spoiled for choice where to start. I begin with his thighs and his cock, which is hard and thick as I slide my soapy hand up and down it. Dax sucks in a breath and watches me as I wash it, followed by his balls, but he makes no attempt to put it to use on me again, and I fight back my disappointment as he takes my soapy hands and leads them to his chest instead.

I let the suds rinse off and run my hands over his tattoos again like that night at his house where he was hurt.

"Now turn."

He stiffens and stares at me.

"Turn around." I look up and wonder if he's still breathing. All the muscles in his shoulders and chest are tense, and a vein is throbbing in his neck beneath the bird's wing. "Dax?"

A muscle in his jaw flexes and then he turns slowly, placing his hands up against the tiled wall so each muscle in his back ripples.

I add more gel to my hands and slide them over his shoulders, soaking in all the tattoos on his back. They're intricate, like his front. A mix of leaves and flowers surrounding a giant, ornate, central cross. Then on his lower back, to one side of his spine there's a sun over water, its rays bursting up into the sky.

"Is it a sunrise or a sunset?" I ask as I trace my fingers over it.

"Sunset." He tenses as I move my fingers lower, over the ripples in the water.

"Dax?"

I run my fingers over the pinched skin again and he stays silent.

"What happened?"

The ripples in the water are distorted where they cover a large scar on Dax's skin.

"I wasn't careful. That's what happened."

"What do you mean?"

He turns and wraps me in his arms, dipping his head to kiss my neck before he sighs. "I was stabbed. In jail."

"What?" My blood runs cold as I turn to face him. He catches my lips in a kiss. "What do you mean? Who did this to you?" I ask, breaking our lips apart.

"It doesn't matter."

He tries to kiss me again, but I move back, flattening my palms over his chest.

"How can you say that?"

"Because it doesn't. The guy's still in there. And I'm out. That's what's important."

"But he hurt you? What's happening to him? Was he charged—?"

"The man responsible hasn't gotten away with it." He looks into my eyes. "You don't need to think about him."

"But did you—?"

"I always see things through, Rose. I'm committed. Okay? I always see things through." He holds my face and takes my lips in another kiss, shaking his head as he draws back and looks into my worried eyes. "Don't think about it."

I blink up at him as my chest tightens thinking about him in there and what it must have been like for him. Away from Jasmin and Logan. His freedom gone.

"I'm so sorry for what you went through. You're so strong."

His lips curl into a half smile.

"I'm not half as strong as you. The external scars are easy. You just turn them into something else."

He kisses me again.

Turn them into something else.

But what about internal scars? He can't have gone through all he has and have none of those. Can he?

I wake from my dream. The room is dark. It's the middle of the night.

Dax's warm arm is wrapped around me, his hand resting on my hip as I lie snuggled into his side with my head on his chest.

After we showered together last night, I washed all of my makeup off and came out of the bathroom to find Dax sitting in bed, his arms stretched up behind his head, staring into space, deep in thought. He smiled when he saw me and beckoned me over, and I curled around him happily until I fell asleep.

There was no need for words. Just holding each other and kissing told me all I needed to know. Dax doesn't see sex with me as something purely for him, like Gareth did. He was right there with me, baring it all. Both of us starved of human touch for so long. Dax from being physically caged. And me from caging myself.

I wanted the fairy tale once. The big wedding and the wedding night sex with the one love of your life. But watching Dax sleeping now, his kissable lips parted as he breathes softly, his bare skin darkened by so much ink, it's obvious. The real princes don't just fight for you. They give you the strength to fight for yourself. And they're your loudest supporter when you do.

I look over at the mirror and press my thighs together as heat pools there.

"Watch yourself. You deserve to be worshiped."

No one has ever said something like that to me. And the way Dax's eyes glittered up at me as he said it... I know he meant every single word.

I run the backs of my fingers down his cheek and shuffle up the bed so I can kiss along his jaw.

"Hey, Sunbeam," he murmurs sleepily, squeezing me with his arm.

"Hey, yourself." I kiss along to his ear and then nibble on his neck.

"Can't sleep?" There's a smile in his voice as I continue sucking and kissing his neck gently.

"I did. But my dream woke me."

"A bad one?" He sounds fully awake now.

I kiss my way down his neck, darting my tongue out to lick where the bird is as my eyes adjust to the dark.

"Kind of. I dreamed Casey was driving toward me in a car... aiming for me. I could see her through the windshield, and she was staring right through me."

"You okay?" Dax presses a kiss to the top of my head as I dip lower and kiss along his collarbone.

"Yeah." I push the heaviness in my chest away. If I refuse to acknowledge it, then it isn't there. At least, not tonight. Not now. "I don't want to think about it," I say as I kiss the top of Dax's chest. "I want to pretend it never happened. At least, until sunrise. Do that for me?" I look up at him and his eyes shine in the dim light.

He tucks my hair behind my ear. "If that's what you want."

I slide my hand over his smooth, hot skin, resting my palm on his chest.

"What I want now is you."

He snakes a hand around the back of my neck, gripping me gently and pulling me over him as he raises his lips to mine and kisses me until my nipples are hard against his chest. I moan as he turns his attention to my neck, his stubble grating against it and making me shiver in pleasure as he sucks and licks my skin.

"I said, I want you, Dax," I murmur as he kisses beneath my ear.

"You're sore," he whispers, his voice full of guilt.

That's why he never touched me again in the shower. He really does think he hurt me.

"It's a nice sore. Not a hurt sore." I slide my leg over him and push up to a seated position so I'm straddling his hips.

"Rose," he groans in warning before gripping onto my hip bones with both hands.

I rub myself over his cock, which is already thick and hard beneath me. The metal from his piercing rubs over my clit and I shudder and suck in a breath.

"We can go slow if it makes you feel better." I rise over him and wrap one hand around the base of him, lining him up. "I just want you again."

"I could still hurt you—" His words die on his tongue as I circle down onto him, only managing to get a few inches of him inside me before my body resists. *"Fuck, Rose."*

The pleasure in his deep growl of my name sends wetness flooding to my pussy, and I sink a little lower. It draws a low hiss that is so damn sexy from him as his fingers flex on my hip bones, that I am able to push myself down all the way, my body stretching around him happily and vibrating with need as his balls finally kiss my skin.

"See? It feels good," I moan as I run my hands over his chest, admiring his tattoos.

I rise and sink back onto him slowly. He groans, dipping his chin to watch where his body disappears into mine.

I'm so full. So deliciously full with him inside me like this.

He digs his fingers into my hips and looks up at me with glittering eyes.

"You control the pace. I don't trust myself with you like this," he groans as I rise and sink onto him again.

"*I* trust you, Dax. You won't hurt me."

There's uncertainty in his eyes as I place my hands on top of his on my hips. Then I pull gently, encouraging him to lift me up and then guide me back down onto him.

He watches me whisper his name. Then he lifts me without my help, groaning deeply as he pulls me back down onto his cock with a little more force.

I tip my head back, my hair flowing down my back as he helps me to ride him. Everything about sex with him is better than I thought it could be. Not that I have much to compare to. But I'm no prude. I've had a vibrator for years and know exactly how to get myself off. And I like watching porn that's made for women.

I shudder as pleasure builds inside me and more wet-ness soaks Dax, running out between us and coating our skin.

Although, I'm sure Dax's cock is bigger than any of the ones I've seen in porn. It's definitely bigger than Gareth's.

And Dax's is pierced.

I bring my eyes back to his as he lifts me faster, fucking me at an angle that hits deep inside, sending pulses of pleasure thrumming through my body.

"Is that—?" I tingle deep inside.

"I promised it would feel good inside you." Dax smirks as my eyes roll back in my head, and I whimper.

Fuck, this new angle makes me feel like I'm turning inside out with intense pleasure. I squeeze my eyes shut and press my fingertips into Dax's chest.

"You need to come, don't you, Sunbeam?"

I manage to nod as I cry out, not quite there, but so, so close.

His hand leaves my hip, and he presses his thumb to my clit.

"Dax…"

He circles once.

I force my eyes open and look at him. His eyes are intense, watching me. His lips are curved into a sexy smile.

He circles twice.

"Dax…"

My lip trembles as I gasp.

He tips his chin up. "There's no better sight to me than watching you come. Show me."

His eyes hold mine and he circles again at the same time as thrusting up inside me. His piercing drags over my G-spot as he pulls back, stealing my breath, and on the next thrust I explode around him at the exact second his balls hit my skin and he's buried deep inside me.

"Dax."

"That's it… good girl," he growls as his cock swells inside me, filling me at the same time as I pulsate around him in deep, consuming waves. He keeps dragging me up and down over his soaked cock with one strong arm as I shudder and shake. He grits his teeth and hisses, circling my clit and spreading our combined wetness over it until it's throbbing again, and my core pulls in tight, taking me by surprise.

"Dax, I'm—"

"You're going to come again? I know."

"H-how?" I pant as the pressure builds inside me.

He groans as he continues fucking me.

"I know your body." He sucks in a breath as I ripple around him and gasp. "The first time, your cunt pulled in tighter and got even hotter on my cock just before you came. It did it again a minute ago." He groans as he thrusts up inside me again. "And it's doing it again now. Fuck."

His grip on my hips tightens as my body does exactly what he says and hugs him hard as I come again with a cry.

"Good girl. *Good fucking girl, Rose*," he growls, his eyes fixed on my face.

He continues fucking me, his cock still hard as he rides the remnants of his orgasm out. Knowing that I'm full of his cum only lengthens my orgasm as I moan and sink down onto him greedily. I gaze down at him, breathing through my mouth, relishing each pulse and wave, until they're all but gone and only a beautiful, calming warmth remains.

"You're beautiful." He places both of his hands on my hips and strokes up and down slowly. "So fucking beautiful."

We can see each other clearly now. The room doesn't even seem that dark anymore now that my eyes have adjusted.

I smile and place my hand over his compass tattoo, tracing the pointer with the tip of my finger. "I think you're beautiful."

I run my fingers over more of his tattoos, and he watches me with an easy smile on his face. Then he takes my hand and lifts it to his lips, kissing it as his eyes sparkle.

"What am I going to do with you, Sunbeam?"

I don't know why Dax asked what he should do with me. Because he didn't seem to need any help in deciding to fuck me a further two times before the sun rose. Each time he was a little less gentle than the time before. He knows he isn't hurting me now. After making me come more times than I can count, it must be obvious to Dax that sex with him is the other end of the spectrum from pain for me.

The more of him I get, the more I want.

I roll onto my side in bed as he comes out of the bathroom with just a towel around his waist, water droplets glistening on his skin like crystals.

"What time's your meeting?"

He rubs another towel over his hair as he comes over to the bed to kiss me.

"Not until nine. But I need to do something first."

I frown as he breaks the kiss and walks back into the bathroom. It's 7 AM. Where does he need to go this early?

Seven o'clock. That means it's still the middle of the night in New York.

"Dax?"

"Rose?" he calls back, making me smile.

"Can I get my phone?"

I gave it to him last night, and getting it back was the last thing on my mind. But like I said to Dax about my dream last night, and not thinking about it until sunrise... well, my brain must have been taking notes, because now all I can think about is how many messages Casey will have left me. Because I know she won't have stopped trying to reach me. *Sandbox to casket.*

I screw my eyes up and take a deep breath as a pang of pain slices through my chest.

"Sure. It's in my jacket."

I slide out of bed and grab Dax's black hoodie that I still have and pull it on as I walk over to where he discarded his jacket last night. I reach into the pocket and pull out the phone.

Marcus: Everything's set. I've got the plans and the gear. These fuckers aren't going to know what's hit them.

I read the message again. And then a third time.

I should put the phone back. I should have put it back the second I saw it was Dax's and not mine.

Plans and gear?

"I like you in my clothes. You look cute."

I drop the phone back inside Dax's jacket pocket in a flash as he walks out of the bathroom dressed in his black suit pants and shirt from last night with the sleeves rolled up.

I lift my eyes to the large mirror as he walks up behind me and sweeps my hair away from my neck so he can kiss it while he looks at me in the reflection.

"So fucking cute," he growls, sliding his hands up my thighs and lifting the bottom of the hoodie, smiling as he sees I'm bare underneath it. "How the fuck am I supposed to get anything done at work now, seeing you and knowing what's underneath all those sexy little skirts you wear."

I lean back against his chest, tilting my neck to the side so he can deepen his kisses against it. "The same way I'll get things done knowing what's underneath yours."

"Under my sexy little skirts?" He arches a brow, and I giggle. "Right." He kisses my neck one final time and drops the hem of the hoodie so it covers me up. "I won't be long."

"Where are you going?" I turn as he reaches the bedroom door.

He smiles. "I won't be long." He pulls his jacket on and then reaches into the pocket. "Here." He strides back over and hands me my phone, then holds my face and kisses me on the lips. "Stay naked underneath this until I get back."

I bite my lip, and he chuckles as he leaves. Then the car engine roars to life outside.

I walk over to the bed and fall back onto it with a huff. What's he even doing at this time in the morning? Maybe he's gone back to the main house for a change of clothes before his meeting. But then why would he come back here after? And why would he tell me to stay naked?

I turn my phone on and gnaw on my lip as it springs to life.

Fifty-three text messages. Seventeen voicemails.

Fuck.

Chapter 19

Dax

"YOU CAN TAKE INSTRUCTIONS, then?"

Rose's face glows as she opens the front door to the cottage and sees me. She's wearing my black hoodie—the same as when I left her—with her blonde hair flowing down over her shoulders.

I wrap one arm around her waist as my lips drop to her neck and kiss her silky skin.

"You were hardly gone long enough for me to get changed, even if I'd wanted to." She tilts her head to one side, sighing softly as I dust her neck with kisses before sliding my nose into her hair and inhaling.

"If I had my way, you'd either be wearing *me*, or my clothes, all the time."

She giggles as I pull back and take her hand, leading her into the kitchen.

"You did have your way. All night." She bites her bottom lip as she slips underneath my arm and curls herself into my side, her hand coming up to rest on my chest. "Is this what you were doing?" She watches as I put the bag I'm carrying onto the counter and unpack it with my free hand.

"Yes."

I place the bottle of juice down and then pull out the tube of cream I picked up from the pharmacy.

"It's a weird breakfast combination." Rose wrinkles her nose, and I press a kiss to the top of her head.

"There's breakfast in there for you too. But this first." I hand her the bottle of juice.

She takes it and frowns.

"We were going at it for hours last night. You need to drink it."

Her expression softens as she reads the label. "Cranberry juice. Okay." She smiles and pops a brow at me. "And what's that?" She points at the tube of cream.

"This." I take the bottle from her and put it down, then grasp her around the waist and lift her up, sitting her on the counter. I slide my hands up her bare legs and spread her thighs. Energy fires its way to my dick as her smooth pink skin comes into view. "This is for you as well." I take the cap off the tube and squeeze a generous amount of the soothing cream onto the tip of my finger. "It'll help... We were..." I roll my lips as I think of how hard we went at it last night, wincing as I recall the blood. "Is it okay?" I arch a brow in question, my shoulders softening in relief as she nods at me with trust-filled eyes.

I slide my fingers inside her and push the cream up high.

"Dax." She gasps, widening her thighs and leaning back on her hands, watching my arm as it flexes between her legs.

"Fuck, Rose. You're soaking."

She looks at me, her eyes hooded as I curl my finger inside her, spreading the cream. It makes her shudder the way she did all night every time my fingers, tongue or cock were inside her.

I ignore the throbbing that my Rose-obsessed dick has started up and concentrate on rubbing the cream inside her.

She squirms on my finger and lets out a breathy moan.

This is meant to be healing for her. I'm well aware of the fact she spent hours stretched around my cock last night when she's only had sex once before. She must be feeling it today.

Once before.

The thought makes my jaw clench and I force away the images my brain wants to conjure up of her and some prick of an ex who didn't deserve her.

I swirl my finger in a slow circle mentally telling my hardening dick to back the fuck off. She needs to rest. Her body needs to rest.

But fuck, she is wet.

"Rose," I growl in warning as her moaning increases in volume and she clenches around my finger.

"I can't help it." She arches her back and shuffles closer to me, sinking herself further toward my knuckle. I let out a hiss which she ignores as she grinds gently against my palm. "It's what happens when you're here. You turn me on, Dax. So much." She drops her head back, the ends of her hair reaching the countertop as she moans again, and her body sends wetness rushing around my finger and out onto my hand.

I told her I could be patient last night. But fuck, I can't. Not with her. Not now. Not ever again.

"What am I going to do with you?" I pull my hand back and unbuckle my belt and push my pants down with lightning speed as the urge to be inside her tight wet heat overwhelms me until I can barely breathe.

I grab her hips and drag her to the edge of the counter, thrusting deep inside her in one powerful stroke.

"Dax," she gasps as I grip her hips and fuck her with hard, committed pumps.

"I'm supposed to be looking after you. You've spent the night stretched around my cock. You need a break," I growl, my words in direct contrast to my actions as I thrust into her, every muscle in my core tensing with the effort of holding back from driving into her harder and deeper until all she will ever feel is me imprinted inside her body forever.

"I just need you." She looks down at where I'm disappearing inside her, then brings her fingers to her lips and sucks two in between her pink lips. "Please." She drops them to her clit and circles it. "I don't want to think right now. I just want to watch. And to feel."

"What's wrong?" Tightness claws at my chest as her brows drop and her eyes pinch at the corners before she brings them up to meet mine.

"Please, Dax." Her eyes are wide and shining as she gazes at me.

Something isn't right. I've been gone less than half an hour.

Her phone.

I gave her phone back before I left.

"Ro—"

I suck in a sharp breath as she lifts her hips toward me, effectively cutting off all further discussion as my piercing gets rubbed inside her, sending the head of my cock into pleasure overdrive, and making me groan long and loud as she coats me with more of her arousal.

"It feels so good." She pulls her bottom lip between her teeth as she watches my glistening cock pull out and drive back in, while touching herself.

"Fuck. I'm going to come watching you do that." I grit my teeth as heat fills my balls.

Her cheeks flush as she increases her pace. "I love it when you come inside me."

That's it. I'm a goner. No fucking willpower. Zero. Obliterated.

"Fuck," I hiss as my cock swells. She moans, and then spasms, coming in waves around me. "Rose," I grit out, grasping her hips, my hair falling forward to my eyes as I watch our bodies merging together.

I pull her onto me harder, relishing the way her body squeezes me as she welcomes her own release. She cries out as I push her hand away from her swollen clit and drop my chin and spit, pressing my thumb to it and rubbing my saliva over her.

I lift my eyes to meet hers. "Come on my cock again. Come while I fill you."

Her clear blue eyes widen as I twist my hips, altering the angle I'm moving inside her. I've got her exactly where I want her. She will come again like this, I've no doubt. I know her body. And this angle tips her over the edge fast.

I groan as she drops her mouth open and pants through flushed lips.

She's beautiful.

We are made to fit. Me and her. I know it. It wouldn't be this good if we weren't supposed to be together.

Heat surrounds my cock as she tightens and then comes with a loud cry. I can't take my eyes off her face as I come hard, heat racing up my cock as I empty all I have inside her. My heart's hammering as pulse after pulse leaves my body into hers, stealing the air from my lungs at the same time.

"Dax," she moans, her eyelashes fluttering as she fights to prevent her eyes from rolling back with pleasure.

It's the best sight in the world.

"Good girl," I groan with awe as she comes in a long chain of deep, hot waves around me, her body shuddering as I wrap her in my arms until the last tremors leave both of our bodies.

I rest my forehead against hers, breathing deeply as calm washes over me. "You're going to need more cream."

She exhales with a satisfied smile. "I don't need it. I'm fine."

I grasp the back of her neck and press my lips to her forehead. "You've looked after me before. Let me look after you. This works both ways. You might not feel sore now. But if you do later, then it's because of me. I'm responsible." I ease out of her gently and pull my pants up.

"Who was responsible that night you got hurt?"

Her words hang in the air as my shoulders tense. *That night I had to show Marcus's friend what happens if you disrespect me,* Rose cleaned me up. She wouldn't have been so keen to wipe up my blood if she'd known why it was there in the first place.

"Who's Marcus?" she asks when I say nothing.

My blood runs cold.

"Just a guy I know." I grab a clean washcloth and run it under the tap until the water is hot. I clean Rose up gently and then throw it aside and grab the cream, avoiding her eyes as I squeeze it onto my fingers. She lifts her hips, granting me easy access to slide my finger inside her and rub it in. She's full of my cum. It's running down the sides of my finger as I try to get the cream to stay inside. "You're going to need to reapply this soon. It's coming out."

"Is he a friend?" Rose searches my face, and I avoid meeting her eyes. I don't want to lie to her. And I don't think I could if I was looking into those beautiful clear blue windows to her soul. She's too pure and innocent for the world I cross into away from the estate.

"No." I put the cap back on and toss the tube onto the counter. "Why are you asking about him? We've never spoken about him before."

She pauses before she speaks. "Haven't we? I thought you'd mentioned him. Maybe it was Logan."

I snap my eyes up to meet hers.

Logan doesn't know Marcus even exists. Neither does Jasmin. No one from the estate does.

Her lips twist, and she looks at me guiltily. "Or maybe I saw his name on your phone earlier? When I was looking for mine."

I breathe out, my shoulders softening with the way she's looking at me. Like she thinks I'm going to be mad. Blame her for something somehow.

"He's just someone I know. He works for another business. Now stop saying other guys' names when I'm rubbing cream inside you, or I'll start thinking you don't like me anymore."

"Who says I do?" Rose smirks as I grab a clean cloth to wipe her with.

"Ouch." I frown as I finish up and then smooth my hoodie back down, covering her.

"Just kidding." She strokes her fingers over the front of my shirt and then pulls me to her by the collar. "I think I like you just fine. Especially when you bring me breakfast." She presses a soft kiss to my lips.

"You want to talk about what you didn't want to think about earlier while we eat?"

Rose stiffens momentarily, then sighs and kisses me gently again, dusting her lips side to side over mine as she speaks. "There's not much to say. Casey just keeps telling me she's sorry. That she loves me and I'm her best friend. That she never meant to hurt me."

I slide my hand up around the back of her neck and stroke her pulse point with my thumb. "But?"

Rose's bottom lip trembles before she takes a deep breath and steadies it. "But I don't know if I can forgive her. I don't know if I *want* to forgive her. All I feel is anger and betrayal. People lie to me, Dax. They lie and tell me it's to protect me from getting hurt. But really, they're just protecting themselves."

I wrap her in my arms, and she sinks against me. Gentle, delicate, and beautiful. Surrounded by dark arms stained with ink and secrets.

I press a kiss to her hair, allowing my eyes to close. *Vanilla and petals.*

Protecting myself is the furthest thing from my mind. But protecting her? I would make a deal with the devil to forfeit my soul in exchange for Rose to be safe. The same way I would for Jasmin.

Some days, it's like I've already signed.

Chapter 20

Dax

"THIS IS AMAZING!"

Rose bounces on her toes and grabs onto my bicep as she stares up at the giant hot air balloon tethered on the lawn behind the main house. It's the Silver Estate open day that Logan and Jasmin have arranged, and there's a buzz of anticipation in the air as we get ready. We've got a band setting up on a temporary stage behind the main house, an outdoor bar and tasting stations. A catering company is putting on a buffet, and the distillery is open for working tours to see the machinery in action. Jasmin even arranged a make-your-own flavor gin class with personalized bottles for each guest.

It's going to be a success. Usually, this would elicit a warmth in my chest that pride brings. That swell of short-lived happiness at seeing something great come together.

And it still does. But those moments in the past when I thought I was happy; they were nothing compared to today. To the cozy fucking log fire that's happily glowing away in my chest at the look on Rose's face when she saw the balloon. It's official. I've entered sappy as shit territory. And I couldn't give a fuck. I like it here.

She wraps her arms around my waist, hugging me as she watches Seth, the balloon pilot, do his checks.

I hold her to my side and kiss the top of her head. It's been two days since I spent the night at the cottage with her, two days and two nights. And all I've wanted to do is be with her, even though I've had a lot of meetings, and late-night commitments taking care of other business. But I've spent both nights—when I did finally make it back to the estate—with Rose in the cottage. I told myself I should let her sleep. Keep away and not wake her. Yet both nights I found myself knocking on her door, my heart lifting into my throat when she opened it and smiled at me. We never even shut the front door the first night. We had sex up against the door frame. Wild, gasping—can't get her panties out of the way fast enough—sex as we grabbed at each other, trying to get as close and as deep as possible to one another. Last night she answered the door with no panties on at all... And we made it as far as the stairs.

"Looks great, doesn't it?" Jasmin comes to stand next to us, folding her arms over her chest as she looks up at the inflated balloon.

"It does," Rose agrees as Logan comes to join us, standing with his hands on his hips.

"You were right about making the logo bigger, Dax." He purses his lips as he looks at the giant black S and E logo on one side—the trademark Silver Estate's logo.

"This is new?" Rose's brow wrinkles as her gaze stays transfixed to the balloon.

"Um, yeah." Jasmin snorts, stopping abruptly when I catch her eye and shake my head.

Rose looks up at me curiously.

"It's been planned for ages." I shoot Logan a death glare as he coughs the word *bullshit* only loud enough for me to make out.

I don't know who's fucking worse, him or Jasmin.

The two of them watch me with smug smirks on their faces, and I scowl back.

"You want to try it out before the guests arrive?" I arch a brow at Rose as she turns to me, her mouth dropping open.

"Um... y-ye-yes! Oh my God, Dax. Are you serious?"

"Deadly." I slide my fingers between hers and walk us toward Seth and the balloon, ignoring the gleeful whispers between Jasmin and Logan. Jasmin was ecstatic when she found out what I had planned.

The two of them chuckle and I hear them high five.

Fuckers think they're funny.

"Hey." Seth smiles at us as we approach. He's a decent guy from what I can tell. The only local qualified balloon pilot I could find. He usually does this sort of thing for events with his own balloon. But the offer of an upgraded truck and trailer and a new balloon, as long as it held the estate's logo, and he was happy to come to a deal about some things with me. One of which is taking Rose up today.

"Good to see you, Seth." I shake his hand and then look at Rose. "Rose, this is Seth. Seth, this is—"

"I'm Rose." Rose takes his hand and beams. If I wasn't convinced that bearded mature guys in plaid shirts aren't Rose's type, then I might be bothered by just how fucking radiant her smile is for him. But as nice a guy Seth is, I'm sure it's the giant silver contraption behind him that's got her so excited. Either that or I'm going to have to learn to pilot a balloon damn fast by myself when I hurl him overboard.

"It's amazing! I bet it's incredible up there." Rose grins as she accepts Seth's invitation to go closer to the basket, which is lifting away from the grass where it's tied down.

She runs her free hand over the wicker, her other still holding mine. She squeezes my fingers in hers and looks up at me, her eyes bright with pure, untainted excitement.

Heat swells in my chest and I pull her into my side and dip my nose to her ear. "You ready?"

"Yes." She turns and plants a fast, breathy kiss to my lips, not caring who might see. But I don't give a shit. My staff aren't stupid. I've been holding her hand for the last hour while she watched Seth set the balloon up. Besides, I like the way it doesn't even register with her to act any differently when we are in public, compared to when we are in private.

Rose Jacobs is mine, and I'm more than happy for the world to know it. At least, this part of my world. The other part—

"Do we climb in using that?" Rose points to a fold-out plastic step to one side of the balloon's basket.

"Ah, yes." Seth goes to retrieve the step, but I've lifted Rose into my arms before his hand even touches it.

"Dax." She giggles as I place her on the edge of the basket, her long legs draping over the side in those black suede over-the-knee boots that have kept my thoughts occupied for many lonely nights.

"You better be wearing panties underneath that skirt when I swing your legs over," I growl in her ear. The idea of anyone seeing anything of hers makes the blood boil in my veins.

"Of course I am." She tuts at me, then leans in close, grazing my ear with her lips. "Wet ones."

She laughs as I curse and help her down inside the basket, then I climb in, joining her and Seth, who is already inside and adjusting the burner that's inflating the balloon.

The heat it's giving off is impressive, and I can't help but gaze up at the giant balloon above us.

"Envelope's good to go," Seth says, reaching over the side of the basket and releasing some sandbag weights that are connected. He says something to his assistant, a guy called Trevor, who is helping to release the ropes. Seth said they work together because it's not like he can turn the balloon around when the passengers have had enough. He's got to fly with the wind direction and land somewhere suitable. These guys know the area and have agreements with local landowners to use their fields where necessary. Trevor keeps an eye from the ground, and follows along with the truck and trailer, ready to meet Seth at the landing site and then pack the balloon up. I've learned a thing or two about ballooning already since meeting them both.

"You ready?" Seth asks Rose. She nods her head and clasps her hands in front of her face as the final rope is undone and the basket wobbles and lifts from the ground.

There's a cheer from Jasmin and Logan as we rise, and Rose grips onto my arm, sucking in a breath as we climb higher.

"Now's not the time to tell me you're scared of heights." I chuckle as she loosens her grip on me and leans forward to peer over the wicker side at the rapidly retreating ground.

"I'm not," she breathes. "It just made my stomach go funny." She squeezes my arm and then lets go, stepping forward and wrapping both hands around the side of the basket as she gazes down at the estate below. "Dax, it's incredible. It looks like a toy." She turns to me, beaming, and my heart swells to at least twice its size as the sunlight catches her blonde hair, making it shine like gold.

Seth's busy firing more flames into the balloon as I move behind to Rose, caging her in between my arms as I hold onto the basket either side of her.

"You like it, Sunbeam?"

She nods, a look of pure joy lighting up her face as her eyes dart left and right at the rolling fields on the horizon, and then down to the ground far below.

"Look at those sheep." She points at miniature white dots inside a field, so small they look like maggots on a leaf.

I press a kiss to her neck beneath her ear as she points out one thing after another after another, her voice never wavering in its excitement.

But other than a quick glance, I don't see any of them. I'm too busy looking at her.

"This is about as high as we'll get." Seth smiles at me as I look at him over my shoulder. He looks at Rose's back, his eyes full of warmth. I told him this was important to me. That coming up here would mean a lot to Rose. Seth is married and has a daughter. He understands.

He tips his chin to me as he turns his attention out over the view to the other side, giving us some privacy. Rose shivers inside my arms as I turn back around and follow her gaze to the clouds around us. I wrap one arm around her upper body and hold her against me. It's cooler up here, but something tells me that's not why she's shivering. Or why she's gone quiet, and her face is now emotionless.

I rub my hand up and down her arm, warming the skin beneath her off the shoulder sweater she's wearing.

"He used to tell me to look for the silver lining." Her eyes shine as she stares straight ahead. "You know, in the clouds."

"I know." I dip my head and kiss the exposed skin on top of her shoulder softly. She sighs as I press another kiss to her skin. "You told me the night of the gong bath."

"Right. At the bonfire." Her focus is still somewhere else, somewhere in front of us, not fixed on a particular thing. Just on space. Air. A memory. She drops her voice to a whisper, the hidden pain in it so heavy that I don't know how my heart falling to my feet doesn't bring us and the entire balloon crashing back to earth. Weighted down by the gravity of the grief and regret held in her words. "He didn't tell me how to do it though." She draws in a shaky breath, her chest shuddering. I tighten my grip around her, afraid that if I let go she won't have the strength to stay on her feet. "He didn't tell me how to do it if he wasn't here," she sobs, clasping a hand to her mouth as she squeezes her eyes shut.

"Hey," I soothe, pressing my nose into her hair and just holding her as she wipes away invisible tears and stares out at the clouds. "I've got you." My chest tightens and I kiss her temple and keep holding her. Because what else can I do? I can't say anything to take away her pain. I can't bring her dad back. I can't do anything other than be here for her now. And the knowledge that it isn't enough to heal her kills me.

Her shoulders straighten as she exhales slowly, gaining composure. "I could hunt my entire life. What if I never find it?"

"You will."

"How can you say that?" She pulls her brows together, turning in my arms to face me. "How can you be sure, Dax?"

She looks at me with wide, shining eyes and more than anything I pray that she will listen to my words. Really listen. Let them reach her soul and truly sink in.

She has to.

"Because I believe in you. Because you are strong, and you're capable. You're Rose Jacobs. The girl who came from New York and crashed into my world like a meteor." My lips curl into a smile as her face softens. "You can do anything. You can find every silver lining, in every cloud, in a whole world of stormy skies. And you'll be stronger for it. You're a warrior. You show up day after day, always hunting for that beauty. For that magic. But it's in you. It's always been in you."

"Day after day... Like the sunrise?" Rose's eyes narrow as she regards me thoughtfully.

"Yeah." My chest buzzes with warmth. I push her hair back from her face and cradle her cheeks in my hands as I pull her to me for a kiss. "Like the fucking sunrise."

We kiss, and I try to convey all my thoughts, the fucking power of these feelings I have for her through the way I take her lips in mine and mould myself with her like we used to be one entity, which was split apart, but has now been brought back together.

I kiss her in a way that shows how these feelings I have for her—that have knocked the air from my lungs and caught me off-guard—are deep and real, and raw. I never expected to meet anyone. Not now. Not with everything that's going on. I *shouldn't* be doing this. I'm risking it all if I lose focus.

But for the first time since I was arrested, I don't give a shit about any of it. One feisty, strong-willed blonde with legs that drive me wild and a quick mouth that renders me in awe some days did this.

She did this.

My Sunbeam.

And the thought of her hurting ruins me. It fucking *destroys* me.

My head spins, and it's not from the altitude. It's from the axis in my world shifting. My priorities changing.

Suddenly everything and nothing makes sense.

I stroke her cheeks with my thumbs, swallowing down her content sighs as she sinks into me, and we continue kissing. We stay completely wrapped up in each other until Seth coughs to mark the final stages of our descent.

Rose's eyes flutter open, and she blinks at me. I press a final kiss to her lips before I slide my hands from her cheeks and hold the basket either side of her, shielding her inside my arms as the ground gets closer. "You okay?"

Her eyes search mine as her lips curl into a soft smile. "Yes... I am... I will be."

I rest my forehead against hers and we stare into each other's eyes as the basket touches down. Seth jumps into action, adjusting the burner and calling out to Trevor who is waiting nearby in the field we've just landed in.

Her pupils dilate as I return her smile with my own, something unspoken passing between us. She's a little lighter, a little freer. It's like she left some of her troubles in the sky and let them float away.

She pushes a loose strand of hair away from my eyes. "Thank you. For doing this. It means a lot to me."

"I know." I press a kiss to her forehead. "You don't need to thank me, Sunbeam."

I take her hand and squeeze it, then turn and move to Seth's side to assist him. In no time we have the balloon safely secured and I'm able to jump out and lift Rose out and back onto steady ground after I've shaken his hand and Rose has thanked him profusely three times.

"Wow, you guys went so high, I lost sight of you for a moment." Logan rushes across the grass to us, a giant grin on his face.

"I thought Jasmin was bringing the car to pick us up?" I look behind him but there's no sign of my sister.

Logan's too busy staring at the balloon—which is now deflating against the grass—to meet my eyes. "She got a phone call. Looked like it might take a while so you got me." He grins as I groan. "Relax. I can get a lift back with Seth and Trev." He turns to Rose with a wink. "You can have him all to yourself on the drive back. Just the way he likes it."

"Fuck off," I grumble with a smirk, catching the car keys that he throws up in the air.

"See you back at the estate. Be back in time for the guests, please." Logan laughs, then heads off to help Seth and Trevor with the final pack up as I take Rose's hand and lead her over to one of the estate's fleet Range Rovers.

"How long do we have to get back?" Rose frowns as I check my watch.

"It's fine. There's plenty of time." I open the door and my eyes drop to her smooth thighs above the top of her boots as she folds her legs inside the vehicle.

"Good." She settles into her seat, kissing me on the cheek as I lean over her and click her belt into place.

I close the door and stride around the hood, sliding into the driver's seat and waste no time getting us out of the field and onto the narrow country track. We drive for a while in silence before Rose places her hand on my thigh and squeezes.

"Dax. Pull in up there." She points to a tiny dirt track that's almost concealed with overhanging branches and overgrown bushes.

"Why?" I slow down as we get closer.

"I need to pee."

"It's too overgrown to get out the car. We'll be back at the estate in five minutes."

Her hand tightens on my inner thigh. "I can't wait that long."

"Ro—"

"Just do it."

I sigh and swing the car into the tiny dirt track that used to lead to somewhere years ago, but now we might as well have just driven straight into a bush.

"You'll not be able to get the door open." I turn to Rose as she unbuckles her seatbelt, but instead of reaching for the door handle, she unclicks my belt and then climbs over the center console and straight into my lap, straddling me.

"I lied. I don't need to pee. I just need you inside me." She grabs my belt with both hands, undoing it and unzipping my pants in record time, pulling my cock free. She glides her hand up and down me slowly, her eyes holding mine. "Being close to you in the balloon... And this whole morning setting up at the estate... it made me miss this. It made me miss being alone with you."

I lift my hands and gently cup her breasts, grazing my thumbs over her hardened nipples, which are visible through the thin material of her sweater.

She tilts her head back and moans, the sound thick with desire as I roll them between my thumb and finger. My girl gets turned on a lot. She's right... this is the longest we've gone without me being inside her. Something she's about to rectify, judging from the way she's grinding her soaking lace panties over me as I lavish attention on her tits.

"Dax." She brings her mouth to mine, her tongue sliding between my lips.

"Fuck," I groan into her mouth as she kisses me and slowly slides her hand up to the top of my cock, her thumb dipping into the pre-cum once she gets there and spreading it around the tip.

"Did I tell you how much I like this?" She smiles against my lips as she rolls her thumb over my piercing.

The sensation it creates in the head of my cock has me biting back a groan as I grab the back of her neck and deepen our kiss.

"Yeah, you did. But I'll never get tired of hearing it."

Rose pulls back and bites her bottom lip, her eyes full of mischief as she rubs the bar again, making my groan sound more like a growl from a starved animal.

"I really, really like it," she whispers playfully, pulling her panties to one side.

I sit entranced as she rises over me, one hand wrapping around the base of my throbbing cock as she positions me at her entrance.

"Fuck yeah." A long moan exits my parted lips as she slides down onto me in one slow move and places her mouth over mine, sighing my name around my tongue.

I run my hands up the suede of her black over-the-knee boots and to the silky skin of her thighs, pressing my fingertips into her soft flesh as she keeps me buried deep inside her and tenses around me.

Then she begins to ride me, her tight body sucking me in greedily each time she sinks down.

"For a girl who looks sweet, you sure can take cock," I groan, grasping her hips as she bounces her gorgeous ass up and down, coating me in her slick arousal.

"Only yours," she breathes, nipping my bottom lip between her lips and then kissing me deeply, swirling her tongue against mine as I growl into her mouth and drag her up and down onto me, my balls kissing her skin with each deep fill of her body. "Only ever yours," she murmurs again.

It's too much. The way she's talking, the way her body is sucking down onto my cock...

I curl her long blonde hair around my fist behind her back and tug gently, arching her neck and watching the way her pulse beats beneath her exposed skin as she takes my cock. I'm going to come before her if I'm not careful.

I stare into her clear blue eyes as I hit the seat control, throwing the backrest down so I can move more freely and control the angle from beneath her.

"Dax." She shudders as I thrust up into her, hitting her G-spot with my piercing at the same time I press my thumb to her clitoris.

"That's it," I hiss as her eyes roll back in her head. "This one's going to feel different."

"What do you—?"

I smirk. "You're so much fun to teach, Sunbeam. Now let go."

I'm transfixed to the unfiltered pleasure on Rose's face as her eyes roll again, before she closes them, and her brows shoot up as she inhales sharply.

"That's it," I encourage as she trembles above me.

I hold my breath as her blended orgasm builds. I've hit her G-spot with my piercing at the same time as stroking her clit before. But there's something about this angle that is more intense, or maybe it's being in the car and the potential risk that anyone could drive down the lane behind us at any second. But I know from the way she's mewling above me, and the way she's rippling around my cock, even tighter than usual, that this angle is hitting differently for her.

And fuck if it isn't the most incredible sight.

"Dax, I think I need to..." She tilts her head back and her eyes screw up as she cries out, her fingers grasping at my shirt and her nails biting through it to my skin as her orgasm takes her.

Warm wetness gushes out around my cock, running over my balls and covering them as they tighten, ready to explode. Her release dripping over me is the final push that breaks me.

"Jesus Christ! I'm coming, Rose."

I jerk violently inside her as I fill her, growling out my release, one hand fisted around her hair as I pull her head back, the other rubbing circles over her clit as she continues to come on my cock, panting my name. My orgasm stretches on to the point of me growing dizzy.

When the final pulse leaves me, I sit up, my lips connecting straight to Rose's windpipe as I kiss the vibrations of her last moans away. Then I slide my lips around to her ear, kissing and sucking before I murmur gently, "You're so *fucking* beautiful. I could watch you all day."

She opens her eyes, trying to catch her breath as she kisses me.

"What was...? That was... Wow." She sighs and smiles at me, before her eyes dart down between us. "I think I made a mess on your pants."

I chuckle and kiss her again. "You can mess up all my pants like that. I'm not complaining. I'll grab a new pair on the way back. You know what that was, don't you?"

She dusts her lips against mine, blinking slowly. "Was it? Did I? Did I squirt?"

The sweet naivety in her voice could make me blow again if my balls weren't drained. "You've never done that before, have you?"

"Another first that belongs to you," she murmurs with a smile.

"Fuck yeah," I groan and pull her closer, deepening our kiss.

Another first that belongs to me. All mine.

"Dax?" She pulls back, stroking the sides of my face with her fingertips before her eyes drop to the bird tattoo on my neck. "Thank you for today. For the balloon. It means a lot that I got to do it. And that I did it with you."

I wait for the pinch at the corners of her eyes to come. The small giveaway of hurt. The... 'but it should have been with my father, not with you,' pain.

But it never comes.

Instead, she smiles at me before pressing her lips to mine again and kissing me until I forget where I end, and she begins.

Chapter 21

Rose

"I swear you've packed more than me." I laugh as Dax loads his suitcase and another small bag onto the baggage cart by the luggage belt.

"It's just some work things I need to go over with Daisy when I get to LA."

"Right. Not you being a secret over-packer, then? Do you have a bunch of British food in there you can't live without or something?" I arch a brow at him, earning myself a chuckle as he wraps one arm around my waist, pulling me into his side, so he can plant a kiss on my neck.

"The only thing I can't live without eating is you."

I giggle as he growls in my ear and turns my chin to kiss me on the lips. We pull back as an elderly lady unwrapping a bright pink candy passes us, grinning at our open display of affection.

"You'll get us banned from entry for inappropriate behavior," I scold with a smirk as Dax releases me.

We are at JFK airport, fresh off a flight from London. Dax had a business trip to see Daisy Anderson in California to talk about Aunt Iris's Blend, and suggested I come with him and visit my family while he's there.

He insisted on getting off here in New York with me, before catching a connecting flight to LA rather than traveling separately. He wouldn't hear of us getting different flights. And despite reminding him that I flew to London by myself only a couple of months ago, I'm glad he insisted. Because flying over with him was fun. We traveled in business class and had two giant seats next to one another by the window. I spent most of the flight with my legs draped over his lap, watching movies as he worked on his laptop, one hand stroking my calves the entire time.

Jasmin is right. Dax is good. He has a good soul. I always knew it. I don't care what some people might think about his criminal record and the way his tattoos might make him look. To me, Dax Silver is the most caring man I've ever known.

I wrap my arms around his neck and pull him in for another kiss, that's over far too quickly.

"Go on through. I'm going to use the restroom quickly." Dax inclines his head to the customs area we need to go through to make it outside to the taxi stand.

"I can wait." I smile.

"No. Go on, I'll catch up." He places one hand on the small of my back and sends me off with the cart, his eyes flicking to a grumpy-looking customs officer, then back to me. "Why don't you smile at Mr. Fun and see if you can cheer him up?"

I narrow my eyes at Dax as he smirks and walks off toward the restrooms. Then I push the cart, grinning brightly and saying good morning to the terse-looking officer as I pass. His face transforms into a warm smile and he tips his head in greeting. "Good morning."

I bite the inside of my cheek as I walk through and wait for Dax, a warmth spreading in my chest as he appears a few minutes later. His lips curl into a smile as he reaches me and pulls me in for a kiss with one hand gripping the back of my neck.

"Thanks, Sunbeam. Now let's get you in a cab."

"I'm telling you; she'll be my date for the wedding." Brett grins across the dinner table at Harley as Mom chuckles.

Reed tips his chin at Brett. "I've already got her name on the seating plan."

Brett leans across the table and fist-bumps Reed as Harley rolls her eyes.

"Does this poor girl know what she's letting herself in for?"

I laugh as I tear a chunk off my bread roll. "I think she would have moved states by now if she had any idea."

Mom chuckles again as Harley fist-bumps me this time, her eyes gleaming as she smiles at me.

I smile back, before looking down at my bread and eating a chunk. Coming home has been much better than I anticipated. The time away seems to have removed the usual tension in the air when my family are together. It's... nice. Great, actually. It's like it always used to feel with us all together. Laughing, joking. Making fun of Brett and his latest love interest. Although, I've never seen him quite so enthusiastic about anyone before. His new physical therapist, Lena, must be special.

Me, Harley, and Mom even went wedding dress shopping yesterday after I arrived from the airport. I think they secretly used it as a ruse to get me drinking champagne in a confined space so they could grill me about England. Harley asked a lot of questions about Dax, which makes me wonder if she's been messaging Jasmin. It wouldn't surprise me. Ever since she started planning her wedding to Reed, she's been obsessing over who I can bring as my plus one. And the fact that he's coming by tomorrow to meet everyone before we fly back has got Mom excited. It's weird. I keep catching her smiling at me with this knowing look on her face when she thinks I'm not looking. And I get it. I must seem happier than the last time she saw me... because, well, I am.

"I've booked Vienna's for tomorrow."

I snap my eyes up from my plate. "What?"

Mom glances around the table, her eyes meeting everyone else's but mine. Vienna's is the restaurant we always used to go to whenever we had something to celebrate. We haven't been since—

"It's time." Mom finally meets my eyes. "Your father loved going there."

I force down the lump of dry bread that's clogging up my throat. Next week would be Dad's birthday, if he were still here.

If we're going tomorrow for lunch, then that means Dax will be coming, too. Our flight back to London is a red eye, so it's a late check in.

"Okay." I manage to get the bread down and offer Mom a small smile. Her shoulders relax and her face softens with relief.

"Good. Well, I'm looking forward to meeting your friend. I hope he has an appetite. I'm told the portions are still huge." Mom busies herself clearing the plates from the table as Brett makes some comment about feeding his super biceps.

And just like that, my family start chatting and joking again.

Dad's been mentioned, and it hasn't ended up with Mom crying, or me feeling like I've let everyone down.

Maybe time really can heal.

I lean into Dax's side, my hand glued to his thigh beneath the table as we have lunch with Mom, Brett, and Harley. Reed had some mayor thing on, so he couldn't make it. Mom keeps flicking her gaze to us every few minutes from across the table, and Harley's not even trying to hide the giant grin on her face as she grills Dax, just like she did to me yesterday.

"I can't believe you got my sister to go to a gong bath. It sounds amazing."

"They're really great for slowing down, taking time out, re-balancing. They help me relax." Dax smiles at her as he sits, happy and relaxed in the seat next to me, his fingers interlaced with mine against his thigh.

They all love him.

To the point where, given the choice, I believe they would seriously consider trading me for him.

Despite everything that's happened the past three years, I've always loved that about my family. They're open and welcoming. Never judgmental. Dad always said he just wanted us all to be happy. He wouldn't have cared about Dax's past or his tattoos. He'd have just interrogated him until he was satisfied he wasn't out to hurt me.

"I'm heading to the restroom," I whisper to Dax.

Mom watches us like a hawk as he turns and smiles at me. "All right, Sunbeam."

I glance in Mom's direction again. She's smiling as I get up and leave the table. I head to the restrooms, which are on the other side of the restaurant, passing the open kitchen on the way. I go in and take time after fixing my hair and makeup, then walk back out into the long corridor that leads back to the dining area.

"Rose?"

I freeze at the familiar voice as the man comes down the corridor toward me.

"Gareth?"

He looks different to last time I saw him, three years ago. His deep brown hair has been cut close to his head, and he seems shorter, if that's possible. But his eyes are the same light brown. The same warmth in them as he says my name. The same friendliness that acts like a mask, hiding what's going on behind.

I never could tell what he was thinking.

"Wow. You look great." His gaze drops over my short black dress and chunky heeled sandals.

I stare at him as he brings his eyes back to my face and politeness wins as I give him a small smile. "Um, so do you."

He grins at the compliment. "I heard you got a new job in England."

"You did?"

"Mom told me."

"Oh."

Gareth's mom still lives locally, so it shouldn't come as a surprise that she knew about me going to England because my mom sees her around town. But the thought of him knowing anything about my life now feels strange, considering I know nothing about his. I've never asked. I didn't want to know how great he was doing while I felt like my life had stalled.

"And you? You're—?"

"Head of sales over at Logify. Youngest in the company's history." He lifts a brow, a self-satisfied smile taking over his face. Modesty never was his thing. He was always the first to boast about his achievements, even if that meant raining on someone else's parade to steal the limelight.

An awkward silence stretches between us as he looks me up and down again.

"Great. Well, take care." I step around him, eager to avoid a trip down memory lane, but he catches my wrist in his hand and stops me.

"Rose. Wait." He lets go of me and studies my face. "It *is* good to see you. You look... you look happy. Last time I saw you..." He exhales, his brows pulling together. "I'm sorry about how things ended between us, is what I'm trying to say."

I jerk my head back. *Gareth's admitting he was wrong?*

"It was a long time ago."

Relief settles over his face as he nods at me. "I'm glad there's no hard feelings. Listen, are you back in town long? I'm staying with Mom a few days. I'll take you out for dinner. We can catch up."

Nausea swirls in my gut. Everything about this feels wrong. Gareth is my past. He's not my present. My present is—

"Hey, there you are."

A warm body envelops mine as Dax curls one hand around my hip, extending the other to shake Gareth's hand.

"Hi, I'm Dax."

Gareth frowns, his brow knitting as I lean into Dax's side.

My nausea vanishes like magic.

"Hey, I'm Gareth. You're British?" Gareth stares at Dax as he shakes his hand. "Do you work with Rose over there?"

"Yes, he's—"

"Dax what?" Gareth ignores me and studies Dax, grimacing as he eyes the bird neck tattoo.

"Silver." Dax straightens, tightening his grip on my hip.

"Right." Gareth's face clears with understanding. "You're the boss. Well, I hope you don't mind me borrowing Rose to take her for dinner. She and I have a lot of shared history." He looks at me and his lips curl into a smile.

"Boyfriend."

"Sorry?" Gareth snaps his eyes back to meet Dax's.

"I'm the boyfriend."

I suck in a subtle breath at the casual way Dax delivers it. But there's no mistaking the undertone. It's the same one that came out when that guy grabbed me in the bar. When Dax called me his girl and then slung me over his shoulder.

I shouldn't like the territorial dominance seeping from Dax's pores, but I can't stop heat firing low in my belly, making me need to clamp my thighs together.

No one has ever claimed me as theirs so blatantly. Gareth certainly never displayed even a hint of the passion Dax does toward me.

My eyes ping-pong between the two of them as Gareth straightens up, noticing Dax's hand curled around my hip.

He laughs, then looks between the two of us. "You're not her type. Nice try though. You one of Brett's friends? Is this a joke?" He looks behind us as if expecting my brother to appear, telling him it's a ruse.

"Maybe her type changed away from selfish pricks."

My eyes bug in my head, and I look at Dax, whose jaw is ticking as he glares at Gareth.

Shit. Why did I have to tell him about Gareth and what he did? I should have left it at 'my ex took a new job and moved away,' not 'my ex tricked me into losing my virginity to him, at the same time as planning how he was going to dump me.' Because now Dax looks ready to squish Gareth like a bug.

I wrap my hand around Dax's tense bicep. "Let's go back to the table."

"Who are you calling a prick?" Gareth squares up to Dax, faltering briefly as he has to tilt his head to look up.

"Dax." I tug on his arm, but he's unmoving.

"She won't be going to dinner with you. Not now. Not ever. She was always too good for you. Accept it." He turns, placing his hand on my lower back to lead me away.

"Rose? You cannot be serious. He looks like he's out of jail after robbing a bank!" Gareth's incredulous voice slams into my back, and I halt, glancing at Dax. He catches my eye, and I shake my head. *Ignore him.*

His jaw ticks before he looks at Gareth over his shoulder.

"GBH, actually."

"What?"

"GBH," Dax repeats. "I got out of jail after beating the shit out of another prick."

Gareth's mouth drops wide, flapping like a fish. If the tension in the air wasn't making my stomach twist with impending dread, then it would be comical. But the heat radiating from Dax has my defenses on high alert. I know he has a temper. But I don't want my idiot of an ex being the reason he gets in trouble with the law again. They'll be harder on him because of his record.

"Dax." I plead with my eyes as he drags his penetrating stare from Gareth. His eyes soften as they meet mine, and he strokes my lower back, walking again.

Gareth snorts behind us. "Fine. But watch out, Rose. He'll probably give you a disease. They all fuck each other in the ass in jail."

Dax rushes Gareth faster than I can blink and has him pressed against the wall with a tense forearm across his windpipe, pinning him in place. Gareth's toes dance against the floor as Dax leans closer and whispers something in his ear.

Gareth's eyes widen.

Then Dax drops him as fast as he grabbed him and is back at my side, leading me away. I glance back at Gareth. He's white as a sheet and rubbing his neck.

"What did you say to him? Dax?" I hiss when he doesn't answer.

He lowers his voice as we weave our way back through the tables of diners. "I told him I got let out early for good behavior. But for him, I'd consider going back in... and that's if I get caught."

"You can't say things like that," I splutter, jabbing him in the side as our table comes into view.

"Why?" Dax smiles easily at Mom, who grins back as we approach.

"Because... because... you can't go back to jail, okay? You can't get in trouble. I need you." I stop and turn to him, not caring if my family's watching. Not caring if the whole damn restaurant is watching. "I need you."

His eyes glitter, and he strokes a strand of hair away from my eyes. "You're strong, Sunbeam. You don't *need* me. But if you want me, then I'm yours."

I nuzzle his palm. "I do. I want you. I want this. You and me. Always." Then I reach up and plant a kiss on his lips, ignoring the stifled shriek of glee Mom makes over at the table as she says, "I knew it."

After the Gareth incident, we have a really fun time. Dax relaxes immediately once we get back to the table, and Mom starts to ask him all sorts of questions about Jasmin, the business, and what the estate is like. I watch him, answering her questions with an easy smile, his eyes lighting up as they laugh together. She even asks about his tattoos, and he tells her the story of the first one he got, when his mom was with him. The same story he told me. Only he doesn't elaborate much on her being gone now, and Mom doesn't pry.

We head back to Mom's house. We've got an hour before Dax and I need to leave for the airport. An hour to say a long goodbye and for me to pack my bag. But the second we pull up at Mom's house and there's a blue sedan parked along the curb; I wish we had gone straight to the airport instead.

"Rose!" Casey jumps out of her car and runs toward me as I climb out onto the sidewalk. She stops suddenly a few meters away as she looks at my face.

Every emotion I've felt since finding out she is the reason the man who knocked Brett down was speeding in the first place must be rushing out of my face, my eyes, my body language, my pores. Spilling out like the blood from a slit throat over an abattoir floor.

Casey takes another step toward me and then abruptly backs up again. Her face crumples as her eyes meet mine.

"I told you I never wanted to see your *lying* face again!" I scream, adrenaline flooding my veins as my chest heaves with shuddering breaths.

What is she even doing here? How did she know I was coming?

Mom, Brett, and Harley are on the sidewalk behind me, and Mom says, "You should go. It's too soon," in a soft voice, a *sympathetic* voice.

I round on her as Dax appears next to me.

"Why are you being nice to her? She's a liar." I begin to shake, pointing at Casey as I glare at my family, who stare back at me like I'm the one in the wrong. "She let me think Brett's accident was my fault. When really, it was hers."

"Rose." Mom looks at me with the same sad eyes I've grown so used to over the last three years. The sad eyes that I was beginning to hope were gone since arriving yesterday. But now Casey has ruined that too.

Sourness creeps over my tongue like a disease. They told her I was coming to visit. They must have. Even they want to forget what she did. They think we can all what? Move on and play happy fucking families?

"You lied." I turn back to Casey, overwhelming grief clawing at my chest and making it hard to get in a full breath as I look back into the tear-filled eyes of my ex-best friend.

From sandbox to casket.

"She lied." I whip my head between her and my family, who are silent witnesses to my breakdown. "I hate you!" I spit toward Casey, who's now sobbing.

"I'll call you later. Go on home," Mom says to Casey gently.

"Why are you defending her? Why are you calling her?" My vision blurs, and I clutch at my chest as my head spins. Their voices swirl around me, taunting me like a haunted merry-go-round.

"Call you later."

"She's still hurting."

"She's not ready yet. She needs time."

"She just needs more time."

"Give her more time."

Time.

Dax wraps me in his arms seconds before I hit the floor, holding me against his chest. His lips find my forehead as he cradles the back on my head in one large hand.

"Breathe."

My fingertips tingle as I suck in a breath, and with it, the scent of him beneath his black shirt.

"Breathe, Rose," he repeats. His voice is so calm, so steady. The only static thing in a world that is twisting and canting out of control around me.

I ball the fabric of his shirt up in my fists, screwing my eyes up against the heat of his chest as he kisses my forehead, whispering to me.

"What can you hear?"

I suck in a breath, laying my cheek against him and reaching past the sound of rushing blood in my ears to focus on what he's asking me. "Your voice. Your heartbeat."

"Good girl," he breathes, kissing me again and taking my wrist in his hand, stroking over my pulse with his thumb. "Now tell me what you smell."

"Your skin." My voice shakes. "The mint you ate before we left Vienna's."

"Good girl." He sounds like he's smiling.

God, I love his smile.

"Now tell me what you see, Sunbeam."

I inch my eyelids apart and blink, looking up at him and ignoring everything and everyone else around me.

Deep brown meets light blue.

"I see you, Dax. I see you."

Chapter 22

Rose

Dax places my suitcase down and walks over to the window in his bedroom, lifting the giant frame and sliding it open so the breeze can float in.

We haven't spoken much since leaving New York. Casey had left once I finally looked away from Dax. And afterward, I went inside and packed while he sat chatting quietly to my family in the kitchen. I told him I was okay and to leave me to do it alone. But now I'm not sure that was the best idea I've ever had. It was obvious from the way they all fell silent when I appeared that they were talking about me.

The family fuck up, like usual.

Dax was the only one who didn't give me a sad smile. Instead, he stood and asked if I was ready, his eyes fixed on mine, gentle reassurance in them as I nodded back, so grateful for him being there. I think I would have collapsed on the sidewalk when I saw Casey if it weren't for Dax.

The flight home was quiet. It was a red eye, so most passengers slept. But I couldn't, no matter how hard I tried. Dax chose a horror movie from the in-flight movies and held me in his arms as he watched it with me. He just held me and didn't try to sleep himself, even though I remember he said he has a meeting to go to today.

"Let's take a shower. Then we can get some rest." He walks over to me, his lips finding the skin beneath my ear and kissing me softly.

"Don't you have work?" I wrap my arms around him, standing on my tiptoes to bury my face in the crook of his neck. He smells so good. Warm and strong, and a little spicy... just Dax.

"I did. But it can wait. I want to stay with you."

"Okay. A shower sounds—"

The loud ping of a new message on my phone comes from inside my bag, and I let go of Dax and retrieve it.

"It's Casey."

My stomach drops as I scan her words. More apologies. More pleading. More attempts at trying to make me think about our years of friendship and how it's worth saving.

I can't. I just can't.

It pings again in my hand.

Casey: I hope in time, you can forgive me.

Time? Fucking time?

An ear-piercing scream leaves me as I stride over to the open window and hurl my phone out of it. I clutch onto the window frame with both hands as it crashes to the driveway below and smashes. Pieces fly off in all directions, their jagged edges catching the light as it splinters.

Broken beyond repair.

Dax wraps his arms around me from behind, pressing his lips to the top of my shoulder. "It'll all work out. You're okay."

I sag back against his chest, content to be held. Content to let the calm only he can create inside me, wash over me, like the breeze from outside.

I stare outside at what used to be my phone. "Shit." I screw my face up. "I told Mom I'd call her when we got back."

"You can use mine. I've got your mom's number stored in it already."

I nod, holding in a sob as Dax tightens his hold on me.

"Why do I feel like you know me better than I know myself, Dax Silver?" I sniff sadly. "I'm the villain of this story. I don't deserve the happily ever after. My family all look at me like I'm going to lose my mind any minute. Sometimes they look at me like I already have."

"That's not what they're thinking. Trust me. They love you. They want you to be happy. That's all. They want you to be happy and safe. The same as I do. And you're no villain, Rose. You're the stitching in the spine that holds it all together. You're holding *me* together."

My laugh is empty as I shake my head. "How'd you figure that? Your life was simpler before I arrived."

He kisses my shoulder, his lips warm against my skin. "My life's never been simple. And if not having you meant it would be, then I'd rather live a thousand lives of turmoil banished to purgatory instead."

"Sounds fun."

Dax chuckles, then spins me in his arms. "Shower, Sunbeam. Then I'm taking you to bed."

"Eyes," Dax instructs as my eyelids flutter closed.

I force them open and gaze back at him as he thrusts inside me. We've spent the day in bed together and still didn't get a minute of sleep. Dax has been taking care of me over and over again. I swear he thinks he needs to wear me out to the point of exhaustion in order for me to sleep, after I struggled so much on the plane.

"I can't," I murmur.

"You can. Just one more. Come for me one more time."

He alters the angle he's sliding inside me so that his piercing drags over my G-spot. I shudder as I struggle to keep my eyes open and on him. I've lost count of how many times he's made me come. The last one was only a few minutes ago. I need a rest, I need—

"I want you to come before I do, Sunbeam."

He kisses me over my shoulder, sliding his tongue inside my mouth and lifting my hips a bit more so he can thrust into me deeper from behind.

"Fuck, you're so perfect." He pushes deep, his balls hitting against me as he strokes my clit with his other hand.

I arch back against him, my mouth dropping open as the familiar waves crash through me and I come with a rush of wetness.

"Good girl." He takes my lips in a searing kiss as he growls out his release deep inside me.

I continue coming around him in deep, shuddering pulses as he fills me, groaning into my mouth and telling me how special I am.

How perfect.

Because to him, I am. And it's the only time I've ever believed it.

Dax wouldn't lie to me.

He's the one person I trust.

Eventually we fall asleep. Only after Dax has made love to me all day long and fed me a delicious meal. Jasmin stocked the fridge up while we were away. I swear I love her more every day. I didn't realize just how much I needed to eat. The last thing I ate was at Vienna's. When I saw Gareth... and then Casey.

I frown into the cool pillowcase as I wake up. I don't even get more than a split second's reprieve before the memories of the last few days crash into me at full speed.

"You okay?" Dax pulls my back against his chest.

"Do you have some sixth sense or something? I just woke up."

He chuckles, his lips trailing kisses up toward my ear, which make my nipples pebble into aching peaks.

"Yeah, maybe I do with you. Or maybe I was just watching you sleep and thinking about how I want to wake up like this every day."

I bite my lip and gaze over my shoulder at him. His eyes glitter back at me before he takes my lips in a tender kiss that sends butterflies racing inside my stomach.

How does he do it? Disperse those memories that were clawing at me mere seconds ago, and replace them with this... this warmth and calmness? This feeling of being exactly where I am supposed to be.

"How was your sleep?" His eyes stay on my lips and he bites his bottom lip as his morning erection grazes the back of my thigh.

"It was well needed." I smile as the final memory fades, until all I see is last night, and the way he looked at me as he slid inside me with my legs draped over his shoulders. I swear he felt deeper than ever in that position. "I was all sexed out."

He groans, sending a vibration over my skin. "That's what I like to hear. My girl, all sexed out and satisfied."

"Did I say *satisfied?*"

I squeal as he bites my neck and presses the weeping head of his cock against me. He holds me still, one strong arm wrapping around my waist as the other slips between my legs, and he sinks two fingers inside me. I'm already wet, always so aroused around him.

I moan loudly as he swirls his fingers inside me and he whispers in my ear about what a good girl I am for being so ready for him, reminding me that I belong to him. Because if these past few weeks together have taught me anything, it's that Dax owns my pleasure. I hand it over to him willingly every single time. I was always good at pleasuring myself. It's all I ever had, apart from that one forgettable experience with Gareth. But even my best efforts are nothing compared to the orgasms Dax gives me. It really is like I told him last night—he knows me better than I know myself.

I moan again, grinding onto his fingers, as a rush of wetness seeps from me, coating his palm.

"See, these sounds you make? They don't sound like someone who isn't satisfied."

I suck in a breath as he lifts my hips and replaces his fingers with his cock, pushing inside me slowly at the same time as he dips his nose into my hair and groans. "Fuck, I love the way you feel wrapped around my cock."

I turn my head, desperately seeking out his lips. He finds them, kissing me deeply as he increases his pace, fucking me with a steady dominance that has me gasping against his lips. He angles my hips upward, making me feel so deliciously full of him that I cry out his name as we both come together in one hot, frenzied release.

"Tell me again that you're not satisfied," he pants into my shoulder as my orgasm continues on around him, clenching around him and milking every last drop from his body in desperation.

He groans, pressing his fingertips to my clit and drawing a second peak from me, extending my orgasm until I'm grasping at his hand to force it away because I'm too damn sensitive to take anymore.

"Fine," I gasp as his hand stays firmly in place, stroking me.

"Just fine?" The smirk in his voice makes me want to turn around and smack him. But I can't, because his annoyingly skilled fingers are still turning me inside out with pleasure. He rolls his hips at the same so that his piercing drags over my most sensitive spot inside, and I almost lose my eyes to the back of my head.

"O... kay," I pant, screwing my face up as my entire body shakes and a bead of sweat runs between my breasts. "You satisfy me. I'm stupidly..." *Gasp*... "Completely..." *Gasp*... "Satisfied."

I swear I feel Dax's smile against my skin as I come again, so hard that my vision blurs and he has to pull me back against his chest to steady me because my head is spinning.

He holds me close, one arm still wrapped around my waist as he kisses my neck and strokes my hip with his other hand until I return to earth and gain control of my body again.

We lie together in silence for a while, the breeze from the open window blowing the long white voiles around his four-poster bed so that they dance around us gently like sails. Dax stays inside me, and I sink back into his chest and sigh at how perfect time with him is.

Time.

"I had a dream."

His eyes soften, and he pulls out, turning me fully so I'm laid on my back beneath him. "Tell me."

I trace my fingertips over the bird on his neck. "It was that same dream I told you about by the fire."

"Where you're trying to lock the door, but the key just keeps turning?"

I bite my lip and nod, warmth, and something else, filling my chest at the fact that he remembered it.

"Only this time, I didn't wake up when it got to the other side." I take a deep breath. "It was vines. Vines with thorns all over. They pushed through the door and were wrapping themselves around me. Scratching me. I was so scared I froze. But then I heard myself tell them to go away. That they weren't welcome. I sounded so calm. So in control."

"Then what happened?" Dax searches my face as I smile at the bird, dancing my fingertips over its wing.

"Then they shrank back. They went back through the door and disappeared."

"Hey," Dax coaxes softly. "You did that. You *are* the one in control."

I drop my eyes to the bird and back up, biting my lip shyly. "I never used to feel it. And seeing Gareth and Casey these past few days... it threw me. I can't deny it didn't. But even after all that, I still feel better than I did before I came here." I take a deep breath, lifting my eyes. "It's you, Dax. You've helped me."

"I've done nothing." The lines at the corners of his eyes deepen with his smile. "It's all you. You allowed yourself to believe that you had nothing to give, that the world got the worst of you. But I've always seen your best. That's always been who you are."

"And I see your best, Dax Silver," I muse as I trace my fingers down to his chest and around the compass that sits over his heart.

"Now that's a trick of the light. It's all how you choose to see it."

"Don't." I continue to trace the hands of the compass that point west. "Don't believe you haven't got goodness in you too, Dax. I feel it." I rest my palm over his heart and splay my fingers out. "Right in here."

He takes my hand, bringing it to his lips. "Did I tell you you're beautiful, Sunbeam?"

"Like a million times." He laughs as I stroke his lips.

"Will you tell me something else?"

"Like what?" He slides his mouth to my wrist and kisses my pulse.

"Why do you call me Sunbeam?"

He looks into my eyes for what feels like forever before dropping my hand and reaching for his phone. Disappointment pulls down inside me, making my chest heavy as he stays silent.

He frowns as he looks at my face, then wraps one arm around me and pulls me into his side. I need to get used to the fact that this is just the way it is with him. He has secrets. Where he goes when he leaves the estate. The 'other world' he's mentioned that he doesn't want me tangled up in. No matter how deep into my scars I let Dax see, maybe he will never let me see his.

He swipes into his photographs and brings up an album. "Here." He hands the phone to me.

The screen is filled with the image of the most breathtaking sunset, the sky a mix of pinks, brighter than I've ever seen.

"Did you take this?" I tilt my face up to him.

"Keep going." He inhales deeply, his eyes locked on his phone as I turn and swipe.

Image after image of beautiful sunsets fill the screen.

"When we were kids, Mom used to tell me and Jasmin that people who died found ways to tell you they loved you. She told us that she would make the sunsets brighter on the days we needed reminding."

"So all these photos—?"

"Were the days I felt like she was up there." A bitter-sweet smile spreads across his lips before I steal it away with a kiss.

"That's why the compass points west, for the sunset." I press my forehead to his, my heart swelling with the depth of feelings I have for him.

"Yeah. It's the first one I got after she died." He snakes a hand around the back of my neck as I sink into him. "I knew on the days I saw those bright sunbeams that there's always something worth being grateful for."

"Sunbeams."

"Yeah." His eyes shine. Then he presses his lips to mine with a whisper, *"Sunbeams."*

Chapter 23

Dax

"It's amazing!" Rose leans closer, inspecting the back of Jasmin's neck. "Why didn't you tell me you could do them?" She turns to me with a grin as Jasmin lets her hair fall back down around her shoulders, covering the script tattoo at the base of her neck.

It's a J and an A, fused around each other. J after our mom, Jessica; A after our dad, Adam. Jasmin asked me to do it for her the week after I was released from jail.

"What other talents do you have?" Rose comes over and slides onto my lap, wrapping her arms around my neck. We're sharing an after-work drink in my apartment.

"Pretty sure you've been experiencing all Dax's talents for a few weeks now." Logan laughs before I fire a cushion at him, hitting him in the head.

Jasmin rolls her eyes with a smirk. "Do men ever mature?"

"Nope," Logan quips, looking pleased with himself, as Rose and Jasmin laugh.

"Speak for yourself." I chuckle as I absentmindedly stroke Rose's legs, my palm slipping over her silky skin fluidly. She looks at me, her eyes glittering, and I narrow mine back with a smirk.

Do you want my cock again already, Sunbeam? I mouth to her.

Her eyes widen and her lips part in surprise before she pushes me in the chest and glances guiltily at Jasmin and Logan who are busy chatting with their drinks on the other sofa.

I chuckle, grasping the back of her neck and pulling her to me for a kiss. "Relax. They know I can't keep my hands off you. I can ask them to leave now if you like. Get you straddling me in this tiny little thing you call a skirt."

"We can hear you!" Logan calls seconds before the pillow I hit him with earlier flies back over and crashes into the sofa next to my head.

"Fuck off, Logan," I grunt.

Rose giggles against my lips and straightens up, turning back around.

"That's nice, isn't it? Telling your friend who picked your jailbird ass up on release day with a cheeseburger meal in hand to fuck off," Logan quips.

"You already ate half the fries," I scoff.

"You were late, and I'd skipped breakfast. Besides, I figured you'd be watching your waistline after all the Michelin dining you'd been getting for free."

"Jerk," I mutter with a chuckle as Logan winks at me.

I pat Rose's thigh and she slides off my lap and onto the sofa next to me so that I can get myself another drink. Jasmin, Logan, and I used to do this a lot. Just chill in my apartment at the end of the week. But ever since I came out and had other things to attend to, we stopped. Tonight was Rose's idea. I'm meant to be somewhere else. But they can cope without me for an hour.

I pour a shot of Aunt Iris's blend, tipping the bottle to Jasmin, who shakes her head. Logan and Rose's glasses are still half full.

"Seth and Trevor called earlier," Logan pipes up as he stretches his arms back behind his head. "They said conditions look good this weekend if anyone wants to go up with them in the balloon."

Rose looks to me, and the way her eyes light up make my heart swell.

"I have to do some work tomorrow. But you go if I'm not back in time."

"Are you sure?"

I smile and nod. Of course, I'd rather be there with her, watching the way her face relaxes as she breathes in the air and gazes at the clouds. But knowing she's happy and enjoying herself will have to be enough. There's a giant shipment coming in soon, and I have to get everything prepared.

"Yeah, they're cool guys. They said it's last-minute again. But they thought it might work."

"Again?" Rose looks at Logan with a frown, and his mouth drops open as he runs his hand around the back of his neck. "I thought the flight on the open day was booked months ago?"

I catch eyes with Logan who shrugs apologetically as I sip my drink and lean back against the sideboard, crossing my feet at the ankle.

Rose darts her eyes between the two of us as Jasmin stands and smiles.

"Come on, Dax. Like it's a secret." She walks to the opposite sofa and drops into the seat next to Rose. "Dax booked that balloon for you." Jasmin grabs her phone and angles the screen toward Rose. "I got some great shots of you going up in it."

Rose is looking at me instead of the screen. "You told me it was a promotional thing."

"It was." I hold her gaze, as her bright blue eyes search mine. I smile softly. "But we could have advertised some other way. The balloon was for you."

"He means, we're all grateful that you came along and put a smile on his ugly face," Logan says.

I flick my eyes to him. He's relaxed back into the sofa cushions again, his feet up on the coffee table as he smirks at me.

Fucker. He's told me multiple times that he likes Rose and is glad she's here. He said it feels like I'm properly back with them now. Not just a shell of my former self, working constantly, and never taking time to have a laugh.

Or have after-work drinks.

"Thank you." Rose bites her bottom lip and then beams at me, before she drops her eyes to Jasmin's phone, and they start scrolling pictures together.

Logan and I drink in easy silence as the girls look through the photographs, chatting happily about each one.

"You want another?" I ask Jasmin when her glass is empty.

"It's okay, I'll get it." She walks over to the sideboard to refill her glass. "It'll have to be my last, though. I'm going out later and need to drive."

"Hot date?" Logan pipes up.

My shoulders tense, and I immediately snap my eyes toward her. But she avoids my gaze.

"No. Just seeing a friend."

She blinks a couple of times, refusing to look at me. It's one thing we used to argue about before I went away. *Boyfriends.* Or men, in general. I know how guys' minds work. And after the things I heard in jail, I would happily cart my sister off to a nunnery, if it meant she would stay safe.

A fact Jasmin is well aware of and likes to argue with me about whenever I voice my opinion too loudly. The only small positive is that as far as I'm aware, there has been no one since before I went inside.

And I'm happy to keep it that way.

"I can feel your disapproval from here," Jasmin snorts into her glass. "Don't worry, big brother. I'm not getting sent dick pics by any older, sleazy businessmen."

I knock back the rest of my drink, sourness coating my mouth.

Julian Young.

Just the thought of his name is enough to have me gripping my glass with white-knuckle force.

"Relax." Jasmin's voice softens and she offers me a small smile. "I'm fine. You need to stop worrying. Leave the past where it belongs."

I huff, slamming my glass down. I know she understands that he gets to me. She's listened to me talk about ways I'd like to kill him often enough. More when I was first locked up. But even now, she's my sister, and she knows me well enough to see when I'm not entirely over something.

Not that I could ever get over what that prick did to me.

Stole a part of my life I will never get back.

Time that's gone forever.

"It's in the past, Dax," she repeats as she wraps her arms around me, hugging me. "I've got you back. That's all that matters."

"Yeah." I force a smile and place an arm around her.

"Hey, Jasmin. Some Alistair just texted you. You want me to read it?"

"No!" Jasmin jumps out of my arms and rushes over to Rose, her arm outstretched for the phone. "No, it's okay, thanks."

"Oh. Now he's calling. Ooh, is this him? He's cute." Rose turns the phone toward Jasmin, but before I can see the image on the caller ID, she snatches it out of Rose's hand and ends the call.

"He's just a work contact interested in an open event booking," Jasmin says as she retrieves her purse from the floor near Logan and shoves her phone inside it.

"Alistair who? Did he fill out an enquiry form?" Logan asks.

I don't miss the 'leave it' glare that Jasmin gives Logan. It's the same one she gave me last week as I questioned the over-friendly delivery driver who was delivering her a parcel. Chancing fucker was relieved to have left in one piece once I'd finished with him.

"Don't worry, I'll handle it." Jasmin breezes over to me and gives me a kiss on the cheek, then blows one to Rose and Logan. "Love you all. But I've got to go. See you later."

I stare after her as the front door to my apartment closes. The hairs on the back of my arms stand up. I know when she's lying to me. Call it big brother intuition.

I have something new added to my to-do list whilst I'm at work later.

Find out who the fuck this Alistair is.

"So, you got a girl, then?"

I turn my back on Marcus, my jaw tightening as I check over the crates awaiting pick up.

He huffs when I don't answer him. "How long we been doing this shit together now? And I still know nothing about you."

"I don't mix business and my personal life." I count off the crates. Twenty in total. Things are progressing. Another ten will arrive in two days' time, and then there's the boat shipment coming up.

The big one.

It's the reason I'm here, in a dingy, damp basement in the shady as fuck end of town, with a guy who smells like BO masked in cheap aftershave.

"I have." He sniffs, moving a crate and placing it on top of another against the stone wall. "Julie." He leans against the crate, a smile spreading over his lips. "She's the one. Cooks a killer steak. Peppercorn sauce… lovely."

Despite myself, my lips curl at the love-drunk expression on Marcus's face.

"I'm getting out of this shit, you know. Once I've got enough to get her a nice ring. I'm going to ask her to marry me, and we're going to move. She's got family up north she misses."

The beginning of the smile drops from my lips. "You're quitting?"

"Yeah." Marcus shrugs. "One day. Won't you? You know, pack all this up. I know it's different for you—"

"How?" I bark, causing his shoulders to jerk in surprise.

"Well… you're…" He glances at me. "You're good at this. You're a fucking natural. I've seen guys piss themselves when you walk in a room. But me?" He clicks his tongue. "You might think it, but I'm not an idiot. I know I'd be lucky to keep my head in this game if I stay too long."

I look at the floor grimly. Marcus is right. I did think he was an idiot. An idiot who only cared about money and the ego he gained playing wannabe gangsters. I thought he was like most of the new, young guys who don't know the shit they're messing with. Coming in all bravado, until they get taken down a peg or two and learn their place.

But maybe I had him wrong. Because he sure as hell is making sense right now.

"I'm no natural. I do what needs doing."

"Sure, whatever, man. If it suits you. But I know this isn't for me. Not forever, is all I'm saying. And this stuff I heard about Mr. Young—"

"Forget him," I snap.

Marcus studies me as I take a slow deep breath in, preventing the anger surging inside my chest from showing.

"You don't need to think about him. Just do your job. Don't listen to anyone else. Don't repeat anything to anyone. Just keep your head down, okay?"

This is the most we've ever spoken outside of the minimum interaction required when we are doing a job together. It's definitely the most I've ever said in his presence, outside of giving him orders.

"Get Julie that ring, and then get out, if that's what you want."

"Yeah." He's still studying me as my phone buzzes in my pocket.

I pull it out and check the message.

Jasmin's not gone to the hairdresser's today like I heard her tell Rose this morning. We went for a run together, like we often do, and she acted like nothing was out of the ordinary. My own fucking sister lied to my face. And then lied to Rose's.

Because the location ping I just got on the fleet car she's using today is nowhere near her fucking hairdresser's in town.

And I'd bet a thousand times the amount of crack in this basement that wherever it is she's really gone to today, there's a person there called fucking Alistair.

I'm swirling the clear liquid around in my glass, sitting in my chair, staring out the giant, ornate windows in my office.

Watching the driveway outside.

Waiting.

Jasmin will be back soon. She's been out at a meeting with a couple who want to host their wedding on the estate. We've told them it's not an option and that the estate isn't even licensed to hold ceremonies. But the guy is loaded and doesn't seem used to being told no. Jasmin can hold her own though. She won't give him anything more than she's willing to. I guess we're alike in that way. Always keeping some cards close to our chest.

But I'm getting closer to seeing her hand.

And I don't like what I've managed to find out over the past couple of days.

She's definitely seeing someone. And I don't buy for a second that this guy, Alistair, is merely a business contact. I get that I'm the over-protective big brother. But what I don't get, is why she's so hell-bent on keeping him a secret.

What's she fucking scared of? She knows one strike and I could get my ass slung back in jail. And she knows my weakness is protecting her. Her... and Rose.

If she's keeping this guy a secret, then there's a reason. She thinks I could lose my head over her being with him. And that only feeds the demon inside me. Because she's right to be worried. All the gong baths and breathing in the world couldn't quell the rage that would explode out of me if Jasmin or Rose were in danger.

"Hey." Vanilla wrapped in petals surrounds me as Rose leans around the back of the chair and slips an arm around my neck. She kisses me on the cheek. "You're so far away, you didn't even hear me come in."

I sigh, sinking into the chair as she comes around the front, her blue eyes finding mine.

"Hey, Sunbeam." I smile, my eyes dropping over her legs in her short dress appreciatively. "You come to talk figures with me?"

She has a manilla folder in one hand.

"I did." She walks over to my desk and places the folder on top, then comes back to stand in front of me. "But it can wait. You want to tell me why you look so serious?"

"It's nothing. Just wondering how Jasmin's getting on at the meeting. The guy... he's persistent."

"Uh-huh." Rose drops to her knees on the cream carpet in front of me, parting my legs so she can slide between them. "And it wouldn't have anything to do with the other man? The one who called her at your apartment Friday night? Alistair, wasn't it?"

I meet her eyes, and one corner of her mouth lifts.

"I know you worry about her. She's lucky to have a big brother who looks out for her."

Rose gathers her long blonde hair into a high ponytail and wraps a band around it.

"But I don't like how stressed you've been all weekend." She licks her lips and reaches for my belt buckle.

"What are you doing?" I hold her eyes as she unzips my pants and pulls the fabric down, taking my cock out. I suck in a breath as she wraps her hand around it and squeezes gently.

"I'm just helping you relax. You always help me. Now it's my turn."

"Rose—"

The low groan from deep in my chest as she wraps her soft lips around me and takes me into her warm, silky little mouth, sends a vibration running through my entire body.

I lean back in the chair as she sucks my now rock-hard cock into her mouth, her eyes glittering up at me.

"It's not fair. I get your cum inside me all the time. But hardly ever in my mouth. And I love the taste of you." She smiles at me as she runs her lips down my length and kisses my balls.

She's right. She's always eager to suck my cock, and fuck, it turns me on. But it usually turns me on so much that I end up pulling her up and fucking her instead. I just can't get enough of her. Of the need to be inside her, and to fill her. Make her understand she's mine.

"I promise not to spread you wide on my desk and fuck your perfect pussy. Is that what you want to hear?"

She blushes at my words and brings her lips back up to the head of my dick. "I still want you to do that too. But after."

"Fuck," I groan as she flicks one end of my piercing with the tip or her tongue, before swirling over it.

She knows what it does to me when she plays with it like this. Especially when she doesn't break eye contact.

"Fuck, Rose," I groan again, wrapping her ponytail around one fist. Her cheeks hollow as she takes me all the way down to the base.

My balls tighten up, throbbing.

"Jesus!" I hiss as she tugs on them at the same time as pulling back and teasing my piercing again. "I'm going to come all the way down your pretty throat if you keep doing that."

She pulls back and giggles. Then she sucks down onto me harder, moaning gently and sending vibrations dancing around my cock in a wave.

I tighten my grip on her hair, and she lets me guide her up and down, slowly at first, then building up pace, until I'm lifting off the seat to meet her, my balls hitting her chin as she takes me happily.

A sound at the door grabs my attention, and I stop, looking at Rose and holding one finger to my lips. She blinks at me, her mouth too full of my cock to do anything else.

"Who is it?" I bark.

"Who the fuck you think, dickhead?"

Logan.

I need to re-think my open-door policy.

I exhale, my shoulders softening as I smile at Rose. I stroke her cheek, and she gazes up at me, then slowly starts sucking me off again, holding my eyes.

"I came to talk about those contracts. We need to—"

"Not now." I shift a little in the seat as Rose sucks on the head of my cock again, and a small moan escapes her lips.

I grip her hair and guide her back down onto me again, stroking her neck with my thumb until I feel myself filling her.

You look beautiful, I mouth to her.

Her eyes sparkle as she rises and sucks back down again.

"Later," I growl as the familiar heat builds in my balls.

"Sure, later. Whatever, Boss," Logan says as his footsteps retreat over to the doorway. "Oh, and enjoy your working lunch, Rose," he calls with a chuckle as the door closes.

Rose increases her pace, her eyes never leaving mine. She sucks me up and down, over and over, as I grip her hair in one hand and stroke her throat with the other.

The sight of her on her knees between my thighs, my cock disappearing into her mouth is too much.

"I'm going to come."

She moans around me, keeping her pace steady as I growl out her name. A long stream of hot cum races out of me until my balls are as light as my head.

I take a deep breath, my chest loosening with a contented sigh as she swallows, then uses her lips and tongue to clean me up as she strokes her hands up and down my thighs.

"I'm definitely more relaxed." I lean my head back against the chair's high back as she rises from her knees and climbs onto my lap, straddling me.

"Good." She smiles against my lips as I grasp the back of her neck and kiss her, sliding my tongue into her mouth where I can taste myself.

"You're perfect," I whisper as I kiss her.

"And you're..." She moans as I slip a hand beneath her skirt and find her wet lace panties.

I rub a thumb over her roughly. Her clit is so swollen, straining against the thin fabric.

"I'm what?" I breathe against her parted lips.

"You're..."

I yank the lace to the side and sink two fingers inside her.

"About to fuck you in my chair? And then again over my desk? Fill you with my cum, so it runs out of you all afternoon while you work at your desk?"

"Dax," she moans as I swirl my fingers around inside her.

"Then if you're a good girl, I'll eat the rest out of you before I take you home and fuck you all night long. How's that sound?"

"It sounds perfect." She shudders against me, and I slide my lips around to her neck, kissing her smooth skin with a smile.

Perfect.

I slide my fingers out of her and press them past her pink lips so she can taste herself on them. The sight of her eyes widening as I lift her and place her back down onto my cock makes me growl in appreciation.

Fuck being relaxed. This is much better.

I lift her, helping her ride me. A rush of her arousal coats me so I can slide even deeper.

This is so much better.

With her, anything feels possible.

With her, I feel invincible.

Chapter 24

Rose

"I LOVE IT. THANK you." I turn the shiny new phone over in my hand, admiring it.

It wasn't enough for Dax to replace my broken phone. He had to get me the latest model that's only just been released. I thought they were impossible to get unless you'd pre-ordered months ago.

"It's nothing." He kisses my neck, then walks over to the coffee machine in his apartment and flicks it on.

We're both going to need it. He did what he promised yesterday and kept me up most of the night. How he still manages to look so good on a few hours' sleep astounds me.

"I already set it up for you. Imported all your data."

He gets two mugs out, a vision in his black suit and matching shirt. I like him in the white shirts too. But all black... it suits him. He looks badass and sexy at the same time.

I smile happily as I turn the phone on and the screen flashes up.

"Dax." I turn to him and grin, then look back at the phone's wallpaper. He's taken a photograph of the tattoo on his neck. The beautiful, feathered bird, hidden between all the leaves and flowers is at the center. "I love it even more now."

He chuckles as he places a cup of steaming coffee down in front of me and kisses my hair.

"Drink up."

"Yeah, yeah." My eyes stay glued to the little bird as he chuckles again and squeezes my ass, before heading off into the bedroom with his mug.

I know he's gone to look out the window again to see if Jasmin's here yet. She never came back to the office yesterday. Instead, she texted Dax and told him the meeting ran over. I know he wants to speak to her, and that he's just being a concerned brother. Brett would be the same if he thought I was keeping a guy a secret from him for some reason.

I don't understand why he's so worried. Jasmin is headstrong and able to spot a jerk a mile off. Maybe she just likes the simplicity of keeping her relationships private. Whoever this Alistair is, I'm sure he's a great guy if Jasmin likes him.

I drop down onto the sofa as my messages filter through.

More from Casey.

I can't bring myself to read them. Not right now. Ever since seeing her in New York, I've struggled to get the look of pain in her eyes as I screamed at her out of my head. She hurt me. I don't even know where to go from here.

I thought the pain of her deceit and lies was the worst.

But ever since we came back, another pain has been growing slowly. And now it's the bigger of the two.

It keeps me awake at night sometimes. Long after Dax has fallen asleep with his arms wrapped around me. It squeezes at my chest, like a vise around my heart.

The pain of missing her.

I drop my head into my hands and sit in silence for a while. Content to not think about anything other than the gentle hum of the coffee machine rinsing itself before it switches off.

Dax hasn't come back yet. He'll be standing at that window waiting for Jasmin.

A loud bang comes from inside the bedroom.

"Dax?" I jump up and race inside.

Dax is standing staring out of the window, his chest expanding with shaking breaths.

"What's going on? What was that bang?"

He looks over his shoulder with darkened eyes at me, and that's when the dent in the wall next to the window comes into view.

The walls in the estate's main house are thick and solid.

Yet he still managed to dent it.

"What happened?" I run over to him and inspect his hand as he glares out of the window, his gaze pinned on the driveway. He lets me turn his hand over in mine. But other than his skin feeling hot and being red, it's fine. He must have hit the wall with the side of his fist.

He's gripping his phone in his other hand, a message still displayed on the screen.

"Dax?"

His nostrils flare and he spins in a rush, stalking from the room.

One of the fleet cars is making its way up the driveway. *Jasmin.*

"Dax?" I race after him, out of the apartment and down the main stairs. All that's left in his wake is the lingering scent of his aftershave in the air. There's no sign of him. "Dax?" I call again, reaching the bottom of the stairs where the main door is wide open.

I sprint outside.

He's there, toe to toe with Jasmin at the side of her car, his face murderous.

"How fucking long?" he hisses as I reach them.

Jasmin's eyes are glassy and wild.

"You're not listening, Dax, it's—"

"How long?!" he roars, making me flinch.

She doesn't falter, but her shoulders sag as she stares back at her brother.

"A little over three years," she whispers, a tear running down her cheek.

Dax's face crumples, and he drags his hands down his face. "*Three fucking years!* The entire time I was inside?"

Jasmin nods mutely.

"What's going on?" I move closer to Dax's side. Something is very wrong. The hairs on the back of my arms all stick up like tiny soldiers standing to attention. The need to be closer to him, to know that he's okay is overwhelming.

"Why him?" Dax drops his hands and stares back at Jasmin.

Her mouth opens as if searching for the right words.

"Why fucking him?" he yells.

Tears run down her cheeks and make her dark hair stick to her cheeks.

"He's not like him... he's..." she chokes. "I'm sorry, Dax."

"Out of anyone. Out of fucking anyone, you had to pick him?"

"I love him." Jasmin doesn't attempt to wipe her tears away. She just lets them run down her face, ruining her makeup.

"You love him," Dax repeats, his voice empty, like he's in a daze.

His chest shakes as he sucks in a deep breath, and instinctively, I allow the back of my hand to brush against his. He turns his head, his eyes locking with mine like he's only noticing I'm there for the first time. Then he grabs my hand in his and raises it to his lips, kissing my fingers and screwing his eyes shut.

"She loves him, Rose. Are you hearing this? My own fucking sister, in love with the son of the man who took me away from her for years."

My eyes fly to Jasmin, and she looks back at me, her shoulders shaking as she cries.

"Alistair?" I question.

"Alistair Young." Jasmin blinks and black mascara smears beneath her eyes, joining the rest that's smudged over her cheeks. "Julian Young's son."

I turn back to Dax. He's staring at Jasmin, his eyes wild.

"I'm sorry," Jasmin says to Dax again. "I never asked for this to happen. I never chose it to be him. But it is."

Dax's hand tightens around my own where he's kept it wrapped inside his palm. I move into his side. His body is stiff, like every muscle in it is primed.

Fight or flight.

I nod gently at Jasmin as I slide my hand up onto his chest, resting it over his hammering heart. She takes a step backward, giving me enough space to slide in front of him and look up into his eyes.

"Dax?"

His eyes are round, more white showing than looks right. He's sucking in deep breaths through his nose like he's barely holding it together.

"Alistair Young," he spits the name like it's poison in his mouth as Jasmin's muffled cries move further away from us.

I take a deep breath to center myself. I can't let him see how shaken it makes me seeing him like this.

He needs me now.

Just like I've needed him before.

"Breathe," I say softly, keeping my hand over his heart.

He sucks in a breath and his eyes seek out Jasmin.

"Breathe," I repeat. "We can talk about it all. But right now, I need you to look at me and listen."

My heart stalls as I wait for the excruciating seconds to pass until he looks back at me.

But then he does.

Deep brown meets light blue.

"Tell me what you smell." I hold his eyes; afraid he won't answer. That he won't let me in. Just like the secrets I know he keeps about where he goes and what he does away from the estate.

What if he can't let me in?

I hold my breath, but then his eyes soften, and he focuses on me.

"Vanilla wrapped in petals," he rasps, lifting one hand to cup my cheek, stroking it with his thumb as his eyes pinch at the corners.

I choke back the relieved sob that's threatening to escape.

"Now tell me what you see," I whisper.

There's a flash of emptiness in his eyes before he blinks it away.

"I see you." He drops his forehead to mine and grasps the back of my neck. "I see a sunbeam."

I wrap my arms around his neck and kiss him. I press myself against his chest and kiss him with everything I have until the hammering of his heart eases against mine. We're panting when our lips part, and I hold his face in my own as gravel crunches in the distance and Logan's voice mingles with Jasmin's somewhere nearby.

My head is dizzy with what I need to tell him. The feelings that are rushing up, straight from my heart, ready to pour from my lips.

Confessions.

Confessions and hopes and dreams.

All with him at the center.

"I—"

"I know." Dax silences me with a kiss, screwing his face up against mine. "Believe me, Rose, I know." He kisses me again. "Thank you for being here. Thank you for being you. For being exactly what I need to stop myself fucking everything up even more."

"You're not fucking anything up."

Dax glances to the side, and I follow his gaze to where Logan has his arm wrapped around Jasmin and is leading her inside. They look over at us, and Dax stiffens, his jaw clenching.

I turn his face back to me.

"Let's go back upstairs. Take a minute. Then you can talk to her."

I cry out as teeth sink into my neck and my cheek squashes against the wall.

Dax grunts as he fucks me hard from behind.

I'm pinned between his tattooed chest and the bedroom wall as he takes out his frustrations using my body as his safe place.

But I don't care. It was my idea. I could see how much rage there was still simmering inside him when we came inside following his confrontation with Jasmin. He tries so hard to rein it in, but the truth is, Dax will always have a temper bubbling away beneath the calm surface.

I've seen flashes of it. He's admitted as much to me before. He promised Jasmin he would work on it. He does what he needs to relieve tension. Gong baths, fish in his office, breathing techniques.

But I've learned that sex calms him too.

And I will do anything to ease the hurt that was in his eyes earlier.

"Dax!" I cry out as he lifts one of my thighs higher, pressing my knee against the wall as he rails me so hard I don't know how his cock hasn't fallen off.

"Jesus," he growls into my neck as I come for him again, wetness rushing out of me as he rubs my clit with his other hand that he's squeezed between my hip and the wall.

I've come once already. He might be using me to fuck out his anger, but this is Dax. My pleasure is still his priority, even when he's shaking with rage.

I moan his name again as my orgasm stretches on almost painfully. He groans and comes inside me with a force that has him cursing and burrowing his face into my neck.

The two of us suck in noisy breaths. Dax takes his hand away from my sensitive clit and grabs my hand, clasping it tightly in his against the wall.

We are two sweating, burning bodies holding each other so tightly, afraid to let the other go.

I stare at the dent on the bedroom wall, inches from my face, as my heartbeat slowly returns to normal.

"Rose." Dax drops his head to my shoulder and his breath skates down my shoulder blade as he pulls out of me and lowers my leg to the ground.

A rush of combined cum runs straight out and down my leg as he spins me in his arms and holds me against the wall, one hand gently cupping my windpipe.

I stare back into his eyes. The fire in them is still there. But it's smoldering now.

He's back in control.

"Sometimes I feel like you know me better than I know myself, Rose Jacobs," he murmurs, searching my eyes.

Buzzing energy takes over my chest as he stares so deeply into my eyes, I swear I leave my body for a moment and float in the space between us instead.

Just my soul and his.

Touching.

"You allow yourself to believe that the world only gets the worst of you, Dax. But I've seen your best. You're the stitching holding me together as much as I'm holding you. It works both ways."

"My sister's in love with a guy whose father I hate," he murmurs against my lips.

He opens his eyes and looks at me again, his eyes red.

The air leaves my lungs at how broken he looks. Like all the fight has left him.

"He took years away from me, Rose."

"And do you think Jasmin would have wanted it to be him? Given the choice? We don't get to choose how love finds us. But when it does..." I stroke the side of his face and he leans into my palm. "When it does, it's breathtaking. Like the silver lining in the shitshow that's sometimes life."

He closes his eyes and exhales, his face nestled in my hand. Two lines appear between his brows.

"Stop carrying it with you. You need to leave it in the past. Yes, you were parted. But you're not now. You're here. And you're free."

He snorts, opening his eyes. "I'm not free. Far from it." His eyes trace over my face and he strokes the pulse in my neck with his thumb. "Jasmin doesn't know the full story. She thinks I beat..." He pauses, as though saying his name is a physical challenge. "*Julian Young*. She thinks I beat him because he sent her dick pics and made some asshole comments. But that wasn't everything."

"What do you mean?"

Dax looks away with a grim laugh. "I heard him, earlier that night. Bragging to another guy that he was taking a girl home. He said he'd got his eye on one, and if she needed persuading, he had something he could slip her that'd loosen her up."

"He was going to drug someone?" My eyes widen as Dax meets my gaze again, jutting his chin out as he sucks in a breath.

"Not someone. *Jasmin*."

My blood runs cold at the idea of Jasmin, of anyone, being spiked. "Did you tell the cops that? Surely that should have been used as evidence. They would have seen you were just—"

"The police didn't care. I always suspected he knew some of them, used money to pull strings... but even the ones who weren't paid off said it was my word against his. There was no evidence. Both guys denied the conversation ever took place. I retracted it from my statement. I didn't want Jasmin to have to live with the what-ifs. To know what that bastard was capable of."

"I'm so sorry, Dax."

My eyes sting. He's carried this around with him all this time. Always being the protective big brother. Always looking out for everyone else.

"He doesn't just import liquor, Rose. He supplies half of the southeast of England with enough street drugs to sink the country."

"How do you know that?"

Dax takes his hand away from my neck, avoiding my eyes. "It doesn't matter."

"Dax?"

"The less you know, the safer you are." He drags his eyes back to mine, his jaw ticking.

"Where do you go? When you leave the estate at night?"

He holds my eyes. "Don't."

I frown, opening my mouth to speak, but he silences me with a kiss.

"Don't ask me that." His voice is full of regret as he tilts my face up and kisses me again, sliding his tongue inside my mouth and stealing my breath. "I won't ever lie to you. But I can't tell you everything. Believe me when I say, it's better you don't know all the sides of me."

"But that's not fair. You've seen all of mine." I kiss him back fiercely, even though part of me wants to push him away for keeping me out of that tiny part of his life.

But it's just something he does. It doesn't change who he is, whatever it is.

He's wrong if he thinks I don't know all the sides of him. Because I do.

I know them all. The good, the bad, the flawed.

And they're all beautiful.

He pulls away from our kiss and rests his forehead against mine with a sigh.

I'm not being fair. This isn't a conversation for now. This is about Jasmin and what he's found out. This is about him feeling lied to and betrayed.

I know how that feels. I know how it tastes. I know how it burns you inside. I know how it can derail your life and your family and your relationships for years if you don't stop it.

"Talk to Jasmin." I stroke his face, brushing my hands lower, over his neck, over the flowers and feathers. "Talk. Don't shout. I'll come with you if you want. You need to hear her side of things. She's your sister. She's the only one you've got."

"She lied to me."

"She loves you. She wouldn't hurt you on purpose. You need to talk to her."

From sandbox to casket.

I shove Casey to the back of my thoughts.

Not now.

This isn't the same. It's not. This is Dax's sister. His own blood.

It's different.

"Shall we go and find her? She's probably still with Logan somewhere. She could have left. But she didn't. She needs your time to listen to her, as much as you need hers."

He wraps his hands around my waist, holding me close. "You're too fucking good for me. Did I tell you that?"

I give him a half smile. "It's a trick of the light. It's all how you see it."

His lips twitch and then flatten as he takes a deep breath. "Come on, Sunbeam. Let's go find this silver lining."

Chapter 25

Dax

JASMIN'S BACK IS STRAIGHT as she sits opposite me on the other sofa in my office. Rose came with me, and we found her and Logan downstairs in the main house. They left us to it. Jasmin just stared at me with this look of devastation in her eyes when she saw me.

It almost tore me in fucking two.

My kid sister, looking like her world just ended. All because of me and the way I reacted. Anger winning out again.

I rest my elbows on my knees as I look at her.

"I hated lying to you, Dax. I'm so sorry that I did."

I'm afraid that if I speak, I will lose it again and say something I can't take back.

Alistair fucking Young.

"Me and Al, we..."

I wince. *Al.* She even says it like he's the love of her life, her voice lifting, her eyes brightening with that one syllable. *Al.*

Her eyes rake over my face, and she inhales and starts again.

"Me and Al got talking after the trial. He was... He came to apologize. For his father's behavior. Not just for that night at the function. But throughout the trial. For him trying to increase the charge to attempted murder. For him pressing charges at all. Al tried to get him to drop the entire thing. Told his dad he was as much to blame after sending me those photos. That you were just looking out for your sister. Al said he thinks he'd have done the same thing if it were him."

"That's big of him," I snort.

Jasmin narrows her eyes at me. "Don't be a jerk, Dax. He's nothing like his father."

"They're blood. Of course he's going to be like him."

She shakes her head. "You're wrong."

Heat fires across the back of my neck. Losing my head will just fuck this all up more. I told Jasmin I would listen to her. I promised Rose I would listen.

So I'm going to fucking listen.

"Go on."

She stares at me for a few minutes before sighing and pressing her fingertips to her temples and rubbing in small circles.

"I didn't see him for a month after the trial. And then I bumped into him in town one day and we got talking."

I clench my fists.

"We ended up going for lunch. He was telling me how he works with his dad. How he used to look up to him as a little boy, idolized him. But then... I don't know. He just seemed sad. Like he'd realized his hero was actually the bad guy. He said he suspected his dad was using the business as a front for other things. Illegal things. When they didn't win the contract for Aunt Iris's Blend, it put an extra strain on everything. Julian started doing things differently. Going out every evening. Being secretive about what he was up to. That's when Al started digging. He doesn't have hard proof yet, but he knows something isn't right."

"He has a personal vendetta against me because we got the contract with the Andersons," I state, because it's not a question. It's a glaringly obvious fact, which Jasmin has just confirmed. I always suspected Julian was pissed we got their business. But now it makes sense.

He wanted me gone.

Maybe he thought he might get a chance at the contract—enough of our staff deserted us after I was sentenced that the business nearly folded—or maybe it was just a jealous revenge tactic. Teach me a lesson for pissing in what he no doubt thinks is his backyard.

"Julian's a weak man. Led by money and status. He's selfish. Al said he cheated on his mother all the time and didn't even attempt to hide it. He would take his girlfriends on weekends away and leave her at home with Al when he was small. But despite it all, his mom just wanted them to be happy, and to have a good relationship. She passed away a few years ago, and that's when he started working with his dad. He thought it would bring them closer."

I nod, tension radiating across my forehead as Jasmin wipes at the fresh tears spilling from her eyes.

"I never meant to lie to you. Or hurt you. I didn't want to feel like I did. But I couldn't help it. I felt a connection to him I can't explain. It's weird. I just felt linked to him somehow. He really is nothing like his dad. I think you'd like him, Dax." She sniffs as I shake my head and curse under my breath. "I think you would. He reminds me of you, a little."

I pop a brow and snap my eyes to hers, still trying to process her words.

"He works hard, and he cares a lot about people. He even...." She looks to the ceiling. "He even helped me out. With the estate."

"He what?" I lurch forward in my seat, my pulse rocketing as Jasmin shakes her head sadly. "You let him come here?" I point to the floor, sucking in a harsh breath as I tear my eyes away from her. They land on the fish tank, and I force myself to concentrate on the tiny bubbles from the filter until the thundering of my pulse in my ears eases.

"Me and Logan... We tried. But it was too much. Staff were leaving daily. We barely kept it going. If we hadn't kept the contract for Aunt Iris's Blend, we would have lost it all. Al helped us lower costs. He found ways we could simplify things. Save money without compromising on quality."

"Knight in shining armor," I grumble. "Did Lo—?"

"Logan didn't know. He thought the ideas were mine."

I nod. At least that's something. My friend didn't lie to me. Only my sister.

Fuck.

"Being apart from you was... it was hard. Al kept me standing when I thought I would break. The trial... he lost his father for good that day. He can't condone what Julian did. What he did to you. To me. All because of greed." Jasmin's voice shakes as she draws in a shuddery breath. "If I could change things, then I would have told you sooner. I know that would have been the right thing to do. But I saw how much you hated Julian. I didn't want you to hate me too."

"I could *never* hate you." I hold her gaze as she wipes away more tears and gives me a small smile.

I drop my head into my hands and rake them through my hair. "I'm sorry for yelling at you earlier. I should never have done that."

"It's okay."

I look up into her forgiving eyes. Her tears have stopped, and she's looking at me with hope in them.

It sears at my heart like a hot poker.

She used to look at me like that when we were younger. When both our parents were gone, and I was all she had.

She used to look at me with hope then. Hope and belief that I wouldn't let her down.

I let her down once, being taken away. I won't do it again.

"It's not okay. It's not." I blow out a breath, my eyes finding the fish tank again, before looking back at her. "Your happiness is everything to me. I love you."

"I know you do. I love you too." She smiles at me, and my heart throbs painfully.

"You said you love him?"

"I do." She searches my eyes, waiting. But I don't know how to respond. So I don't. I just nod mutely. "You know what that feels like, Dax. To love someone who comes into your life unexpectedly."

My mouth goes dry as I stare at her.

"We don't choose love when it's convenient, or when we think we're ready. It finds us," she continues.

I drag in a rough breath as Jasmin gets up and comes to sit next to me, wrapping her arms around me.

"I know you understand."

I lean back into the sofa and wrap her in my arms, closing my eyes as we hold each other.

I understand perfectly.

Because it sure as hell isn't convenient. And I wasn't ready. I had things to take care of. Things that no one else can know about. Things that seemed like the most important things in the world not so long ago.

But now I'm questioning everything.

All because of the unexpected.

All because of Rose.

"You go first." Rose hands me the notepad and pen, then looks away, giving me privacy.

"Here." I write something on the paper and then hand it back to her.

Her eyes widen. "You didn't tear yours out?" She looks at the pad, and at the word *forgiveness* written in black ink.

"I don't want to keep secrets from you. I just need a little time to take care of some things. And then we can talk, okay?"

She nods, complete trust shining in her eyes. "Okay."

My eyes rake over her face as she looks down at the pad, pulling her bottom lip between her teeth as she writes.

She is beautiful. I could stare at her for eternity and never tire of the pure good that radiates from her. It radiates calm and serenity when there's a war raging inside me. No one has ever been able to talk me down before. I've got good at controlling my temper myself. I've had no other choice. My decisions are controlled now, measured. I planned as I left jail about what I wanted, and what I needed to do to get it. Playing the long game and keeping my head was part of it.

But Jasmin's revelation threw me through a loop.

Of all the fucking people... It had to be him.

But as everything screamed around me, Rose appeared.

My Sunbeam.

Her voice, her skin against mine, her light blue eyes.

With just a few words, and her presence, she brought a calmness and control back to me, when I thought I was losing it. Really fucking losing it.

And ever since, the same questions have been spinning in my head. *What am I doing? What the fuck am I doing?* Even Marcus has his shit together better than me. He and Julie are going to live out their fantasy together, eating steak and peppercorn sauce. And me? Where the fuck will I be?

A few months ago, I could see a glimpse of my future. And it all boiled down to one thing.

Revenge.

I never considered what came after. What else there was.

As far as I've been concerned, there was nothing else. I only saw that. I made my entire existence focused on one thing. One man. A man I hate.

"Okay, I'm done." Rose looks over at me, her lips lifting into a soft smile as she passes me my piece of paper. "Do you want to see what I wrote?"

My chest is light as her eyes sparkle at me. "Tell me."

She turns the paper in her hands and holds it up.

Blame.

"I'm letting go. Right this moment." She folds the paper, her gaze moving to the small fire we have set up on the lawn behind the main house. "Dad used to say holding blame and hurt is like you drinking poison and expecting the other person to feel sick. I'm fed up with hurting, Dax." Her eyes narrow as the flames dance over her face, casting shadows in the evening light. "I need to stop blaming myself. I need to stop blaming—" Her voice cracks. "I need to stop blaming Casey... I miss her." She wrinkles up her nose. "I've spent years existing in this bubble of hurt and blame. And I'm done. Coming here..." She sighs. "You've no idea how much coming here and meeting you has helped me."

I pull her underneath my arm and press a kiss into her hair, staring at the fire as I inhale. "I told you already. It's you who helped me."

She hums and leans into me. "Maybe we were supposed to help each other."

"Yeah." I press another kiss into her hair as she flicks her paper into the fire and watches it burn. I throw mine in next to hers and we sit listening to the crackling of the wood.

"Did you choose forgiveness because of what happened with Jasmin today? How did you even find out?"

I run my hand up and down Rose's arm. She's wearing my black hoodie again. It suits her. I hope she wears it forever.

"Through a friend. I asked around."

Rose doesn't ask who, and I'm relieved. I told her I won't lie to her. And I won't. But I can't tell her who pulled strings for me. That in return for the favor I'm doing for them with regards to this big shipment that's coming in, they looked at Jasmin's phone records and pulled the name and number for me. I'm not proud of invading her privacy. But I would do it again in a heartbeat to know that she's safe. No matter the cost. But it's just another reminder that the other world I step inside is no place for Rose. She's too good for it. She's too good for any of it. She always has been.

"I chose forgiveness. But not only for Jasmin. Yeah, she lied." I blow out a breath, willing the tension in my shoulders to leave me. Let me rest for one fucking second. "I chose it for me as well."

Rose lifts her face to meet my eyes. "You?"

"Yeah." I clear my throat. It's felt thick and clogged all day. Like realization has sat there, forcing me to acknowledge it before it will allow me to breathe properly. "I've thought of one thing since I came out. And that's the man who put me in there in the first place. But it's more than that. Yeah, he was the cause of why I lost it that night. And he's the reason the trial went the way it did, and I got a harsher sentence. But it was still me, Rose. I did it. I'm the reason Jasmin was left alone."

She slides an arm around my waist, hugging me. "You want to know what else my dad used to say?"

"Sure."

She gives me a small smile. "He used to say the best revenge is living your life and being happy. He told me that after Gareth ditched me."

Just the name Gareth has me tensing. Rose must notice because she reaches up and strokes my neck. I dip my head and kiss her wrist.

"Your dad was a wise man."

"Yeah. He was. What was yours like? You've told me about your mom, but you haven't talked about him as much."

"My dad?" I murmur, looking back at the fire as her fingertips trace over my bird tattoo. "He was... He was great. The best dad I could have hoped for. He met Mom when I was a baby, and he treated me like his own son. He gave us everything he could. He was always bringing Mom her favorite flowers and playing with me when he came home from work. He never raised his voice. Ever. He'd talk things out with me instead. Help me learn. Grow. When Jasmin was born, he told me how lucky we were to have two amazing women in our family. And how it was our job to love and protect them."

"He sounds incredible." Rose slides her hand away from my neck and finds my hand, interlacing our fingers.

"He was." I try to ignore the thought that always enters my mind when I think about him, and about how calm he always was. How he never had a temper bubbling away below the surface.

I'm nothing like him.

"So are you." Rose snuggles into my side.

I laugh softly.

"Believe it." She turns to me, and the moment her eyes meet mine, my chest swells and I grab her face between my hands and kiss her.

"*You're* incredible," I whisper against her lips as she parts them, inviting me to kiss her deeply. "I wasn't expecting you to come into my life."

"I wasn't expecting you either," she breathes as I rest my forehead against hers. "I feel like I had to go through the past couple of years to bring me here. To meet you. Is that stupid?"

"It's not stupid." I stroke her cheeks with my thumbs as she blinks up at me. "It's not stupid at all."

Time stretches between us as we just look at each other, our shared breath in the tiny space between our lips.

"I..." Rose bites her bottom lip, her eyes searching mine. She doesn't need to say anymore. I'm thinking the exact same.

I've loved her for a long time before we ever got to this point. I'm so in love with her that for the first time since I was released, I'm starting to understand what freedom might feel like. Freedom to live. Freedom to love. Freedom to leave the past behind.

I run my thumb across her bottom lip, swiping the pad against her teeth. "You've re-set time for me, Sunbeam. I didn't even see how stuck I was, until you came along."

I lean forward to kiss her again, but she gently pulls back, reaching to the bottom of my hoodie and pulling it up over her head. She holds my gaze as she silently takes her camisole off, and then unhooks her bra, discarding it on the grass.

"Can we stay outside a little longer?" She looks at me with a darkened gaze as the flames from the fire set shadows dancing over her breasts.

"We can spend as much time out here as you want."

I grin, and she giggles as I wrap my mouth around one of her perfect, rosy nipples. It puckers against my tongue, and she tilts her head back to the night sky and moans.

"Eyes, Rose," I whisper.

It's selfish, but I love her eyes on me. I love the way her pupils widen as she feels pleasure that I'm giving to her. I love being locked in that moment with her. Like nothing else exists.

I like to pretend that it doesn't.

I live for these precious moments with her when I don't need to worry about all the shit I'm involved in.

I just get to have her. To enjoy her.

To love her.

She slides her hands into my hair and watches me in silence as I suck and swirl my tongue over one nipple, and then the other.

"Please, Dax," she murmurs as I return to the first nipple and circle my lips around it.

"What is it?" I suck on her nipple, groaning from deep in my chest as she shivers from my touch and arches into my mouth.

"I want you inside me." She twists her hands in my hair and whimpers as I nip her gently with my teeth.

"Okay... but let me enjoy this first." I inhale slowly, then ease back and peel her black leggings down her long legs, pulling her panties off with them. "You know I love doing this."

She leans back on her elbows, her teeth sinking into her bottom lip as I spit onto her pussy. Not that she needs it. The glistening on her skin already tells me she's wet. *She gets so wet for me.*

I lift my eyes to hers. My dick strains in my pants as I lower my mouth and drag my tongue over her, circling her clit. She sucks in a breath and gazes at me. I could so easily close my eyes and get lost in her taste. But I want to watch her. I want to watch her and know that she's mine. She was about to tell me exactly how much she wants to be mine. I know that one word was so close to leaving her lips, as much as it was close to leaving mine.

I can't say it yet. But I can show her.

"Dax." She sucks in a breath as I flutter the tip of my tongue over her, and a rush of wetness flows out of her body, coating my chin.

"You taste so good," I groan against her, keeping my movements slow and deliberate.

She strokes my hair softly as I eat her out like I have all the time in the world. I groan with each new rush of arousal she sends to my tongue, and each move of her body as she quivers beneath me. But my eyes never leave hers. And hers never leave mine.

I bring her to a slow, deep orgasm. And we stare at each other as she whimpers my name, her eyes pinching at the corners. We don't need anything more in this moment than each other.

And I've never felt so fucking euphoric.

She's still breathless, riding her pleasure out, as I sit back on my heels and pull my t-shirt and my black sweatpants off.

"You're everything." I climb over the top of her and grab her chin, sliding my tongue inside her panting mouth as I force one of her legs up with my knee. Then I push my way inside her, burying myself deep like I have every right to do it. Like she belongs to me.

"Dax," she cries out against my mouth as I fill every space inside her, leaving room for nothing else. No doubts, no blame, no past.

Nothing but me and her.

She cups my face and her lips part as we look at each other. I thrust inside her, setting a steady pace as my piercing rubs deep inside her. She shakes beneath me, while I tremble on my arms.

I know her body. She'll come like this. And I won't be able to hold back when I feel the perfect moment that she lets go.

I push inside her over and over, swallowing her moans with kisses. But our eyes never close. We watch each other the whole time, the words we haven't said being communicated silently instead.

"Dax." She tenses, the heat intensifying around my cock as her body hugs it tight.

"Do it," I rasp, barely holding it together. "Come for me. Come for me, while I come for you."

She nods, her breathing quickening as the first wave hits, pulling me under with it.

I groan into her mouth as she cries out my name. My body switches to autopilot, and keeps moving, keeps sliding inside her as we come together. Breath, lips, tongues, words, hearts... all tangled together in one.

All existing for the other, and for this exact moment in time.

Nothing more. Nothing less.

We ride it out, until exhaustion finally wins over. Not only physical, but emotional. The emotional weight of today and all that's happened.

I pull out and roll onto my back, keeping one arm around her waist so she comes with me, nestled into my side.

We lie back against the blanket, and I stare up at the completely darkened night sky. Rose sighs and rests her head over my heart, tracing my compass tattoo absent-mindedly.

"Get some sleep, Sunbeam," I whisper into her hair with a kiss.

It doesn't take long until her breathing slows.

Then I close my eyes and tighten my grip on her.

The fire's almost burned out when I wake up. And my hoodie is still over us, where I covered Rose during the night. It must be around five thirty, because the first rays of orange are lighting the sky behind the estate's treeline. Soft, glowing beams signaling a new day.

Rose shuffles in my arms, sleepy noises making way for a yawn as she blinks her eyes open.

"Morning."

She twists her face to look at me, and her eyes light up. "Morning you."

The corner of my mouth curls into a smile and then I lean down and graze her lips with a kiss.

She kisses me back, sighing happily against my lips when I suck on her bottom one.

Something has changed between us overnight. Maybe not changed, exactly. But grown. Grown and embedded itself. Until it's no longer small enough not to acknowledge out loud.

Last night, I made love to Rose. It wasn't sex. It wasn't fucking. Not that it's ever been just that with her.

Last night changed something.

I knew what I had to do before I even wrote that note and burned it in the fire.

But now I don't just want to do it. I *need* to do it. Every part of me is screaming at me to do it now. To let go of the past and to grab on to something else.

Her.

Rose rests her arm over my body, her fingers curling around my side and stroking my stab scar.

I force away the memory of the blade sinking into me that day. It's still as fresh as the day it happened. The sound of the *flick* as he extended the blade behind me. The sour smell of his breath against the side of my face as the blade broke my skin and he kept pushing it deeper. Then the metallic taste in my mouth, and the bright red blood on my hands as an alarm was set off, vibrating off the concrete walls of the dining hall we were in.

I can't prove Julian was responsible for paying the guy who did it to me. But I know it was him. Instinct tells you everything sometimes. He didn't just want me locked up. He would happily have had me dead. All for what? Money and the chance to take over the estate and business if Jasmin had to sell?

Rose continues stroking the healed skin and I take a deep breath of morning air.

Another sunrise. Another new day.

"Dax." Rose's eyes move between mine and I know what's coming, because it's on the tip of my tongue too. It's been on the tip of my tongue all night. And at the front of my mind a lot longer. "I lo—"

"Shh." I kiss her, cupping her neck in one hand and tracing my thumb over her pulse. "There are some things I need to do first. I need to be completely here for you when you say it. Because fuck, Sunbeam, I want to tell you too. I want to tell you so fucking much."

I screw my eyes shut as I kiss her again. "Do you understand what I'm saying?"

She kisses me softly, letting her lips graze over mine. "Yes, I trust you."

I let go of the breath I'm holding, my shoulders dropping in relief. I don't want her to think I don't feel it. Because I do. God, I fucking feel it in every part of me.

"How about for now..." She traces her fingertips over the compass tattoo over my heart, running them in the direction of east. The morning sun shines off her hair, making it look golden. "How about for now, I just say, I promise you every sunrise, Dax Silver?"

Jesus. My heart expands, threatening to break out and float away like the hot air balloon. So full and light. And *free*.

I grab Rose's hand, pushing it against the tattoo as I drop my forehead to hers. She must be able to feel my heart thundering. "And how about I say, I promise you infinity, Rose Jacobs?"

Forget time. It's not enough. It has to be infinity.

She sucks in a breath, and then giggles, the sound lighting up the air around us like the morning sun. "That sounds better than what I was going to say. I'll take it."

I grasp the back of her neck. The joy in her eyes is infectious, making me smile as my lips meet hers again in a heated kiss.

I roll on top of her, redirecting my attention straight to her neck, beneath her ear, as I breathe in her scent and she wraps her legs around my waist, welcoming me inside her again.

I sink into her as I inhale.

Vanilla wrapped in petals.

A scent I could surround myself with every day, and it would never stop smelling sweet.

Never.

Not even if I were to be surrounded by it for infinity.

Chapter 26

Rose

DAX BRUSHES A THUMB over my bottom lip. His eyes are dark and intense.

"You sure about this?"

"Uh-huh."

"Rose," he growls. "Use your words. I'm only going to do this if you really want it. You have to have forgiven yourself. Be ready to move forward."

He rests his forehead against mine, and I place my palms flat against his chest, the beating of his heart creating a gentle thrum against my skin.

"I have," I whisper. "I'm ready for the future. No more blame. It's time to start living again. Dad would have wanted that. You made me ready, Dax."

He curses under his breath, squeezing his eyes shut as he snakes a hand around the back of my neck and presses his lips to my forehead.

"But if you don't want to, then it's okay. I can ask someone else—"

"Rose." His grip tightens on my neck, and he drops his head, his eyes snapping open. "No one gets to lay a finger on you, on your skin. Except me. Understand?"

I bite my lip to hide my smile. The truth is I wouldn't let anyone else do this for me. It has to be Dax. But I love the way he gets possessive over me. The way his heartbeat increases. The way his eyes flash. The way he sucks in measured breaths through his nose like he's trying to control himself. And especially the way his neck muscles tense, and the wings of his bird tattoo ripple on his skin.

All at the thought of anyone else touching me.

But he should know by now that I only trust him enough to do this.

"I understand." I press a gentle kiss to his lips, and he exhales.

"Fine."

"Fine?" I bounce on my toes, excitement fizzing in my stomach.

He narrows his eyes at me, the corner of his lips curling the slightest amount as I wrap my arms around his neck and reach up to kiss him again. He drops his hands to my waist and groans as I press my breasts up against his chest and suck on his bottom lip.

"Take off your top before I change my mind," he grumbles.

I move back and grin as I grab the hem of my off-shoulder t-shirt and pull it up over my head.

"Fuck, Sunbeam. Are you trying to kill me?"

I giggle as Dax's eyes drop to my bare breasts.

"What? I can't wear a bra with it, you can see the straps."

He curses under his breath again as he takes my hand and leads me over to the bench.

Dax said Scott, the guy whose shop we're in, has been a friend of his for years. From way back when they were kids. He's who taught Dax how to do this.

"Do you know what you want?" Dax asks as I get comfortable, face down on the bench.

"Whatever you choose. I trust you."

"Rose," he scoffs. "This is permanent."

"I know." I give him a soft smile as he frowns at me. "Okay, fine..." I allow my gaze to wander over the bird and flowers on his neck. The ones just like his mother's favorite mirror that he gave me. "Give me something that will make me remember Dad."

Dax purses his lips, studying me for a heart-stopping moment.

Please don't say no.

Finally, he nods, his expression somber. "Where?"

I don't think I've ever stayed so still for so long. I'm terrified if I move, I might break Dax's concentration and he'll make a mistake. He looks so serious, his eyes fixed on my shoulder as he works. He glanced at me once a while ago, and I swear he was about to smile, but then he got all straight-faced again and his full attention returned to his task.

To the surprise he's creating for me. A symbol of the future Rose. The one who isn't going to live in the past anymore.

I wish Dad could see us now. He'd like Dax, I know he would. And he'd never for a second believe that I am actually here, doing this. I've never wanted one before. Never really liked them that much.

Until Dax.

He's changed everything.

"Almost finished." His warm breath flows over my skin with how close he is.

I turn my head as much as I can without moving my shoulder. The needle buzzes as Dax passes it over my skin. It stings. But it's going to be worth it.

"What is it?" I try to read his face, but he gives nothing away as he finishes and turns the machine off.

"Patience," he tuts, earning himself a huff from me. He dabs at my skin with a wipe, and finally smiles as he looks from my shoulder to my eyes. "Okay. It's done."

I sit straight up, ignoring the heat in my skin and turn my head, but although I can see some of it, I can't make it out properly.

"What is it?" I ask again, twisting and pulling my arm down.

"Stay there."

He moves away and then returns with a small mirror and hands it to me. "Go stand in front of the one on the wall and use this."

I take it and rush over to the large wall-mounted mirror and spin around, not caring that I'm still naked from the waist up. I angle the mirror until I can see it.

My new tattoo.

"Dax..." A smile stretches across my face as I study the delicate design.

He's drawn the outline of a cloud, and inside, the word *Silver* in beautiful, fancy script.

"You gave me my own silver lining." I blink and swallow down the lump in my throat.

"*You* are the silver lining." He comes to stand next to me, his eyes fixed on mine, his voice serious. "It's always been you. Look at this if you ever need reminding."

I nod, pressing my lips together as my eyes mist over. I won't cry, even though my chest is burning with emotion. I never cry. My ability to disappeared after Brett's accident. I used to think it was because I didn't deserve to cry. Why should I do something that might cause people to show me sympathy when I deserved none?

I need to forgive myself and move on, and I intend to, I really do. I'm in a much better place since coming to England. Yet somehow, I still can't give myself that. I can't give myself tears.

Not yet.

Dax stands next to me, close enough for his warm body to provide a comfort to me, that only he can, but also with enough space for me to take in this moment for myself. Take it in and understand how much it means.

"I know you'll still have days when you think the world only sees your worst. But I'll always see your best. Always." His eyes meet mine in the mirror and emotion overpowers me, making me turn to him, wrapping my arms around his waist and burying my face into his chest.

"Thank you," I whisper. "For everything."

He strokes my hair, holding me as I sink into his strength, his calmness, his love. Because although he hasn't said it—even though I thought he was about to say it at the campfire a couple of nights ago—I know he does.

I mean, I *pray* that he does.

Because if I love him as hard as this, where I feel like I would splinter into a million pieces if this were to ever end between us, then he must feel something too.

He *must.*

I breathe in his scent, content to stay wrapped in his arms for longer. He's been distracted since the campfire. Quieter. More serious, even for Dax. And he's not mentioned anything else about what he needs to do. What this big thing is that he needs to sort out.

I don't want to doubt him. I trust that he'll do it, whatever it is. Because he's always kept his word.

But the gnawing sensation in my gut tells me it isn't that easy.

Whatever Dax has been keeping to himself, it's big.

What if he can't walk away easily? What if it's not up to him? What if he's in too deep? Or in trouble?

I tighten my arms around him, and he runs one hand up and down my back.

"You'll need a dressing on it for a few hours," he murmurs into my hair.

"Okay." I squeeze him one more time and he extracts himself from my arms and goes over to the counter to get a sterile covering, keeping his back to me. "Why are you avoiding looking at me?"

He shakes his head with a grumble as he flicks through a box of individually wrapped dressings.

"Rose, you just let me ink your virgin skin. And I've spent hours beside you while your incredible tits are bare. I'm a man on the edge here."

"You are?"

The muscles across his shoulders ripple beneath his t-shirt, straining against the fabric, before he glances at me over his shoulder. His eyes drop to my nipples before he turns away again. "Hanging over the fucking edge," he mutters quietly.

I walk over to him and gently slide his t-shirt up his back so that I can press my nipples to his bare skin. Then I wrap my arms around his waist.

"Rose," he hisses as I drag my hardening nipples over his skin.

"Dax," I hum back playfully.

He grumbles as I press kisses between his shoulder blades. I don't know why he's acting all virtuous. He fucked me against the wall in the shower this morning. And he showed no mercy while he thrust into me so deeply that he made me come three times before he finally let himself explode inside me.

I can still feel him, making my panties wetter as my body slowly releases what he left inside me.

"You need to rest your shoulder. You can't lie on it or press up against it."

"Then get behind me," I whisper, snaking my hands up over his pecs and then running my nails down his abs.

He sucks in a sharp breath, tensing. I love the effect I have on him. I've gone from only really knowing my own body since meeting him, to being this insatiable sex-addict who can't get enough of him. I want to touch him all the time. Feel him. Kiss him. Have him inside me.

"Please," I purr, dropping a hand to palm his rock-hard cock through his jeans.

A low growl leaves his chest as he spins and grabs me around the neck, smashing his lips to mine. He walks me backward toward the bench, his other hand unfastening his jeans on the way.

"Why can't I say no to you?" he grumbles.

"Because you don't want to," I breathe against his lips.

His eyes darken and he squeezes my neck enough to send a buzz of electricity racing through my veins as he curses. Then he kisses me, his tongue seeking mine. My body softens, sinking into him, completely under his control.

"You want it, huh? You want this?" He pulls his cock out, which is hard, and glistening with pre-cum. His piercing catches the light and glints.

I lick my lips. "Yes."

"You want me to fuck you? Fill you with my cock? Make you come all over it?" He turns my head and groans into my neck as I reach out and stroke him up and down, spreading the wetness around his tip.

"Yes, please," I whimper as he sucks my neck.

"Then turn the fuck around and spread those pretty legs."

I scrabble to do what he says, resting both palms on the top of the bench, my body tingling with anticipation. I arch my back, pushing my ass toward him.

"You might be a good girl," he says, lifting my skirt and squeezing one of my ass cheeks hard until my skin stings. "But you love me fucking you like a slut too, don't you?"

I cry out as he holds the back of my head and pushes it down until my cheek is squashed against the cool surface of the bench. Then he rips my panties to the side and slams inside me. His other hand grasps my hip and holds me still while he presses as deep as he can, hissing, as I stretch around him.

He pauses, buried to the hilt. Then he starts moving at his own determined rhythm.

I cry out with each hit he delivers. Punishing, hard fucks, which have my toes dancing against the tiled floor, and my pussy dripping for him.

Dax owns it all. I couldn't possibly pick how I like it with him best. Slow, hard, fast, soft. Sex with him is an adventure I never want to end.

"You love it, don't you?" he grunts as he fills me to perfection.

I pant as my orgasm builds. "Uh-huh."

"Words, Rose." My ass stings as he slaps it and then drives down, fucking me harder. He lets go of my head and grips onto my other hip so he can really push himself deep.

I twist to look at him over my shoulder. His eyes slide from mine to my new tattoo and back again.

"Fuck. You're mine, Sunbeam. Fucking mine."

We hold each other's eyes as he pumps into me, and I pant with my mouth open. Then he looks at my tattoo again, and something dark and possessive fills his eyes.

Something primal.

"Fuck."

He snaps his eyes back to mine and comes hard, growling my name like he needs it to exist.

I pant beneath him as heat explodes inside me, filling me.

"Rose," he hisses. His forearms shake with the force at which he's coming.

"Dax." I clench around him, and his eyes squeeze shut for a brief moment, before he forces them back open. I moan beneath him and my body hugs him tight.

"Jesus," he utters. "I couldn't stop." His movements slow and his arms stop shaking. "I was looking at you. At your skin. Knowing I did that. You let me do that." His brow knots like he's struggling to make sense of it. "*Fuck.* I never come before you."

"It's okay." I gather my breath, relishing the fullness inside me where his body is still buried in mine.

"It's not okay." He pulls out and lifts me, turning me to face him. He strokes my cheeks. "*You* are my priority."

"It's fine, Dax." I press a kiss to his frowning lips. He looks so angry with himself.

"It's not fucking fine!" He grabs my neck and kisses me, running his thumb over my pulse. I whimper into his mouth as his other hand slides inside my soaking panties and he pushes two thick fingers straight inside me. "Jesus, you're full of my cum. It's running out of you."

"I love it," I murmur as his eyes drop and watch where I'm seeping all over his hand.

He looks back up, his eyes burning into mine. Then he drops to kneel at my feet and slides both hands up my thighs.

"Panties off. They're ruined anyway."

I look at him but make no attempt to move.

"Panties. Off." His nostrils flare.

I stare back but stay rooted to the spot, enjoying the sight of him on his knees for me. All dark clothes, dark inked skin, dark eyes… dark temper. Some would call it passionate.

I do.

He's so beautiful.

"Fine," he mutters. His pupils widen as he digs his fingers through the thin lace and tears the lace strip clean in two, leaving it hanging in shreds from my hips. "Is that what you wanted? For me to rip your panties off before I fuck you with my tongue?"

He leans forward and sucks on my clit, maintaining eye contact. "Answer me."

"Yes," I breathe, dropping one hand to his hair and parting my thighs wider for him. *"Yes."*

He makes a muffled noise of appreciation against me as he runs his tongue all the way from my asshole, over my pussy, and to my clit. He looks up at me, and there's a shimmering puddle of his own cum cradled on his tongue.

"Dax."

He holds my eyes and slowly brings his lips together and swallows. His neck contracts, and I stare at it as my clit throbs painfully with need.

"I'm going to clean you up. And then you're going to fill my mouth with *your* cum. Understand?" His voice comes out gravelly.

I nod as my entire lower body shudders in anticipation.

"Words, Rose."

"Yes." I twist his hair between my fingers. "Please."

He looks at me again, and then he sinks into me, sucking, licking, kissing, devouring. And each time I think he's about to stop, he starts again, with even more determination.

He cleans me up until I'm grinding onto his face with need.

"You ready to soak me, Sunbeam?"

"Y-yes," I moan as he sinks two fingers inside me and strokes my G-spot with a beckoning motion.

"Don't hold back. I want you as wet as you were in the car after the balloon ride."

I nod, inhaling with a gasp as Dax presses the pads of his fingers expertly against me inside and sucks on my clit.

"I—"

"Do it," he growls, his eyes dark as he watches me.

I gasp again, climbing higher, every movement of him inside me, every flutter of his tongue against me forcing the pressure inside me to grow and grow.

"Fuck!" I scream, forcing myself to let go and not hold back against the feeling of complete submission as my body releases a gush of fluid over him. The tension in my clit bursts at the same time, sending my pussy into frenzied spasms.

Dax groans, pressing his mouth against me as I shake and pull his hair so tight, I'm scared I will pull it out of his scalp.

"Keep going," he hisses as he buries his face in me and laps at my clit.

I continue coming over him in pulses, and he doesn't slow his movements until I come again, crying out his name.

"No more." My inner thighs tremble as the final waves begin to leave me and I struggle to keep my balance. "Dax. I..." I pant as my body turns to jelly.

He's on his feet in a flash, holding me to him, his strong arms keeping me upright. I drop my face to his chest, my cheek resting against his t-shirt. Some of it is damp from soaking up the overflow of my release. Dax drank the majority up like he was dying of thirst.

"You taste so good. I want you to do that every day for me."

I giggle against his chest. "Okay."

"I'm serious." He presses a kiss to the top of my head. Then he sweeps my hair away from my shoulder and grows quiet. "Let me cover this for you. I should have done that first." His voice is full of concern as he studies my skin.

I remain quiet as he takes care of me. He applies a dressing and helps me put my t-shirt back on, being careful not to disturb the bandage. We don't say anything. But I catch his eye and he gives me the most breathtaking smile that has warmth blanketing my stomach.

When he's done, he takes my chin between his thumb and forefinger and tilts my face up to him.

"You okay?"

Deep brown meets light blue, and I stall for a second, soaking in the way he looks at me.

"Rose, are you—"

I smile. "Yes. Are you?"

His face relaxes, and he smiles back. Then he kisses me on the forehead with a soft sigh. "Never better, Sunbeam. Never fucking better."

Chapter 27

Dax

"Why isn't it that fucking simple?" Fire burns in my veins, and I whip my head to the side, staring out the windshield and down the dark, abandoned alleyway.

"It's not what we agreed."

"Fuck that!" I slam my fist onto the dashboard, then let out a deep hiss. "You know what else we didn't fucking agree? That I'd still be here, nine months later. Still doing it."

I clench and unclench my fist, forcing in a deep breath before I squeeze the guy's neck who's sitting in the driver's seat next to me. He may have helped get me Alistair's name as a favor. But we both know it was more like a sweetener. He could sense I was distancing myself from him, from our agreement. And as much as we are both chasing the same outcome, he's also got his boss breathing down his neck wanting results.

Still, the idea of snapping his neck isn't completely unappealing right now.

But that'd be all I need, getting sent back inside for murder. Although, from what I know about guys inside, and how they view the man—and the other members of his 'gang'—next to me, I'd get a warm reception and deserve a fucking medal in their eyes.

But that's not who I am.

I'm not like them. Even if I fucking feel like the biggest criminal of them all some days.

Nine months of lying to everyone. Hiding this part of my life.

And for what?

To be told that even though I'm already three months over what we agreed that I still can't walk away? I still can't be free. I might not live in a cell sixteen hours a day anymore, but freedom still seems like something for other people.

Something still out of my grasp. Like a balloon floating in the air, its string out of reach. Until it's gone. Behind the clouds. Forever a memory.

"C'mon, Dax. We're close. So fucking close." The guy next to me exhales stale cigarette breath and leans his elbow on the doorjamb of the car. "We just need this one shipment to go down, and then we've got him. Julian Young will no longer be your concern."

I melt back into my seat as I stare out the window at the trash-lined alley. This is my life. Middle of the night meetings in dingy alleyways full of other people's shit. I was stupid to think I could ever leave it all behind.

I squeeze my eyes shut and picture Rose. Her blonde hair, her clear blue eyes. Her trust in me. Misplaced, clearly. She's so much better than I deserve. She believes in me. But I'm a man hell-bent on revenge. Or at least, I was.

Now I want out.

I want her.

I want to be worthy of her.

But the guy in the crisp gray suit next to me has other ideas.

"It's just a few days. Then you'll get what you wanted. Young will be finished, his business wiped out. He'll be looking at years inside. And you can dance off into the sunset with the American."

My eyes fly to his face, and if the heat of a glare could kill, then he would be a simmering pile of ash in the footwell.

"It's my job to know what you're up to. Don't take it the wrong way. She looks nice."

"Get her out of your fucking head." I spin in my seat, launching out one arm and pinning him by his throat to the opposite window. He doesn't flinch. He knows I can't hurt him. Not if I ever want to live a normal life again. He's higher up the food chain than me. And despite my disgust at the situation I'm in, I don't blame him. He's not a bad guy.

But I also dream of the day I'll never have to see his face again.

He isn't going on any fucking Christmas card list.

"She's got nothing to do with this." I release my grip on his neck, and he takes a couple of subtle deep breaths, straightening his collar with one hand.

"Of course. And I want to keep it that way." He side-eyes me as I clench my jaw and concentrate on the sound of my heartbeat in my ears, breathing deeply until it quietens. "So just do this last shipment. Finish the job you set out to do. Get the closure. And then move on. You never have to speak to me again."

"Best fucking news I've heard all year," I mutter.

He snorts and shakes his head. "You've come this far. Don't bail at the final hour. You can have everything you always wanted. Young won't be your problem anymore. And you can do whatever you want to do." He glances at me. "Three more days, that's all."

My jaw ticks as I stare out of the window.

Three more days.

I can do it. It'll be fucking worth it.

Julian Young gone. A future with Rose.

"Three days," I snap as I open the door and climb out. "And not a fucking second longer."

The guy inside smiles at me before I slam the door shut. I pull my hoodie up over my head and shove my hands into my pockets, walking off into the night's shadows.

***

"Rose showed me. It's beautiful. You did a good job."

I grunt in reply to Jasmin's praise. I've never been good at accepting it. Especially from her. I still struggle to stop the image of her crying in the courtroom coming to me. Every once in a while I dream about it.

Can't even escape in sleep.

I turn and lean back against my desk, crossing my legs at the ankle as my sister laughs.

"You need to learn to accept compliments." She rolls her eyes as she walks over to the fish tank and sprinkles some food from a pot into it. She bends down to look at the small clown fish that swims up first to eat.

She's got her long dark hair tied up today, and the top of her tattoo I did for her is visible above the neckline of her blouse.

J&A.

Pretty fucking cozy.

"What is it? I can sense your brotherly disapproval from here." Jasmin straightens, placing the pot down and turns to face me.

"Your tattoo. Was it really for Mom and Dad?"

Her lips part as she stares at me. "Yes. Why would you even ask that?"

I shrug. "It's just... J and A. Jasmin and Alistair also fits."

My biceps tense as I fold my arms over my chest, the idea that my sister asked me to tattoo her lover's initials on her neck, making out it was for our parents, has acid running through my veins.

"You're a real prick sometimes, you know that?" She glares at me and then sighs, rubbing at her temples.

I purse my lips. "Sorry."

She looks at me from under her brows. "You know I miss them as much as you, right?"

I sniff and lift my chin. I don't want to get heavy right now. We both fucking miss them. I know that. Our life would be so different if they hadn't died.

"I know you do."

Jasmin sighs. "The coincidence with the initials did occur to me, yes. I'm not going to lie and say it didn't.

But I wanted a reminder of them. Just like you have one." Her eyes go to the bird and flowers on my neck, and then to my chest, where the compass is concealed by my shirt. "I was going to ask you after... after that night at the business dinner. But life had other plans."

"Didn't it just?"

Jasmin meets my eyes, and her face softens. "The tattoo was for Mom and Dad. But then I met Al, and it felt..." She glances at the fish. "It felt right. Like it held a new double meaning. One for the past. One for the future."

I nod in silence.

A double meaning. Just like the tattoo I did for Rose. Her past. And her future. She just needs to look and see. It's all there waiting for her.

Jasmin's gaze moves around the room as she breathes softly. "I know that's not all that's on your mind. So, what is it? What's really wrong?"

"Nothing." I fold my arms and roll my neck, the cracking only providing the merest relief to the tension that's been clouding my head—and the rest of my body—for the past day.

Two days to go.

Forty-eight hours.

Then the past becomes the past.

Time moves on.

Except, call me a pessimist, but after all that's happened to me, I'm not ready to start believing it yet.

"Have you and Rose had a fight?"

"What? No. Why? Did she seem upset about something?" I push off my desk.

If Jasmin thinks we had a fight, then maybe she saw Rose, and she was upset. Or there's something wrong.

I'm halfway to the door to race to Rose's office when Jasmin's words stop me.

"You love her."

I still, turning to face her. Her eyes are lit up like Fourth of July fireworks. I glance at the doorway. Rose is just down the hall. Too far to hear any of this. Yet, I want to go down there. Just to look at her face. To soak in the energy that races around my body when I'm near her. To check if she's okay.

"Rose was fine when I saw her. She looked… She was glowing." Jasmin flicks her eyes up and down my body with a smile. "Like you do when I say her name. I've never seen you like this before. You're different around her. Calmer. Freer." She claps her hands with a small squeal. "My brother's in love."

I abandon any idea of visiting Rose as Jasmin comes over to me and pulls me into a hug.

"I'm so happy for you, Dax. You deserve someone wonderful. And Rose is."

I hug her back. She's tiny in my arms. Much more like Mom than me, with her long dark hair. I inherited Mom's eyes. But that was all.

"Yeah. She is."

Too good for me.

Jasmin moves back from our embrace and smiles up at me, a weight of emotion held in her eyes. "It's time someone got your love, Dax. Because I know there's a whole lot to give inside that giant heart of yours."

"Don't go getting all soft on me, Sis." My lips curl into a half smile as she searches my eyes and takes a deep breath.

"I want you to meet him."

"What?" The smile slides from my face in a flash.

"Alistair. I want you to meet him." She blinks up at me. "I think you'd get on, if you can just—"

"No!"

"Dax, please. He's nothing like his dad."

"Nothing like the man he shares blood with?" I snort, raising one brow.

Jasmin and I have been good in recent days. Finding out about Alistair was a shock. But I've been slowly coming to terms with it. She's happy, and she's told me constantly about what he did for her when I was in jail. How he kept her going.

When I abandoned her.

I at least owe him for that.

"He isn't. He's... he's *my* Rose, Dax." The light in Jasmin's eyes dims, making guilt curdle in my stomach.

I'm an asshole.

My sister is happy. She's fucking happy. And I'm ruining it for her. All I ever wanted was for her to be happy... and safe. I just wish a new puppy, or a new car made her happy. Not the son of the man I hate.

I run a hand around my jaw as I hold her eyes. She must sense my guard slowly slipping because she takes a step closer.

"Julian doesn't know about me. You know that. Alistair has kept our relationship a secret too. He doesn't trust his dad, Dax. You know he's been looking into the business. Gathering evidence that he finds."

Jasmin's told me this already. Alistair is working on building a case against his dad. She said he loves him, but he can't forgive him for the way he treated his mother. And for the way he's using what started as her family's business that he married into to fund his less than virtuous sidelines.

But can I really believe that? He's still Julian Young's son. And they say the apple doesn't fall far from the tree.

"I can tell what you're thinking," Jasmin huffs. "I know you."

"Fine," I grit. "I'll meet him. I can size him up for the grave he'll need if he lets you down."

She snorts. "He said a similar thing to a guy who tried it on when we were out once."

"He's going up in my estimations. Maybe I'll give him some extra space to stretch out whilst he's talking to the worms."

"Dax." She laughs.

I smirk. Nothing makes me happier than seeing my sister happy.

And seeing Rose happy.

These two women have got me by the balls, and I'm sure Jasmin knows it.

"We can set something up." She pulls out her phone and taps out a message as she spins toward the door.

"Sure. Can't wait," I mutter as she throws me a look of undisguised delight that she's finally wearing me down.

I shake my head as she leaves and then walk over to stare out of the large window at the fountain below, shoving my hands into my pockets.

Alistair is working against his own father. And Jasmin is helping him.

I could laugh about it. Throw my head back and really fucking laugh.

We've been doing the same thing.

All this time, I've been plotting my revenge against that asshole. Yearning for the day I can take Julian Young, and everything he cares about, down. And Jasmin and his own son have been doing the exact same thing. Granted, I doubt Alistair will be as ruthless in his efforts as I am. I doubt he pictures his hands around his dad's neck, wringing his pathetic soul from his body. But he's hardly going to win an award for son of the year, either.

Different approaches.

Same outcome.

Alistair might be building his own case against Daddy Dearest. But mine is almost complete.

Two more days.

Forty-eight hours.

My fucking freedom.

And it's about time.

Chapter 28

Rose

"YOU STILL HUNTING FOR the right girl?" I grin at Logan as he flops into the chair opposite my desk, scrolling through his phone.

"Nah. Just window shopping." He turns the screen to me and raises his brows in question. I nod at the picture of the smiley brunette on the dating app, and he looks back at the screen, tilting his head before swiping to save her profile.

"You know those things go purely on looks, don't you? They're superficial. You need to meet a person face-to-face to know whether there's a connection or not."

He smirks and slides the phone into his suit pants. "What's wrong with going on looks first? I need to find her attractive enough to want to rail her, otherwise what's the point?"

I roll my eyes. I can see why Jasmin looks exasperated whenever Logan and his dating life come up in conversation now. It's like trying to train a dog to meow.

"You can't tell a person's attractiveness from one photo. What if they're really unphotogenic? And what about the energy and vibe they give off in person? You can't tell any of that from a dating app. Basing everything on looks isn't going to find you a soulmate."

"Go on, then."

"Go on what?" I look up from the paperwork I'm doing. I love the open-door policy the offices have on the estate. But it leaves it far too easy for Logan to slink into my office and distract me from work multiple times a day. He's so laid back; I'm amazed how he gets any work done some days. But he does. And he doesn't just get it done. He nails it. The estate events are going from strength to strength, bringing in a huge amount of revenue. I've seen the accounts and the figures speak for themselves.

Maybe he's just one of those cocky guys everything turns to gold for. Because judging by the money he's bringing into the business, he's certainly living up to his name, Logan Rich.

"Go on," he continues. "Tell me what you thought of me that first time you saw me. Looks only." He leans back in his chair, a broad grin on his face.

I toss down my pen and mirror his posture. I'm not going to get any work done if I don't indulge him in his game.

"Fine. Well, I thought you were Dax to begin with."

"Except I'm better-looking."

He winks as I snort.

"You're funny."

"Is that what you thought of me? Or are you trying to tell me you actually find Dax hotter than me?"

He smirks as I roll my eyes.

"Okay..." I chew my lip as I think. "First impressions? I thought you were good-looking. Tall... I liked your sandy hair. The waves... they suit you. And you smelled amazing. But then I had been traveling for the best part of twenty-four hours, so a skunk dipped in pond water might have held the same appeal."

His chest rumbles with a laugh. "So, you wondered what I looked like naked, then?"

"Idiot, I did not." I catch his eye and laugh. He reminds me of Brett. He's always had a cocky charm about him. Even the accident never changed him. He's the same larger than life guy he's always been. "You're not my type, Logan. Not in a million years."

He pretends to look offended, before he laughs. "I know. Your type is moody and currently pacing up and down his office down the hall." He jerks his thumb over his shoulder.

"How's he seem to you?" I glance toward the doorway as if I'll be able to see the answers in the air, floating up from his office. Floating up from the man who is embedded in my soul.

He keeps telling me he has things to sort out, but that once he does, everything will be good. That we can make plans for the future. He even suggested we take a trip together. Go somewhere hot where we can relax and just be together.

It sounds amazing.

"He'll be fine. This is what he does." Logan falls serious. "He sorts shit out. He thinks about it. Plans it out. Then executes it. It's the way Dax has always been. He's had a lot to contend with since becoming Jasmin's legal guardian."

"I know, I just... Do you think he seems okay, though? I feel like he's got a lot on his plate. What if it's too much for him to do alone?"

"Then he has us to help him. But, Rose, I've known Dax years. This is just the way he is. He gets all intense and enters super-boss mode. And then he gets on with it. He likes to do a lot by himself. He's always been that way. But he also asks for help when he needs it."

I lay a hand over my chest, rubbing at the tightness there. Logan's right. Dax does ask for help when he needs it. Jasmin told me how he asked Logan to look after her and the estate while he was inside.

He doesn't shut everyone out. Not when it really matters. I need to stop worrying about whatever it is he's said he needs to sort out. Maybe it's some big contract or something? I've let it morph into my head into something bigger, something scary. But this is just Dax and the way he does things.

I have nothing to worry about.

"He's a lot like his grandad in that sense."

"You knew him?"

"Not really. I mean, as a kid, I saw him. My parents knew him and their grandmother, being that they both ran businesses locally. I remember Dad saying what a great businessman he was. Always got the job done."

I take in this new information. Dax rarely talks about his grandparents, except to say that he and Jasmin didn't meet them until after his mom and dad passed away, and even then, they were only starting to build a relationship when they died too, passing the estate onto Dax and Jasmin.

"I've seen his name on some old accounts I've been sorting out. Things weren't left in the most ordered manner in here."

I cast my eyes around my office. It's neat now, not a sign of the piles of paperwork and boxes of files that were here when I first arrived. It's taken me since I arrived to get it like this. I'm almost on top of it all. There's just one last box to sort through, and the date on it is over thirty years old. Dax's grandad sure liked to keep records for a long time.

"Yeah? It's a shame it's just accounts and shit." Logan looks at the final box I'm staring at. "I don't think Jasmin or Dax got to know much about them before they died. Not what they were like, who they were, you know?" He shrugs his shoulders. "Then again, the shit that goes on in some families, maybe that's a good thing."

"Talking from experience?"

He winks at me as he stands. "I'm not going to tell you all my secrets, Rose. Got to maintain my air of mystery."

"Right." I giggle as he heads out the door.

"Do you think I'd be even better-looking if I swept my hair to the other side?" His face pops back around the doorframe.

I snort with laughter. "You're so vain. Go, please. I have work to do."

He tips his head to the side. "Nah. I think it's good. My left side is my best side."

I'm still laughing as he walks down the hallway, whistling to himself. God help the woman he sets his sights on. She's going to have her work cut out for her. But I know his heart's in the right place. He's loyal to Dax and Jasmin, and to the estate. And he always goes above and beyond for what's needed from him.

I spin in my chair so I'm facing the final unsorted box head-on. That's what I need to do. Dax offered me the job to come here to sort out the historical accounts, and to get everything up to speed. But the offices downstairs are on top of the day-to-day running of things now. And once I sort this final box, then everything will be complete. Neat and tidy, and I'll have a bit of spare time.

I can do something nice for Dax. Like Logan said, he doesn't know much about his grandparents. Maybe there are some boxes in the attic with more personal items in. They must have still held on to things because they had Dax's mother's mirror. It makes sense they would have more memories packed away somewhere. Ones Dax hasn't had the time to sort through.

That's what I'll do. I'll tackle this final box, and then I'll see what I can find out about them. It'll be a nice surprise for Dax and give him something else to think about. Because the way he's seemed distant and distracted this past day or two has made my heart go out to him. He's so used to doing things himself. This will be something I can do for him.

I walk over to the box and carry it back, placing it on top of my desk, then lift the lid to get to work.

"I'm sorry I'm such a shit cook." I drop the burned pan into the sink in the cottage's kitchen and turn to face Dax. His dark eyes gleam at me as he holds back a smirk.

"I like you for more than your cooking abilities."

"Or lack of them." I giggle as he walks over to me and grasps my hips, pulling my body against his.

I wrap my arms around his neck and my body relaxes, letting out a contented hum as his lips skate over my jaw and onto my neck, where he kisses me beneath my ear. I wanted to come back to the cottage tonight to get some things. I've been spending every night in Dax's apartment in the main house, but it's nice to be back in the cottage. It's cute and homely. And it's the place we first spent a night together. Even though it was only a few months ago, it seems like a lifetime.

So much has changed.

I've changed.

I smile as Dax brushes my hair away from my shoulder and kisses my skin, his lips only a couple of inches away from my tattoo. It's all healed now, and it's beautiful. I couldn't love it more.

It's a symbol of the future.

I tried to send Harley a photo of it, but I couldn't get the angle right in the mirror. I need to ask Dax to take one for me. She sounded excited when I told her about it. Her, Brett, and Mom. We've all been speaking more since Dax and I visited. They haven't mentioned Casey again, and I haven't asked. But I'm sure Mom has been talking to her, hoping for a reconciliation. Mom never could hold a grudge for long. Just like Dad. They always said life is too short, you never know what time you have.

Maybe they're right.

Sandbox to casket.

I should talk to her.

Just not yet.

"You all right, Sunbeam?"

Dax kisses my forehead.

Sunbeam.

I used to think he was being condescending calling me that.

Now I love it. I wish he said it more.

"Yeah, I'm good. Can we sleep here tonight?" I gaze up at him. We were going to go back to the main house after my disastrous attempt at risotto was eaten. But now, being here with him like this, has memories of that first night flooding back to me. I press my thighs together as he looks at me.

"Whatever makes you happy."

"You don't have to go out?"

A flash of something passes over his face and his brows flatten over his eyes. "Not tonight."

"Good." I stroke the back of his neck and bite my bottom lip.

"What's that look for?"

"Nothing."

"I know when you're lying." His hands flex on my hip bones and his lips curl into a playful smile as I giggle.

"What is it?"

"I just…" I glance down at the open neck of his black shirt, the delicate artwork disappearing out of view beneath the fabric. "I like being here with you. It makes me think of that first night."

"You feeling nostalgic?" His eyes sparkle as I nod shyly. "You want to go upstairs and watch in the mirror as I make you come again?"

"Dax!" I gasp, but secretly, my pussy's started throbbing like a brass band just started a world concert between my legs.

He chuckles and tightens his grip on me, and it only makes my already tingling skin scream out for him even more.

"Come on. Let's go." He bends and scoops me up, throwing me over his shoulder.

I laugh as he strides to the stairs and takes them two at a time.

"Don't say you didn't ask for it." His voice is a deep, sexy, sinful growl as he slides one hand up my thigh. He spreads his fingers around my ass cheek and squeezes as he takes us into the bedroom. "I'm going to enjoy watching your face as I fuck you from behind."

Oh God.

I suck in a deep breath. When Dax fucks me from behind, he really goes for it. Like he does the rest of the time. But behind me? That's going to be so hot watching him like that.

He drops me onto the bed and wastes no time in stripping us both out of our clothes. His eyes drink in my body and then he dips his head and spits on my pussy.

He rubs the wetness around me and pushes it inside me with one finger, groaning as it slides in easily. "Are you dripping because of me? Because you want to watch yourself get fucked?"

"Uh-huh." I squirm beneath him as he crawls over the top of me, his eyes intent on mine as he adds another finger and fucks me with them slowly until I'm panting with need.

"Words, Rose. Or do I need to teach you a lesson to help you remember?"

I gulp as he flips me over in one fast move and pulls me up onto all fours. The mirror is right in front of me, and I meet his eyes in the reflection as he kneels behind me.

"Do I need to make you wait a little longer for this cock?"

I whimper as he casts his eyes down and uses his hands to pull my ass cheeks apart. A smile crosses his face and then he bends and places his tongue on me.

"What—?" I jump forward instinctively.

He growls and lifts his head, his stormy eyes meeting mine in the glass as he grabs my hips and pulls me back to him. "Get your ass back here."

I suck in a breath and try to relax as he lowers his head again, his tongue finding its way back to my asshole.

"Jesus, Rose. I want every part of you," Dax groans as he laps at me, tracing around the tight hole with the tip of his tongue.

It feels weird. A nice weird.

"Dax," I moan as he presses the tip of his tongue inside me. Then he slides his fingers inside my pussy, and my body sends a rush of arousal to them.

I think I've gone to heaven.

Being fucked by Dax's thick, skilled fingers as his tongue explores me is like nothing I've ever felt before.

"We'll work up to you taking my cock here," he says as he licks me again and rises to his knees.

Oh.

His face softens as he looks at me in the mirror. "You don't need to worry. You know I'll take care of you."

I know he will. He'll take care of me. I trust him.

"You ready to watch now?" He runs a hand all the way up my back and wraps it over my shoulder with his palm placed over my tattoo.

"I'm ready."

I hold his eyes, my body practically vibrating with need as he pushes the tip of his cock inside me. His mouth goes slack, and I'm hypnotized by the look of pure unfiltered pleasure that paints itself over his handsome face as he pushes further and further, until I'm so full of him that I need to take a breath as I wait for my body to fully accommodate him.

"You're so tight. If you didn't get so wet, there's no way my cock would fit inside you so easily. You're fucking stretched wide open to take me." He glances down and flexes inside me, as if to prove his point, and I moan as I throb around him. "That feel good?"

"Uh-huh." My lips part, and I whimper as he flexes again and cants his hips so that his balls kiss my skin.

My eyes meet his in the mirror, and they're dark and glinting as he begins to move.

"How many times?" He pulls back and sinks into me again with force.

Thrust.

"How many times do I have to tell you?"

Thrust. "Use." *Thrust.* "Your" *Thrust.* "Words." *Thrust.*

I'm panting. Panting on shaking arms as Dax pumps into me from behind, his eyes holding mine and burning like black fire in the mirror. He fucks me without apology. Rough, deep, hard.

And I can barely catch my breath enough to get the words out.

"It... feels... good," I cry.

Strands of his blond hair fall forward toward his eyes as he groans and drives into me, his hips smacking my skin with each thrust. The muscles in his stomach are tense, causing the tattoos to pull tight over his skin.

His pecs are rigid too, the beautiful compass set like stone over his heart. And his neck... it's solid and tense, the leaves, and feathers too far away to see in full detail from this angle. Or maybe it's the fact that my vision is starting to blur with the intense pleasure that's building in my core.

I look back into his eyes, my mouth hanging open as I cry out with each hit. He strokes his thumb over the skin on my shoulder.

Over my tattoo.

My cloud.

My silver lining.

"You're squeezing me, Sunbeam. You about to come for me?"

I gasp as I stare back into his eyes. They pinch a little at the corners as he alters the angle, and his cock piercing hits the sweet spot inside me.

He knows my body better than I do.

I'm about to explode at any moment.

"Y-yes!" I gasp as he continues to fuck me, stroking my shoulder.

"Good girl."

I cry out as the first pulse builds inside me, threatening to detonate at any second. I fight to keep my eyes on his, the urge to squeeze them shut and succumb so strong.

"Dax!" I moan as he keeps his delicious rhythm going.

"Come for me, Rose."

I nod, our eyes locked together.

The first wave is right on me as I search his eyes.

And something in the way he's looking back at me makes my heart swell.

This is it. No matter how long I were to search, I would never find someone else who I feel so connected to.

I know it.

Dax Silver is everything I ever need. Everything I could ever want or wish for or hope to find.

"Every sunrise," I whisper as I hold his eyes.

He inhales a sharp breath, his eyes more intense than ever before as I come around him with a loud cry. I come in waves that shake my arms, and make my entire body feel like a forcefield just passed through it.

And the entire time our eyes are glued on each other.

I keep coming, the sound of my wetness echoing around the room until Dax's growl drowns it out.

Only he isn't just growling.

He looks deep into my eyes as he comes inside me, one word ripping through the air as he fills me with liquid fire.

"Infinity."

He keeps thrusting deep inside me, as our orgasms stretch on together. And the words whispered on his lips heal those final parts of me that I thought no amount of time could ever repair.

"Infinity, Sunbeam. Infinity."

Chapter 29

Dax

"What are you thinking about?" Rose traces her fingertip absentmindedly around the compass on my chest as we lie in her bed, her cradled in the crook of my arm.

I allow my eyes to fall closed as I press my lips to her forehead and breathe in her scent.

Vanilla and petals.

For the rest of my life, I swear the scent of her will calm me like nothing else.

Even when my head feels like it could explode with the amount of shit that's swarming around inside it.

"I'm thinking about where I'm going to take you."

"You mean on vacation?" She lifts her head and the delight in her eyes makes my heart pang with guilt. I wish I could give it to her now. Give her everything. Hell, I wish we were there now, and this was all over. All in the past.

Forty-eight hours.

Two days.

"Yeah." I chuckle as she grins and grabs either side of my face and plants an excited kiss on my lips.

"I can't wait. Where will we go? Will it be hot? Will I need a new bathing suit?"

"No."

"No?"

Her face falls briefly, and I reach out to run the pad of my thumb over her pouty bottom lip.

"You can swim naked. I intend on you being naked the entire time we're there."

Her eyes light up again before she places her head back into my chest and sighs happily. "I can't wait. Our first vacation together."

She takes one of my hands in hers and threads her fingers through mine, holding our entwined palms in front of her face. "I've got a surprise for you, too. Although I shouldn't tell you about it. It's not ready yet, I've only just started working on it."

"Does it involve you being naked? Because I know I'll love it if that's the case."

"Dax!"

I smile and tighten the grip of my arm around her. Hearing her happy is like food for my soul. Or like a beam of sunlight on the darkened parts. Warming up the cold corners that I thought were beyond redemption.

"When do I get this surprise?" I dip my nose into her hair and just rest there, contentment washing over me for the first time in a long while.

It's like I'm finally starting to breathe again.

So close.

"I don't know. A day. Maybe two." She brings our joined hands to her lips and kisses my knuckles one by one. "It'll be worth the wait. I hope."

Two days.

My mouth goes dry, the sliver of ease from moments ago disappearing once again. I can't have it yet. Not until this is all done.

Until it's over.

"Two days," I murmur, kissing her hair. "In two days, I'll have a gift for you as well."

She stops stroking my chest and tilts her face toward me, her light blue eyes finding mine.

She really is beautiful. Pure and good. Too good for me, yet here we are. She wants me, and I want her. God, do I want her. I've never wanted anything more. And from the past few years, that's saying something. In a few short months, she's become everything to me. The reason I want to move forward. The reason I want to leave the past behind.

The reason I need two more days.

"You will?" She looks at me, and I swear if I were a crying man, I would well up at the adoration and trust in her eyes.

I have to be worthy of her. I have to do this. Close the door so that we can have a fresh start. It's the least she deserves.

I extract my hand from hers and cup the side of her face, tracing my thumb over her cheek.

"You make me want to be a better man, Rose. I thought I knew what I wanted. Then you came along. Give me two days. Then our future begins. We both leave our past behind. Give me that time. *Please.*"

She nods once. "Okay."

Okay.

Just like that. She doesn't ask for anything more. She just smiles softly at me and angles her face toward me as I hold her chin and bring my lips to hers.

I kiss her, savoring every sigh from her as she kisses me back and strokes my neck. Then I roll on top of her, wrapping her legs around my waist.

"Hold on to me, Sunbeam," I breathe against her lips as I sink inside her.

She wraps her arms around my neck, her eyes holding mine as I hold her tightly in my arms and pump into her slowly, over and over again.

Our breath mixes in the fraction of an inch between our lips, and time becomes immeasurable. It's just me and her. Two souls, so close to being free together. Both tainted and stained by lies and the shadows of our past. But both gripping so tightly on to the other, never wanting to let go in case it all ends. In case it was all a cruel trick.

"Dax," Rose whimpers as I slide deep inside her again, setting her body shuddering beneath me.

I struggle to hold back the swell of pleasure threatening to burst out of me at the way my name sounds on her lips.

She blinks up at me and cups my face, searching my eyes as I hold her tight and thrust into her.

Yes... two souls... both with a promise for the other.

A promise of every sunrise for infinity.

"You're everything," I whisper, catching her lips in mine as her first orgasm rolls through her and she moans my name.

Then I come, groaning with a deepened kiss as I fill her. The strength of the emotion churning up my chest makes my eyes water, and I grip Rose tight as I empty everything I have deep inside her.

"Sunbeam," I murmur, kissing her over and over. Her cheeks, her lips, her eyelids, her neck.

Anywhere and everywhere my lips reach.

I keep my body inside hers, kissing her and stroking her face, running my hands through her hair, until my cock starts swelling again.

"Dax."

Her voice melts my last reserve until I'm painfully hard inside her again. I hold her eyes, and she nods.

Then we make love again.

And again.

And again.

I never leave her body.

I don't ever want to leave her.

The thought alone is enough to destroy me.

I make love to Rose all night long, hoping my body conveys the words I can't say to her yet.

But soon I will.

Our bodies are a tangled, sweaty mess as the sun's first early morning rays shine through the cottage's small window.

"You're close. I can feel it. Come. Come for me," I encourage as I drive inside her again, dragging my piercing over her G-spot on the outward thrust, the way she loves.

Her cheeks flush as she lets go, allowing another orgasm to steal the final threads of energy she's been holding on to.

Her eyelids fall low in exhaustion as she fights to keep her eyes on me. But she still manages to squeeze me, hugging me tight inside her wet heat. And it's the final push I need to join her. I hold her neck, stroking her pulse as pleasure surges through me, and I spill inside her again. I've lost count of how many times I've poured myself into her tonight.

Each time has stolen my breath more than the last.

Her eyes flutter closed, losing the battle.

One day to go.

"Everything okay?" Logan looks at my white knuckles as I sit back in my office chair, trying to concentrate on the latest update he's giving me.

"Yeah. Fine." I uncurl my fist that's on top of the desk and take a slow deep breath in.

"You sure you want to do it, then?"

"Yeah, of course," I mutter, nodding.

Logan's been talking about this guy, who's been anchoring after privately hiring the estate grounds for the day to hold his wedding. I was against it for a long time. But he's pulled out the big guns and is offering an eye-watering amount. Enough to cover all the lost revenue from when I was inside and the business suffered. It's enough for the entire staff to retire.

An obscene amount.

But the truth is, I don't care about the money.

It was when Logan told me that the guy's fiancée had dreamed of this place since she was a little girl that did it.

The guy said he didn't give a fuck where he married her, as long as he did. But her heart is set on the estate for some reason, and he wants her to be happy.

Meeting Rose has turned me into a sap. Because if there was something that would make her dreams come true, but I couldn't get it for her… it would eat away at me.

I told Logan to tell the guy yes.

Spread a little fucking light and positivity.

"All right. I'll let you know what date they want. We can insist on a premium if it's peak time."

"Whatever they want. Just let them pick."

Logan looks at me like I've grown two heads. "O-kay. You sure you're all right?"

"Never better." I put my hands onto my thighs beneath my desk and flex them.

It's the truth. Sort of. I am never better. Because soon this shit I've been chained to will all be finished. But tomorrow when it's all done and over… That's when I will truly be never better. When I can look into Rose's trusting eyes and know that I never have to leave her at night again. Never have to crawl back into bed in the early hours of the morning and miss her falling asleep in my arms. Never have to lie to everyone.

And Julian Young will finally be where he belongs.

Dead, or behind bars.

Either way, I don't care. As long as he's gone.

"Fine." Logan stands, sensing he won't get anything more out of me. "I'll call him. He's going to be happy. I told the fucker there wasn't a hope in hell."

"Tell him to think of it as a silver lining. Because the amount he's paying, he could buy the whole fucking sky as well as hell."

Logan smirks as he heads toward the door. "All right, Boss. Catch you later."

I stand and walk over to the window. The cottage is sitting behind the treeline, but I can see it from here and make out the front door.

I told Rose I want us to sleep there again tonight. After I get back, that is. It seems right that the first morning we wake up together with it all behind us will be in the cottage. My mind is already full of all the ways I want to show her what she means to me. Starting with in front of the mirror again. But this time, I won't be saying infinity. I'll be using other words. Ones I've never said to anyone before in my life.

After tonight, it will be done. Time to start over. Time to tell Rose how I really feel.

Time to fucking live again.

Chapter 30

Rose

I wring my hands in front of my body and then give up and wrap my arms around myself instead.

I can't stop shaking.

This isn't real. This isn't happening. Only it is. Because I've checked more times than I count. And it is happening.

It's fucking real.

I get up from my desk chair and pace the room again, gnawing on my bottom lip until it stings and the sharp tang of metal pokes at my tongue.

Now that I know, I can't un-know it. I can't pretend that everything's fine. That I'm not sitting on a bomb that has the strength to rip this entire estate apart.

To rip Dax apart.

I drop my head forward, nausea crawling up from my stomach. I've been sick twice already, there's nothing left to come up. I'm just grateful that Dax was out of his office earlier and never noticed me going to the restroom twice in a short time period to freshen up. The first time I never even made it that far. The potted plant from the hallway is now enjoying its new home in the composter around the back of the main house.

Fuck.

I drag in a shaky breath as I hug myself. What will Dax do? This will hurt him. I know it will. I'm already anticipating his pain when I tell him. And it's suffocating me. This could destroy him. He's the most amazing, kind person beneath the fiery exterior he can show.

What happens to a person when they find out something like this?

I've spent all day reading and re-reading the documents I found in that last box in my office. But the bank statements and letters in the attic of the main house cemented it to me. I wish it weren't true. Sitting in the dark, on the old, rough wooden boards of the attic, I wished with every part of myself, that it isn't true. Families have secrets. And the Silvers are no exception.

But now, because of me, a secret that has been hidden away in forgotten boxes, pieces scattered about like a jigsaw, is about to come to light.

I could have left it there. Hidden. Forgotten. But I couldn't live with myself knowing what I know and lying to Dax every day. I couldn't have looked into his eyes and pretended. I couldn't have promised him every sunrise.

He should have been told a long time ago. Years ago. And right now I hate his grandparents. Because they hid this. They covered it up. Paid for secrets to be kept.

They should be the ones who have to live with the look in Dax's eyes when he finds out. Live with that pain.

Not me.

My stomach lurches again, and I dart my tongue out to wet my dry lips.

I'll tell him after work. Show him everything I found.

And pray that I haven't made the biggest mistake by telling a secret that isn't mine.

"I'll be back as soon as I can." Dax wraps me in his arms, and I bury my face into his chest, nodding silently.

I meant to tell him already. But he ended up on a call and worked late. Then he came down to the cottage to find me, with only a few minutes to spend together before he goes out to whatever it is he has to do tonight.

I've tried to stop wondering where he goes. He says it's better that way. That he's fine, and that I don't need to worry.

But I do anyway.

And my worry has multiplied by a billion with each passing second of today, thinking about telling him tonight.

"Do you have to go now? I've barely seen you all day."

His grip on me tightens. I don't care if I sound needy. I wish tonight, of all nights, he didn't have to leave.

"I'll be as quick as I can. But Rose"—he pulls back and tilts my chin up with two fingers beneath my chin—"I'll be thinking of you the entire time. Thinking about coming back to you. About waking up next to you tomorrow."

I nod.

Dax curls his hand around the back of my neck, his thumb stroking over my pulse, and I lean into him on instinct.

"Time is about to reset, Sunbeam." He smiles softly at me. "Tomorrow is a new beginning. No more leaving you at night. No more being stuck in the past. No more being held back." He pulls me to him and presses his lips against mine. "Infinity."

"Every sunrise," I whisper back before I sink into his kiss.

It's different, weighted somehow.

But when he pulls back and his deep brown eyes shine as he looks at me, I understand.

For him, it's weighted by the promise of the future and the excitement that it brings.

And for me, it's weighted by the secrets of the past and the power they hold.

Dax leaves. I keep standing in the cottage doorway long after the taillights from the Range Rover disappear.

The next couple of hours, I try my best to not think about him. Where he is. What he's doing. I put a horror movie on, and then flick the TV off when it doesn't hold my attention and walk to the window to gaze out into the dark instead.

That's something so different here, on the estate. It's so dark at night. No lights from other properties. There's just a faint glow of the light from the main gates.

"This is ridiculous," I huff.

I'm so annoyed at myself. I should have told him earlier. Not wimped out. Maybe he would have stayed so we could talk. Maybe whatever he's doing tonight could have waited. I mean, this is important. There's nothing that could be more important right now, is there?

I grab my phone and bring his number up, hitting dial before I can doubt my actions. I've never called him when he's out at night. But I've also never been unable to sleep because I'm sitting on something that's the equivalent of the iceberg to the Titanic.

He answers on the second ring.

"Rose? What's wrong?"

Even Dax knows. I've not said a word yet. But he knows something isn't right. It's crackling in the air.

Tension. Unease. *Fear.*

"I..." I walk over to the sofa and drop into it, resting my forehead in one hand. "I just wanted to hear your voice." I sound weak, desperate. I know I do.

There are muffled sounds on the other end and the sound of wind as though Dax is outside.

"I'll be back soon." The regret in his voice makes my chest burn. I'm calling him and making him feel bad about leaving me. He told me he needed tonight. Whatever he's doing must be important to him.

I need to trust him.

"Okay," I whisper. "I just miss you, that's all. I'll leave you to get on with what you're doing. I'm sorry for interrupting."

"Don't. Don't ever apologize. Not for wanting to speak to me." His voice softens. "Rose, I don't think you know how much... Jesus." He blows out a slow breath. "I don't think you know just how much I love that you call me when you need something. I want to be the first person you call, whatever the reason."

"You are." Despite the aching force pulling down inside my chest, I still manage to smile at the happy sound he makes in response.

"Good. And from tomorrow, you won't need to call, because I'll be there. I'll be there with you. I've just got this one last thing to do. Then Young, my past, it's all behind us."

"Young?" The hairs on the backs of my arms stand up as my skin prickles, sending goosebumps skittering up my arms. "Julian Young? Dax... Where are you?"

The silence stretches on for a few excruciating seconds.

"I'm—" He exhales. "I'm at the dockyard. It's just work, nothing to worry about."

"Is Julian Young there?"

"No."

My shoulders sag with relief. Dax has a temper, I know that. For a second I thought he's doing something stupid. I don't know why, it's just this feeling I have. This unease that's settled low in my gut.

But of course, Julian wouldn't be there. Dax doesn't know what I know.

Yet.

"But he will be later."

"What?" I bolt upright, my body balancing on the edge of the seat. "What do you mean? Are you meeting him? Are you...? Dax, what's going on?"

"Nothing." His voice drops as though he doesn't want to be overheard. "Trust me, okay. I'll tell you everything tomorrow. It's fine. It's all going to be fine."

"Why are you there? Why is he coming? You hate him. I don't understand."

Panic sends adrenaline racing around my body. The dockyard? Why would he be there? Why would he mention Julian Young?

The nearest dockyard is forty minutes' drive. My body is working faster than my brain, and I jump up from the sofa and scoop up the car keys from the table by the door.

"Don't worry." Dax's calm voice does nothing to ease the thundering of my pulse in my ears as I yank the front door open. "I'll be home soon. And this will all be finished."

"Okay," is the only response I manage to croak back before I end the call. I wait until it disconnects before I slam the front door of the cottage shut and run to the Range Rover outside. Thank God I left work today while Dax was on his call. He indicated he'd be awhile, so I drove into town to buy food for dinner. Food we never got to eat because he was so late finishing. But it means I have a car. Otherwise, I would have walked back to the cottage after work, and I would be losing precious time now. Maybe the universe was working on my side for once. A silver lining to the shit I found out today.

I snort at the idea as I press the ignition and the engine roars to life.

Whatever Dax is doing, if Julian Young is there, it can't be good.

Nothing to do with that man is good.

Nothing except...

I press my foot on the gas and gravel kicks up behind me as I pull away.

Please don't do anything stupid, Dax.

Chapter 31

Dax

I GRIT MY TEETH as Marcus huffs again.

"Makes sense. Why the fuck would you be on time when you're the boss? The rest of us can just wait around like we have no lives of our own."

I look over the top of his head at the row upon row of shipping containers, lined up like dominoes.

All Julian Young's latest import.

But like dominoes, you only have to have one person pushing on one and then the entire arrangement will fall.

Tonight, I'm that fucking person.

"Julie arranged for us to go to her sister's tomorrow. Fuck that. That's one thing with coupling up. You have to take on the entire family." Marcus turns and spits his gum out onto the floor, then glances at me. "Another good talk." He chuckles as he's met with silence. "You're full of the best chats."

I cross my arms.

He's late. Julian Young doesn't have to do shit on schedule if he doesn't feel like it. Marcus and I are mere minions, the bottom of an elaborate system that he operates. A system so big, that guys like us are disposable, replaceable.

Anonymous.

It's a small blessing that comes with the level of greed that fucker has. He has no idea who's working lower down the chain.

A carefully constructed profile, a fake name. It was easy to slide right in and hide in plain sight. Maintain enough respect that I reached a level where I could find out key information but stay inconsequential enough that I never had to be in the room with the prick, face-to-face. Because there's no doubt he would recognize me. I expect my face is as burned into his memory as his is in mine.

Two and a half years in a cell does that to you.

Gives you time to plan. To think about this day. The day you finally get to watch your enemy burn. To lose something they care about.

This business, the money that's rinsed through it. It's all he fucking holds dear. I hear enough to know that. Even Alistair doesn't want to protect him. Surely, a son would never want to turn his own father in if there was a good relationship there.

Julian Young only puts his cold heart into what he cares about most.

Himself.

And that has made this so much simpler, a silver lining, even if it's taken longer than it should have.

I roll my shoulders, then rotate my neck, the tension cracking through my bones. Rose sounded lost on the phone. She's had a bad day. Maybe she's missing her family in New York. Maybe it's something more. But I haven't even been able to talk to her about it. I had to leave her with turmoil filling her eyes. My beautiful girl is at home, waiting for me, *needing* me. And I'm here, in a grim, concrete yard, waiting for the man who stole something from me that I can never replace.

Time.

But starting tomorrow, all my time will belong to her. To Rose.

The clock resets.

A new sunrise.

"Why don't you head off. I can wait."

Marcus's brows shoot up. "We're both supposed to be here. Everything's done in pairs. Those are the rules."

I shoot him a look that has him shrinking back.

"But I would like to get back. Julie asks questions when it gets too late. She knows the only bars open after two are titty ones. And it's never a great day after if she thinks I've been in one of them."

I force the image of Rose having a lap dance out of my mind. I can't lose focus by remembering how turned on I was watching her explore her own pleasure as she experienced something new. Every fucking thing she does turns me on. I only have to look at her walking around at work in those swishy little skirts, with her incredible legs on show, to get a raging hard-on at my desk.

"Go," I grunt. "We've checked everything together and it's all been sealed. The only difference is Young's dropping in tonight because it's a big shipment. Wouldn't you rather stay off his radar anyway?"

His eyes dart around the still deserted yard. "You know... that sounds..." He rolls his lips. "Yeah. You got this, haven't you? Doesn't need us both just to wait around like fucking losers."

His left eye twitches. It happens when he's on edge. Like the night his 'friend' was helping himself to Young's latest delivery. The asshole could have gone nice and quietly, but he had to make a scene. And then I was forced to leave him enough of a memory to ensure he never spoke about it to anyone. I couldn't risk having my cover blown.

His wounds will have healed by now, anyway. But if he'd brought Young's attention onto things Marcus and I were given to handle, then there's no telling what would have happened.

I wouldn't be here tonight. About to see him finally go down.

Marcus looks me over, his eyes settling on the bulging vein that's pulsating in my neck.

"I'll see you soon then, yeah?"

"Yeah." I nod in response as he backs up and then turns and walks away.

He won't.

He won't see me again. But he doesn't know that. He won't have a job come tomorrow morning. Julian Young and his entire shady enterprise will have been brought to its knees. And if Marcus has an ounce of sense about him, then he'll take it as his chance to leave this life behind. Go off and live with Julie and her home-cooked steaks.

Have a fucking happy life.

Because it's what I intend on doing.

I'm going to go back to the cottage and slide into bed with Rose.

Pull her into my arms and never fucking let go.

Headlights appear on the far side of the shipping yard, slowly drawing closer as the vehicle drives up the wide lane between the rows of containers. I stay where I am, off to one side, hidden in the shadow of one container.

I don't want him to see me yet.

The vehicle rolls to a stop and kills the headlights.

What the fuck?

Ice threads through my veins. The Silver Estate logo emblazoned on the side of the Range Rover is clear as day, illuminated by the moonlight.

The door opens, and one long leg steps out, followed by another.

"Dax?" A whisper-shout. She's uneasy, being here in the dark. It's in her voice. And she fucking should be. What the hell is she doing?

She leaves the Range Rover and walks over the oil-stained concrete floor, her over-the-knee boots making her footsteps echo around the yard. She's glancing around, not paying attention to where she is, to who could be watching her.

"God!"

Her eyes widen as I pull her down the gap between containers and push her up against the cold metal of one with my hand over her mouth.

"What are you doing here?" I crowd her body with my own, pressing right up against her, one hand still over her mouth, the other pressed flat against the container next to her head.

"Fuck, Rose. What am I going to do with you?" I grasp her neck and press my thumb to her pulse. It's pounding beneath her soft skin as her chest rises and falls quickly between us.

"You shouldn't fucking be here," I hiss, letting go of her mouth now that she's seen it's me and she's not going to scream.

"I..." She stops and tries to catch her breath.

"Breathe." I cup her cheek with my other hand as I lean toward her, embracing her scent as it washes over me. "Breathe."

She nods, her face relaxing as she breathes in deeply and then lets it go. "I was worried. When you said Julian Young was going to be here. I thought—"

"You thought I was going to do something to him?"

She nods, and I clench my teeth, tension rippling through my body again as I glance over my shoulder.

We're still alone. For now.

"If I could kill him and not go back to jail, I would." I look back at Rose. "But I would never do anything that could take me away from you. You understand?"

"Then what are you doing here?" Confusion clouds her gaze.

"I've been working on taking him down." I glance over my shoulder again, shielding Rose with my body. We haven't got long. He could arrive at any moment. And I doubt he goes anywhere without carrying a gun. Not when you get to his level. I'm one in a long line of people who would happily have his head. His operation stretches across the entire southeast of the country. It would be worth a lot to anyone who could take control of it.

But that's the last thing on my mind.

My motivation is purely personal.

"That's what you've been doing every night?"

"Yes. I've been working for him, for his drug operation. But he doesn't know that."

She stares at me, her brows pulling together as her mouth drops open.

"You've—?"

"Been preparing to finish him from the inside."

The disbelief in Rose's eyes has acid churning in my gut. Now she knows. She's finally seeing it with her own eyes. Seeing the man I really am. One scarred by his past. One hell-bent on revenge. One who needs to finish this so that I can love her in the way she deserves.

"But what changes tonight? You said it all finishes tonight. Dax, what are you going to do that—?"

I clamp my hand over her mouth again and move us further into the shadows of the container.

"We've got company," I hiss.

She murmurs beneath my palm, panic flashing in her eyes as the sound of another vehicle approaching grows louder.

"You need to stay here. Don't come out. Let me deal with it."

"Da—"

I force my lips against hers in a kiss to silence her. "Don't let them see you, Sunbeam. Please don't fucking let them see you." I kiss her again, squeezing my eyes shut before I turn and walk away without looking back.

As I reach the edge of the container, there are three voices. Julian's and two other males'. They're already out of their black SUV and standing next to the open door of Rose's Range Rover.

Fuck. This isn't how it was supposed to go down. They were supposed to turn up while I was out of sight. I would have had the element of surprise. I know which container they'll check first. The one with the diamonds. Because as I've learned, Julian sneaky-prick Young isn't content with only supplying street drugs to a quarter of the country. He wants to get his filthy hands on blood diamonds too. The greed of this man is unbelievable.

And Jasmin still wants to believe Alistair is different. The tail I've put on him will uncover it soon, if he is as dirty as his father.

"Well, well." Julian sneers with a laugh as he looks at the logo on the Range Rover. "Tonight will be better than I expected."

I stay pressed up to the container as I peer around the corner of it.

Open the diamond container, asshole.

It's all I need. Him to open it. Show that he knows the combination of the lock. The final piece of evidence. The nail in the coffin that I've been building for nine months. He needs to be caught red-handed. The one final action that will signal the end of him. And I *need* to see it. It's why I'm here.

But then, Rose....

Julian runs his hand over the hood of the car.

Of course, the prick isn't going to grant me the satisfaction of making it simple. Not now he's seen the logo.

He knows I'm here.

And if he hasn't worked out by the sight of the car that I'm one of the two guys from his payroll he was expecting to meet tonight that took the delivery in, then he's not as smart as I've been giving him credit for. There's no welcoming party here for him. No trusted members of his operation, like he was expecting.

It's just me.

And he knows it.

"Aren't you going to come out and play, Silver?"

Fuck. How do I do this? Why can't he just open the fucking container? My heart pounds up into my throat as Julian laughs again.

"Wasn't one warning enough? You want to know what I do to squealing little pigs?" He looks side to side around the yard, his dark eyes almost black and seeming even darker against his blond hair. He nods to one of his henchmen, who disappears from sight. "I string them up and bleed them out. Let them be a lesson to everyone. But with you, Dax..."

Rage boils inside me at the easy way he says my name.

"With you, I'd have some fun first. Maybe give you a matching scar to that one on your back. You won't need your kidneys when my boys here throw you into the sea for the fish to pick apart."

I press my back into the container and glance at Rose at the other end. Her eyes are wide and shining from where she's standing, rooted to the spot I left her in, realization dawning in them at the small part of that story I omitted when she first saw my scar.

Julian Young paid someone to try and murder me while I was in jail. I always suspected he was behind me getting stabbed. Now he's confirmed it.

"But I'm not a monster," Julian continues. "I'll let you watch me with your girlfriend first. See if she screams louder for me than she does for you."

Rage floods my veins like lava and my chest swells as every muscle in it tenses.

Rose shakes her head at me and clamps her hand over her mouth. She wants to run to me. I can see it in her eyes. They're pleading with me. But I can't walk out of here with her. Not until it's finished. He'll come for me. He'll come for her. And that's the only thing I care about.

Her.

He cannot be in any kind of state when I leave here tonight that means he can come for her.

I hold a palm up and indicate Rose to stay still, and she nods.

I whip my head back toward Julian. He's holding something that the other guy has handed to him from inside the Range Rover.

Nausea gut punches me as he raises the black hoodie to his nose and inhales with a perverse groan.

"I wonder if she tastes as good as she smells."

My reserve snaps. He's got his filthy fucking fingers on her things. He's smelling her. *Vanilla and petals.*

The one scent in the world that calms me. The abuse of that one thing is what finally pushes me over the edge until all I can hear is my own pulse thundering in my ears.

"You'll never fucking find out!" I storm out from my hiding place, only meters away, and go straight for his legs, barreling into him and bringing him to the ground with a satisfying *thunk* of bone cracking against concrete. "You'll never lay one disgusting finger on her! Or anyone else, you piece of shit!"

I pound his face with my fists. Each hit like sweet fucking therapy to my soul. Therapy for the words he said that night, all those years ago. The comments he made about Jasmin. The realization that men like him exist. Vile, despicable predators that will take what isn't theirs and feel nothing while they do it.

Euphoria spreads through my body with each connection my fist makes. But this wasn't part of the plan. He should have just opened the fucking container. Then everything else would have been put into motion.

Julian laughs, spitting blood up into my face, momentarily blurring my vision. Long enough that his piece of muscle he brought with him can land a punch into the side of my head, knocking me off balance and allowing Julian to roll out from beneath me, still laughing as he spits more blood onto the floor.

I jump to my feet and position myself between the two of them and the gap between containers where Rose is hiding.

"She's not here. She left that in my car."

Julian's on his feet again, and he scoops Rose's black hoodie up from where it's fallen to the ground.

"You wish that were the truth." The corner of his mouth lifts, and his eyes glitter as he looks over my shoulder. "Nice boots."

All the air leaves my body in a rush. I don't want to turn around. Because I know. The dread threatening to make my heart stop inside my chest is enough to know.

"I'm sorry, Dax," Rose whimpers.

I turn, meeting her wild eyes from where she's being held with her arms behind her back by Julian's other guy. A guy whose face looks like it's taken its fair share of beatings in its lifetime. He grins at me and one gold tooth glints.

"Get your fucking hands off her!" I yell, sweat running down my back as I advance on him.

He pulls a gun from his belt and presses it to Rose's temple.

The click of the safety being released signals the sound of my soul breaking as I freeze.

No. No, no, no.

"Let her go. You can take me," I spit as I whip my head back toward Julian.

Where the fuck's the backup? They've got a fucking gun to Rose's head, for God's sake. How is nothing happening?

Realization settles in my gut like lead.

They've left me here to rot alone.

I wanted out. I told them... I wanted out. I should never have let them talk me into it. Finish the job, they said. You'll get what you wanted. Julian out of the picture. You'll be free, you'll get justice.

And it's all I wanted.

Once upon a time.

Before her.

Rose cries out as Gold Tooth pushes the gun harder against her skull.

"Let her go!" I roar.

She drags in shaky breaths, her lips trembling as she blinks at me with shining eyes. The tip of the gun is pressed deeper into her skin.

"Every sunrise," she whispers.

"No!" I shake my head, my eyes burning as I stare into her pure, light blue ones. "No. Don't say it like you're fucking leaving me. You're not fucking leaving me!"

She can't. She's all I want. I'll forget about revenge this second. *Dear God, are you listening? I don't need anything, apart from her. Not one damn thing.*

Julian laughs behind me. "Bring her here first. I've got something for her."

Gold Tooth places the safety back on the gun and marches Rose toward the Range Rover. She struggles to keep up and loses her footing, so he drags her the rest of the way.

Julian's other thug has a gun pointed at me. He'll shoot me before I even make it halfway to Rose.

My mouth goes dry as they reach the hood of the Range Rover and Gold Tooth throws Rose down onto it face-first. He's restrained her hands behind her back with a cable tie.

"Uh-uh." Julian walks over to her and strokes her hair, turning her head to the side so that she's facing me. "I want you to look at him. I want him to see the moment your eyes widen as you get your first feel of a real man's cock inside you."

Rose cries out, but Julian smacks her head against the hood, pressing down hard and holding her there as he reaches for his belt with his other hand.

I'd rather die, have my brains blown across this filthy dockyard for the gulls to eat than stand by a second longer while his hands are on her.

I lurch forward, a microsecond before a shot fires out, making my ears ring and my head pound. I don't look to see if I'm hit. I just know I'm still moving. I'm not dead. I can still get to her.

Julian's loosened pants have him off guard, unable to reach for his own gun that I'm sure he must have. And it gives me valuable moments to reach him, shoving him away from Rose and pushing her across the hood behind me. I still have one arm on her as he turns to me, so I act on instinct, rearing back and headbutting him square in the face.

"Fuck!" His hands fly to his face, and I grab the gun attached to his belt and point it at his other guy, who's standing staring at the lifeless body of Gold Tooth, bleeding out on the floor.

"Your gun!" I shout. "Throw it! Now!"

He reaches into his belt, his eyes coming back to mine as he drops the black metal to the floor and kicks it across the floor, away from himself.

I turn the gun back onto Julian, who's wiping at the blood pouring down over his lips. The whites of his eyes shine as he stares down the barrel at me. I've dreamed of this moment. Revelled in the feeling of standing here, with him at my mercy, knowing I have the power over him, finally. The power to destroy him. To take every-thing from him.

"Dax."

Rose has stood from the hood, and her voice is shaking. I glance to the side. Her hair is matted, her makeup smudged beneath her eyes.

"Don't do it. This isn't you."

I move so that I can wrap my other arm around her waist and hold her into my side.

"You okay?"

I kiss her hair, inhaling deeply.

Vanilla and petals.

My grip loosens on the gun, then I tighten it again and look back at Julian as I take the safety off.

"I'm fine." She leans into my side. It's all she can do with her hands bound like a fucking prisoner.

"Close your eyes, Sunbeam. Then it'll all be over."

I kiss her head again as she buries her face into my neck.

"Don't." Her voice is a faint whisper. *"Please."*

Movement in the corner of my eye steals my attention as thug number two makes a dive for his weapon. But he's too late. A bullet rips through his skull, and he falls to the ground in a flash.

Rose screams, and I grip the back of her head, forcing her face into the crook of my neck so she can't see.

I straighten the gun, aiming it back at Julian. He looks at the two bodies on the ground, the same question in his eyes as held in mine.

Who?

"Listen to Rose, Dax. Put the gun down."

I stop breathing as Marcus comes into view, his own gun pointed at Julian.

Only he sounds nothing like Marcus. His voice is different. And he's holding the gun like it's second nature to him.

And he knows my real name.

And Rose's.

"The fuck?" I stare between him and Julian, keeping my gun firmly aimed still.

Rose twists her head, her lips brushing over my neck.

"Don't do it, Dax."

I train my eyes back on Julian as Rose lifts her lips to my ear, her next words turning my body to stone.

"He's your father."

Chapter 32

Rose

I can pinpoint the exact moment that my words register in Dax's brain. The exact moment that all he knew implodes. All blown apart.

My beautiful man, hit with a force that has the power to destroy him.

The air leaves his lungs, a groan and a gasp all in one. Then silence.

Silence as his grip falters around the gun.

"No."

I squeeze my eyes shut against his skin. "I am so sorry."

"It's not true, Rose. Who told you that?"

"I'm so sorry," I sob. "I wish it weren't."

I look up at him and his eyes are round and pained.

"I found old accounts. Transactions to an account in his name. Your grandparents paid him off when your mom and him began dating. They had suspicions about him. They were trying to protect her. They didn't want him anywhere near her. I didn't want to believe it. But then I found letters from your mom in the attic. They confirmed it. She told them it was their fault her baby had no father. That she knew what they'd done. She said she knew they'd forced Julian away. He *is* your father."

"No." He screws his face up and looks back at Julian, his arm shooting out straight again. "Don't fucking move!"

Julian's staring at the two of us, listening to every word.

"Dax, please."

He glances at me, then back to Julian. A vein throbs in his temple and his jaw is set solid.

"I can't share this asshole's blood, Rose." He sucks in a breath, his eyes growing wide as he trains them on Julian. They're dark, darker than I've ever seen them. Intent on target. Like a killer. "I can't be anything like him."

"You're not!" I cry, twisting my wrists in the tie until warm stickiness drips into my palms. I need to hold him. I need to show him that I know he's nothing like Julian, blood or not.

"Jessica?"

"Don't fucking say her name!" Dax roars at Julian as he stares at Dax like he's seeing him for the first time.

"The Jessica I knew was never pregnant. And she wasn't Jessica Silver," Julian says.

But the narrowing of Julian's eyes as he studies Dax's face gives away his uncertainty. Despite all the blood, it's there. The blond hair. The height. The strong jawline.

Dax looks like his father.

The man he hates.

He looks like Julian Young.

"She would use my grandmother's maiden name when she went out. She said she only attracted pricks after her money if she told them she was a Silver," Dax spits.

Julian's eyes bug in his head before he recovers. Then slowly he begins to laugh. And it's a sound that will haunt me. Worse than any crazed laugh of any horror movie I've watched. The sound of true evil. "That money... that *anonymous* fucking money. She was a fucking Silver?" Julian continues to laugh, distorting his bloody face further. "I would have left her for nothing. If only they'd waited."

"You won't be laughing when your brains are on the bottom of my shoes." Dax keeps the gun perfectly aimed.

"Put the gun down."

I glance at the stranger who appeared earlier. The one who knew my name. The one Dax seemed to recognise. The one whose gun was aimed at Julian but is now pointed at Dax.

"Listen to him," I plead, pressing my lips to Dax's throat, and squeezing my eyes shut as I kiss his skin. "*Please*, Dax. We can talk about everything. Don't make me go home alone." His neck relaxes a little with my contact, and he swallows, setting the movement flowing past my lips as I kiss him again.

"Step back, Rose," the stranger says.

I shake my head, my eyes burning. "Why? So you can shoot him?" I move closer to Dax, pressing myself against his chest, my lungs burning as I suck in the night air. "You'll have to shoot me too."

I turn my attention back to Dax, my lips grazing his cheek as I speak to him. "Put the gun down. You're nothing like him. You will *never* be anything like him." I move back to study Dax's face. He's still staring at Julian, his nostrils flaring as Julian continues to laugh.

"You're no son of mine," Julian finally snorts, his laughter ending abruptly. "I've already got one son who can't shoot a gun to save his ass. I wouldn't be cursed enough to have two. If you were mine, you'd have pulled that trigger by now."

Dax stiffens.

"Never were able to finish a job, were you? Not when you almost had me three years ago. And not now, either." Julian spits a globule of blood and what looks like a tooth out onto the ground. "Tell you what. I'll let her live." He looks at me. "I'll let her and your sister live. My *actual* son seems to like her. Idiot thinks he kept it a secret, but I know what goes on. Kind of poetic, really. He falls for her. I take your business. She won't be able to handle it all once you're locked up again. She'll sign it over to me faster than your mom could spread her legs."

"You bastard! I'll kill you!"

I use my body to hold Dax back as fury erupts from him like a fireball.

"Dax." I struggle, forcing myself in front of his eyeline so he can't aim the gun. "Dax."

He finally focuses on me.

Light blue meets deep brown.

Time stalls as I soak up the pain in his eyes. If I take away as much as I can, pull it away, like a magnet. Draw it to me. Then maybe he won't look so broken.

Maybe I won't feel broken.

His lips part, and he lifts his free hand to my cheek, his palm barely making contact before he's ripped away by two men in black SWAT style uniforms. *Armed cops.*

They grab his arms, disarming him and pulling him away from me.

"Stop!" I shout, but I can't do anything. "Stop!"

No one is listening.

Blue and red flashing lights make it hard to see. Stinging my eyes. And the sounds of sirens and screeching tires ringing in my ears as the yard fills with squad cars.

"Stop!" My voice grows hoarse as hands appear and take hold of my arms, pulling me in the other direction.

Away from him.

"We're police officers. You're safe. You're safe."

Why are they saying that? Why are they taking me away from him? I was never in any danger. It's Dax. He would never hurt me.

I fight against the hands to get to him. He's thrashing around, trying to fight off the officers as he calls to me. Two more join in to overpower him.

"Rose!"

I pull as hard as I can, trying to get to him.

"Don't take him. He hasn't done anything wrong. Get your hands off him!" I scream and I fight as hard as I can while Dax does the same.

Then the stranger with the gun, the one who shot Julian's men walks over to Dax and says something to him. And it's like a light turns off. Dax's chest caves in on itself and he stares at me.

"What's wrong? Dax!" I struggle to try to get to him, but he turns his head and lets the officers push him down into a waiting squad car. "Dax!" My chest burns as my body is stripped of oxygen from all my screaming.

I gulp in deep breaths as I'm pulled further away and over to the back of an ambulance where I can no longer see him.

"We'll get you checked over. Your wrists need attention."

"Where are they taking him?"

A female medic begins checking me over while one of the officers still holding onto me says, "He's been arrested."

The medic smiles at me kindly as the other officer cuts the tie behind my back, and I bring my bloodied wrists forward. *I could make a run for it.* The officer who's still holding me tightens their grip on my upper arm as if reading my thoughts.

"But he's done nothing wrong."

The medic extends one of my arms and examines my wrist. It should hurt.

But I feel nothing.

"He hasn't done anything wrong," I repeat.

But no one is listening.

"Tell us again about what happened when you went to New York?"

"I've already told you." I drop my head into my hands, exasperated, as the officer repeats the same question.

Jasmin places a fresh cup of coffee down on the table and wraps an arm around my shoulders as she sits next to me on the sofa in the cottage's living room.

"She's told you already. My brother's innocent. He was only pretending to work for Julian Young to get evidence to use against him. You should be dealing with him, not wasting your time here. He's the real criminal."

"We're aware of Mr. Young's business he was running, and that's being dealt with."

Jasmin snorts.

"But," the plain clothed officer continues, "we're still conducting inquiries into missing items related to our investigation."

"What's that supposed to mean?" Logan stands in a rush and drags his hands back through his hair, pacing up and down as the officer looks at him with a raised brow. "You're not suggesting Dax smuggled shit for that asshole, are you? He wouldn't do that. I know him."

"Could you please answer the question, Miss Jacobs?" The officer looks back at me.

I drag in an exhausted breath. I've barely slept. I was taken to the hospital for a check-up last night, despite insisting I was fine. And Jasmin came to collect me from the hospital while Logan went to the station to talk to Dax. But they wouldn't let him see him. The three of us are all bloodshot-eyed and running on caffeine this morning.

And Dax is still in a holding cell somewhere.

I press my fingertips into my eye sockets and try to ignore the pounding at the base of my skull.

"We flew in. We both went through customs. Dax helped me get a taxi outside. And then he went back inside to check in for his flight to LA."

"Did he seem on edge?"

"No."

"How about his luggage? Was he carrying more than you'd expect for the length of the trip? Was he acting unusual? Being extra protective over it?"

"No." The back of my neck burns.

"You really think my brother would do anything like that? What is it you think he had?" Jasmin asks.

"We can't disclose that information," the officer answers.

Jasmin curses under her breath beside me as goosebumps scatter up my arms.

New York.

The officer asks some more questions, which Jasmin and Logan answer, while I sit in stony silence, and then he and his colleague finally leave.

"What the hell was that all about?" Logan walks back into the living area after showing them to the door.

"Ridiculous," Jasmin mutters. "They're being ridiculous. Dax always said he's looked at differently since he was convicted. He's done his time. Why can't they see that? This all started because of Julian Young, he's the real criminal. Dax isn't... he's..." She covers her eyes with her hand and lowers her head as tears drop onto her cream skirt.

"We know that. And they'll see that. They will," Logan says, his voice stronger than I feel.

"He'll hate it in there. It'll be eating him up. You know how he was when he was first released. He'll hate it." Jasmin cries harder as I lift my puffy eyes to meet Logan's.

"I'll head down to the station again." He looks from me to Jasmin. "See what I can find out. See how he's doing. The lawyer's there now. She's the best there is."

I nod at Logan as he leaves, grateful for any information he might be able to get for us.

My gorgeous Dax, I hope you're doing okay. Just hold on. You'll be out soon. Just hold on.

Jasmin lifts her head and dabs under her eyes. It's just the two of us now. The two women who care about Dax the most in the world, left with more questions than answers.

"I'm worried about him, Rose," she sniffs. "He won't be doing well. Not if they're holding him in a cell."

It's my turn to wrap my arm around her in an effort to provide some comfort. Because I know that that's exactly where Dax will be. In some cold, drafty cell. Or worse, in a windowless room being interrogated.

He hasn't done anything wrong.

Jasmin's phone vibrates on the coffee table, and she picks it up with a trembling hand.

"It's Alistair."

"Do you want me to leave?"

She shakes her head and presses connect, putting the call on speaker.

"Jaz, Honey? Are you there?"

"I'm here." A soft smile crosses Jasmin's face at his warm, deep voice on the line. "You're on speaker. I'm sitting with Rose."

"Rose," the warm voice says, "I wish we were talking for the first time under different circumstances."

"Me too." I curl my lips as much as I can manage at Jasmin as she grabs my free hand and holds it.

Alistair sighs. "I'm so sorry. Dad, he... Shit."

The agony in his voice is palpable. It reaches through the phone and joins us in the room as though it's sitting here with us. A dark force taking up a seat on the sofa. I bet Alistair's eyes are red and puffy too, and that he didn't get any sleep last night either. Jasmin told me they spent hours waiting together at the hospital.

I hope someone made sure Dax got checked over. He wasn't hurt, *but*... I squeeze my eyes shut as they sting.

"They've arrested him," Alistair says. "His entire business, his assets, they've all been frozen. They've been working on getting him for years. Fuck, I even wanted him to get caught. I was even looking into things, I was—"

"But he's still your dad," I finish for him, opening my eyes and inhaling slowly.

"Yeah." The line crackles as his breath vibrates through the speaker. "Yeah, he's still my dad."

Jasmin squeezes my hand tighter, her eyes shining with fresh tears as she looks at me.

She knows.

Everyone knows now, including Alistair.

Dax is Julian Young's biological son. And Alistair's half-brother.

It's all too crazy to believe. But after everything that's happened with Brett, and Dad, and then Casey before this... Crazy seems like my new normal. Anything less wouldn't fit.

"The police have just been here. They already asked Rose and I a load of questions at the hospital."

"They've been here too, Babe. Going over the same stuff," Alistair says.

"They kept asking about the trip to New York, making out Dax took something there." Jasmin looks at me in disbelief as she talks. "It's the craziest thing I've ever heard. They wouldn't even tell us what they think it was." She looks at the phone and Alistair's photo on the screen. He's got brown hair and green eyes. He must take after his mom. But his jawline is similar to Dax's. And his nose too, come to think of it.

The longer I look at the screen, the more resemblance he has to Dax. I stare until I'm forced to turn away and look out of the front window instead.

It's all too much.

How is he?

"He never would," Jasmin continues talking. "He just wouldn't. And besides, he's not stupid. He knows if he got caught with anything, he'd be straight back to jail with his record."

I sit as the two of them continue talking, no longer listening, my entire body blanketed in numbness. The kind that your body might use as a survival technique when you've had a shock. When the reality is too horrendous to process without you becoming hysterical.

"Go on, I'll catch you up."

I sit frozen as my mind replays that day.

"Why don't you smile at Mr. Fun and see if you can cheer him up?"

Dax didn't take his bags through customs in JFK airport.

I did.

Because he insisted I go ahead without him while he went to the restroom.

He came through afterward.

With nothing.

I took it for him.

Whatever it was. He had it. And he made me his mule. His pawn.

If he lied to me about that, what else has he lied about?

Chapter 33

Dax

THE CLOCK ON THE wall ticks by with each passing second. Marking another second of my life where I am trapped. Caged like an animal.

Kept apart from her.

"They're holding you on making a threat against life while in the possession of a firearm, and for resisting arrest."

I look up at my lawyer, Sophie, as she walks into the interview room. It's bigger than the cell I was in before. That just had a metal bed frame bolted to the floor and a low-level WC that stank with the dried-on remnants of the last lucky inhabitant's bowel contents in. At least this room doesn't stink of shit, even if all it has is a depressing-looking gray table in the center of the room, with a chair on either side.

"He was going to rape Rose." I curl my fingers into my palm, until my nails bite at my skin. "He was going to fucking *rape* her. And all they're worried about is the fact that I came close to doing the world a favor and ridding it of an asshole like Julian Young?"

Sophie doesn't flinch at the venom saturating my voice. She will have heard it all before in her job. And much worse.

"That's something I will bring focus to in the interview this afternoon. He's a sexual predator and danger to the community alongside the other charges being brought against him. Mr. Young's been on their watch list for years, as you know. I'm confident we will get all the charges against you dropped. Especially given the surrounding circumstances."

She walks over to the table and places her briefcase on top of it, sitting opposite me.

Sophie Havers. Best lawyer in South England. Logan persuaded her to help me out. He met her once when he was set up on a double date with our mate, Drew. But Drew had a better connection with her. Something Drew's been trying and failing to explore since. And looking at her now, all professional and confident, I can tell she isn't a woman who will be talked into doing anything she doesn't want to.

Apparently getting Sophie to agree to take you on as a short-notice client is as hard as finding the fucking Holy Grail. She's known for choosing who she represents on a case-by-case basis without care of the monetary gain at the end. She already gets enough high-profile cases to have herself set up nicely.

Perhaps I'm the charity case. Because despite the estate doing so well, there's no way I could afford her. I gave Logan my budget. I'm not eating into Jasmin's future financial security because of Julian fucking Young. He's already taken enough from her.

"The lab's running the test now. We should have confirmation of paternity within the hour." She takes some paperwork from her briefcase and places it on the table before snapping the lid shut.

Within the hour. Just like that, I'll know for sure. I don't see that it's relevant to Young and the business he's been running, or the fact his ass should be thrown in jail, never to see the light of day again. But Sophie insisted on a test as soon as she arrived and fast-tracked the samples to a private lab.

The acid simmering low in my gut tells me I already know the answer. I don't need a piece of paper to tell me it's true.

"He's your father."

I clench my teeth, a throbbing pain exploding across my forehead and blurring my vision.

Rose looked convinced. She wouldn't have told me something like that if she wasn't certain.

Yet, a small part of me still clings to the shred of hope that she was wrong. That she made a mistake. Because I'm nothing like him. I *can't* be anything like him.

"It must have been a shock finding out. After everything that's happened. I've read your file. About how you came to start working for Young." Sophie fixes her gaze on me.

She knows. She knows it all.

"But I'd like to hear some things from you."

I know where this is headed. She's read my file. But that's facts. Dates and stone-cold facts.

She's asking about things those files don't tell her.

She's asking about how Mom never told me a lot about my biological dad. Only that he left before she could tell him she was pregnant. Adam was my dad as far as I'm concerned. He raised me. I never felt any different to Jasmin in his eyes. He loved us both the same.

Maybe he wouldn't have if he'd known whose blood I have running in my veins.

A rapist's. A criminal's. A blot on society who shouldn't be allowed to taint the air with his breath.

Tension claws its way through my body like a disease as I look back at Sophie.

"What do you want to know?"

There's a knock on the door to my cell. Marcus walks in, carrying a tray of food and drink.

"It doesn't taste as rank as it looks."

I snort as I lean forward with my head bowed and my arms resting on my knees.

He walks in and places the tray down on top of the thin, stained mattress and steps back.

I glance at what looks like cottage pie slopped onto a plate.

"What? No steak and peppercorn sauce?"

Marcus snorts, his easy chuckle that follows sounding strange and out of place within the concrete walls. "Nah, no girlfriend. Doesn't really mix with the job. My mom, though, now she makes a killer chocolate fudge cake."

"And you?" I lift my eyes to meet his, and he folds his arms over his chest, widening his stance a little.

"James Harris. SOCA officer. Undercover for eighteen months."

I nod, pursing my lips. He looks more like a James than a Marcus. And minus the long, greasy hair and accent I'd grown accustomed to, he's like a different guy altogether.

"We were both after him."

"Yeah." James nods in agreement. "We were. And now we've got him. Even if it did go down a little differently. We both got what we wanted."

I shake my head with a supressed laugh that holds no humor. "If you say so."

Julian Young may be unlikely to wriggle his slimy ass out of this one, but there's still what he did to Rose.

The look of fear in her eyes will haunt me to my last breath. She really thought he was going to do it. She thought that she was going to have to look me in the eye whilst that vile scum forced himself onto her. And after, when he'd had his fun, he'd have shot us both.

"I know what he was going to do," James says as though he can read my mind.

"Yeah? You didn't put a fucking bullet in his head though, did you?" I grit out, dragging my hands back through my hair and screwing my eyes shut.

Clear blue eyes. Clear blue eyes that looked into mine as she thought I was about to watch her be...

"I couldn't. I didn't know he was armed at that point. Not until you took his gun and threatened to kill him yourself."

"Maybe I should have." I open my eyes and meet James's with a long exhale. "Thanks. For what you did. I might not have made it. He was going to—"

James presses his lips together and nods. He knows as well as I do that Young's henchman could have easily shot me if James hadn't acted fast and taken him out first.

Rose would have had my brains splattered all over her face.

I put her in so much danger. All because I was too fucking weak to stay away like I should have.

"Listen, I'm going to have a word. See what I can do. We both know that prick's where he deserves, and after everything..." James looks at me with something akin to respect in his eyes. "After all you've done up until this point, I think it'd be wrong for you to have any further action taken against you. And threatening to kill with a weapon only sticks if someone actually heard you threaten to kill." The corners of his lips lift into a small smile. "And it was windy last night, my hearing was compromised. All I saw was a guy who'd already been assaulted himself trying to save a woman in danger."

I nod silently, my mouth in a grim line.

A woman in danger. Placed there because of me.

Rose. *Sunbeam.*

James continues as he walks toward the door, "Although I'm not sure my statement will even be required at this rate. Your lawyer has it in hand. I've never seen the officers in this station move their asses so fast as when she asks them for something. You'll be out of here in no time."

I nod again, my voice thick, as I manage to get out one word. "Thanks."

"Hey, Dax?" I look up and meet his eyes as he stands in the doorway to my cell. "I think this is the most we've spoken in all these months."

I smirk. "All that time you knew who I was. And I thought you were a guy who was even more stupid than he looked and stank of stale sweat and feet. Don't take it personally, but I was there for one reason. And it wasn't to make friends."

James smirks back and holds his hands up. "Hey, I'm not offended. We both had our roles to play. It's all part of the act. Although, it felt fucking good finally getting a haircut this morning."

I meet his eye as he runs his hand around the back of his neck and newly styled hair.

"It's an improvement. But you somehow pulled off the oily look. I had no idea you weren't who you said you were."

"Same to you. If I hadn't been clued in, that is. I could have easily thought you were one of them."

Bile lodges in my throat at his choice of words.

One of them.

James was there. He heard what Rose said. I *am* one of them. It's running in my veins. *His* blood. His tainted, evil, warped—shouldn't-be-allowed-to-exist—blood.

"Mmm," I grunt, the smirk falling off my face.

"Eat up. And you'll be out of here before you know it. Back to that girl of yours. I heard she's already called the station five times for an update in the last hour."

James hovers in the doorway for a moment. Maybe he expects this nugget of information to please me. To bring a genuine smile to my sour face. The comfort that someone is waiting for me, worrying about me. Wanting me home with them.

Wanting me back to watch the sunrise with them.

Someone who I could so easily have lost forever yesterday. All because I was too selfish to stay away until Julian Young was gone.

I wanted to move on with my life. Reset time.

With her.

But I'm still in a nightmare I can never escape. I spent years hating that bastard, dreaming of the day I saw everything taken from him. Only to find I share the same blood with him. It's flowing through my body, giving me life.

Giving me life at the same time as stripping away every reason that I want to live.

My heart hammers as my breathing speeds up, each intake of air becoming shallow as heat flares across the back of my neck. Rage swells in my chest like a rough tide crashing onto the shore and washing up the corpses of fish, caught in old, gnarled nets.

Caught. Trapped. Their freedom a mere memory, lost forever.

James shuts the door. The sound of his boots hitting the tiled floor as he walks down the hallway is drowned out by an almighty *crash*!

Adrenaline courses through me like I'm hooked up to it directly into the vein.

Brown goo slides down the wall of my cell to join the broken plastic food tray and its remnants on the floor.

I was never good enough for her.

And now I never can be.

Chapter 34

Rose

THE SILVER RANGE ROVER glides up the main driveway toward the house. I knew it was coming. It's why I'm standing in the bedroom window of the cottage, looking out.

Watching.

Waiting.

Yet even though I knew to expect it, the slash across my heart at the sight still steals the air from my lungs in a rush, drawing out a sob that I quickly rein back in.

He's back.

I turn, catching sight of the wide-eyed girl. Skin that's pale and lackluster, lips that have forgotten how to smile, eyes that are dull. *Dead.*

I turn away from the giant ornate mirror, its beautiful, gilded bird like a taunting reminder...

Two days.

Two whole days since I last saw Dax.

Two days of him refusing to see me while he was being held in jail.

Logan went. Jasmin went. Even Larry who brought the mirror to the cottage for me went.

The entire fucking world was allowed to visit Dax.

But not me.

I was told by multiple police officers, and by Logan and Jasmin that Dax didn't want me to visit him. He didn't want me to see him in there. Locked up. But as my despair grew, so did the pity in their eyes. They didn't know what to say. How could they? By the second day, he didn't just not want me to see him *in there*, he didn't want to see me—period.

The last few years of my life has been one great big shitshow. But never for one second did I expect Dax to deliver the cherry on top of it.

I sit on the end of the bed, dropping my head into my hands. But memories of Dax making love to me here flood my brain cruelly, so I jump up and head downstairs, reaching the bottom step as there's a knock at the door.

My heart lifts in hope, then promptly drops as I open the door.

"Oh. Hi."

"Well, it's better than some welcomes I get, I suppose."

Logan walks inside, then closes the door behind himself as I wander over to the front window and gaze out. I can make out parts of the top floor of the house through the trees. Dax's bedroom window being one part. But it's too far to see whether he's in there. Whether he's looking out at the cottage.

Is he thinking of me like I'm thinking of him?

Because he's all I've thought about. Ever since that night in the dockyard. Ever since the light dimmed in his eyes when I told him Julian Young was his biological father. Ever since he was ripped away from me.

Gone.

Except I thought I would get him back. Once it was all sorted. Once the police had questioned him and realized it was all a mistake. That Dax is a good person. He was just protecting me. He was never going to shoot Julian.

But the cold bile settling low in my gut as I glance back at Logan's face tells me...

I'm never getting him back.

That Dax Silver is gone. He disappeared that night. Died on the cold floor next to Julian's two men.

"I'm sorry, Rose." Logan shakes his head as I nod mutely and turn back to the window.

I thought being released and having all charges against him dropped would help. I thought coming back to the estate would help.

I *prayed* that coming back home would change whatever it is that's keeping him from seeing me.

I blink my dry, stinging eyes as Logan speaks.

"He said to tell you he's terminating your contract early."

"What?" I whip around and gape at him. He looks as drained as I feel, the burden of having to deliver this news himself evident in the absence of his usual bright eyes and cheeky smile.

This whole situation is sucking the life out of all of us.

"He actually said that?"

Nausea rolls in my stomach, as Logan whispers, "I'm sorry, Rose."

"He's... it's a shock. He's still in shock. Jasmin said he's meeting Alistair later. To talk. He's thinking about that.

And coming home. And..." My shoulders drop as I stare at Logan. "Why is he doing this?"

"I don't know. I wish I did. Nothing makes sense."

I turn back to the window again as Logan walks up behind me, his strong, warm body stopping behind me and bringing a sliver of comfort with it as it evokes a memory.

Dax wrapped me in his arms in this exact spot once. He buried his nose into my hair and inhaled. Breathed me in. Kissed my neck and whispered in my ear. *Infinity.*

The muscles in my back tense as I tear my eyes away from the main house and Dax's bedroom window and spin to face Logan.

"How was he when you dropped him off? Is Jasmin there now? Or is he alone?"

"He's alone, but..." Logan's eye pinch at the corners.

He's too nice to say it. Too nice to tell me not to go there, that Dax still doesn't want to see me. Logan probably thinks I'll cry. But he doesn't know that I don't ever cry.

Dax knows that.

At least the bastard knows I won't be shedding any tears over him.

"Give him some time. He'll get over whatever shit he's got going on inside his head."

"Time. Yeah," I snort.

I appreciate Logan trying to make me feel better, I do. But the fact is, Dax has chosen to shut me out, for whatever reason. And being told to give him time? It's like hearing my family telling me that's all I needed, over and over again. I heard it for months... years... on repeat. But after everything, it wasn't time that helped me.

It was Dax.

He made me feel calm for the first time in years. He taught me to let go. To stop blaming myself. He showed me how to forgive.

And now he's treating me in a way I'm not sure I can ever forgive him for.

He's shutting me out.

"He's terminating your contract early."

"Look. Let me make you a drink," Logan says, his eyes raking over my pinched expression.

I shrug my shoulders. "Sure. Coffee, please."

He places his keys and phone down on the coffee table as he heads down the hallway toward the kitchen.

I take a seat on the sofa as he moves around in the kitchen, fixing us both a drink.

The past two days I've survived on coffee. I couldn't bring myself to eat. Every time my phone beeped, or someone knocked at the door, I thought it was Dax. Or, at least, news about Dax. A message from him. Confirmation that he was allowed visitors and had asked for me.

Something.

Anything.

But all I got was nothing. Nothing followed by more nothing.

Sophie came over when Jasmin and Logan were here. She said she was certain the charges against Dax would be dropped. But she wanted to understand more about the entire situation first.

She confirmed the DNA results. Julian Young is Dax's biological father. Something I already knew, yet still made me want to throw up when I heard her say it. And she also told us that the guy at the dockyard, James, was an undercover cop. He'd been working as part of a team investigating serious and organised crime—specifically Julian Young and his business—for the past eighteen months. Apparently, James knew who Dax really was the entire time. Which makes no sense to me at all. How could an undercover cop allow a civilian with a vigilante revenge motive to get so close to a case like that and do nothing about it for months? But Sophie brushed off my concerns with confidence. Jasmin and Logan seemed happy with her explanation, or lack of one.

Maybe I'm overthinking it. My head's been all over the place.

I pick up Logan's keys, turning them over in my hands for something to do as he continues crashing about in the kitchen. I swear he can't do anything quietly. I'd do anything to hear one of his funny dating app stories right now. Take me back to a time when things seemed normal. When I knew how it felt to laugh.

Before I found out my boyfriend's grandparents anonymously paid off his dad to leave their daughter alone. They may have seen what Julian was capable of back then. But Jessica didn't. Protecting their daughter cost them their relationship with her.

And their relationship with Dax and then Jasmin.

All that time they could have spent together... lost.

Lost because of secrets.

Lost because of lies.

Jasmin's since learned from talking to Alistair that Julian met Al's mom shortly after leaving Jessica. They married and had Alistair within a year. And Alistair's mom came from a wealthy family. Julian used money from them to start his business. The business that's now been seized as part of the criminal investigation against him. Thankfully, Alistair was only ever involved in the legitimate side of things, so the police have cleared him from any involvement. Alistair said Julian always had his eye on the Silver Estate. It's another reason he and Jasmin kept their relationship a secret. Only, Julian knew somehow. He admitted as much in the dockyard. He probably thought it was a brilliant twist of fate in his favor that they fell for one another. He always planned to get the business somehow. Whether that was by getting Dax out of the picture with a jail stabbing, or some new plan for Jasmin, the thought of which makes my skin crawl and blood run cold.

That bastard will stop at nothing for what he wants. I saw it in his eyes that night. I *felt* it in his hands when they were on me, holding my face down against the hood of the car.

I wrap my arms around myself, rubbing my hands up and down my upper arms where goosebumps have formed. He didn't do anything to me. Dax made sure of it. He could have been shot for trying to save me. He could have died in front of my eyes.

And now he can't even bring himself to see me. I wish I knew what was going on in that confusing head of his.

Dax hot-and-cold Silver.

"Here you go." Logan walks in and places the steaming mug in front of me on the table and scoops up his keys that I've placed back down, and his phone.

"You leaving?"

"I can come straight back. I just need to get some things for Dax." He looks at me with guilt-ridden eyes.

"Oh."

Dax could have asked me. It's exactly what I could have done for him. I would have loved it. Picking up some things for him for when he comes home, stocking the fridge with things he likes, getting more fish food for his office.

I would have been excited to do it, knowing that I was about to get him back again.

"It's fine." I force a smile onto my face and stand to walk Logan to the door. "There's no rush. Take as long as you need."

"I'll be an hour, max." Logan steps through the front door.

He looks at me with uncertainty.

"Really. I'll be fine."

He takes in a deep breath, his brow furrowing, before he reaches out and squeezes my upper arm. "Call me if you need anything."

"I will."

He walks to his Range Rover and drives off.

I don't even close the door before I'm striding out through it, my coffee forgotten.

The only fuel I need is the fire that's started burning in my gut from Dax pushing me away. *Canceling my contract.* Who the hell does he think he is? At least have the guts to say it to my face. Whatever he's going through, he can't shut me out. He's not the only one in this.

I curl my fingers around the jagged metal in my palm. Logan won't miss his spare key to Dax's apartment. Not yet anyway.

I've got an hour.

An hour to make Dax speak to me.

It's plenty of time.

Chapter 35

Rose

I FIND HIM ON the roof terrace, standing by the stone railing, staring out over the estate's main driveway. The muscles in his broad shoulders are tense, taut, and solid beneath his black t-shirt. He would have seen me stomping up to the main house. He could have come down to let me in. But he didn't.

He really doesn't want to see me.

My step falters, and some of the raging fire that's burning low in my gut eases in its intensity at the sight of him.

He looks... broken. He's still the same tall tower of dark clothed intensity he's always been. But there's something else there now. It's like something has shifted in the energy around him. He always exuded strength, control... passion. Now the only waves I sense coming off him are impregnated with regret.

Regret over us?

"Dax?" My voice betrays me, pitching unnaturally. I came here prepped for a fight. Ready to scream and shout my hurt and confusion at him for pushing me away for the past two days. But just seeing him again... despite being so hurt and angry over what he's done, all I want to do is run to him and feel his arms wrap around me. Hear his breath as he inhales with his nose pressed to my hair, the way that he does. And feel his lips against my forehead.

"You shouldn't be here, Rose."

Rose. He calls me Rose a lot. But somehow, in this moment, it cuts deep, like a stake through my heart. He could have used Sunbeam. It's the first time I've seen him since the cops took him away... *he should have used Sunbeam.*

"My contract's over, then? Just like that? Were you even going to have the decency to come and tell me why?" My hurt morphs into anger, and I welcome it. Anger is better than this gut-wrenching pain that's threatening to consume me if I let it.

Dax drops his head, inhaling deeply, causing his entire back to widen and fill out. He really is a sight to behold. Dressed entirely in black, his inked forearms solid as he holds onto the guard rail with a fierce grip.

Silence.

"Two *fucking* days, Dax," I hiss at his back. "That's how long I've been waiting to see you. To know that you're all right. And then you send Logan to do your shit for you."

My words hit his back like missiles. But they just seem to roll off as he remains impassive.

"At least look at me, you selfish asshole!"

His head snaps to the side and our eyes connect for the briefest moment, his flashing with something. Then he moves faster than I can blink, strides over and wraps a hand around my neck, his eyes almost black as he glares at me. I blink up at him, licking my lips, hope blossoming in my wrung-out heart.

He's still in there.

My passionate, broken man is still in there some-where. He didn't leave me that night he was taken away. Whatever James said to him that made him stop fighting and get into the squad car, it didn't change the way he feels about me. It's running through his skin into mine, buzzing like static electricity.

"You have no idea who you're talking to," he growls, his eyes raking over my face and pausing on my lips before he rips them away.

"Don't I? You don't think after everything we've talked about and done together that I don't know the real you? That I haven't seen who you really are inside?"

Dax sucks in a breath through his nose, his wild eyes meeting mine once more. "I'm his *son*," he spits out the word like it's poison. "His fucking *blood* runs in my veins. And you want to be near that? You want to be near someone who has the blood in him from a man who was going to rape you over the hood of his car and then probably shoot you like an animal? Throw your body away like it's trash?"

"You're not him." I struggle to speak. Dax's grip is tight on my throat. Tighter than he's ever held me before.

His haunted eyes search mine, then he screws his face up and crushes his lips to mine, kissing me forcefully. I wrap my arms around his neck, kissing him back with desperation for the precious few seconds it lasts.

Then he takes his hand back and wrenches himself from my grip, leaving me gasping as he steps back, away from me.

I rub the tender skin on my neck as I take a deep breath, my lungs burning. "Dax?"

"You need to leave." He takes another step away from me, his face closing off, as he avoids looking into my eyes.

"I'm not leaving. You're being ridiculous. You're nothing like him. You have to know that. Dax?" I step toward him, but he pulls an envelope from the back pocket of his jeans and thrusts it into my hand. "What's this?"

"Your plane ticket. You're going back to New York."

"What? I am not!" The paper burns into my palm as he looks away. I rip it into tiny shreds without even opening it and hurl it at him. It flutters over his t-shirt like confetti. "Fuck you! You can act like a prick all you want. But I am not leaving you."

"It was all fake."

It's not his words that make me freeze on the spot. It's his eyes. It's the way they've finally met mine again, but they're full of... nothing.

Whenever Dax looks at me, even when we first met, there was always something there. Always some fire, some light. Something that told me he felt *something*.

Now there's nothing.

Empty, emotionless dark brown meets heartbroken blue.

"You're lying."

"I'm not. Believe me." His lips curl down and a muscle in his neck twitches, drawing my attention to the tiny, delicate bird on his neck.

"I can't," I croak. "I know you."

"You don't know shit."

I snap my eyes back to his, and the darkness in them has me choking back a sob. He's looking at me like it was all one big act. He's detached. He doesn't even look like Dax anymore.

"I've been lying to everyone for nine months. My own sister didn't even see through it. And you think you can? Some girl who only arrived a few months ago? You don't know me. I wanted one thing... revenge for what he took from me. I wanted to watch Julian Young get locked up, lose a part of his life like I lost mine. It's all I ever wanted. You were just a pretty distraction along for the ride."

I drag in a broken breath, and it's like breathing in jagged shards of glass, each one ripping me apart more. "Don't say that. Don't make out like it meant nothing. Don't lie to me, Dax."

My body swirls with a combination of hurt, anger and pain. I'd rather him be a stone-cold murdering criminal who really was working for Julian Young than lie to me.

I can't take anyone else lying to me.

"Don't lie to me," I repeat, my voice sounding strong, considering the surge of vomit I'm only just managing to keep at bay. "Anything else... *anything*. But don't lie."

Dax screws his eyes shut, a vein in his neck bulging and pulsating.

I take a step toward him, and he opens his eyes and stares at me, regret filling them once again.

Please don't lie.

"It wasn't an act. Don't ruin what we had, don't make out I'm stupid. You might have fooled Young's gang, but you can't fool me. I know you."

I take another step toward him.

I just need to make him understand that I'm here for him. Finding out about Julian was a shock, I get it. He's hurt. I can help him like he helped me.

"You don't, Rose."

"Stop saying that."

Another step.

"I do know you, Dax. You're a good person. You knew someone needed to stop Julian. But you weren't really involved in what he did. You were just getting evidence against him. You never smuggled anything, like the cops said."

"What?" His eyes go round, and I drop the foot I'm about to take another step with back to the floor.

"They asked me loads of questions about New York. About your baggage."

I pause, searching his face for a clue. I've been thinking about it ever since the cops interviewed me. I wondered if there was any truth to it. But then, it just didn't make any sense. Dax isn't a criminal. He was trying to take Julian down. The cops know that now. They let him go free without charge. It was just part of their questioning. They were just doing their job.

"They probably thought if you were guilty of something that I would give you up accidentally if they probed deep enough."

"It's true."

"Exactly. It's how they always play these things. Ask lots of quest—"

"No, Rose. It's true."

Now it's my turn for my eyes to widen as I gape at him. "What is?"

He pauses, his eyes raking over my face and then pinching at the corners as though he's mentally preparing to deliver the kill shot.

"I did use you. I gave you my bags to take because I thought you were less likely to be searched. I told you to smile at the customs guy because I knew he'd be too busy looking at your beautiful face to even consider you might be carrying something you shouldn't."

"No. You..." I snap my head back. "You wouldn't do that."

He watches me as sourness settles in the pit of my stomach and the sound of my own heartbeat racing echoes in my ears.

"I used you to get things into the country illegally. You know I'm not lying now. Look at me." Dax nods slowly as I search his eyes, and I suck in a sharp breath.

He's telling the truth. I can tell. He was lying before about it all being an act with me. I can tell that from his eyes, even if he won't admit it. But this? He's not lying about this.

He lied to me when we went to New York. He used me.

"You said you were going for work, to visit the Andersons in California, and that I should visit my family."

"Sounds a lot better than telling you I needed to move something out of the country, doesn't it?"

I stare at him, my brain firing out explanations one after the other, desperately searching for one that will make this all stop.

None make any sense.

Except one.

That it's the truth.

"You wouldn't put me in danger like that. If I'd been caught with drugs, then I would have been arrested, I could have gone to jail."

He flinches, then recovers himself, his face closing down as he holds my eyes.

"You need to let the sun set on any romantic notions you had of us. Because I'm not that man. I never will be. Go back to New York, Rose." He drops his head and begins to turn away.

"What? Go back and call up Gareth? Tell him I'll go for dinner with him after all?"

I'm shaking with anger, but I don't miss the sudden flex of Dax's jaw as he brings his eyes back to mine.

"Is that what you really want? For me to go back there and be with someone like him? When you're the only one I want?"

The thick muscles in his neck contract, making the bird tattoo on his neck move in a way that makes it look like it's waving with its wing.

Waving goodbye.

"You're free. Do whatever the hell you want. Just do it back in New York." His voice is low, quiet. But each syllable is said with precision. And each one is like a bullet in my chest.

"Don't do this." My eyes sting, and I blink rapidly as he pulls his phone out of his pocket and taps something into it.

My own phone vibrates in my hoodie, and I pull it out and open the email from him. It's a copy of a plane ticket to New York. Just one ticket. With one name on it.

Mine.

He walks past me, his arm brushing mine and forcing a sob from me that I claw back in before it fills the surrounding air on the roof terrace.

"Don't come crawling back to me when you've finished your pity party for one!" I spin and scream at his back as he walks to the stairway door. "Whatever shitty denial you're living in right now is your own fault. I am here, Dax. I am here. For you." My chest heaves as I gasp in air before screaming again. "You don't fucking deserve me right now. But I am here, like you have been for me. But if you walk down those stairs and shut me out, then that's it!"

He stops, his hand wrapped around the door handle.

My heart lifts, and I take a step toward him. Ready to run to him. Because even though this is fucked up, it's Dax. He is Dax. I know him. There has to be a reason he would take drugs to New York. He isn't a criminal. He's good. He has a huge heart. Just like Jasmin told me.

She isn't wrong about her own brother.

I *can't* be wrong about him.

I can't.

He inclines his chin over his shoulder, but not far enough for our eyes to meet.

"You need to forget about me, Sunbeam."

Sunbeam.

"Your flight leaves at nine."

Then he walks through the open door.

I stand in shock for a few minutes, until the sound of an engine roaring into life snaps me from my trance and I rush to the edge of the roof.

Dax's Range Rover tears down the main driveway, leaving me alone on the roof terrace.

I grip the stone railing until my palms sting. The view reaches far across the estate up here. It's almost like being up in the clouds, looking down at everything like this. I used to love being up high. Walking up that hill with Dad. He'd say our troubles were far below us.

But what if the cause of my trouble was up here with me until just a few minutes ago? What if that trouble was the thing that was stopping me from crashing all this time? Holding me up?

And now it's gone.

Chapter 36

Rose

"I'VE MADE YOU A coffee." Mom's voice carries through my bedroom door. "I'll leave it out here."

There's a shuffling, and then her footsteps retreat back downstairs again.

I roll onto my side on my bed. Three days. It's been three days since I had that fight with Dax on his roof terrace. Three days since I ran out of his apartment and tore down the driveway to the cottage. Three days since I yanked my suitcase out from under the bed so hard that it swung into the giant mirror he gave me and smashed it.

Jasmin told me not to worry. That it was just the glass, and it could be replaced.

I found a tiny shard of it that must have gotten caught up in my clothes when I threw them in during my angry, hurt-fueled packing. The jagged edge of it sliced right through the skin of my forearm when I was unpacking back at Mom's house—I can't even call it home anymore. I don't know where I belong now. I didn't even react when the blood started pulsing from the cut. I stood and reveled in the sensation. I welcomed it. Because although it was pain, it wasn't the pain I've felt in my heart since Dax left me alone on that roof. It was a relief to feel a different pain for a change.

"Rose?" Mom calls up the stairs to me as I'm running my fingers over the edge of the thin dressing that's covering the cut. "There's someone here to see you."

The pathetic loser in me jumps up from the bed as my heart lifts.

It could be him.

He could be here to take back what he said. To explain everything. To... Fuck, I don't know what he could say to make any of it better, but just the thought of seeing him is enough to get me to leave my room.

He didn't fight for me. He said we were an illusion. A trick of the light.

But I saw in his eyes he was lying.

Has he come to fight now?

I know I told him once that love was just dopamine. But I stopped believing that a long time ago. Dax made me change my mind about a lot of things.

He changed me.

I rush downstairs and into the kitchen.

But it's not Dax hovering by the table.

"What's she doing here?" I turn to Mom, my pulse rocketing.

"You two need to talk. It's time."

I glare at Mom and then bring my eyes back to Casey, who's looking at me with tears pooling along her lower lids.

"It's so good to see you, Ro."

I clamp my mouth shut, my teeth grinding together.

Breathe, Sunbeam. Breathe.

I shake my head, trying to get his voice out of it. He always knew how to calm me.

Well, fuck you, Dax Silver, because you aren't here now, are you? Where are you when I need you?

I take a deep breath, concentrating on the sound of it passing up through my nose and filling my chest. And I take in the scent of Casey's familiar perfume, the same one she's worn for years. It immediately transports me to my twenty-first birthday with her, singing and dancing all night at the party Mom and Dad threw for me at Vienna's restaurant.

That was such a happy day.

"Why don't you girls go and sit on the porch? It's a beautiful day outside." Mom nods gently at me. "Go on, Rose. You need the fresh air. You haven't left your room since you came home."

I turn back to Casey who's holding her breath, her bottom lip pulled into her mouth as she looks at me.

"Fine. You first," I say to Casey.

I frown at Mom before following Casey out to the front porch. This used to be one of our favorite places to sit together, talking about school and boys, and putting the world to rights.

Back when we were both younger... and naïve. Before lies tore us apart.

She sits in her usual spot on the long wicker sofa, but I slump into the chair, as far away from her as possible instead of sitting next to her like I always used to.

Her shoulders droop and she looks at her hands in her lap. "What's it like being back?"

"Shit," I answer without missing a beat.

Her lips curl down. "I'm sorry about what happened. Your mom told me. It sounded like things were going well last time we spoke. You... sounded happy there." Casey lifts her eyes to mine, and I look away as my heart constricts painfully.

"I was... while it lasted."

"She told me about the police, about that man... Dax's dad... about what he tried to do to you."

I stare out over the front yard as a breeze blows over my arms causing goosebumps to scatter up them. "So everyone knows all about my shit, then? Fuck up of the family like usual."

"Don't say that. She told me because I care about you. I call every day and ask about you. We haven't spoken in weeks. And I know that's my fault, and I..." Her voice cracks. "I am so sorry." Casey drops her head as she wipes the tears from her cheeks.

I wish I could cry like that. I imagine it's a relief, to let it all out. I just have this constant pressure inside that makes me feel like an overinflated balloon that could pop at any moment. It makes my head pound. It makes my chest so tight I struggle to breathe. It makes the very essence of me vibrate like a corked bottle that's been shaken violently.

"I didn't know he was married. I swear. He... he was so nice to me. He made me feel beautiful and intelligent, and worthy of his attention. He made me feel alive." Casey looks at me, her eyes still full of tears. "I loved him. At least, I loved who I thought he was for those few months. Before the lies all unraveled."

I swallow as the hard lump in my throat throbs force-fully. I remember all those months when Casey would have been seeing the man who knocked Brett down. I wasn't there for her. I was too busy dealing with my own shit to notice that my best friend needed me. She was in love, and I had no idea.

"I'm sorry I was a shit friend." The words fall from my lips, causing Casey's eyes to pop wide. I mean them, every one, despite how angry I've been with her. "What-ever has happened since, it doesn't change the fact that I should have been there for you, and I wasn't."

"You had your own stuff going on with Gareth, I get it. And... I don't know. I think deep down, I knew something wasn't right from the beginning. Otherwise, I would have told you about him. The way you told me about Dax."

I snort. "Yeah. I wouldn't shut up about him on some of our calls."

Casey sniffs and then giggles. "I can't blame you. He's one of those pretty bad boys. And older. And your boss. It's like the law that we should have spoken about him as much as we did."

A sad smile creeps over my face as I pull my legs up underneath me and curl into the chair. "Yeah, I guess."

I glance over at her again. She's relaxed a little and her tears have finally stopped. The two of us sit in silence for a few minutes, and we wave as a neighbor passes, walking their dog.

"When did you find out he was married?"

Casey tenses. "The day that Brett..." She sighs, and for a moment, I worry that her tears will start again. "I found out that morning. We had a huge fight and I told him his wife deserved to know. Then I left. I don't know if I would have told her or not. My head was a mess. I just needed to get away from him, to let it sink in. But he had gotten it into his head that I was on my way to see her. To ruin his life. But it was him who ended up ruining everyone else's that day instead. Because of me."

"No. Not because of you." I take in a deep breath. There are so many things I wanted to say to Casey. So many hurt-filled words I wanted to launch at her. To make her feel as empty and broken as I do. But looking at her now, I can see... She already is. We're both as empty as each other.

"I don't blame you for Brett's accident."

I've been such a bitch. If time with Dax taught me any-thing, it's that forgiveness is one of the strongest things you can give yourself. And one of the most meaningful things you can give to someone else. Being angry at Casey was a deeper reflection of the anger and blame I still held against myself. And it's only sitting here with her now that it's starting to make sense.

"I don't blame you, Case. It wasn't your fault. And it wasn't mine." I have to stop and take a breath. It's the first time I've said those words out loud.

It wasn't my fault.

"But what hurt me is that you lied about it. I would have still felt the way I did about Brett's accident. I would still have blamed myself all these years. But you were there for me, by my side all that time, knowing something about it that I didn't. That's what hurts. That you didn't trust me enough to tell me." I look over and into her eyes. They're shining with emotion.

"I do trust you. I just didn't know how to tell you without causing you any more hurt. Seeing what your family went through was awful. Seeing what you went through, I'd never wish that on anyone. I was so helpless."

Her voice cracks, and I turn away.

"You were the one person who kept me functioning," I confess, leaning my head back against the back of the chair and gazing up at the clouds, unable to look at her until I've gotten everything out. "I just wish you'd told me. You must have been hurting too, finding out that about him."

"Yeah." Casey's voice is small. "Yeah, I was. But mostly I was angry at him for making me fall in love with a lie."

Tension spreads through my shoulders as I allow her words to sink in. We've both been burned by love and lies.

"You don't think any of it was real? The way he was with you?" I stare at a cloud that's shaped like a balloon, willing it to break apart so I don't have to keep staring at it. I could look away, only some twisted part of me wants to look. To remember Dax. To believe that it wasn't all a lie like he wants me to think.

"You're Rose Jacobs. The girl who came from New York and crashed into my world like a meteor. You can do anything. You can find every silver lining, in every cloud, in a whole world of stormy skies. And you'll be stronger for it. You're a warrior. You show up day after day, always hunting for that beauty. For that magic. But it's in you. It's always been in you."

Those are the words he said to me in the balloon that day. When we were high up in the clouds together. That wasn't fake. No matter what Dax wants me to believe, I know none of it was fake.

Which means he *is* a liar.

I swallow as I squint at the sky.

"I mean, yes. Honestly, I do think it was real at the time for him," Casey says. "But none of that matters now. It was over the minute I found out. And things are going pretty good with the new guy I'm seeing. And I've met his family, so there's no secret wives he's keeping hidden."

"Thank fuck for that."

Casey laughs quietly. "Yeah, thank fuck."

I watch the balloon cloud until it's moved out of sight. "Dax was lying to me too. He didn't tell me what he was doing every night. He didn't tell me he was on this revenge trip to catch Julian and get him arrested."

Casey was a great listener, ever since we were kids. She would let me get it all out without interrupting. She knows everything there is to know about me. My best friend. *God, I've missed her these past weeks.* Being in England it was easier to ignore the gaping hole her absence left inside me. But it's not that easy now I'm back here.

I don't want to ignore it anymore. I want to fill it. I want that hole to be gone. Because I'm so full of holes that any more and there'll be nothing left holding me together at all.

"I get why Dax didn't tell me. He probably thought I was safer not knowing," I continue.

"Yeah, you'd have followed him and insisted on help-ing."

Casey and I look at each other, the corners of both of our lips lifting at the same time.

"Yeah. I would have," I snort. "But before I left, he tried telling me that everything was fake. That none of it was real. That's what hurts. That's why when I think about him, I want to scream until the sky rips open. He's trying to make out that everything I felt for him couldn't be real, because it was all fake for him."

"It's like he's invalidating your feelings by pretending he never had any."

"Exactly." *She gets it. Best friends always do.* "And I... I want to smack him in the jaw, and pound my fists against his heart, the way he's done to mine. He knows how I feel about lying. But he's still chosen to do it. I think it would hurt less if he really had never felt anything toward me. But then I think, surely if his feelings were real, then he wouldn't be able to do this either. He wouldn't be able to hurt me like this. Nothing makes sense anymore."

Casey shuffles along the sofa so she's closer to me, then reaches out and curls her fingers through mine. She stills as I stare at our entwined hands.

Then I squeeze hers gently.

"I keep thinking how my family told me I needed time. So they sent me there. And now I've come running back again. More fucked up than when I left."

"You've never been fucked up, Ro. It's just a fucked-up situation."

I hold Casey's eyes and smile gratefully. Her eyes shine, and she stands, pulling me to my feet. Then she flings her arms around me.

And there isn't even the tiniest measure of time that I don't consider hugging her back.

I hold her like I always have through all the years of our friendship. Because I meant what I burned on that paper at those bonfires with Dax.

Forgiveness. Blame.

It's time I start living like I intended to when I burned those two words. Dax may not be a part of my life anymore. But I don't have to lose everyone I care about. Not if I can live my life like I should have been doing for the past few years.

"Thank you for talking to me again. I've missed you," Casey says.

"No more lies," I say, hugging her harder.

"None, I swear."

"Ever."

"From sandbox to casket," she whispers.

I squeeze my eyes shut as gratitude that she's here flows through every cell in my body. I haven't admitted everything to Mom, Brett, and Harley. I blamed my mood on jetlag. But they're not stupid. They saw how Dax and I were together. But I still haven't spoken about it with them. I haven't told them just how much my heart weighs me down with every single movement I try to make. They don't know just how much Dax meant to me.

They don't know that I was willing to trade my life for his that night, had Julian given me the choice.

I would have done it in a heartbeat.

I screw my eyes up more until they sting and grip on to Casey. She didn't give up on me. She kept trying. Because friendship is worth fighting for.

And I need my best friend more than ever right now.

I open my eyes and look at the sky behind her. "Yeah," I whisper. "Sandbox to casket."

Casey moves back from her hug and smiles at me, then her eyes land on my skin in my off-shoulder hoodie. "What's that?"

"Oh." I twist my head, but I never can see it from this angle. "It's a tattoo. Dax did it. I'm getting it covered over with something else. I already made the appointment."

If I had spoken to Casey, returned her texts and calls, then she'd know about the tattoo. It's exactly the type of thing I would have called her about straight away.

I dust my fingers over my shoulder, and she steps closer, rising onto her toes to take a better look.

"Why? It's beautiful."

"It is. But I don't want the word *Silver* on me. It just makes me think of him." I tug at my top. I don't know why I chose an off-the-shoulder one. I'm going to make sure it's covered everyday now until my appointment to get it fixed. The idea of having a permanent reminder of him on my skin makes me want to throw up. And so does the fear that even if I cover it up, it won't be enough to erase him. He's kissed every inch of my body. He's made love to me all night. He's consumed every part of me.

No matter what I do, a part of me will always belong to Dax Silver.

"Huh? It doesn't say silver. Turn around." Casey spins me so she can look at it from behind me. "Oh, it's one of those ambigram ones. Oh, they're clever."

"Ambi what?"

She turns me again. "You know. A word that reads one thing one way up, and something else the other way up."

I pull at my shoulder again, craning my neck uselessly. "What does it say?"

"This way." Casey spins me again. "It says Silver. But this way." She makes me bend so she can look over the top of my shoulder again. "This way, it says Rose."

"Rose? Are you sure?" I yank my phone from the hoodie pocket and thrust it into her hand. "Show me. Take a picture from there."

My phone clicks as she snaps an image over my shoulder and hands it to me. On the screen is my delicate black cloud tattoo. But in the center, in intricate, scripted font is the word *Rose*.

"How is that possible?"

"He must have known what he was doing. They're not easy to design. I bet it took him ages."

I stare at the phone screen. It did take Dax hours to do. But that was when he was using the needle. How long had he thought about the design before that?

"You are the silver lining. It's always been you. Look at this if you ever need reminding."

He even told me before he did it. How can I not have seen this until now? He was trying to tell me something, the same thing he was always trying to tell me.

I am my own silver lining.

My throat thickens as I blink rapidly. How could he do this? How could he be so fucking amazing and beautiful... and *him?* How could he have been everything I ever wanted and needed?

And then he pushed me away like it all meant nothing.

He told me he just needed two more days. Two more days and then our future would begin. He begged me for that time. Two days later was when I went to the dockyard and found out he'd been working to bring Julian down. It was all meant to be over that night. But then something changed. Was it me telling him Julian was his father? Am I the reason he shut me out?

But if that's true, I would make the same choice again. I couldn't live with myself knowing that and lying to him. Even if it might be the reason, he's now writing our time off together to history.

I click out of the picture and my screensaver shines back at me. The one he put on my phone. *His neck. The bird tattoo.* I screw my eyes shut at the sight of it and drop my phone onto the chair cushion.

I might have burned the word forgiveness and be trying to live by it now.

But the jagged grief tearing open my heart right now isn't something that will be easy to forgive. And that's if he was even here trying.

Which he isn't.

You're a bastard, Dax Silver.

You let me fall in love with you and then you slashed the ties that held me to you. You let the wind carry me away after you used me for what you needed.

Maybe that was his plan all along. Use me to smuggle things. Keep me at a distance. Even though I know from his actions, he didn't manage it. His feelings were real, I have to believe that. But despite them, he kept saying he was no good for me. He told me that over and over.

I should have listened.

Because we both fell too hard and too deep.

And whatever rises must come down.

But we didn't just come down.

We crashed.

Chapter 37

Dax

"She said Brett's still trying to work his magic on his physical therapist. He's persistent. Kind of reminds me of Logan and his obsession with that dating app," Jasmin chirps as she flits around my office, straightening cushions and moving files.

She's been doing this every day for the past week since Rose left. Coming in and harping on about what the two of them have been texting to one another and talking about on their phone calls.

Each word is like a dagger to my chest. Knowing she's out there and not where she should be. Where I wish she was.

Next to me. In my arms. In my bed. Buried so deep, just like she is in my heart.

"And then her sister, Harley, she's in full wedding planning mode. Apparently marrying the Mayor of New York is big news. Rose said Harley has journalists following her about to all the planning appointments asking about colors and seating plans. Rose is maid of honor. She's going to look amazing. Her dress is silver."

Silver.

I curl my hands into fists on the arms of my chair as I stare out of the window and down the driveway to the estate's main gates.

She isn't coming through those gates again. Not today. Maybe not ever.

She'll never forgive me for what I've done. I wouldn't if I was her.

"I told her Julian hasn't spoken much when he's been questioned and that he's been denied bail." Jasmin sneers his name in disgust as she walks around the front of my chair and positions herself in front of the window, blocking my view. She crosses her arms and arches a brow. "Aren't you going to ask how she sounded?"

A muscle in my jaw ticks. "How did she sound?"

Jasmin narrows her eyes at me, then lets out a sigh. "As miserable as you. For God's sake, Dax, what the hell are you doing?"

And there it is. My little sister's ball-busting fire she's always had. I may have been her guardian since she was young. But she's always been the one who has no problem dishing out the tough love.

"What's needed," I grunt.

Her eyes widen as she throws her arms wide. "What's needed for who? I don't get it. I've always known you, Dax. But right now, I can't even begin to understand what's going on in your head. Is this because of him?"

She means Julian. And the fact that he's my father. A fact that I've gone over and over in my head, and it still rips at my gut every time like I'm hearing it for the first time again.

His blood. I share his blood.

"Because you know that means nothing. You never cared who your biological dad was before. Don't start now. You're nothing like him and you know it. Dad brought us up. Mom and Dad. And they did a great job."

Jasmin looks at me with glassy eyes. No matter how many years pass, she always gets sad talking about losing them. I know she's right. But the rage that's burned through me since Rose told me is still there. It's lying low in my gut, threatening to erupt spontaneously.

How can I be related to him?

But that's not why I've been a moody bastard the past week. I mean, fuck, yes, it is to an extent. But there's more. More that Jasmin doesn't know yet. More that Rose doesn't know.

And until Julian's men are all rounded up, I can't tell them. James whispered those words to me that night. About how we were being watched. How he didn't know who to trust. That there might be a rat.

I had to let them arrest me. And I had to let them take Rose away. She was safer far away from me.

She still is.

Because until everyone who has a part in Julian's operation is found, she's at risk. He paid a guy to try and shank me in prison. All to get the estate. If he knew Rose was still around here, he would try and find a way to get to me, using her again.

The image of her face as he held her down against the hood of the car comes into focus in my head. I will never be able to unsee it as long as I live.

He will pay for this. Shared blood or not. Knowing how he left Mom for money only makes me hate him more. I wondered as a kid sometimes what my real dad was like.

Some things are better left unanswered.

"Look," Jasmin continues, fixing her gaze on me. "You looked after me when we lost Mom and Dad. You built up a business. You survived prison. You survived a stabbing. You're capable of anything, Dax. You know that."

I look at her and pride swells in my chest. I'm so fucking impressed by the person she's become. But she's still my sister. And she could still be in danger too. It's why she has a police protection detail following her in secret. She'd hate the idea, which is why I didn't tell her. But Alistair knows.

My brother.

I'm still getting used to that shit-bomb too. I have a *brother.* And the day I got released, I met him properly, face-to-face. Jasmin sat like a peacekeeper the entire time, probably worried I would jump him for being Julian's son. But if I wanted to hurt his own flesh and blood, then I could just watch in the mirror as I slit my own throat.

He actually surprised me by how much disdain he seems to have for his own father. And how much he really does care for Jasmin. We both agreed on one thing, at least. And that's that Jasmin must be safe. Which is why he called me privately afterward and we set up the protection for her.

He cares about her. And the rest... time will tell how our relationship pans out, I guess.

But out of all my relationships, it's not the one I'm fucking up the most.

No clues needed for which one that is.

"Do you want her back?" Jasmin walks over and crouches in front of me so she can look into my eyes. "Dax? Do you want Rose back?"

"She'd never forgive me." I hang my head, tearing my eyes away from hers. She sees a good man when she looks at me. And it's more than I can handle because I'm far from it.

"That's not what I asked." She tilts my chin up so my eyes meet hers. "You have to try. Your heart's too big to be wasted."

As if reading my mind, her brows pinch, before softening, and a smile dusts itself over her lips. "She doesn't love you for your blood. It's your heart. Your soul. The way you make her feel."

I stare back at her, the weight of regret pulling on me with such force that it's like I'm sinking into the ground, about to be swallowed up entirely. "Even if I could go to her, which I can't... Even if I could... Would you forgive me? If you were her, and I admitted I'd lied to you and then I'd told you to go, would you forgive me?"

Jasmin searches my eyes, her shoulders dropping as she smiles sadly. "No. I can't say that I would."

"At least you're honest. Which is more than I've been," I snort as she wraps her arms around my neck and holds me.

"But I'd like that you tried," she whispers. "It would mean something to me that you tried. I've watched you look after me all these years, Dax. It's time you lived for you. Don't waste any more days wondering what could happen. Don't trap yourself in the what-ifs."

I let my eyes fall closed as she strokes my back.

I don't want to be trapped any more than she wants me to be. But freedom has never seemed like something meant for me.

I needed Rose to leave to keep her safe. She isn't safe near me. Not yet. Not until this last thing is done. And it could take months until the last guy is found. The rat. Ironic really, considering what I am. And I have to tell Rose the whole truth. She deserves that. Even if that's all I can do, I owe her that. But I'm still not in control of when I can tell her.

I'm never in fucking control.

James said it'll take time.

It always takes fucking time. Time I'm fed up with wasting. Time I'm never in control of.

I want to be in control of my future.

And I pray to God Rose will be a part of it.

I always used to say to her, *what am I going to do with you, Sunbeam?* But I was wrong, because there's no doubt in my mind since she left that I should have been asking a different question.

I should have been asking, what the fuck am I going to do *without* you, Sunbeam?

Because I have absolutely no fucking idea.

All I know is that time has no place for me without her.

Without her, I'm nothing.

Chapter 38

Rose

"IT'S FOR YOU," BRETT calls, wheeling backward from the front door with a brown box from the mailman resting on his thighs.

He turns, and I stare at the box as he approaches me in his wheelchair.

"It's not going to bite. Or maybe it will." He moves one thigh and makes the box jerk.

"Idiot," I snap as I jump and grab the box.

His laugh trails behind him as he disappears into the family room. He's moved into our garage now. Dad started converting it for him after the accident, but progress slowed after Dad passed away. In the end, Harley and Reed helped Mom, Brett, and I to get it finished. But Brett's still waiting for his new obnoxiously large TV to be delivered. So until then, I have the delight of my older, annoying brother spending more time in the main house. And he's grown more irritating since I left for England. His new physical therapist, Lena, has been helping him, and he's made amazing progress. He can lift each thigh now. He's still got a long way to go to walk again; if he ever will. But his regained movement

447

is making it possible for him to play new tricks on me. And to laugh like an idiot when I fall for them.

I carry the box up to my room. It's light. I bet there's nothing in it. It's probably Brett's idea of another joke. Send me an empty box. But he's gone off to watch TV. If it were from him, he would probably want to watch my reaction as I open it.

I grab some scissors and score through the tape holding the lid of the box down, before lifting it off.

I yank my head back before I'm hit in the face by the pale blue thing that floats out. It heads straight for the ceiling of my bedroom, settling there with a gentle *bob*.

A balloon? What the hell?

Confusion threads its way through me as I reach for the long silver ribbon trailing from it. Pinned to the end is a photograph. I'd recognize the stone railing visible in the bottom of the image anywhere.

It's been taken from Dax's roof terrace.

I turn the photo over and the writing on the back steals the air from my lungs in one giant whoosh, like the popping of a balloon, causing my chest to cave in as I lean over and grip the image in both hands.

Sunrise number one without you. I'm so sorry I lied to you, Rose. It's the biggest regret of my life. Everything I felt for you. Everything I told you. It was real. But I can't be the man you deserve right now. I can't keep you safe.

I can explain what was in the bag in NYC. But not yet. I hope when the day comes, you'll let me try. Until then, know that I will be thinking of you. Every day. Every minute. Every second. For infinity.

He hasn't signed his name. But I know it's from him. Without a doubt. It's in his handwriting. I turn it back over. The date stamp is from one week ago.

The morning after I left.

He took this on that first day. The morning after I flew back to New York. I had probably only just gotten off the plane when he was taking it.

The pink and orange hues look spectacular, lighting up the Silver Estate. The sight of it makes my stomach cramp painfully. It's only been a few weeks since I woke up by the campfire in Dax's arms. After he told me he promised me every infinity.

After I promised him every sunrise.

It's a promise I would have kept if he hadn't pushed me away. Now we're both facing each one alone.

I let go of the photograph, and it hangs, suspended mid-air, twirling in taunting circles at the end of the silver ribbon.

I knew his feelings were real. They had to be. He risked his life to get to me when Julian had ahold of me. He could have been killed right in front of my eyes. That's not the actions of a man who feels nothing for the person he's trying to protect. But he still lied when we flew to New York. He was hiding something from me. What couldn't he tell me? What can he still not tell me?

He says he can explain. But he's right to hope I will let him try. Because with each day that passes, the dull ache that's in my gut grows.

Time makes the heart grow fonder, supposedly. But all I feel is mine closing him out more and more.

What choice do I have? I ping-pong between being so mad at him I want to call him up just to scream at him, to also knowing that if I did, the sound of his voice could be the final thing to break me.

And I've spent so many years being broken.

It's time to leave it in the past.

Four weeks later

"This guy's turning into a simp for you, Sis."

"Shut up, Brett," Harley scolds as she carries in the box from the porch and walks past him to hand it to me. "Aren't you going to open it?" she asks when I put it down on the kitchen table and go back to making my sandwich.

"Don't need to. I know what's in it."

"The question is, will this be white or blue?" Brett grins, waggling his eyebrows.

"For someone who's supposedly intelligent, you're a real dork, you know that?" Harley tuts as she starts to open the box.

"He's all excited like a puppy because Lena's back from her vacation." I stick my tongue out at Brett. He's been a nightmare these last two weeks while Lena's been away. He had a stand-in therapist while she was gone, and I swear I've never heard him complain so much. The poor guy who had to work with him sure had his work cut out.

"She didn't decide to stay away, then? Escape while she could."

"Ha, the fuck, ha," Brett says to Harley as she lifts the lid off the box.

A single white balloon floats out until it reaches the ceiling. I glance at it and then go back to spreading jelly on my bread.

"For infinity," Harley hums.

She's holding the photograph on the end of the silver ribbon between her fingertips with a museful smile on her face.

"He's romantic, I'll give him that. Makes me think of Reed singing to me."

"Oh, God," Brett groans, but Harley ignores him. She knows he approves of Reed. Everyone does. My family loves him. They welcomed him the second she brought him home to meet everyone.

The way they did with Dax.

I cough, attempting to dislodge the lump. I've been back from England for over a month, and the damn thing still isn't budging. I'm going to have to start charging it rent for taking permanent residence.

I spin, sandwich in hand, and walk across the kitchen toward the door.

"Where are you going?" Harley asks.

"Out with Case," I reply through a mouthful of peanut butter and jelly sandwich. "We're going to the mall and then the movies."

Harley looks at me and nods happily. Casey's been amazing since I came back. We've spent hours talking. About everything. Even her new boyfriend, Josh. Everything that happened with Dax. I told her that Jasmin said he's been going to therapy to talk about finding out Julian is his biological father. And that Sophie said Julian isn't getting off. She's sure of it. She says they have enough to put him away for years.

But despite all that, Dax still hasn't come.

He hasn't come to explain, like he said he would in that first note. All I've gotten are balloons. Hot air when all I want is the truth.

Harley stops me before I pass her. "Don't forget this."

"Thanks," I mutter, taking the silver ribbon from her.

I take it to my room, letting go of the ribbon as I enter. It floats up to join its friends, which have covered half of my ceiling. It's like walking into an over-the-top kid's birthday party. I have to fight my way through the hanging silver ribbons to make it in and out of my bed now.

I scoop my purse up from the floor and make the mistake of looking up. I try not to do this. Because I know what he's doing now. And the sight of it still makes my heart stall as much as the first time I understood.

There are more blue balloons than white.

It's a sky.

A bright blue sky with white clouds.

Dax Silver is turning the ceiling of my bedroom into my very own cloudy sky, like that day in the hot air balloon with him. And he's doing it with balloons.

Clever bastard.

But a fancy display doesn't mean shit. Not when he hasn't tried to call me once since I left. Not a single text.

Nothing.

He's just continued to send these balloons. Day after day. Each with a new photograph numbered with the sunrise we've been apart. Each with a note on the back, always ending with the same words.

I weave my way through the silver strands, stopping at today's on my way out. Curiosity gets the better of me, and I lift the attached photograph to have a closer look.

Sunrise number thirty without you. I feel closer to you here. The sheets still smelled like you, vanilla and petals. And that may have faded now, but my thoughts of you never have. Know that I am thinking of you. Every day. Every minute. Every second. For infinity.

I turn it, and the bright colors leap from the image. He must be lying in my old bed at the cottage, because it's taken from a distance, looking out through the open window. In the corner of the photograph is the edge of his mom's mirror with its beautifully intricate frame.

The glass is fixed.

It's brand-new and shining, like nothing ever happened.

I drop the photo, allowing it to flutter down and join the others.

If only people were as easily fixed.

Chapter 39

Rose

THE BALLOONS KEEP COMING.

He could have gotten bored by now.

Ninety days.

Ninety days. Some days blue. Some days white. Every day a sunrise photograph.

But still not a word spoken.

"This is ridiculous," I mutter, parting the silver ribbons with my arms like I'm swimming so that I can get to my bedroom door.

Ridiculous, yet I've kept every single one. I've not tied them into bundles or cut their ribbons shorter. I've left them like a sky above me. Just like he planned. Because a pathetic part of me—my heart—won't let me do anything else with them. Not when looking at them tells me he's thinking about me too.

Because I still think about him.

All. The. Time.

I can't escape it. It hasn't gotten less frequent with each passing day. In fact, I'd say it's gotten worse. When I first came home, emotional exhaustion from all that happened, combined with jet lag, meant that I slept, albeit at odd times. But now, just getting to sleep at all is a struggle. Memories of him, of us, play on a never-ending loop in my head.

Bonfires, sunrises, tattoos, smiles, laughs... kisses... deep brown eyes...

Dax Silver has fucked up my head so much it no longer feels like my own.

And it just confirms to me that I was never in love with Gareth all those years ago. Because all I felt after we broke up was hurt and humiliation. But since being parted from Dax, I also feel an indescribable loss. Loss for what could have been. And I know that he could do anything, literally anything to me, however awful, and a part of me would still feel like it has died without him. A part of me would still want to forgive him and be with him.

Because everything makes more sense with him around.

I feel like me; the me I'm supposed to be.

But he's not here asking for forgiveness. So I'll never know which part of me would win. That part, or the part that curses his name every time another balloon arrives.

"Rose?" Harley calls as she walks up the stairs toward me. She's come to meet me so we can go to Manhattan today for another wedding dress fitting.

"Hey." My stomach sinks as she appears, holding another brown box.

"Oh, wow." She looks behind me into my room. "They've taken over."

I shrug. She's right. The ceiling of my bedroom is no longer visible.

I take the box from her to leave on my bed until later, but the sound of something scraping around inside it takes me by surprise.

"I know. I noticed it making that noise. What do you think is in it?" Harley looks at the box as I put it down on the floor.

"I don't know," I mumble, grabbing some scissors. "Maybe some firewood for me to start a bonfire with and burn all the photographs he's sent me."

"Rose!" Harley's eyes pop wide. She's such a romantic. If I wasn't joking, then I know she would save every photo and refuse to let me have them. She still likes Dax, I can tell. She still hopes things will work out. But any hope I had has slipped further away with each day.

I remove the lid of the box and a balloon floats out like usual. But this time it stops a little outside the box, weighted down by the photograph, and a key tied to the ribbon.

"It's silver," Harley gasps, looking at the balloon.

I snap my eyes away from the key and to the balloon as Harley pokes it with a finger. The whole thing shimmers, and I squint my eyes to study it.

It's full of silver glitter.

"Why's it different?"

"I don't know." I look at Harley and then at the photograph of another sunrise.

Sunrise number ninety without you. I've watched them all. And soon I'll have watched more pass by without you than I spent with you. I want to explain. I want you to understand why I wasn't honest with you about New York. It's time you knew everything... because

I've been missing you. Every day. Every minute. Every second. For infinity. You are everything to me, Sunbeam.

A vibration rips through me, causing my fingers to shake. I drop the photograph back into the box and there's a dull thud as the key hits the cardboard base.

Sunbeam.

It's the first time he's called me it since I left.

"It's got a tag," Harley says as she fishes the key out of the box and detaches it from the ribbon. The balloon flies up to the ceiling without the added weight and nestles itself between two white ones.

A silver lining in a cloud.

He sent me a silver lining.

"You bastard," I whisper, my eyes glued to the glittering silver contents of the balloon. "You complicated, selfish... *beautiful* bastard."

"You okay?" Harley wraps an arm around my shoulders, and instead of tensing, I sink into her and squeeze my eyes shut. But even the backs of my eyelids are shimmering like fucking silver particles.

Why is he doing this? It's been three months. And now he's decided it's convenient for him to finally tell me the truth? Send some cryptic message and a key like this is a treasure hunt and not my life.

Not my actual life. And my actual heart. And my actual feelings.

"We can go there. I'll come with you."

I open my eyes and look into Harley's kind ones. She's holding up the key and note. It's the name of a bank with a safety deposit box number on it.

"Sure," I sniff, straightening my shoulders. "It's near the dress fitting place, isn't it?" I look at the bank's address on the note. "We can go after your appointment if we have time."

I don't care if we can't fit it in. He's made me wait this long. I'm not going to trip over myself to do as he wants. I'm not going to act like I care. Like him pushing me away isn't the worst thing anyone has ever done to me.

I wipe underneath my stinging eyes, even though my cheeks are dry, and take in a ragged breath.

Harley's arm tightens subtly around me. "You know, I think we have time before the appointment, if that's okay with you? It'll actually help me out. I needed to go there anyway."

"You don't use that bank."

I know this because I've seen all the forms at Harley and Reed's house that she has ready to complete with her new married name to get their accounts changed.

"We're thinking of moving some money around. It's one of the ones I wanted to look into," she insists, unable to meet my eyes as she pretends. She just wants me to go there. To see what Dax is up to.

"Fine, thanks." Sourness creeps over my tongue. I would have happily stalled going there. Avoided it for as long as possible.

Because I know that silver balloon is the last.

Dax isn't sending any more.

He taught me how to forgive myself. But I don't know if he taught me how to forgive him for what he's done.

Once I find out the truth there's no going back in time.

The bank is busy. We have to wait to be directed to the correct person who has access to the private safety deposit boxes. With each passing minute, the back of my neck grows hotter, and the likelihood of me throwing up all over the shiny tiled floor increases tenfold.

But once the serious looking bank clerk arrives and leads us to a private viewing room, I'm focused. I can just look in the box. See Dax's excuse and leave.

And that's it. I don't have to do anything else. I don't have to process what's in that box today. I can store it away until I'm ready.

I can hold myself together.

We take a seat at the long table and wait. The clerk returns with a long silver box, and I snort internally.

It would be silver.

"You have the other key," he says as he uses his key to open one of the two locks on the front of the long box. "So whenever you are ready, you can open the box. There's a bell on the wall." He points to a button by the door. "You can call once you are finished. Please, take all the time you need."

"Thank you." Harley smiles brightly at him.

"Thank you," I say, my eyes trained on the box.

He closes the door behind him as he leaves, and we sit in silence as I continue to stare at the box.

Harley places her hand over my trembling one. "Do you need me to?"

"No, no. I've got it."

It takes me three attempts to get the key inside the lock. But with a deep breath, I manage to slide it in and turn it.

The contents are ordinary. I half expected a balloon to float out. But it's just a couple of envelopes and a memory stick.

I take the first envelope out and open it. It's copies of accounts for Julian's business, some photographs of him looking shady with some other guys, and lots of different shipping container details and codes.

The deepening of my scowl makes my jaw ache.

Ninety days... for this?

I know Julian was running his own illegal drugs import business. The police knew. Alistair knew. None of this is news to anyone. It's evidence that the police must have themselves.

I open the other envelope and slide the contents out onto the table. Harley gasps as she sees a piece of paper with my face on. It's dark and I'm looking over my shoulder by the main gates of the estate. A cold dread sends goosebumps scattering up my spine as the hairs on the back of my arms stand up.

It's the night I got separated from Jasmin and Logan when the estate had a work's night out. The night Dax stormed down to let me in and made me promise never to be out alone at night again.

I thought he was overreacting.

The back of my neck burns as I lift the paper and read the accompanying text. The photo is part of an email chain that's been printed out with instructions to find out 'who the girl is'.

Julian was watching me all that time.

There are more photos. Me out in town, drinking in the bar alone after finding out about Casey. They must have been taken before Dax arrived. There's even a grainy image of me having a lap dance at the club, while Dax watches me.

There is image after image. All of me.

And beneath them all, a passport.

"Dawn East?" Harley's brow wrinkles in confusion as she holds it open.

It's my picture.

"Dawn for the sunrise, rising in the east," I murmur as I frown at the name. "He got me a fake passport."

"And an escape plan by the looks of it." Harley holds up a card of a private plane company with a name of who to ask for should I call it.

"I don't understand." Dizziness makes my head swirl.

"There's so much evidence here," Harley says as she sifts through the documents. "It's like he was building up an insurance policy in case the police's investigation didn't work."

I snort. "Sounds about right. Dax didn't trust the police. Not since Julian pulled strings at the trial and got him sentenced more harshly. And then someone was paid to stab him in jail."

She continues reading. "And the documents for you. He thought you were in danger. Oh, God, Rose." She drops the paper on the table and covers her mouth with her hands. "Do you think you still could be? But Julian is in jail. So it's over, right?"

My heart stalls. "No... I'm definitely not." I take a deep breath. "His note wasn't a warning. The only reason he would have me come here and see all this, if it wasn't because he thought I needed to use it, is if he knows the threat has gone. That has to be it. It's been months. He wouldn't have waited all this time to show me this otherwise. He's trying to explain. But it still makes no sense."

"What shall we do with it?" Harley lifts another piece of paper and scans the details of the overseas bank account that's been set up in the name Dawn East. The amount deposited in it makes my eyes water.

"We put it back in and we walk out of here," I say, my voice coming out calmer than I expect. "I don't need it. I'm not going anywhere. And the only one who can explain what it all really means is Dax."

"You're sure?"

I gather up the contents of the box and place it all back inside, closing the passport and placing it on the top.

"I'm sure. When I last spoke to Jasmin, she said Julian wasn't getting bail. He's miles away, back in England. Just like Dax. I'll call Jasmin when we get outside. But it's fine." I take another deep breath as I lock the box and then press the bell on the wall. "It's fine."

Chapter 40
Dax

TENSION RIPPLES THROUGH MY shoulders, the sweat on my back making my dark t-shirt stick to me.

She'll have seen it now. She'll know almost everything. She was never safe with me. The minute she stepped onto British soil, Julian had his eye on her. I shouldn't have been so naïve to think he wasn't keeping an eye on what was going on at the estate. He's made no secret over the years of how he wants to take it over.

It's a miracle he never realized where I was going those nights if he had people watching.

It's about the only piece of good luck I've had.

A car pulls up on the driveway, and I stand from the porch step. Blonde hair is visible as the driver steps out of the car.

Fuck. My heart's firing off faster than an AK47 in a gangster movie. Ninety days. Ninety nights. Ninety sunrises without her. It's a miracle I'm still in one piece. Being apart from her like this has been a worse hell than being in jail ever was.

My breath lodges in my throat, as the driver looks over at me, her brows shooting up in surprise.

It's Harley.

I open my mouth to call out a greeting, but then the passenger door opens.

And there she is.

My Sunbeam.

Looking so radiant, she steals the words from my mouth as my tongue dries up.

Her eyes connect with mine and there's a brief light in them as they widen, and she stares at me. But it dims instantly. She looks almost the same as she did the last time I saw her. But her hair is a little longer, the soft waves falling around her shoulders and reaching toward her waist in her jersey dress. And she's wearing her black over-the-knee boots. *Her favorite.* The ones she wore that day in the balloon. The day she made me pull the car over so she could climb into my lap.

Back when she wanted to be close to me all the time.

Back when she looked at me with a brightness in her eyes that isn't there now. It's been replaced by a cold wariness. And it makes my heart plummet to my feet.

It can only be a couple of seconds, but it's like time is standing still as I stare back at her, my eyes roaming all over her face, studying it, drinking it in, trying to convey a million thoughts and feelings silently.

I'm so sorry. I fucked up, Sunbeam. I fucked up. But you mean more to me than the air I breathe. You mean more to me than my own life.

You are everything.

She slams the car door and storms around the trunk. Harley races after her, reasoning with her—telling her to slow down and think.

But this is Rose, *my* Rose. She'll fire out all her passion and think later. It's one of the things I admire about her the most. That she's strong and independent. That she won't allow anyone to walk all over her without calling them out on it. Without calling them—

"Bastard!" She flies up, stopping toe to toe with me, her eyes wild, her cheeks flushed as she pants. "What the hell are you doing here?"

"I—"

"Ninety fucking days!" she screams, the whites of her eyes shining as she places both palms on my chest and shoves me until I step backward. "You don't get to waltz back here without a text message, a phone call. Who the fuck do you think you are?"

"Rose..."

Her eyes stay trained on mine, angry breaths pushing past her parted pink lips.

She jerks her head back, then shakes it. "Don't. Don't even say my name. You..." She screws her face up. "Why are you here? You just sent me on some twilight zone treasure hunt to see all your lies and secrets. Is that it? Now you want me to give you my time?" She slaps her palm against her chest. "You want me to listen to you because now you're ready and it suits you? Well, guess what? You're about ninety fucking days too late." She throws her arms wide.

"Rose, why don't you talk inside—" Harley cuts in behind her.

"No!" Rose snaps, inclining her chin to her sister over her shoulder, but keeping her eyes firmly on mine.

Harley nods and gives me a regretful look as she heads to the front door. "I'll give you both some privacy." She heads inside, leaving Rose glaring at me.

Rose's shoulders are trembling, and even though I know it's from rage, the sight is like a stake through my heart. I did this to her. I forced her away from me. I thought making her hate me would be easier. But easier for who? Because looking at her now, the last ninety days have been just as hard for her as they have for me. Harder, in fact. Because I knew the truth. She's only known fragments of it. Broken pieces that didn't fit together without the missing ones.

"You think you can just turn up here?" The volume has dropped, but her voice is still shrouded with the iciness that was there when she first spoke. A cold, hard distance to it. Separating herself from me.

And it's the least I fucking deserve.

"Would you have been here if I told you I was coming?"

She flinches, pain flashing in her eyes as though the sound of my voice is cutting her as deep as hers is doing to me. Then she steps backward, creating more distance between us.

Her lips flatten into a grim line as she meets my eyes.

She doesn't need to answer. I know she wouldn't be. It's in her silence. If she knew I was coming, she wouldn't have been here. She would have kept herself far, far away from me. Just like I should have done with her when we first met.

Kept her safe.

But then I'd never have felt the warmth of her shining on my stained soul. And the selfish part of me would never want to let that go once I felt it.

She is everything.

Just like I told her.

Rose Jacobs came into my world and set it spinning again. I'd been stuck. Banished to the shadows. Dark motives for a darkened soul. But she came and spun it back around to face the sun.

And I've never fucking wanted to be a good person so much in my life. To be worthy. Worthy of her.

"And I would deserve that," I say. "If you hadn't been here. I would deserve you never wanting to see me again. Never being close enough to see the way the sun makes your hair shine like gold, the way your pupils dilate when you're excited. The way your lips part the tiniest bit before you take a deep breath. I would deserve never to be close enough to smell your beauty—vanilla and fucking petals," I whisper. "I would deserve all of it."

Her eyes drop to my neck and my tattoo. I'm fighting back every urge and instinct that's telling me to reach out for her. To pull her into my arms and crush her to me so she can't get away.

But I can't. If she wants to listen to me, then it must be on her terms. I know that.

And so does she.

"But I would still have found you. Wherever you went. I would never have given up until I'd found you."

"So you could lie to me again?" She draws her eyes up from my neck to meet mine. "Would you have searched for Rose Jacobs? Or Dawn East?"

"Sunbeam—"

"Don't. Don't call me that. *Don't ever fucking call me that!*" Her voice cracks as she blinks rapidly. "You don't get to walk back into my life after three months, Dax! You don't get to come and think that you can say sorry—which you haven't even fucking said yet, by the way—and what? I'll forgive you? That I'll swoon into your arms like some pathetic idiot? This isn't some corny movie where the guy turns up ten minutes before the end and they kiss and make up and sail off into the sunset!"

"You don't think I fucking know that?" I take a step toward her, but she bristles, wrapping her arms around herself. I move backward again, letting her have that distance between us, even though it physically hurts me to increase the gap and not close it.

"Are you still watching the horror movies?"

She glances away, then back at me, twisting her lips. Then she shrugs one shoulder. "Sometimes."

I take the opportunity of her facing me to caress her face with my gaze. "You're even more beautiful than I remember," I say softly.

"Stop." She drops her eyes from mine, turning her shoulder toward me, and takes a deep breath in through her nose as she stares across the front yard and out to the street.

I keep my eyes on her face. Small lines appear by her eyes as I speak, but she still doesn't turn back to me.

"I am sorry. I am so *fucking* sorry. Everything I did was to keep you safe."

"All I can hear is what you want, Dax. What about what I want? Like being told the truth?"

"That's why I'm here."

"Three months too late!"

"I should have sent you away months ago. I should have known what he was capable of." I can't even bring myself to say his name. *Him. My father. My own blood.* "I should have protected you. That night. He was going to—"

"I know." She rounds on me, her chest heaving. "I know what he might have done, okay? You don't need to tell me about it. What you need to do is tell me why the fuck you used me to bring things into New York for you. You need to tell me why you lied about it. You need to tell me why you pushed me away, and why you waited three fucking months to come and see if I was okay. Three months to show even a hint that you care!"

"Rose."

Heat fires across the back of my neck and disgust coils like a deadly snake in my gut.

She thinks I don't care.

"I pushed you away to keep you safe. I pushed you away because I love—"

"You don't!" she screams, dropping her hands to her side and balling them into fists as her entire body shakes. "You don't. So don't even say it. Don't you dare say it, Dax Silver!"

Her chest heaves with giant breaths as she fights to stay in control.

And I want to tell her to breathe.

I want to place my thumb over her pulse on her neck or on her wrist. I want to press my lips to her forehead and hold her close to me. Tell her to breathe. Ask her what she can hear. Taste. Smell.

I want to do all those things.

But I can't.

Instead, I have to watch the girl who means everything to me fight alone to cope with the pain I've caused her.

And I've never hated myself so fucking much.

"If you felt anything for me, then you wouldn't have left me for three months with nothing but balloons and photographs and words. Empty fucking words! I needed you. I needed *you*."

"I'm sorry," I choke out, my chest burning so damn much I could spontaneously combust. Be reduced to ash at her feet, like our burned notes in the last fire we sat beside together.

Forgiveness and blame.

I'm the one to blame for this. For why we're standing here; a giant ravine between us. And forgiveness is a word I've prayed for every second since she left. I've prayed that when the day came and I could come for her, that there'd be a chance, no matter how minute, that she might forgive me.

"I'm sorry," I repeat, willing the light to come back to her eyes as she stares at me.

But it doesn't.

"Why?" she whispers. "I get you don't trust the police, so you kept copies of evidence against Julian. But the passport for me? Why didn't you just tell me he was watching me?"

"I couldn't." Regret's thick in my words as Rose snorts and looks away. *"I couldn't."* I reach for her and gently place two fingers beneath her chin and turn her face back to mine. She shakes my hand away, but lets her eyes meet mine.

"I wasn't working alone, Rose. I was working for them. For the police. It's how I got out of jail early. They wanted me to be an informant for them. Maybe they suspected I would be going after him myself anyway. I don't know. But they said if I agreed to six months of working on their operation to bring Julian down, then I could go free earlier. I should have been done before you even came to England. It should have been all over. You wouldn't have been in danger. Julian would have been locked up. But six months became seven, and then eight, and then nine." I blow out a long breath, the weight of the secret falling off my shoulders a relief like no other.

She knows everything now.

"I was working for the police. Even though I didn't fucking trust them." My laugh is empty as I glance at the sky, then back at her. She's still watching me, her eyes fixed on my face. But I can't get a read on what she's thinking. "I didn't trust them one fucking bit. It's why I kept my own evidence and brought it to New York, somewhere they'd never find it. I wasn't going back to jail if they screwed it up or double-crossed me."

"James? The police officer who shot Julian's men?"

"Marcus. I didn't know he was undercover. I thought he was just some guy who'd chosen wrong and got pulled into it all. But that night when Julian... when he..." My eyes drop down Rose's body as the image of her being held facedown over the hood of the car flashes in my mind. "That night... I was supposed to have backup. They were watching, ready to arrest him once he opened one of the containers. But it wasn't there in time. If James hadn't been there, then..." Acid burns a hole in my chest.

"Then it could have been really different," Rose whispers.

"Yes." I search her eyes, my heart lifting as her pupils widen a little before she drops her gaze to the floor. "It could have been so different."

"Why? Why weren't they there watching when they should have been? Why did they leave you alone?"

"There was a rat. Someone on the inside, working for Julian. I didn't know. But whoever he was, he delayed the backup. James realized while working undercover. He told me that night as they took me away. I couldn't rely on them to protect you until he was found. The less you knew, the safer you were."

"It's why you stopped fighting to get to me?"

"I have *never* stopped fighting to get back to you. Never. And I will never stop."

She rolls her lips but says nothing.

"But I knew you weren't safe until he was found. Jasmin had a police protection unit placed on her. And she had Alistair. But I knew it was you Julian would tell him to go after. All those photographs..."

He was watching her. He had his disgusting eyes on my girl the whole time.

"He knew in order to get to me, to really *hurt* me, he needed you. I would have signed the estate over to him without question to make sure he never touched you. I would have fucking *killed* him with my bare hands if I could have, Rose. You are everything to me. Please tell me you know that?" I plead. "Every moment with you has been a gift. *You* were my gift. I've been stuck for years. Then you came along, and you freed me. You are the reason I wake up every morning. You are the reason I want to see another sunrise. *Please*, Rose. You are everything to me. And more."

"You lied to me, Dax." Her voice is small, quiet, but the strength in it is undeniable. She's a fighter. And right now, she's still fighting against me.

I've ruined everything.

I broke the best thing I had in my life.

"Remember how I told you that I hate people making decisions about what they think is best for me?" She doesn't wait for me to answer. "You know I hate it. And yet you did the exact same thing to me. You should have told me Julian was watching me. You should have told me what you were doing when you pushed me away that day. Because all I've felt all these months is betrayal. I'm not helpless. You don't get to dictate my life. You don't get to make decisions for me."

"That's not what I was trying to do. I never want to do that. I was doing what I thought I had to. Everything I did, every mistake I made... I did it all to protect you. The passport... the money... I wanted you to have a get-out if you needed it. I had to know you'd have that if anything happened to me." I press a finger and thumb into my eye sockets until my head throbs. "If anything happens to you... I... *Nothing* can ever happen to you. It would ruin me. In fact, *I'm already fucking ruined*. I have been since you left."

"And you think I'm not? You think I've been living this amazing, happy life without you? I gave you everything, Dax. Because I believed in you. In us. Now I don't know what to believe."

"Please. I swear to you. You know everything we had was real. You know how I feel about you. You know that." I drag a hand down my face, fear pricking at me like a thousand scalding needles.

What if she doesn't believe me? What if she never forgives me? How does the earth exist without its sun?

"I just had to keep you safe. You were never safe with me."

She takes a slow, deliberate breath in, looking over my face, her eyes softening, and hope blooms in my chest. Then she parts her lips and whispers her next words so softly that I have to focus to hear them.

"You're right. I was never safe with you. But it wasn't because of Julian. Or a rat inside the police. It was all because of you. Lying to me. Pushing me away. The people closest to us have the power to hurt us the most. *And you're mine, Dax Silver*. You're my weakness and my biggest threat. Because with you, I am never safe."

"God." I drag in a splintered breath, my eyes wet. "Please don't. Let me prove it to you. Just give me one more sunrise before you close that door on us. *Please*."

She shakes her head sadly and the fight leaves her in a final, dry-eyed sob. "Go to hell," she whispers.

I blink through the tears pooling in my eyes. "I'm already there without you."

Her gaze passes between my eyes and then down to my lips before she looks to the front door where her mom is watching us.

"Don't invite him in, Mom. He's leaving now." Rose's voice regains its strength as she rushes past her mom and into the house without looking back.

Her mom gives me a sympathetic smile. The same smile she gave me when I arrived hours ago.

Then she follows Rose inside the house and closes the door.

Chapter 41

Rose

I RUN UP THE stairs and into my bedroom, slamming the door behind me. Ninety silver threads grab at me, wrapping themselves around my arms and my neck. Entangling me like a web of lies.

He came.

It's what I wanted. Him to come and say it to my face. But seeing him again has ripped the floor from beneath my feet. I knew it wouldn't be easy and that seeing him again would send emotions raging through me like a storm.

But what I didn't expect was how much I wanted to throw myself into his arms. To tell him I forgive him and that it's okay. That it's all okay, *because he came.* Because he came for me, and all that matters is that we are together, where we belong.

And even though I'm shaking from how mad I am, I'm beginning to understand. Everything he's saying is starting to make sense.

He wanted to protect me. He wanted to keep me safe and from harm. It's like what Harley and Reed went through before they got engaged. So much shit was thrown at them. But they came out of it stronger than ever.

And their story gives me hope.

But that's their story, and this is ours. It's not simple. And I am so angry. At Dax. At Julian Young. At the world.

At everything.

A silver ribbon wraps itself around my neck, and I yank it free, choking back a sob.

Fucking balloons!

Even if what he says makes sense, it doesn't change the last three months. It doesn't change the fact he thinks he can come back here and make my heart feel like it's been ripped out and torn to shreds. To say sorry, and that I'll just what? Forgive him and that'd be it?

I pull another ribbon from my arm as my breathing quickens.

The balloons swell against the ceiling, pushing lower and lower, sucking the air from the room. Ribbons wrap around me like the vines from my recurring nightmare. Pulling me in different directions, threatening to burrow through my limbs and rip me into pieces.

Sweat pools along my hairline and a bead rolls down my back as I gasp for air.

I stumble over to the window, climbing onto my bed to throw it wide open as I grab at the ribbons, scrunching them inside my fists and then force them through the opening.

Blue and white surrounds me, bouncing off the window frame, the rubber making a high-pitched squealing sound that makes my ears ring as I force them outside.

I push and push, shoving balloon after balloon through the window.

The sky outside the house is overcome with blue and white as each handful of ribbons and their accompanying balloons are thrown out.

I don't stop.

I keep going, my muttered cries of unfairness and heartache burning my lungs as more and more are set free, soaring off up into the sky.

Nothing stops me.

Not the little kid across the road pointing with delight and tugging on his mother's sleeve to show her.

Not the neighbor walking his dog as it barks excitedly at the scene.

And especially not Dax, who's looking up at me from the porch below, his eyes not on the balloons, but on my face.

Always on my face, never leaving. He doesn't look mad. He doesn't even look shocked.

He's just Dax. Dressed all in black, the mesmerizing ink on his arms and neck visible in the t-shirt he's wearing. He's watching me with those deep brown eyes that I've spent so many nights losing myself in. Those eyes that belong to the only person I've ever loved. The person without whom the last ninety days has felt like the worst punishment for a crime I never committed.

He watches me with a strange calmness until only one balloon is left.

The silver one.

I grab the ribbon and push it through the window, but it catches on the latch, and I tug at it as I look down at

Dax. My traitorous heart lifts before I cut down any hope it's trying to raise in me that it'll all work out in the end.

Because what if it doesn't?

Ninety days.

"You warped reality, Dax Silver. You are the worst kind of liar. Whatever the truth is... you're so far from it, it could smack you in the face and you wouldn't know!" I yell.

I give the balloon one hard tug to free it, and the motion rips it open, sending silver glitter cascading down over the porch below, and all over Dax. Then it hangs there on the outside of the window, like a lifeless body.

Just like me, seeing him again.

"This is what you did to my heart."

He looks back at me with such a sudden and intense loss in his eyes, silver sparkles shining all over him, splintering the light around him, that it steals the air from my lungs.

Even covered in glitter, the bastard is beautiful.

He opens his mouth to say something, but I wrap my trembling hand around the window ledge to support myself.

"You think I'm going to forgive you that easily?" I grab the window frame. "You can think again. Fuck off to infinity, Dax. And when you get there, fuck off some more!"

Then I slam the window shut, causing it to rattle in its frame.

I don't eat dinner with Mom and Brett. Harley already left to go back to Manhattan. She came to say goodbye and gave me a hug before she left. But there wasn't much else to say. I heard her talking outside, then the deep timbre of Dax's voice as he responded.

He's still there.

It's been hours and it's getting dark.

And he's still out there.

Maybe he's thinking. Like me.

Because all I've been able to do is think.

About him. About how fucked up this all is. About how much my body still reacts, just knowing he's near to me.

I hate it. All of it.

I hate the way my heart lifted when I saw him. I hate how heat fired low in my stomach when I looked into his eyes and remembered the way he would hold my eyes as he made love to me, or when he fucked me from behind in front of the mirror.

I hate how my core clenched with need as I saw his tattoos on his neck. How I love knowing that when I kiss them, especially the bird, that it makes him suck his breath in. That he rasps out his nickname for me—*Sunbeam*—like it's the most precious word in his vocabulary.

And I hate that when I got changed into my pajamas for bed, my panties were soaking for him.

That even when I want to hate him so much for pushing me away, my heart and my body still want him.

Every part of me still wants him.

I can deny it as much as I want. But I know it. And he knows it.

Something about us just fits.

We were supposed to find one another. As stupid as it sounds, I know it's true.

No matter what happens now, I know I was meant to meet him.

Despite everything, he's still helped me. Brett's accident, Dad's death, Casey... It all hurts a little less because of Dax. I'm living again because of him. I'm no longer stuck in a time loop of blame and self-loathing. And I have him to thank for that, regardless of what else has happened since.

I open the window gently and then lie back on my bed, breathing in the night air as it flows into the room.

He thought I was in danger. He found those photos somehow. He knew Julian was watching me and the estate. So while he was building his own insurance policy of evidence against Julian should the police let him down, he was also building an escape for me. Even back then when we went to New York.

He was thinking of me.

I get that he would have had to keep being an informant a secret from his friends and family. And I understand that Dax, more than anyone, wouldn't trust the police fully, and probably knew we were all safer not knowing. It's a small comfort knowing that no one else knew. Not even Jasmin. It wasn't only me he was shutting out. He took it all on himself. He carried the burden alone.

Just like he's lived so much of his life. Being the protector. The big brother. The adult. Having to make hard decisions and put other people first.

I told him I was here for him on the roof terrace that day. I tried to fight for him. I was ready to fight straight away. And in his own way, he was fighting for me too.

Even if it didn't feel like it.

"You could have called me. I haven't heard your voice for three months. *I love your voice*," I choke out, loud enough for my voice to carry through the open window.

My eyes sting as I stare at the ceiling as a deep exhale floats up from the porch.

"Just hearing yours would have made me cave, Rose. I would have come for you and begged you to come back with me. I would have put you straight back in danger again. I couldn't risk it. Not until the inside guy was found. I'd never forgive myself if something happened to you because of me."

The porch sofa creaks below.

"I am sorry, Rose. I'll say it until my tongue bleeds. I'll tell you every day until you believe me. I did everything because I thought it was the right decision at the time. Not because I didn't want to tell you the truth. Not because I wanted to shut you out or push you away. I did everything because I didn't see any other way. I..." He curses low, but I still catch it. I still catch the emotion brimming in his words. "I promised you infinity. And I meant it. I will tell you I'm sorry for the rest of my life if that's what it takes."

I clamp my hand over my mouth to stifle my sob and turn onto my side, curling up into a fetal position.

We've never spent the night close together like this and not been wrapped up in each other's arms. I would have my head resting on his chest, over his compass tattoo. I would be listening to his heartbeat as it calmed me to sleep.

But tonight, all I have is my cold pillow beneath my cheek and my duvet twisted into a creased mess.

And I have Dax... two stories below me. His heart seeming as heavy as mine.

I press my face into my pillow, not wanting him to hear my raggedy breath as I sob without tears.

Until eventually he says, "Good night, Rose."

Chapter 42

Dax

"DAX?"

"Why aren't you sleeping?"

"Why aren't you?"

My heart cracks at her voice. It's lost all its fight. *My beautiful girl.*

I rub my eyes with one hand. "I never sleep well since you left."

"Neither do I."

I stare up at the night sky and the stars as I wait for her to speak. Because I know there's so much more she still wants to ask. I can feel it hanging in the air between us. Unspoken feelings. Unanswered questions.

Unparalleled hope.

"You remember the night you came back covered in blood?"

"The night you cleaned me up?" I smile at the memory of her exploring my skin with a gentle dusting of her fingertips as she told me she thought my tattoos were beautiful. But I saw deep inside her that night, to who Rose Jacobs really is. And she's always been the beautiful one.

"Yeah."

"Another member of Julian's gang was going to bring attention on us by being a prick and stealing gear for himself. I couldn't risk having more eyes on me and my small part in the operation. I just gave him a warning, that's all. He's fine."

I flex my arms behind my head as I transfer my gaze to Rose's window. Her bed must be right by it because I can hear her clearly. Knowing that she's so close has my body fighting with my head. I could stand on the sofa. Maybe put the chair on top of it to make it higher and then grab the window frame and hoist myself up. Climb through it and get into bed with her, pull her into my arms where she belongs.

If she's going to listen to me, it has to be on her time. I can't force her, or I will lose her forever.

Maybe I already have.

"Who knows?"

I stare at her window, still imagining her lying on her bed, her long, blonde hair splayed across her pillow.

"Just James and a select few police who are working the case. And Sophie."

"Jasmin and Logan?"

"No." My chest sinks as I exhale. "I can't tell them yet. I might never be able to unless it's going to be shared in the trial. I'm not supposed to tell anyone."

"But you're telling me."

"Because I had to. I hated you not knowing the whole truth. Jasmin, Logan... They don't need to know if I was working alone, or for the police to get Julian. But you? I hated looking into your eyes and knowing there was something I hadn't shared with you. Because you're the only person in this world who's seen all of me, Rose. All my parts. Including the dark, ugly ones."

"Don't talk about yourself like that," she snaps.

The tiny glimmer of hope in the air lodges itself inside my chest at the fire in her voice.

She's still fighting for us.

Somewhere deep down, it's still there. An ember. But I'll take it. She hasn't let it burn out entirely.

There's still a chance.

"So you waited until the last guy was found?"

"Yeah. I didn't trust the police to do their job properly. My trial was fucked up, I was stabbed in jail. Julian had people working for him on the inside. As long as there was a chance Julian could wriggle his way out of it, then I couldn't come for you. Even though I wanted to. I swear to you, Rose. I've never wanted something so badly in my life."

I watch the window, hoping she might look out. Allow me a glimpse of her. Meet my eyes so I can look into hers as I speak.

So she can see that I mean it. Every. Single. Word.

But the space remains dark and empty.

"How do you know he won't still find a way?"

"He won't. Alistair found more evidence hidden at his house. And he got him on tape, admitting to things. Admitting to wanting me dead. Wanting the estate. Staging an 'accident' for me in jail." The hairs on my arms prick up. He would never have stopped. I had to stop him first. "Julian won't be getting out. He gave up his inside man when they told him he was looking at a conspiracy to commit murder charge. He begged like the coward he is. And he's not going to have many friends in jail. No big henchmen protecting him. He'll be a sitting duck for all the people he's crossed over the years to get ahead."

The thought spreads sourness over my tongue. If Julian makes it through his sentence alive, then he's a lucky man. And if he doesn't? Then I've already been to my father's funeral. I won't be shedding any tears, shared blood or not.

It's something I'm working on, but I'm getting there. I am not him. I never will be him. And I believe that. And knowing Rose believes that too, and that she told me over and over again before she left, it's enough.

Blood means nothing.

"What's he like? Alistair, I mean."

"A total sucker for Jasmin."

"Of course he is." There's amusement tinting Rose's voice that has my lips pulling into the beginnings of a smile as my heart swells.

"He's a good guy. He loves her. He worked hard to help her when I wasn't there. He helped her take on the business, gave her the strength and confidence to make difficult decisions. I owe him a lot."

"He looked a bit like you when I saw him on Jasmin's phone."

"Yeah, poor fucker."

When I first met Alistair, it was like looking into a mirror but knowing it wasn't me reflected back. We have the same face shape... but different eyes. We both have eyes like our mothers'. A fact I'm grateful for.

I don't have his. Rose doesn't have to look into Julian's eyes and see him when she looks at me.

"Don't you mean lucky? Hot like his big brother? But not as hot, obviously," Rose muses, making a chuckle rumble inside my chest for the first time in over ninety days.

"You still think I'm hot?" I'm met with silence, and my chuckle dies. "I'm sorry, I didn't mean—"

"My body and my heart will always be yours, Dax. For infinity." She sighs, as though speaking is draining her energy.

"But?" I hold my breath.

"But... nothing." She pauses. "We should sleep."

I wait until I'm sure she isn't going to say anything else. Then I close my eyes, even though it's pointless.

I can't sleep without you, Sunbeam.

I can't function without you.

Time means nothing if it isn't spent with you.

"Don't give up. She forgave me." Casey smiles at me as she passes me on the porch sofa on her way out the following afternoon.

"Not planning to." I tip my chin at her as she passes.

Rose hasn't come out today. From what I can tell, she's been in her room most of the morning and then out in the rear yard. I could hear music playing through the side gate. Then after Casey went into the house, the sounds of screaming and tense music came from the living room on the opposite side of the wall to where

I've been sitting. And I smiled as I realized they were probably watching a movie together.

Brett invited me into his guesthouse in the converted garage to use his shower. But I was so scared of missing Rose if she left the house that I took it as fast as I could and then went back to the porch sofa, still damp beneath my clothes. And their mom must have felt sorry for me because there was a plate of food and drink waiting for me when I returned.

I take up my position on the porch couch again, pulling my phone out to text Logan and call Jasmin. They both know I'm here. They're taking care of everything at home, along with Alistair. I couldn't ask for more. They are my family. It's the people who are there for you no matter what.

And I'm going to be here for Rose, no matter what.

I'm going to be here for as long as it takes.

I busy myself with some work emails to pass the day, and I wave as the neighbor with the dog passes again. He gives me a questioning thumbs up as he looks at the house behind me, which I reply to by tilting my palm in a so-so movement. With a hopeful smile, he moves past.

I'm becoming a local spectacle.

The heartbroken man sleeping on the porch. Maybe they'll make a movie about me. If it was a horror, maybe Rose would even watch it. I've not seen her once today. She's probably trying to ignore the fact I am still here. But she needs to get used to it. Because I'm not leaving.

Brett brings me out some dinner and even stays to have a beer with me. I really am the fucking charity case.

Desperation must be seeping from my pores like the silver glitter that I keep finding everywhere.

As the sky darkens, I lie on the sofa, ready for another night. It's uncomfortable and there's a loose spring digging into my back.

But it's closer to her.

So that makes it fucking paradise in comparison to anywhere else I could be.

Day ninety-two. Tomorrow will be sunrise number ninety-three. More without her than with her.

"Give me one more, *please*," I whisper before falling silent as one by one, lights flick out in the houses up the street, leaving me in darkness. All the lights in Rose's house went out half an hour ago.

A sound above draws my eyes. Her window opens briefly, and something is thrown out. Then it's slammed shut again.

I get up from the sofa and walk over to scoop up the bundle, carrying it back to the sofa.

I unroll it, spreading the blanket over me, its scent enveloping me as I stare up through the dark at the closed window.

Vanilla and petals.

Chapter 43
Rose

It's still dark as I tiptoe barefoot out onto the porch. His breathing is rhythmic and slow and the sight of him—blond hair ruffled from sleep, tattoos that look darker in the moonlight—has longing pulling at my heart, willing me to take notice, to finally admit to myself—life without him will never be as bright as it could be with him. If I can't forgive him, then it's all been for nothing. This whole journey, finding myself again, learning to forgive myself. It's like it was all training me for this moment.

All training me for Dax Silver.

The sofa creaks as I perch on the end of it by his feet, and the movement makes him open his eyes. His find mine straight away, instantly brightening in undisguised hope.

For a few seconds, we just stare at each other.

He's unshaven, dark blond scruff scattering over his defined jawline. And it suits him. Nothing doesn't. He looks equally as good in a suit at work as he does in black sweats and mussed up hair and a few days' worth of growth on his chin.

"Hi," I breathe.

"Hi." His brow creases as he rises to a sitting position, his eyes staying on my face.

"Did you sleep better?" My eyes drop to my blanket, laid out over his legs.

He follows my gaze. "A little. But it's not the same as the real thing."

"Nothing ever is," I whisper.

I study his face. The warmth of his body burning next to mine makes me suck in a breath. But that only brings with it the scent of him. His scent. His warm skin, a subtle masculine fresh sweat. *Strong, inviting, intense.* The scent I first noticed that night he stormed down to the estate's gates in the dark to let me in. It's even on my tongue as I swallow, bringing with it a comfort low in my stomach. Because as much as there is passion and fire when we are together. There is also this.

Peace.

A peace in myself that has never been there before. A peace he created.

"Won't they be missing you? At the estate?"

Dax takes the blanket off his legs and wraps it around my shoulders, which are bare in my camisole and shorts pajama set.

"Maybe. But they're doing a great job. They don't need me."

"They might soon, though. You should go home." I pull the blanket around me and drop my gaze away from him. Looking into his eyes is a glaring reminder of how we used to be. Of how deep we fell into each other. Because he is all over me. Inside and out. He always will be.

"It's not home anymore if you aren't there." He shifts in the seat, causing his thigh to press up against mine. I don't move. Instead, I stare at his leg in his dark sweat-pants next to my bare skin. "There will never be anyone else." He runs his fingers through his blond waves. "Never."

He drops his hand to his thigh and turns his head to the side, his eyes following mine as I frown at his skin next to mine. He flexes his hand and the flowers and vines that run down his forearm and over his wrist move in the moonlight.

"You're so perfect next to me, Rose. I love your skin. I hated that you wanted me to tattoo it at first. Like nothing should be allowed to taint it. But then I saw how much it meant to you. And I knew that if anyone was ever going to leave a permanent mark on it, then I wanted it to be me. It could *only* be me."

"I made an appointment as soon as I came back to New York to get it covered."

Dax sucks in a breath and turns his head away from me. *"Jesus."* His shoulders drop as he runs a hand around his jaw and screws his eyes shut as his voice splinters. "Fuck."

"I'm sorry," I murmur.

He shakes his head but still can't look at me. "You have nothing to say sorry for. It's all me. I'm the one who's sorry. I'm the one who doesn't fucking deserve you. I never have."

Guilt weaves its way through my veins at the devastation on his face as he fights to take in a ragged breath.

Just the thought of me doing it is crushing him like he can't breathe.

He turns back to me, his eyes dark and shining. "What did you get?"

I shrug the blanket off my shoulder and twist so he can see.

He drops his head with a low exhale, his entire chest sagging in relief. Then he grabs my thigh as if on instinct. The feel of his fingers digging into my skin sends electricity racing through me.

"I couldn't do it," I whisper, covering my cloud tattoo with the blanket again.

"Thank you." His voice is thick, heavy. "I would have understood if you had... but I'm so glad you didn't."

"You're the only one who I'd ever trust to do it."

He squeezes my thigh, and then pulls his hand away like he's realized what he's doing. "It feels so wrong being close to you and not touching you. I think about touching you all the time. I remember everything about the way you felt in my arms. The way you tasted. I remember everything."

"So do I," I whisper.

"I'd do anything to have it all back."

"I believe you."

Dax once told me he always sees things through, once he's committed. And now I understand; he will sleep on this porch for as many nights as it takes until I talk to him again. *Really talk.*

I reach over and take his hand, threading my fingers through his. The contact sends a vibration running up my arm, and Dax's breathing stalls as he stares at our entwined skin.

The marble in my throat shifts suddenly, dropping into my stomach.

And it's like a dam has been blown apart.

"Don't think this means it's all good." My voice cracks as I begin to tremble, until I'm shaking so much I struggle to speak. "D-don't t-think that this means—"

Dax pulls me to him, and his lips find my forehead as I sink into him, fighting to breathe past the giant sob building in my chest.

"Don't think..." My breath leaves me as I choke out a strangled sound. "Don't—"

He shushes me with such tenderness that I screw my eyes shut, my chest burning. "I've got you, Sunbeam."

I sob out loud. *Sunbeam.*

The first drop of hot, salty liquid rolls over my skin, the sensation so foreign to me that I forget to breathe as another joins it.

Then another.

And another.

"Dax." I hiccup as I try to breathe.

He kisses my forehead. "I've got you. And I always will, Rose. Whenever you need me, I will be here. Even if you can't stand to look at me. Even if you can't ever forgive me. Know that I will be here for you without question. Anywhere. Any reason. Any time. Okay?"

I bury my face into his neck as hot tears rush from my eyes.

They keep coming. Harder and faster. Until I'm sniffing and shuddering with the force of them taking over my body.

More than three years' worth of tears.

All flowing out over the beautiful bird tattoo I love so much.

Dax crushes his lips to my forehead again, then he cups my face in his hands and wipes the tears from my cheeks with his thumbs as he looks into my eyes.

Dark brown meets light blue.

"I know all these tears aren't for me. But some are." Lines appear at the corners of his eyes. "I don't deserve them, Rose," he whispers. "I'm not worth your tears."

He brushes more away, but they fall faster, running over his hands until they're wet too.

"You've got them though."

His eyes pinch, glassy with his own unshed tears as he strokes my face.

"I love you."

I suck in a breath, looking through my tears as I blink at him.

"I promised you infinity, Rose. And I meant it. Even if you never forgive me, I will never stop. Months, years, decades... I will love you through them all. Because time itself will run out before my love for you ever will."

I open my mouth to speak. But the words in my heart aren't the ones that come out.

"Come with me. I want to show you something."

The walk to the top of the hill takes us an hour with only a flashlight for guidance. And by the time we reach the top, the first light of a new day is beginning to color the sky.

"Dad used to bring us here as kids. It's where he told us that our troubles would seem smaller from up high," I say, pulling Dax's hoodie around me as I turn, and he comes to stand behind me, looking out over the horizon.

"It's quite something."

"Yeah," I agree as orange bursts up behind the distant hills like the flames of a bonfire, signaling a new day, burning away the past.

I turn to Dax and look up at his face. "Sunrise number ninety-three."

His expression is tense as he looks at me. "Yeah."

I take a deep breath, pulling my bottom lip into my mouth. My heart flutters from the way he looks at me. No one else stands a chance.

Even if they were given infinity to try, they would never be Dax.

It's all I thought about as we walked here. How it will only ever be him for the rest of time.

And infinity is a long time not to forgive someone.

Especially someone who you love.

Especially someone who the thought of living without makes you feel like you might physically retch. Like you'd cease to have any kind of meaningful existence if they weren't a part of it.

"I love you too." I blink, new tears threatening to form in my eyes. It's like the gates have well and truly opened for them now. "I promised you every sunrise. And you're getting number ninety-three, because I love you too. And I'm still mad at you for lying to me. But I understand why you did it. And I'll probably go wild and smash something up if you ever lie to me again." Dax places his hands on my hips and pulls me toward him, his eyes glittering. "But I love you too. Time with you did something to me. Because I'm not the same now. You changed me."

His eyes caress my face as he matches my smile with his own soft one. "I didn't do anything besides falling for a girl with virgin skin and a smart, fiery mouth."

"You did so much more than that and you know it." I place my palms on his chest, splaying my fingers out over his heart through his t-shirt.

His grip on my hips tightens, and he pulls me against him. He pauses for the briefest moment as if seeking permission. And I lean closer, giving it without words. Then his hands are on my face and in my hair and curling around my neck as he kisses me with a force that has my knees buckling.

And I kiss him back with everything I have.

I kiss away ninety-two days of separation. Ninety-two days of pain. A ceiling full of popped balloons and lost sunrises.

And as I kiss him, I welcome every day with him I will get from now on. Each one that I will cling on to with both hands and be grateful for.

Dax holds me as I grab fistfuls of his hair, parting my lips and welcoming his tongue inside my mouth, his teeth against my lips and his groans into my body, as he kisses every bit of air from me until I'm gasping against his lips.

"I love you, Sunbeam. I love you so fucking much." He trails hot kisses up my jawline, allowing me to catch my breath, as his mouth reaches my ear, and he whispers, "Let me show you. Please, Rose. I've been dying more each day without you. I *need* you."

My agreement is an incoherent nod as desire thrums through me from the sensation of having his hands and lips on me again.

"Words, Rose," Dax murmurs against my neck. "Please say it."

"Y-yes. I—" I moan as he sucks on my neck at the same time as he slides a hand up underneath my camisole and circles my nipple with his thumb.

"It's not enough," he groans into my neck, pressing his groin against my hip so I can feel just how badly he's missed me. "I need you to say all of it." His voice is heavy, laced with pain and regret. *Desperate.*

He needs me.

A soft moan leaves my lips as he pulls me closer, until his erection digs into my stomach.

"I... I need you. I want to feel you back where you belong... *Inside me.*"

"Fuck," he chokes out, emotion clogging up his throat as he caresses my hard nipple gently between his fingers.

"I don't want to think about the last ninety-two days without you. Make me forget we were ever apart. Make me remember how good we are together."

The ground underneath my feet disappears as Dax lifts me into his arms, encouraging me to wrap my legs around his waist as he lowers us down onto the blanket we brought.

"I've missed you so damn much. I'm fighting the demon on my shoulder that wants me to fuck you until you see stars," Dax utters as his hot body hovers over mine.

He kisses me again, his breath stalling.

"Dax..."

I arch my back so he can pull my hoodie and camisole off in-between desperate kisses.

"Do it. Make me see a whole shower of stars," I plead as he drags my shorts and panties off.

A deep line puckers the skin between his brows as he balls the soaked cotton of my panties in his fist and lifts them to his nose. His eyes hold mine as he inhales deeply.

"Jesus..." He closes his eyes and inhales again before placing them down. "I've missed every fucking thing about you."

I pant, completely naked beneath him. His eyes roam over my body. He sucks in a breath, a muscle twitching in his jaw as he continues his assessment of me.

"Dax, touch me, please." I reach for him, but he pulls back, and there's a look I can't place in his eyes.

"I don't want to hurt you, Rose. It's been months and…" His fingers dig into his sweatpants on his thighs until his knuckles turn white. "And *fuck*, I'm scared I'm going to lose control. You deserve me to be gentle. I want to be gentle. I *should* be gentle."

I reach up to stroke his cheeks with my fingertips. "I want you to be you. I know you can be gentle. You don't have to be anything in this moment other than what feels right."

His eyes are dark and wild.

I whisper, "I trust you."

A deep growl leaves him as he smashes his mouth to mine, biting my lips and sucking my tongue. He pulls back for mere seconds, long enough to rip his t-shirt up over his head and yank his sweatpants off. Then he crushes his hard body against mine, one hand finding mine and entwining our fingers together tightly, the other cupping my neck and seeking out my thundering pulse with the pad of his thumb.

I take a deep breath as he caresses the beating vein softly, his eyelids hooded with lust.

"I need to feel you, taste you, be surrounded by you. I've thought about you, pictured your face, obsessed over the scent of your skin for every moment we've been apart. All I've been able to think about is how much I love you. How much I miss you. How much I need you to fucking survive."

"Show me."

I widen my legs, desperate to lift my hips so Dax can sink inside me. But he moves back, far enough for me to gaze into his eyes. The haunted depths of them makes my breath stall.

He croaks hoarsely, "My life would be darkness without you, Rose."

"Stop," I breathe, my heart breaking as I see how deeply this is affecting him. "I'm here now. *We're* here *now*."

He kisses the inside of my wrist as I blink back the threat of tears. It isn't only him who needs me. I need him too.

"We are," he whispers. "We are, Sunbeam."

I pull him into me, kissing him in between fevered gasps as we press ourselves together, re-connecting, too scared to let the other go. I fuse our hot skin together as we try our hardest to climb inside each other and erase all the pain. Dax lets out a low hiss as the metal of his piercing grazes my entrance, and a shiver runs through me.

"Please," I whimper, pulling him closer.

"You're always so wet for me," he groans, pushing an inch inside me and then stopping.

I moan and wriggle, willing him to sink more of himself inside me. To fill me and make me stretch around him.

His hand tightens around mine, and he pauses, his eyes holding mine. "You like that, Sunbeam? You missed this cock?" His eyes pinch as if he's still fighting to push the pain away.

I capture his lips in another kiss, and he pushes another inch inside me, then retreats. I writhe beneath him with a muffled sob.

"Say it." His voice has a tremor like he's barely holding himself together. *"Say it."*

"Yes! I want it. I want *you*. I love you. You've got me, I promise."

The relief in his eyes grips me by the neck and steals the air straight from my body. He really has been broken by these months apart.

Scarred.

"Please, Dax," I urge. "We need this."

He groans and thrusts in deep, his pupils blowing wide. Both of us catch our breath with parted lips and stare at one another.

"I love you." He dips his lips to my shoulder and kisses the top of my tattoo.

"I love you too," I whisper as he starts to move, never taking his eyes off mine as he pushes deeper and deeper inside me.

A deep moan of appreciation leaves my lips, and Dax groans while kissing me again, his balls pressed against my body as I hug every inch of him inside me.

Ninety-two days, but my body remembers him like it was mere hours ago that he was last inside me.

"Hold on," he whispers, nipping my lower lip with his teeth. Then he slides one of my knees higher up the blanket and begins thrusting into me with all the energy of a man who's been waiting his whole life for this moment, not three months.

With each thrust, the haunted look in his eyes clears more, like the morning mist being burned away by the rising sun. Until all I see is love shining back at me as he claims my lips again.

I cry out as he drives into me with a relentless rhythm, his piercing sliding over my G-spot with each drive of his hips. His body hits my clit each time he's buried deep, sending shockwaves vibrating through my body.

"Dax." I shudder beneath him.

"Do it, Rose. I can feel you squeezing me tighter. *Do it.*"

He kisses me as I gasp out his name and come around him with a wet rush, my vision blurring so much I screw my eyes shut.

"Fuck," he hisses, canting his hips so I'm forced down against the ground even harder. The increased pressure on my clit and the angle he's driving inside me at makes my orgasm roll into another one that steals my breath until I can't control a single muscle in my body anymore.

I hand them all over to Dax.

It takes all of my energy to drag air into my lungs as he drives into me, whispering into my ear, "Good girl, you know just how to milk my cock. I'm going to fucking explode."

"Yes," I pant as he strokes my pulse with his thumb again, his other hand still entwined with mine. I'm gripping his so hard I worry he'll have nail marks in his skin.

"Give me one more first. I need one more."

"I ca-can't..."

"Yes. You. Can." Dax strokes my pulse as he encourages me softly in my ear, his body connecting with mine with each deep push. "Yes. You can, Sunbeam."

Light flashes in my eyes as the sun pushes up over the horizon, and I squeeze them shut, the backs of my eyelids filled with bright orange spots as one final burst of pleasure rips through me, and I come.

He kisses the garbled moan from my lips, and he trembles as he comes with me, pouring himself into me.

"I love you. I love you. Fuck, I love you," he chants as he thrusts inside me, filling every tiny part of me with him. I swear that with the force he's just come with, he must have tattooed his name inside me with his cum.

"Dax."

"I love you." His lips connect with my tattoo again, and he kisses the skin there as the final waves of pleasure leave his body, and he halts his movements inside me, burying his face into the crook of my neck. "I don't deserve you. But I will love you with every breath I ever take. I promise you that."

"I know," I whisper as his lips travel up my neck and back to my lips. "Because you promised me infinity, Dax Silver. And I intend to make you good on your promise."

He chuckles and kisses me while the sun continues to rise around us. "You promised me every sunrise."

"What do you think this is?" I breathe, still catching my breath as calmness paints itself through my body as the sky lights up.

Dax kisses me again, then turns his face to the horizon. "Do I get tomorrows?"

His brows pull low over his eyes as he looks back at me.

The view might be breathtaking. But it's not a patch on the beautiful man holding me in his arms and looking at me like I'm the most precious thing in his world.

Not a damn patch.

"You get them all." I lift a hand to his face, and he kisses my inner wrist. "Every single one. They could only ever be yours. Do you remember me telling you love was a chemical?"

"Dopamine?" He cocks a brow, a smile pulling up his lips.

"I was wrong. It's you."

He stays inside me and places both elbows on either side of my head so he can stroke my face with both hands.

"It's you for me too. It always was."

His eyes shine as he rises onto his arms, moving back enough for me to see his chest. And I stare at his compass tattoo. Because where there used to be one arm pointing west for the sunset, a memory of his parents, now there is another.

I trace my fingertip over his hot skin. Over the new dark ink on it, and all the way to the end of the rose stem where the petals bloom around the E for east.

"When?"

His heart beats out a steady rhythm beneath my palm as I lay it over his chest.

"The day you left. I couldn't go a day without having you close."

I roll my lips, my chest burning with emotion as my eyes threaten to make more tears.

"I think I'd like it really slow and gentle now," I whisper.

Dax's eyes soften as he kisses me. "Anything you want, Sunbeam."

Then he wraps his arms around me and makes love to me, wiping the tears from my cheeks and gripping me tight as I come for him again and again.

Until I lose all sense of time.

Chapter 44

Dax

"This is even better than last time."

Rose bounces up on her toes, leaning over the side of the basket. I abandon the burner and slip an arm around her waist from behind, pulling her back against my chest.

"You're going to kill me, Sunbeam. Step away from the edge."

She laughs and spins in my arms, snaking hers around my neck. "You weren't this bossy last time."

"Last time I was holding you the entire time and not trying to pilot this beast by myself." I reach out to the burner and adjust it, keeping her firmly in my grip with my other arm.

"I think it's possibly the most romantic thing you've ever done. Learning to pilot yourself so that we can do this." She throws her arms wide to the grounds of the estate spread out below us. The movement makes her wobble in my arms, and she giggles as I curse.

Her sweater dress slips off her shoulder as she regains her balance, and the cloud tattoo peeks out. I reach up and run my thumb over it.

"Knowing you thought about covering it up when we were apart…" I force away the sourness creeping over my tongue. "It made me realize how much I fucked everything up."

"Hey." Rose turns and grabs either side of my face and brings my eyes to hers. "Don't. It's in the past. And I would have never done it. I told you that. We don't need to think about the time we were apart. It's gone. It's done."

She swipes her lips over mine in a gentle kiss. I do well most days not to curse myself for almost losing her. It used to creep up on me sometimes. But time and talking about it has helped since Rose came back to England with me.

Jasmin persuaded me to try therapy to process finding out about Julian being my biological father. Rose came with me once and talked about Julian and what he almost did to her. But she seemed content to let it go, burning the word fear on the bonfire afterward. For the first time, we burned the same word at the same time. I can't be afraid that I almost lost her anymore. I can't let the past stain our future. Time is too precious.

She is too precious.

Julian's still awaiting trial. The bastard shows no remorse at all, and I cling to the certainty Rose has in her eyes each time she tells me I am nothing like him. She believes it, so I have to. I have to be the best man I can be for her.

And Sophie's confident Julian's going to be locked up for years. Maybe the trial will act as closure. Alistair said as much to me. My half-brother wants to see our father go down as much as me.

Rose strokes my cheek, reading me. She always knows when I'm torturing myself. Blaming myself.

"Don't," she whispers against my lips.

"I can't help it." I squeeze my eyes shut and kiss her back, allowing her scent and her touch to center me again. The way they always do.

It's strange how things work out, when given time. Sometimes the estate is so busy I can go an entire day without remembering all Rose and I have been through. And other days, like today, it can hit me at any given time. Some days, it hits me the second I wake up.

But now I wake up with Rose in my arms, and nothing can ever distinguish the way my heart pounds with joy when I see her face first thing in the morning. When I kiss her, sink myself inside her, love her with everything I am.

Because I do. Fuck, I do. And I'm determined never to live in the past again.

I kiss her again, and she nips at my lips playfully, making me groan. She giggles as my fingers flex on her waist, and I curse softly at the way she feels beneath my palms. She always makes it better, makes it sting less. Just by being her.

I kiss her once more, then spin her, wrapping my arms around her from behind as I leave the burner and allow us to float through the clouds.

"Go on then."

"Go on what?" She leans back against my chest and sighs happily as she looks out at the view.

"Look for the silver lining."

I wait for her to scan the clouds and pick one. But instead, she turns inside my arms and looks straight into my eyes.

"I'm staring right at it."

"Nope." I shake my head with a small smile and try to turn her again. "I'm not accepting that answer."

"Stop." She balls my shirt in her fists. "Remember what you said to me once?"

"That I'm going to marry you." My lips twitch. I've made no secret of telling her that she will be Rose Silver before the year is over.

She thinks I'm joking.

I'm not.

She rolls her eyes with a smirk. "I mean when you said that I thought the world only saw my worst. But that you saw my best. That's what I mean, Dax. I see yours. I see the beautiful shining parts of you that light up like glitter."

She bites back her grin as I narrow my eyes at her. I was finding silver glitter for weeks after we came home from New York. Rose thought it was hilarious.

"It's a trick of the light." I look up at the envelope of the balloon.

"It's not. It's magic." Rose pulls my face back down, her lips spreading into a face-splitting grin. "It's magic and I won't let you say otherwise, Dax Silver."

She giggles as I hold the back of her neck and kiss her. "What the fuck am I going to do with you, Sunbeam?"

"I'm sure you'll think of something." She steps out from my arms and spins toward the edge of the basket again, pointing at a cloud shaped like a fish, neither hand holding on as she turns to see if I've seen it.

I'm behind her like a shot, one hand gripping her hip as the other slides around her waist and holds her tight, pulling her back to the middle of the basket with me, away from the edge.

I dip my nose to her ear. "Will you fucking stop before I spank you?"

She bites her bottom lip and looks back at me over her shoulder, her eyes lighting up. And I know that look. I call her Sunbeam because she's the light to my darkest parts and she's the best start to my day. But maybe it should be because of the firecracker heat she has inside her.

Life is certainly interesting with Rose Jacobs as your girlfriend.

"Lean back." She turns and drops to her knees and pulls at the zipper of my suit pants.

"Rose, I'm flying a giant bag of hot fucking air here," I reply, setting the burner going again so we don't float too low.

"You telling me you don't like me sucking your cock?" She pulls it out, and the bastard is already hard with pre-cum pooling at the end and covering my piercing.

"God, give me strength," I mutter, tilting my head back to the sky.

"He won't help you." Rose giggles as she takes me inside her mouth and sucks.

"Fuck!" The burner fires up as I pull on it too hard.

She giggles again before sucking down hard on my cock, taking me all the way down to the base.

My eyes roll back in my head, and I drop one hand to her hair and stroke the blonde strands between my fingers. She sucks me off with enthusiastic moans until my balls draw up and I'm shaking with the effort of holding my release at bay.

"Keep doing that and I'll be coming down your throat any second," I groan.

She draws back, flicking her tongue over my piercing, which sends shockwaves pulsating down the length of my cock. Her blue eyes are bright as she blinks up at me. Then she smiles and sucks me all the way down again, tugging on my balls gently.

I grit my teeth, a playful warning in my eyes as I growl, stroking her cheek as I release streams of hot cum into her mouth.

She gazes up at me as she swallows it.

She knows she'll pay for this later.

And knowing Rose, she's already counting down the time until I fuck her hard as punishment. There's nothing that this girl won't let me do to her. She wants it all the time. She wants *me* all the time.

But it's never as much as I want her.

There's no measurement of time that could accurately portray just how much I want her. How much she means to me. How much I love her. How fucking grateful I am that she chose forgiveness.

That she chose me.

She came back to England with me days after I went for her. On the understanding that Casey could visit whenever she wanted, and that I would go back with her for an extended vacation for Harley and Reed's wedding next month.

Like I would have ever said no. I'm never letting her out of my sight again. And I love how excited she gets talking about it. She said Brett's convinced Lena to go as his date. And the way her eyes light up as she talks about him now, instead of clouding over like they used to, it fills every fucking crack that my soul once had.

"Do you think they'll be happy?" Rose asks as she rises to her feet, licking her lips.

I fix my pants and pull her to me, kissing her and tasting myself on her lips.

"I only care about whether you're happy."

She laughs and places her hands against my chest as she gazes down at the estate and the hive of activity going on as the team brought in for tomorrow's wedding race around to make everything perfect.

Whoever this guy is that Logan and Jasmin have met up with—the one who I caved to and let host a wedding on the estate—has a fuck load of money. There's even a giant ice sculpture that's been flown in from Switzerland.

Rose places her head against my chest over where my compass is, her hand reaching up to stroke the bird on my neck. It's her favorite position. It's how she sleeps, wrapped in my arms. And she sleeps well now. We both do.

"I know there's a romantic in there, Dax Silver. One who learns to pilot balloons and tattoos a rose over his heart. One that lets strangers host their wedding here because he heard it was the bride's dream."

I smirk as I wrap a hand around her neck and stroke her pulse point. "I think all the sunrise sex is going to your head."

"I like sunrise sex." She pouts.

I chuckle against her lips. "And I love making you come every morning. And day. And night. And after balloon rides."

"Is Logan going to meet us and then drive the balloon back?"

"Yep."

"The bush on the drive home?" She bites her bottom lip.

I pull her snagged lip free with my thumb and kiss her again. "Yep. And then again when we get home. I can't fuck you the way I want in the Range Rover."

"The mirror?" Her eyes light up.

"Yes, Sunbeam. My fucking *favorite* mirror."

She laughs as I descend on her neck, groaning into her skin as I kiss it and inhale.

Vanilla. Petals. *Infinity.*

The (Almost) End.

Chapter 45

Rose

Extended Epilogue – Sunrise number two hundred and twenty

"How was the wedding?"

I grin at Logan as he looks between me, Jasmin, and Dax in Dax's office.

"That good, huh?" He chuckles as I sink into Dax's side. Dax dips his nose into my hair and inhales, wrapping an arm around my waist.

I've already told Jasmin everything there is to know about Harley and Reed's wedding. It was perfect—romantic, fairytale-worthy—perfect. But I knew it would be. They've been planning it for ages, even though they changed venue at the last-minute to this amazing private island for extra privacy. Reed gets followed everywhere being Mayor of New York, so they wanted to keep the ceremony private and intimate, and the island was perfect for it. Then they had a formal reception back in New York that the press went wild over. Reed was a man possessed, ensuring it was perfect for my sister. He adores her.

I used to envy the two of them and think I would never know how it felt. I thought I was destined to watch from the sidelines forever.

But then...

I grin goofily up at Dax, and Jasmin giggles as Logan groans.

"You two were fucking in the chair again before we came in, weren't you?"

The look Dax gives me as he curls his palm around my hip and pulls me closer to him says it all.

Logan mutters something good-naturedly.

"The wedding was amazing. The island was out of this world. I've no idea how Reed set it up. Griffin must have had something to do with it. The guy's a billionaire." I wave a hand in the air. Logan and Jasmin already know about Harley's boss and his hotel in New York where she works. He's loaded, and I assume it was him who arranged the island off the coast of Italy that we had all to ourselves.

"Reed gets followed about by the press wherever he goes. So it meant it was private, you know?"

Jasmin nods.

"It was almost over-the-top luxury, if that's even a thing." I giggle, recalling Dax raising an eyebrow at not just a pillow menu, but the option of having a personal, ergonomically designed mattress flown in and installed in your room. We had a four-page form to complete of our preferences.

"It's probably owned by some rich guy with a small dick," I muse as Dax coughs, sounding like he's about to burst into laughter.

Jasmin smirks and opens her mouth, but Logan shoots her a look that makes her close it.

"Or..." Logan looks at me. "It's owned by a guy with one so big, having its own zip code wasn't enough, so he had to get an entire island instead."

"Huh?" I narrow my eyes. "What do you know?"

He holds his hands up as he backs out of the room. "I've got to go or I'll be late for my date."

He disappears with a grin as Jasmin shakes her head. "I can't believe he's still using those apps."

"I think there's a romantic under there somewhere," I say.

She looks between me and Dax. "Yeah. Maybe." She smiles before heading to the door. "But this is Logan. All we can do is pray for the girl that he finally sets his sights on."

Dax is still smiling as she leaves.

"What are you finding so amusing, Mr. Silver?" I brush my thumb over his bottom lip, and he grabs my wrist, pressing a kiss to my pulse point.

"Nothing, Sunbeam. I just want to get you home."

I gaze up at him. It's Friday night, and that means it's cottage night. We spend most nights at Dax's apartment in the main house. But we always spend our Fridays in the cottage. It's become our thing.

The sunrises look better there.

I stand on my toes and press my lips over his. "Come on, then. Let's go."

"Let it go, Rose. Soak my cock again."

My arms shake, struggling to hold my body up as I look up into the mirror and into Dax's eyes that are darkened with lust.

"I—"

"Don't tell me you can't," he warns as his grip tightens on my hips, and he pulls me back onto his cock again. "When we both know you can."

I pull in a breath, biting my bottom lip, as he leans forward, sliding wet fingers onto my swollen clit.

"I want your cum running down your legs for me before I explode inside this perfect cunt. Then I'm going to drink that shit up."

I shudder as his hot breath on my ear infuses his crude words with my senses. He means it. Dax loves *cleaning me up*. This man will literally do anything for me.

I'm worshiped daily.

"Fuck!" I cry out as the pressure peaks, causing another orgasm to flow from me, drenching us both.

"Good girl," Dax breathes, the satisfaction in his voice matching the smile spread across his face as I look up into the mirror.

He holds my eyes in the reflection, tilting his lips toward my ear again. "You feel this?" he growls as the telling jerk of his cock inside me gives away his orgasm.

"Uh-huh."

"Words, Rose," he growls as his cock swells, bringing heat with it deep inside me as he thrusts hard.

"Yes." I stare into his eyes.

I love sex with him like this. It's always hot and intense. But since we came back from New York, in the mirror is when he likes to get really dirty.

And I'm totally here for it.

"This is me showing you that—"

"That I belong to you?" I cry as he continues pumping inside me, making my core clench around him.

He smiles, the sight of it making my heart lift. He is so beautiful. My man with all his story told in the dark ink over his skin.

Then he kisses the cloud on my shoulder. It's still the only tattoo I have, and the only one I need. My new story began with him.

He thrusts into me one final time, and I sigh happily as he kisses beneath my ear as the final shudders leave his body.

"I won't argue with that. But it isn't what I was going to say."

"It isn't?" I tilt my neck so he can kiss higher and there's a smile in his voice as his words roll over me.

"I was going to say you are everything to me. And as much as you're mine, I'm yours."

"Dax?" I turn my face, and he catches my lips in a soft kiss.

"I belong to you. I'm yours, Sunbeam."

"For infinity." I kiss him back as he grips my chin, holding me to him.

"Infinity," he repeats. *Fucking infinity.*

The (Actual) End.

Elle's Books

Time with Mr. Silver is book 7 in 'The Men Series', a collection of interconnected standalone stories.
They can be read in any order, however, for full enjoyment of the overlapping characters, the suggested reading order is:
Meeting Mr. Anderson – Holly and Jay
Discovering Mr. X – Rachel and Tanner
Drawn to Mr. King – Megan and Jaxon
Captured by Mr. Wild – Daisy and Blake
Pleasing Mr. Parker – Maria and Griffin
Trapped with Mr. Walker – Harley and Reed
Time with Mr. Silver – Rose and Dax
Resisting Mr. Rich – Logan and Maddy
(Also available by Elle, Forget-me-nots and Fireworks,
Shona and Trent's story, a novella length prequel to The
Men Series)

Get all of Elle's books here: http://author.to/ellenicoll

About the Author

Elle Nicoll is an ex long-haul flight attendant from the UK.

After fourteen years of having her head in the clouds whilst working at 38,000ft, she is now usually found with her head between the pages of a book reading or furiously typing and making notes on another new idea for a book boyfriend who is sweet-talking her.

Elle finds it funny that she's frequently told she looks too sweet and innocent to write a steamy book, but she never wants to stop. Writing stories about people, passion, and love, what better thing is there?

Because,

Love Always Wins

xxx

To keep up to date with the latest news and releases, find Elle in the following places, and sign up for her newsletter below;

https://www.subscribepage.com/ellenicollauthorcom

Facebook Reader Group – Love always Wins –

https://www.facebook.com/groups/686742179258218

Website – https://www.ellenicollauthor.com

Acknowledgments

I will start as I always do, with the lady who started this all...

TL Swan.

You are the reason these stories exist. I will be forever grateful for your support and giving me the push I needed to write that first word just over two and a half years ago. And to all the Cygnets, thank you for being the amazing, supportive group you are.

To my author friends Vicki Nicolson and Sadie Kincaid, you inspire me every day! (and you haven't blocked me for the multiple daily messages – yay!) Love you ladies.

JR Gale, my morning coffees and your voice messages are the best start to my day.

Sara, my PA, and all-round amazing, organized lady. How did I get so lucky to have met you? I told you you're stuck with me now. I'm never letting you go!

My beta readers; Sara, Taye, Rita, and Kelly. Your feedback on those early drafts is everything. Thank you for being with me for book after book.

Zee, the most amazing editor who feeds my praise kink when you tell me you can't find any danglers. You are the

most incredible teacher. All those deleted throats and swallows were in your honor.
Thank you to Abi and Sherri for always amazing me with your beautiful covers.
Thank you to the amazing ARC readers and street team, bloggers, bookstagrammers, booktokkers, and everyone who has shared my books. I am so grateful.
Finally, to you, the reader. These stories would stay in my head if you didn't encourage me to share them with all of your love and support. I'm always overwhelmed by how many messages I get about the books. And I appreciate Every. Single. One. Thank you so much. And may reading continue to bring you joy.
One last please from me;
if you enjoyed Time with Mr. Silver then please leave a review on Amazon and share it with your book besties.
Thank you, and until the next book...
Elle x